I Hear Men Talking

and other stories

by Meridel Le Sueur

I Hear Men Talking

and other stories

by Meridel Le Sueur

Edited, with an Afterword, by
Linda Ray Pratt

West End Press
1984

Portions of **I Hear Men Talking** have been published elsewhere in altered form as short stories. They are:

"Our Fathers," *Intermountain Review of English and Speech*, Feb. 1, 1937, pp. 1 passim. Reprinted in **Ripening**, ed. Elaine Hedges, Feminist Press, NY, 1982.

"Fudge," *Fantasy*, Winter 1933, pp. 9-17. Reprinted in **Harvest**, West End Press, Cambridge, 1977 (subsequently in combined edition, **Harvest and Song for My Time**, same publisher).

"Milk Went Up Two Cents," *Black and White*, April 1940, pp. 26-29.

Other stories in this volume first appeared as follows:

"The Bird," *New Caravan*, edd. Kreymborg, Mumford, and Rosenfeld, NY, Norton, 1936, pp. 177-223.

"The Horse," *Story Magazine*, July-August 1939, pp. 66-104.

Cover: "Unemployed Men in Minneapolis," Edwin Nooleen (oil), 1933.

Reproduction of painting courtesy of the Minnesota Historical Society

LC 84-51769

ISBN 0-931122-37-6

$5.95

This project is partially supported by a grant from the National Endowment for the Arts, a federal agency.

Printed in the United States of America

Contents

To Rachel and Deborah

Foreword

It was the Fall of 1978, and I was fairly new at doing books. After months of going over the manuscript, working with the typesetter, sending last-minute galleys back to Meridel, the time had come: We had gotten out her novel **The Girl**. It was at the point of publication, and exhaustion, that Meridel emerged from her basement one night carrying a large, old, faded manila folder, stuffed with a ream of browning paper. "I found this," she said, a flicker of a ·smile on her lips. "I thought maybe you'd like to see it." It was the 288-page manuscript (a few pages were missing) of **I Hear Men Talking**.

I photocopied it, helplessly watching the corners crumble off the old paper. I read the copy as best I could. There were lines lost as well as the missing pages near the beginning. It was a novel of life in a farm community and a town. There was a superficial resemblance between the girl Penelope of the story and the unnamed Girl of the novel I had just published. Because the poor quality of the paper and the idiosyncracies of the typing in the manuscript were very similar to the ms. of **The Girl** that I had just worked on, I surmised that the final date of composition was about the same (around 1940). I recognized a few sections of the story, because they had appeared elsewhere as separate pieces. I had published one, "Fudge," in the collection **Harvest**; another, "Our Fathers," I recognized from earlier magazine publication. (In the manuscript I had, Meridel had removed parts of this story, suggesting that it was written early, then cut back as the main design of the novel grew.)

But most of the material was new to me. It introduced themes that were striking: the fleet figure of Penelope, her running feet carrying her about the Town as she gathered up its parts; the ruined Mr. Littlefield, recalling brokenly vestiges of the Midwestern tradition of eloquence, learned from its populist orators; the self-deceived and bitter Miss Shelley, whose story was a puzzle for Penelope to unravel; the farmers talking behind closed doors of the house, stirring up a brew of revolt. And in the figure of the mother, Mona, and the grandmother, Gee, there appeared to be autobiographical images, people close to Meridel's own family in her growing-up years. (Linda Ray Pratt, in her Afterword to this edition, explores the autobiographical matter along with the other characters and themes in the novel.)

Also present was a characteristic vein of faith and humility that Meridel Le Sueur has carried in her throughout her long adult life as a writer—faith in the words of common people and humility expressed in her belief that the writer is a scribe of those people. The title and main narrative thread of the novel suggests a subordination of the listener to those common voices, teasing and puzzling their way to a new truth about the land, the community, the possibilities of success or failure in the future. We know from other materials, such as the film "My People Are My Home," how Meridel says she spent her youth listening to the people of the towns she lived in—of status high and low, and moral character good and bad. She was a collector of tales, gossips, intrigues, secrets, and a student of both their content and structure, long before she began to write them down. Later she came to feel that these words and the stories they told had special power, really a life of their own, and finally that the role of the artist was to return them to the people.

In a short story published in the McCarthy period, in the midst of her own persecution and despair, she wrote:

> The source of American culture lies in the historic movement of our people, and the artist must become voice, messenger, awakener, sparking the inflammable silence, reflecting back the courage and the beauty. (S)he must return really to the people, partisan and alive, with warmth, abundance, excess, confidence, without reservation, or cold and merely reasonable bread, or craftiness, writing one thing, believing another, the superior person. . . . ("The Dark of the Time," 1956)

The novel **I Hear Men Talking**, never before published, shows this aim and this facility in its early stages of development.

With this novel, in the same volume, we print two other pieces, conceived in the Twenties and written in the Thirties, the novellas "The Bird" (a grotesque story of a young man's initiation to life while on shipboard), and "The Horse" (a tale of a wealthy young girl in revolt, which ends in disaster). The stories share the general theme of initiation; they are highly accomplished, and have been noted elsewhere, even while long out of print following early magazine publication. For a full discussion of their significance I leave the reader to the two Afterwords, by Professor Pratt and by the author herself. Here I will only note the remarkable fusion of democratic, symbolical and personal concerns that Meridel had accomplished, in diverse ways, at a young age. Influenced deeply by non-establishment American writers (Twain, Whitman and Dreiser were important; her Midwestern counterparts Sherwood Anderson and Jack Conroy perhaps crucial), she also read widely and eclectically, finding, for instance, a key to sexual liberation in the works of D. H. Lawrence (again, see the Afterwords) and other resources in such nonliterary material as hymns, sermons, and the great orations of the day. The fusion of her reading and experience cannot be schematized simply: The need of a story, not her reading matter, dictates its style. But she had cast a wide net, and by the time these pieces were written had come up with rich treasures.

The Afterwords, again, deal with the politics of these pieces. But I should like to point out that there is a political life in the very act of going to the people and writing down what they say. What distinguishes Meridel from many Left writers is her ability to avoid the stance of what she calls, in the quotation cited above, the "superior person." She does not believe that socialism requires or awaits a stone tablet brought down a mountain; she believes it emerges in the thoughts and actions of people seeking a better world, and she is true to her belief in her writing. (For those familiar with the literature of Left thought, it is significant that she cites most often the works of the Italian Communist Gramsci—who believed in a popular voice governing political conduct—and the Brazilian teacher Paolo Freire, whose pedagogy rests on the notion that the intellectuals must trust the people and return to them their language.)

Manifestly, these early pieces are not in perfect conformity to the beliefs of Meridel Le Sueur as they have ripened and matured in her to this day, at age 84. She herself is quick to point out that her life did not proceed, never did and never could, by a series of conscious choices, dictated by a superior, foreknowing intelligence. She did not embrace a political creed at a given time as one would sign a contract or marry someone; she did not become subject to a set of doctrinal rules and work *from* them, ever. Rather she ingested what was there, did what she believed best at the time, and thus participated in' many of the grand and terrible moments of the century. And this came about by necessity: the necessity to eat, to live, to celebrate life in order to stand it. The writing comes out of the hard, uncertain, querulous reality of a daily struggle for existence, both material and of the human spirit. If the result is profound and worthy of our study, it is *because* it is imperfect.

As she nears 85, Meridel Le Sueur is turning to new writings, with her customary eloquence, optimism and lucidity. As her publisher and friend for the last seven years, I salute her effort, and honor her fierce reaffirmation that the point of such labor is not simply to understand the world but to change it.

John Crawford
Publisher
West End Press
July 1984

I Hear Men Talking

for my mother

Invocation

The Summer was enfolded complete in the first morning of
Spring, curve upon curve, fold upon fold encircled within itself,
waiting only for those days of heat when the earth would swell in
the Iowa sun, grains of wheat yellowing, straining in the kernel,
toward that day when the threshing machine would come down
the highway, when the milk trucks would be held up by young
and old farmers in blue overalls, and what had been young in the
first Spring would be then ready to harvest in the full Summer.

Penelope blowing down the prairie from a far seed, interloping
in the fields, hearing the voices of men in the towns speaking from
a greed that made a bad odor over the country but promising the
growth of a new speech that had not been before. Penelope
standing bound, ready for flight and without it, turning her eyes in
fright and anxiety towards a past that gave no word, looking for a
growing time good to her bones, fertile to the seed that lay in
ambush from old countries, carried into mid America by such as
Nancy Hanks and Johnny Appleseed, by men and women going a
long jounrey, walking the tall wind of Indian prairies, bursting in
sudden flights, then falling back and back . . . waiting.

Penelope standing, startled in a moment of anxious rest between
one moment and another; and the Town waiting for that day of
heat when the cyclone would stand on the horizon and the wheat
would be mowed down by a hand that would not gamble it on the
Exchange; and the child that Pete Swillman, the leading banker,
had planted in his wife the week before Easter would be ripped out
by the wind, and he had meant to sell and barter it, too; and Mrs.
Littlefield would see her hate chiseled off Mr. Littlefield, and him
lying in the morgue clean as a whistle, the whole town seeing him
too, clear of their hate, washed slick as a man three days in the sea;
and before that time when the lambs were dropped Mrs. Fearing
would give birth to a son, with the doctor sitting on the floor,

pulling the head until it was black, and Miss Shelley looking around the door, then clacking out the news to the waiting Town, hungry enough for what it could get and saying—Three months too soon. . . . Well, well . . . that's more than we expected. And a right smart chap too, not an incubator one, eh Fearing?—So that the father-husband would have to look at his guilty face in the mirror and knock it off his body with a close shot, and Cora Fearing screaming in the street so the whole Town heard its own cry echoed back upon it, saying too—Is there a winging between this time and that, between a winging up and a bringing down? Is there any one makes a flight? And answering too—We made no flight between breaking this land and spawning a hard generation and selling wheat, hogs, corn, and there shall be no flight now.

Close to that time of the cyclone Ezra Littlefield would have to let his finger rise and point to where Penelope was, so the Sheriff could find her, and Bac Kelly would turn hot as a hound upon her, knowing what he had said in the pool hall, "I'll bet ya five to one I can make her."

O Towns, O Towns sunk in stillness, in that darkness farthest from the moon where there is no stirring of the human spirit, with the secret unremembered seed waiting in the furrow for a new planting and a fresh Spring. . . . Oh ghost of a dream in your wooden houses so straight upslanting, their sides blank, their interiors like a nut where the pith has gone, mildewed, so that a dust fumes out when it is opened, but still the ghost of a dream there, O Town, and all your dense body needing a crevasse of dawn to break some thick rind and let a good wind adown your streets. . . The limbs of your People turning in soured pain and all the Eyes looking from you—the crafty ones, the gimlet eyes, measuring and calculating eyes looking at wheat, scales, the body of child, wife, husband, at receipts, with a cunning that closed the door too close behind a man's coming in. . . . O let that tall wind come along your prairies, blow your shambles away, uproot your dead. O let that wind come upon your stillnesses in a tide of people, opening those dreams of avarice that have been too small for a man's stature, that have made the flesh of your women spare and brittle, and have given the eyes of your children the look of old men and anxious women. . . .

O let that wind!

Part One

Chapter One

The cocks were singing their first call to the earliest dawn. Penelope lay sleeping, her thin uncurving arms stretched above her head. She looked as if she were listening, waiting to bring her arms down over whatever would come to her, waiting for the slow Spring to mature and bring what it would have to bring. . . . For from that moment, the first dawn of Spring a week before Easter, many seeds were planted that Summer would cradle, and each would be mysteriously itself and not another, so that there was nothing to stop them becoming what they would become.

All the Town sleeps from the gigantic routine which has made their lives too small for a man and a woman. Now they are locked in embrace in the passing night, through the course of the moon, sleeping before the cracking gleam of old light on the world, over the prairies that are now breaking into a race. They sleep bitterly locked together, folded over and back, the unspoken green love given over, weaving close in the night, over an anxiety and fear of what is not known or anticipated. The night odor of Main Street opens to a wind of terror between the successful past and the successful future, exhaustion creating a crevasse for gigantic dreams amongst them, a cracking open in the floor below.

Penelope sleeps, knowing the house in every part of it like her own body; knowing the Town, surrounded by houses full of sleepers, and she seems to be listening to them all, searching them before she is settled upon by what will happen to her before the wheat is harvested.

Across the street in the yellow house, Mr. and Mrs. Fearing sleep; and in the house with drawn blinds sleeps Miss Nina Shelley, as if keeping watch over Mrs. Fearing all the time, saying: *They haven't been married long enough. Everybody knows that. That Mrs. Fearing is too large, as everybody can see. And wasn't the marriage a hasty one though? My!* Smiling in that black shadow that lay on her lips with the only joy she knew.

Mr. Littlefield now sleeps in his shack on the outskirts, because he never went to bed until late and couldn't sleep then for going over what had come to him, why he had lost his business, his wife and everything that he had been taught to expect would be his, taking his dreams from history books and the myths of Abraham Lincoln and Jefferson.

Mrs. Littlefield in her one room sleeps like stone, her grim mouth set saying: *Why does Penelope go to play chess with Mr. Littlefield on Saturday nights? Why? Why?* And putting upon it a reason she herself knew could not be so.

Further out the Kelly road, on the other side of Mumsers' Orchard and the Roselawn Cemetery, Bac Kelly, who would get up soon to milk the cow and do the chores before starting into Town for the Saturday market, would be sleeping as if caught in the act of running or boxing, his long body powerful like a man's, but quicker, with more lightning in it, and his wrists and hands like a boy's, for uneven he was, and lanky, but handsomeness was in him and power. He was like a hound now, set hot upon something so that Penelope could not even dream of him, thinking he would be set upon some trail, hound fashion, and she could not look at what he would be after. The moment of that future satisfaction would be set upon his face like fire and sun.

All the farm boys with names she did not know or put importance upon sleep in the lonely prairies, the dawn flowing in like milk. They would be coming into town to the meeting hall, to see what was to be done about the farm situation. There would be hunger for them and sun and labor, the hot hound fire of beast and prey making them subtle as fire and taut as bowstrings.

At the second cock crow Penelope stirred, sat up listening, seeing the bare boughs of the apple tree jutting up into her window, over the kitchen lean-two, tapping its naked boughs outside as the milk of day began to flow. She listened to her own house, seeing if her mother stirred or if her grandmother would get up to prepare breakfast. There was not a sound and had not been since in the night she had heard the heavy sound of men's feet going out the door, and men's voices now drunken saying goodnight . . . goodnight.

She looked at the apple tree, saw it getting ready to let its sap run and saw the moment when it would be like a lowered cloud of blossom out the window. Then lying back on her pillows she let her mind go from her mother in the next room, her grandmother lying in a huge unstirring mound beyond that, into the Town, running past the sleeping houses like a frightened hare, seeing Littlefield too, and not knowing him or what would happen to him; seeing the closed door of every house . . . Pfeiffer's door, and Babcock's, the superintendent of school's, and Swillman's, who always asked her to come to Sunday School, and the menacing door of Miss Shelley, passing that by swiftly, knowing there a danger stood that had been raised up by them all from their own evil. Then into her own door, seeing the bottles on the tables downstairs, the marks of men's muddy boots on the threshold where they had come in and gone out again. Then coming back to herself she felt her own thin arms over her hair like corn tassels, her long thin legs, now stretching beneath the sheet, that would walk the earth, not knowing she would lie a long time seeing herself unused, coming to no fire or fruit. And seeing that in every house each performed himself without love or audience, wedded each to himself and every one an enemy of the other.

In despair she knew that figure sleeping in the house, the mound of Mother whose windy sides had stretched over her, wild, dark and angry; she could see her sleeping as if running between violence and violence.

And her grandmother whom she called Gee sleeping covert in her flesh, buried long in the accretion of her own desires that were upon her layer upon layer coming to nothing. She had been thrown forward deep into the flesh from violent pioneer loins. cursing, striding, thrown like a meteor that has buried itself in the earth's crust from outer space and there lies saying nothing, revealing no source, speaking of a far and unknown place. She had been thrust out from huge and powerful women and men who were in fear and terror of a flight they had to take, behind them failure and mutilation and before them death and hazards unknown to them, unwritten prairies having no myth and no speech, upon which they were forced to engage in endless action without word, fighting, brawling, conceiving without song.

The slight girl thrown off in that swift action waiting, the dark prairies waiting too, its fields heavy and lush, its people poor and frightened, waiting too, mad and covert, thrown too from a past of extreme danger and peril into a new soil, now waiting.

All in the Town turning now before waking, hearing the cocks crow . . . Judas . . . Peter . . . breaking open the shell, shaking bright combs . . . the dawn coming quickly. The wind goes invisible down the streets; the lusty dawn comes in with light. The sky green and paling, a terrible rustling coolness coming from the ground, running into the sap, waking trees that are going to bloom—despite what will happen to these now waking, stretching, scratching, yawning, putting feet in slippers—going to bud and hang rich, meeting over the streets under which Mr. Littlefield will go every day for a can of sardines; under their branches will move all these awakening, tossing up to sour and stagnate, stir and sleep and foully breathe. Dawn coming from something not listed, from out the margins, not charted in Washington, D.C. from the sky, the only part of the prairies not yet fenced around; the cold light washing in the tide of day.

Penelope crept out of the house walking on her toes, carrying her shoes, though there was slight danger of waking her mother and Gee, who would not fill the house with their windy bodies until around noon. But her thin shoulders were raised, held tense to her neck as she creaked down the stairs, stopped, listened, opened the door, the sun now glittering on the fresh street. Then she was out in the air as if she had stepped into a sea that flowed around her like milk.

She stooped, wobbling and gawky, to put on her shoes that were her mother's, fitting her but little, sticking out ahead of where her feet stood. She was looking at Miss Shelley's still house. The blinds were drawn clear to the bottom, but the sides of the curtains were pushed out and hung loose as if they had been pulled back. They gave a sense that Miss Shelley was always peeking around them. The house of Mr. and Mrs. Fearing was very still too, yet holding what would happen there. Running down the wooden steps she thought: If there's any violets up I could take her some because in the Spring she'll have that chap . . . and turning down Maple Street past houses, half-dim yet in night sleep, although the sun had a bright glitter through the naked trees. Down another street, unseen, she could hear the clop clop clop of the milk horse going the rounds. She walked swiftly under the trees, her jacket clutched together at her neck, swiftly, her hair loose, her head thrown back, her wide mouth open as if she drank the Town, her eyes looking, asking, her whole body and arms out as if to embrace, to find out what was there, to be fed.

The birds hopped in the street, rose, and settled behind her. The robins were already fattening on the pale green lawns. She went past the school house where she would have to go on Monday; past the church where she would have to go on Sunday. This was Saturday, and bright happenings would be in the Town. She was headed toward the market now, going swiftly even if it was early, in order to be where Bac and Jenny would soon be; to have a foretaste of what might happen.

When she heard any step on the walk far or near she stopped, excitement shaking through her, and she stood, her head back, mouth ready to speak, waiting for steps lonely sounding in other streets, approaching turning and lapsing away, but she met no one. Horses sounded down other streets, turning away from her; autos wheezed to a start, chugged away, going where they must go. She kept walking, swiftly, past many houses, knowing some small tidbit about every person in them, gleaned in her mind like her only harvest and treasured and rehandled there.

A low night wind still crept the ground, whipping her skirts that hung about her thin shanks. Her Gee had let out the hems that week, making them longer so that now she could not walk without becoming tangled in them. Gee had said, looking strange, "You are getting to be a big girl now. Things will happen to you. Your skirts must be longer." There was chill and foreboding in it, like there was in what Jenny was always whispering by the school yard fence, "Listen kid . . ." and Penelope would listen, her head nodding heavy on her shoulders, her eyes staring back in fright, afraid she would hear what Jenny was saying, afraid she would not hear. What could be happening so that her skirts must come swirling longer, making swift running a hazardous thing, so that she could not climb the fence at Kelly's, but had to open the gate and walk through, feeling her ways strange even to herself. Something is happening . . . something is happening, she sang to herself, stepping over the cracks in the walk:

Step on a crack
You break your mother's back.

She stopped, listening. Around the Town went the shuffle, shuffle, shuffle of the Six-Ten echoing straight through the fiber of the village and falling out into the prairie on the other side. Shuffle, shuffle, shuffle, HOOT, Hooooot at Kelly's crossing. Were they waiting to cross, Mr. Kelly and his squat wife sitting on the seat, Jenny and Bac on the potato sacks? Now it hooted for Littlefield's crossing, after passing the cemetery and Mumsers' Orchard; then in a change of sound and tempo it took off over the town in a great black gleam. That snorting engine rearing into the Town mornings and evenings, and going off again, shuffle, shuffle, shuffle, HOOT, out into the prairie. How many miles of prairie before the mountains or the sea Penelope didn't know. She thought, they might all of them be on a sea; each house rocking on a sea.

But there was something in the air as if suddenly, upon one morning, it could happen—Spring could come! There was the river cold and slow, the country locked away and the tight Town;

the farmers coming in, red faces peering out of mufflers, the ruin and desolation of corn stalks, the fields cold upturned, the sense that all life had gone with that seasonal fertility. And then upon one morning like this there would be writing on the world as if some peasant had come in with an indecipherable note, saying that it was happening in the ground, in the seed, that it would again be Spring.

Stopping, sniffing, Penelope knew it, and started running down the street. Mrs. Pfeiffer taking her hair out of curl papers saw from her upstairs window and said bitterly, turning down her thin lips, "I declare, there goes Penelope. It's my opinion she's an idiot! Racing through the streets at this hour . . . at *this* hour."

Now Penelope was saying to herself: the fields in clover, alfalfa blossom on the Summer air.

She ran, and eyes looked at her from behind curtains, women standing up from sleep, acrid, bitter, peering out at her, "Well I'll declare. Such goings on."

She kept running and running as if she knew that only two ways goes beauty, shut up forever, or shaken out.

Then as if she knew and felt those peering eyes she was slowed by fear, or as if they had let wing an invisible arrow from their own hate and had laid her low; she slowed and stopped, with a foreboding of unknown dangers, of unspoken malady, as if the prairies were not going to hold her up, as if she would not live to fullness; and the day became suddenly so tenuous in substance, as if it were an old fabric slowly falling to pieces, while the wooden houses around her were being eaten by worms.

She saw the face of Swillman coming down the steps without seeing his body, and his smile pinned her to her fear so she could not move.

"Hello, my girl," he said, buttoning up his coat as if he had dressed hurriedly. He was going out to see why his trucks could not get through the blockade the farmers were putting up on the highway, which he still considered just a lot of nonsense.

Penelope looked at him, her eyes flaring, startled.

"What is your mother up to, letting you race around all the time? The boys say they see you at all hours running around the country. Don't you know, my girl, you'll come to a bad end?"

"No," she said, feeling her body thick, coiling back from what was meant in the words that came from his fat mouth. Then he patted her on the shoulder, her body fleeing his touch though she could not run, knowing what he stood for in the Town, fearing it, knowing fully the power that was in it.

"Come," he said, "we don't see you at Sunday School."

"No," she said, "I have to help on Saturday nights, you see I have to . . . I have to. . . ." All language fled away from her in her fear she might say a thing her mother would berate.

He patted her, and she saw pity and flailed down pity. "I know," he said, "It's no life for a girl, is it? Something ought to be done, I think. Perhaps you don't come to Sunday School my girl because it's only a girl's class?" And he laughed unpleasantly, so that she stepped away from his freckled hand. "Well, don't forget your duty to God," he said, buttoning the lower button of his coat, "We have a fine class."

He went around to get his car, looking back at Penelope who started walking slowly, seeing her a moment strange, and for a moment wondering who they were, the three females who had come to Town, the handsome flaunting woman called Mona, the fat and obscene old lady and this sly slender girl who seemed to roam the Town and the country like one possessed; seeing the wooden house where they lived, with lights burning all night and the sound of men's voices coming out into the street after all good people had been long in bed.

Penelope bound her jacket tight around her, looking back at Swillman going to his garage around his neat little lawn, seeing in him a death and a stricture that would turn, unknown even to him, into an evil that might wrack down what he had been trying to grow.

She did not know which way to be going, whether back or forward, and death seemed to be in the very ground as if the wolf of Winter would never leave that part; as if the hunter and the black cold plains had come amongst them for good; and the wind began to blow suddenly off the prairies, as if the Town did not exist at all, as if it blew right through the flimsy houses that were never built to house anyone even for one's own lifetime, blew and stomped on the streets from the cold fields, as if bringing the winter death, locking them in, mowing down the first Spring, a remembering . . .

Back in the rooms above the barber shop, after the funeral, Mona was sobbing, but not for him; for some obscure loss of which even she was ignorant. Her Gee pouring the milk out, smiling, licking her lips, outdarting with her thin tongue, her bad eye running water as if weeping unknown to her.

"A good riddance," she said. "A good riddance. Men . . . men," she said bitterly. Saying "men" murdered them for her. "Men" . . . and the milk ran out on the table, trickling down on the floor and no one wiped it up.

Penelope sat, not moving, ground out between the two great women, one whose bitterness soured the space, the other whose wild untrammeled sorrow had not a man to weep for.

Then a darkness came over her . . . *Who are we? Where have we come from? What movement of lost seed in a new country. . . .* There moved these two women, Gee going to set the milk on the window ledge; Mother beating her breast in that ambiguous sorrow. . . . *Who are we? Where? Lost?* Wandering from this lost city to another. . . .

Gee stood, looking cunningly at her daughter who wept so voluptuously for a man she had never known . . . Gee looking around her fat jowls, light coming off her great flanks. Penelope became dizzy, the room faded away, went out of her; yet she had to look back, drawn to those gimlet eyes in the bulky shadow, radiant skin falling in rolls of thick and oily flesh, moving slowly upon itself, changing, silent; the small and crafty eyes looking round, the thick lips . . . a greed come to corruption in a thin stream habitually fouling the face . . . what was buried there? what girl? what bright youth? The flesh so rampant, swelling, moving as if without eyes. "Come drink your milk," the lips said, grinning, "come on, Pen, and drink your milk . . . you know the living . . ." a smile cunningly curved on the thick flesh.

Penelope turned her face away. "Oh, I couldn't eat . . . I couldn't."

Mona strode the floor, "Poor Tim . . . poor, poor Tim. When we were married and went to Buffalo, what a man he was. . . . Remember how everybody used to turn and look at him on the street? What a handsome Irishman . . . what a looker. . . ."

"Yes, mother. . . ."

"No one appreciated him . . . no one . . . oh my God."

And then her mother was eating. Crouching, she saw both women eating as if death was not in the world.

"Eat, eat," said her grandmother, "for God's sake, eat."

"What's the matter, Pen," said her mother, "why don't you eat? God knows you're skin and bone. . . . Get some meat on you. What man is going to look at you twice?"

"What man would look at her?" said her grandmother, not looking.

Someone knocked on the door. "I brought you some soup, Mrs. Shriven. I thought . . ." the prying eyes of a neighbor woman looking in.

10

The room was filled then with a torrent of words, Mona feeding her sorrow from the neighbor woman's face. "Oh yes, oh yes . . . we been married a long time . . . we gone a long ways . . ."

"Well, these things must be . . ."

"I wisht he had a dress suit . . ."

"A dress suit!" snorted Gee, helping herself to the soup which steamed and smelled of meat, "You can't make a silk purse . . ."

They all laughed. Penelope looked up, startled, as they reared and stood in the room, woman bodies and woman throats thrust back, wild laughter and wild grief festering in them. Penelope sat, hands clasped close between her thin knees, thinking: the many dead in each, the many dead lying in mounds, rotting in their flesh as in the earth. *Who lies dead in you? Where are cousins uncles . . . where are faces to see, hands to touch? Where?*

"Why, you have cousins in Butte, in Des Moines. . . . Let me see, doesn't that fifth son of Uncle Eb live in Kentucky now?"

"God knows, mama, God knows . . ."

Yes, sir, it do beat all how they scatter, it do beat all. . . . Yes sir, we ought to write, now, ought to write and that's a fact. . . ."

But they had gone from town to town, never writing, with only what could be carried in Gee's old wooden trunk, that trunk holding all of the past that could be known.

"It sure beats all," Gee would say, "It beats all how they've scattered. Why they're not two of them in one place . . . my children are all lost somewheres as if they never came."

"There's us," Penelope would say.

"Us!" her Gee would snort. "For the Lord's sake . . . two women and a half!"

Mona never looked into the trunk, but slept or moved in a wild dark squalor, saying nothing.

Who would speak for them then? Penelope would lay away the pictures and stand, her mouth open, the breath coming sweetly into her living body, looking up, wanting to be; hearing Gee saying, going on with her talk, fingering what had been, minutely:

"I tell you we come of a good family. Your grandfather on your father's side was the best veterinary in Ramsey County, puncturing the bellies of colicky horses, and his brother was a lawyer. And don't let nobody tell you different."

Hearing her say: "That no account Samuel . . . I couldn't stand him. A no account, and I guess my kids're just like him; took after him, every hide and hair of 'em. I never saw him after I left him, except lying dead. My youngest come in and said 'Father's down behind the hedge' . . . come back as big as you please! . . . 'wants to see you' Jerry said. It was Jerry'd been talkin' to him, the spittin'"

11

image of the old man. 'He wants to see you' says the boy. I recollect it was just supper time. . . . Did I go? Well, not so's you could notice it, and him leavin' me everytime I had a chap, him leavin' and goin' off God knows where. . . . I says, I remember the exact words, I says, 'You tell your father that what I says to him before holds good now. I'll have no truck with him. Until he turns over a new leaf, leastways, until he reforms.' That's what I says. That's what I told him right out, and I never seen him again until the day he was dead in Joliet. Then I done the decent thing by him, I must say, I done the decent thing."

Gee told about when she was a young girl and had gone to a camp meeting near Green River in the Cumberlands; how the fires blazed, and how murderers, horse thieves, highway robbers, debtors, fugitives had come down the long valley of the Appalachians, how they got religion and wallowed in the dirt, crying and sobbing, hearing the message of Doom, as she said, and being washed whiter than snow. And she told how she lay on the ground as if it was her bridal bed, and that it was alive with writhing men and screaming women; and how from then on she had been in the bosom of the Lord. As if this was her only love story, her only remembrance of love. My Redeemer liveth—but in Heaven; the Bridegroom cometh—but only after death.

Come evening wherever they were Gee sang the songs, the songs of a jealous God—Come Thou Almighty King. Golden Harps Are Sounding. Hark Ten Thousand Harps and Voices. . . . Singing: There Is a Land of Pure Delight . . . There Is a City Bright . . . and never seeing them, or making them in a new time, but saying: I'm But a Stranger Here; Heaven Is My Home! . . . singing plaintively the only love songs she had . . . Jesus Is Tenderly Calling Me Home; and O Tender and Sweet as the Master's Voice . . . and then, if there was a piano, playing the cords with her stiff fingers:

Just as I am without one plea,
But that Thy blood was shed for me,
And that Thou biddest me come to Thee
O Lamb of God, I come, I coooome . . .

These her only love songs; this her only urgency; I'll Go Where You Want Me to Go, Dear Lord . . . and never going an inch along with Samuel; My Life and Love I Give to Thee, she quavered in the evenings, and gave her life to no living one though they hungered. Rigid, embarrassed she turned away, her head lowered, broken off from the living ones she most longed to touch, saying: Lord Jesus I Long To Be Perfectly Whole. And instead of having a courtship to speak of in the evenings she sang to Penelope: When I Walked with Jesus . . . Stand Up, Stand Up for Jesus . . . and Samuel so

derided, her will mowing him down, like a Spouse of the Lord
being betrayed by earth's little men. . . .

> Now wash me and I shall be whiter than snow,
> whiter than snow, yes . . .
> whiter than snow . . .
> Now wash me and I shall be whiter than snow.

and

> I need Thee,
> O, I need Thee,
> Every hour I need Thee

and Samuel sitting in the corn fields of Iowa, fled away. . . .

An anguish would come into the girl, listening. *Your husband
is down behind the hedge. . . . Let him lie. . . . He is drunk behind
the broom bushes and the sun is going down, won't you go? No. . . .
Don't let the potatoes burn, Mark. Don't let the beans boil dry,
Luce. . . . Where? Where? There, right below that flowering broom
to the right of the pear tree there he's waiting. . . . Trim your wicks.
Fill your lamps with oil. . . . The Bridegroom cometh. . . . That
couldn't be Him down behind the hedge now, could it? That bum?
That wastrel? That living man? God preserve us! That no account;
not worth the powder and shot to blow him up with. . . . That
couldn't be Him. . . .*

And Mona, rocking and crying now . . . "Poor Tim, Poor Tim"
magnificent and wild, her anger flaring behind weeping not for
the living man but only for the dead. . . .

Our Father Who Art in Heaven . . .

And Father . . . who art in earth!

In the Town, storekeepers were coming to their doors now,
sweeping off their sidewalks, looking at her curiously. Passing so
swiftly gave her courage and daring. Good morning . . . she smiled,
walking on, passing swift with her long gawky legs, lifting her
hand, raising her face on her long neck . . . Good morning . . . Good
morning . . . Good morning.

The wind was blowing so her words did not fall steadily or drop coldly but seemed to lift and be blown back behind her like her hair. The wind was cold, and yet she had not been wrong; there was that message in it for the first time; she smelled it, dilating her nostrils, she smelled it unmistakably, the first sign of Spring. It went strong into her living body, the signal of her last Spring. And it made her feel sure, certain of her own beauty that was secure and incorruptible; for she could be crippled or shot down but not corrupted, and this she knew, threading the sharp and light slanting wind, saying Goodmorning and swiftly going by, seeing a face, a horse, a dog, seeing yesterday's *Herald* blow along the gutter, seeing the faces of men at windows, at doors, taking a look at her, speaking after she had passed, and she felt that speech keenly though she did not hear it.

A picture of Joan Crawford blew loose, flapped gigantic down over the street from a billboard, colossal lips, breast, teeth, eyes of woman. The Town seemed beneath the portent of some terrific happening, everywhere a movement larger than the living one, roaring, pitching in a frenzy strong and unpitying.

Pfeiffer opened his grocery store, saw the girl coming down Main Street, clutching her coat, so tall, the wind blowing her skirts about her, and he saw her for the first time as part a woman, remembering what he had heard Mrs. Pfeiffer say of her; and he looked at her coming down the wind for a moment, wondering.

He nodded to her and saw her look at her half-running reflection in the plate glass against the vegetables. She's looking at herself, he thought; she knows it too, that there is a change. But he felt her shy away from him, veer off from his gaze. He watched her. Too thin, he thought. Not like the mother. . . .

They stood, watching from their doorways, stopping their brooms, watching her go up the street, the wind whipping, worrying her too close.

The sun shone ominously pale, and clouds rode over it swift and white. A dust haze rose, stirred up fuming from the wind, lifting skyward toward stormkernelled clouds, the trees bent over knocking their limbs, getting ready to bud. And old leaves from an old year rose and blew, rattling down the streets like ghosts out walking.

Chapter Two

Penelope saw Jenny and Bac standing by the Kelly stall, and she tried walking as if she had not seen them. Jenny stood talking to a farm boy, teetering on her toes, legs curved back from the fruitlike buttocks. Pen went in a circle around, waiting to be noticed, and there was Bac lifting down the sacks of potatoes and corn, bracing his swift legs, showing through his jersey the powerful wedged back, the head going up swift and his neck flashing as he lifted.

"Hi, kid," Jenny said.

"Hi," said Pen.

Jenny slung an arm around her. "This is my girl friend," she said to the boy who flushed but was heated to Jenny, their eyes riveted.

Pen was lost in agony of love and the swift repulsion of Jenny's sharp, sensuous body, the strong feel and odor of her, as if she were swift, haunched in knowing, from her brown stalked body, teetering, blooming suddenly for one season, to her sensuously sunned face, always with pimples on it, dusky full lips, the flower-thick mouth, the purple black hair tight to the little skull.

"So long, kid," they said to the farm boy.

"I'll be seeing you," he said.

"Listen, kid," Jenny kept an eye out for prey.

"Hello, Pen." It was Bac.

She stopped as though her feet were tricked. "Hello Bac."

"Say girl," he straddled her way, "when you coming out? When you going with me to the back woods?"

Jenny giggled, punching her with an elbow.

"Oh, I don't know," Pen said, flushing, "I don't know."

"Well what do you know?"

They both laughed, then Pen laughed, looking at them with fright and longing.

"I want. . . . I want . . ." she said.

"C'mon kid," said Jenny. "Leave her alone," she said, winking at Bac, "you leave her alone," winking, saying: I'll fix her for you. . . .

Pen felt that arm around her shoulder. Girl . . . girl . . . I have a friend. . . . And she let her head fall back, touching the arm; let her hand lift, touching that swift brown hand of friend.

Pen saw Mrs. Kelly, her wrinkled face looking out of the stall. And Mr. Kelly, a short Irishman dumping out the potatoes into bushel baskets. "Hello Pen," he said grinning at her, too, as if she were in a conspiracy of which she knew least of all.

"Hello," she said, trying to be easy.

"C'mon kid," Jenny pulled her, greeting all the men who spoke to her, shouted at her, half-following, pleasantly at ease, and she turning, lifting her hand, pulling Pen past the stalls.

"Listen kid, I've got something to show you. . . . You've got on that old jacket again. I told you to come down to market in your best bib and tucker. You'll never get asked. . . . Listen, don't tell a soul, kid. . . ."

They went around behind, where the rotten apples and potatoes and old vegetables were dumped, and sat on a crate of shipped oranges from California with pictures of suns rising upon full orchards. Pen looked toward the front, thinking of Bac lifting out sacks of potatoes, and Jenny whispered, chattering into her ear, giggling, her eyes goggled, her breath warm, her hands quick, moulding in the air excitements. It was all about a sort of an actor who had been with Reading's Carnival last Fall at Halloween, on the edge of Town. And he had left his address with Jenny and they had kissed outside the flare of torches and the call of the tricksters. He had left the address when the carnival moved on to Joplin and she'd been writing to him.

Penelope listened half-hearing, hearing mostly the ways of the girl, the sound of her flashing body, the tinkle of her voice, the shaking of her blood like bells. And Jenny had been writing to him all this time, letters to Houston, El Paso. . . . Penelope had seen the letters bearing these names of far places; Jenny had wanted it known she had a person to write to in such places, had a part in a strange life. All the girls had seen those letters, leaning on Jenny's shoulder, smelling the powder she got at the Five and Ten, seeing the curve of her breast. . . .

And she had put on the letter "Dear Hubby," just for fun, to see how it would go, and sent the letter and afterwards could not call it back. And he had written then, saying that him and Joe Manning were going to start a show and would she go on stage with him—a sweet girl like her, a smart girl, buried like that on a farm, it was a shame—and he said he would buy her clothes and support her.

"I haven't told anybody," she said, half dancing up and down, "and I said send me five bucks and I'll meet you and talk it over, see? I could go this evening on the Five Ten, when I'm supposed to be gaffing with you kid, and I can take a look what it's about."

"Are you going?" Penelope said, clutching Jenny's hand, "Are you going?" Knowing Jenny would go. She seemed ready and it seemed simple, as if she could not help going . . . like the things Jenny had told her, speaking of those happenings with her mouth dark and smiling.

Jenny was holding out his answer. "This is what he says, see . . . duck it if Mom should come out, or Bac; Bac smells something in the wind." Penelope could hardly see the letters, could hardly know their meaning:

> You will get here about eight fifteen. Joe and I will be there. I thank you very much for the lock of hair. I wish I had your pitcher. Tell your pal I said Hello [that must be me, Penelope thought]— Let me know if you received the money order. I'm just dying to see your sweet face. Anytime I say anything sweetheart you can bank on it I mean it. Honey you can get anything from me that your heart desires for I love you baby and there isn't another girl that can take your place in my heart kid. I am writing this at one twenty and it will come over the N.W. RR and you will get it Friday evening. Well kid, I don't know anything else to say only see you Sat. Goodbye from your dear husband excuse the mispelled words take all mistakes as kisses. . . .

Penelope looked up holding the letter tight as if it might blow away. "You ain't married, Jen?"

"Sure not. That husband business is just you know, well. . . . Listen Pen," Jenny came close, worming her warm body near. "Why don't you go, see? We could both go on this, you and me both."

"Me?"

"Sure. Willya?"

Penelope never took stands. She grinned, hardly knowing what her face was doing. "Oh, I don't know if I could."

"Sure you could. Tonight is Saturday night. Your ma and grandma won't even miss you till tomorrow about noon or umpty ump . . . say, what a swell time we'd have."

"Sure," she said vaguely.

Jenny leaned close, whispering, watching the back door that led into the stall. "I'll see you. It's only the station that'll be bad. Somebody'll see us, but we can say we're just going for the day, can't we say that? I've got things to do, places to go. . . . Gee kid, I'm so excited to get away from here, to have a chance. . . . We're too swell kids for this place. Ain't that so?"

Penelope smiled and nodded.

"Mum's the word," Jenny said, and already upon her seemed to be what was going to happen to her. Penelope saw it on her body as if it could not help but happen.

She sat on the crate after Jenny had gone, feeling the wind

around her, seeing the images of Jenny's life in her mind for a moment, feeling her shoulders and breast flare like Jenny's, feeling that she herself might get up and move altogether, in one piece, with one destiny upon each movement, so that men could see and follow, and no terror in her but desires blooming up and going to death without any word, without any knowing.

And then, like a flame going down, Jenny left her as time went through her, threading her own time, her own destiny close, threading her down to the way her own body went lank and frightened, the way her own hands went out to touch, to embrace, her own mouth waiting for words, her breasts waiting to come like young horns, and her own ways were good to her in the wind, in the first pale day of Spring.

She got up and let the wind blow her around the corner, and into the new thick of the morning buying and selling, and she heard talking:

"Seventeen cents for corn . . . I got twenty-six cents for my wheat? What's a man to do with these prices?"

"I couldn't get a man to bale my hay and haul it to town even if I gave him the hay . . ."

"Try to borrow money . . . I'm worse off than I was . . ."

"I had to sell my livestock that might have et the grain and hay."

"I reckon you know Barnett failed in the hardware and is goin' to work at Jones down the river a piece. That man's been here for fifty year. . . . My father bought his first tools from that man. . . ."

"It's a shame and that's a fact."

Something was happening that day different from other days. Men were saying:

"They're holding up the milk trucks on Highway Twenty."

"What will happen?"

And some were standing, not committed to what was being done, but keeping an eye on it.

She heard men talking, pro and con, gathered in clusters like black bees upon the hive, clustered at a point where danger was, or disaster.

Women gathered in bitter black gatherings, hook and eye fastening them close, a black fume of women, bitter and rearing upwards, dark wild and dry, rearing up bitter against the men, the men seeming timid and gentle when the womenfolks scourged them with black tongue and sharp word. Penelope saw them for strong sick women; they all looked as if they should have been aged, yellow and pale. And no one spoke to her, but looks came after her, turning as she passed.

She saw the hot glance of Bac like a hound after her, saw him standing chewing a straw, one leg crossed over the other leg bearing his weight staunchly, and the strong curve of the haunch, the thigh, showing his strength, his slumbering back showing beneath his jersey; saw the way the muscles wedged down cruelly and swelled up to his neck, and the hands were large that went to his mouth and his face wide and cruel and handsome because of that, looking after her so she could not walk, like a noose crippling her, his glance like a dog going at her feet, confusing her walking.

She hid behind Barnett's wagon, looking at Bac who stood now quite still in the noon sun, chewing a straw and looking at everything. She looked at him unseen, knowing the cruelty of his ways, how his look was a hunting, how standing still he was cruelly gutting the scene for himself, seeing what craft he could do, seeing what young bucks were in for Saturday night, what girls; speaking to boy and man, seeing what car they could get to go over the border; laughing, showing his great smooth teeth, his face flushing, the blood going up to his black hair in a streak along the jowl, his hands grabbing shoulders, punching ribs. She had heard he was a good fighter, quick with his fists. She had to crouch, watching him for a long time, even when the market thinned, people going to early lunch, making ready for the town wives who would come shopping after.

Mrs. and Mrs. Kelly went down town together, and seeing them, she remembered what she had forgotten: that Jenny was going away. The train came at five and they didn't know, and Penelope with that knowledge. . . . She sat on the sacks behind the wagon. A horse chewed hay, shaking his head, pulling it from the bale and chewing it into his mouth slowly, his long face sadly showing, the great jaw moving, and a sadness came out of his hide to her. The market was almost empty; some were eating their lunches in the stalls. She could hear talk and see the skirts of a woman moving in and out of the shadow. The wind blew and blew down the street, and she saw a bevy of dead rabbits blowing, hanging down from their legs tied up high, along with some dried peppers and corn.

Penelope got up and drifted through the crowd, her head down to make her less tall, not wanting to speak; walked swiftly, cutting across Main Street, going past the station where she cut down the track, walking the ties not missing one, balancing, stepping, holding out her hands. She thought fleetingly of how the train would come across at five o'clock, that Jenny would be here not knowing that she had passed that way earlier, not knowing her thought. As if the occasion were there and the time arrived, she knew Jenny would get on that train; she could not count the disaster that would come, but she knew there would be change coming upon love or disaster. That was the way, she knew— disaster first, then change. The wind weaving stillness and stillness afloat upon the wind.

Penelope's face in the wind was a mask of death, of virginity that, caught between those millstones, could not break into the windy word of flesh, or froth upward into ecstacy of the deathly ideal, so she should be naked and responsive only to God whose articulation was death, and her face raised in an ecstacy of mysterious love, Jesus Lover of My Soul, striking down in a wonder of love that could never lodge now in her body or çlash with the flesh but must sour her then or break her into pieces.

"I wouldn't let anyone kiss me, only Jesus," but Jenny had laughed, her mouth, her hungry red mouth, opening in derision. Jenny would go on that train, and it would be sin . . . she would taste then of sin and she could be redeemed; she could stand up in camp meeting and hold out her arms and all the people could moan and sway, holding her up upon their own sin-laden bodies, loving each other at last in sin. And Reverend Stevens would take her to Jesus, holding her in his arms, letting her sink into that water that washed you pure as snow. She saw Jenny at the station dressed in scarlet, Satan and his angels lifting her downward into sin that shone and clashed and ran rivers of blood, and then angels white as the wool of the Lamb waiting to take her up, to walk with her through that river, that Jordan, and she would be fair of body and shine and her wet hair falling, her face lifted and a light shining around her head. Penelope went on over the trestle.

She then left the track and went through the hobo jungle, where there were signs of a fire, and cans, and pressed-down grass when men had slept. No one was there. She parted the stiff naked brush and went through, cutting away now from the town into brush that led to the fields, to the wild creek where it would be as if no one were on earth but Penelope. She parted the brush with her hands, stepping carefully. Mud lay heavy and thick in some places. The wind was sharp; the boughs cut her if she didn't take care, whipped her chill flesh in a cruel pain that must be like sin, too. . . .

Alone she had an ecstacy, cut off, bound in herself, a heedless ardor of a girl under an enchantment. Her loneliness turned to fortitude, defiance, love. She spoke to everyone in the Town. She lay down on the dead grasses that crackled under her and felt the icy ground, and saw the market, the way people were moving, moving in her and the faces lifted, smiling, and they were looking after her with admiration. *There goes Penelope. How lovely she is. How beautiful. Penelope. Ah, Penelope*, and she bent her head to them, smiling, her mouth smiling and smiling.

Sorrow and love filled her with a voluptuous sensuality. She lifted her arms and saw people touching her, and she touching herself, speaking to herself as if enclosed forever. Then in her high voice she began to sing: "Jesus Lover of My Soul, Let Me to Thy Bosom Fly. . . ."

Chapter Three

Saturday nights she always ended up at Littlefields for their chess game after supper, and she liked eating with him because he was awkward, and she could snatch the jam dish from him, laughing like her mother and ordering him about, setting out the dishes so he looked pleased, grinning, patting her shoulder, falling into his chair helplessly, for once enjoying it. She would set out the table, give the old curtains a shake as if she lived there, while he sat in the gloom outside the lamplight, smacking his loose lips, talking disjointedly, shaking his long bony hand in the shadow, mumbling, swearing, weeping.

She saw fragments of him as if broken he fell through space, part of him falling past her, a hand, a mouth, a dirty cheekbone, an eye full of matter, words, phrases suddenly turning from being flat and making images instead, his mother bending over him; a tall boy with shoes too little, poverty gnawing his vitals; a young man listening to Bryan who ate too much, talking about the gold standard. Then they would close up again and be lost in the sharp-edged falling of his words, in his orations, phrases he had crabbed from Bryan's own silver tongue.

They always had stale bread, tea and jelly. She sat opposite him, sitting very straight, holding her hand over her mouth as she chewed, smiling at him. He ate voraciously, drivel falling from his mouth, jelly on his coat. He was ashamed, too, when he saw her looking, and he would cover the lower part of his face, or put his dirty coat sleeve over his face, just his frightened pleading eyes looking at her.

Penelope could see out the tiny window Littlefield had made himself. It sat crookedly in the wall, putting the lane, the country road, the railroad track, the gently sloping hills askew, and the Town on a slant, smoke coming from the chimneys.

The sun was sinking and the wind had grown more chill. It was bending and shaking the bare trees in a last convulsion of death. Over the hillock the sun hung, white rays darting from it. Everything seemed to turn and face this white light on the hill, waiting. There was no outcry; the earth, dim, turned back to its bright burden, to its heavy life, flowering the shrub, breaking the iron. The trees, the shrubs, the hills all still within the wintry world. There were birds flying in the half-frozen air as if melting, delicate, terrible and fatal.

Littlefield said, "Man looks at the earth now on the square. No more of this mystical nonsense about it. I tell you, Darwin. . . . " She did not hear.

She saw the clock on a shelf he had built crookedly: five minutes to five. She stood up.

"Where are you going?" Littlefield said, peering up at her, a piece of bread waiting for his loose mouth.

"I was . . . suppose there was something . . . happening. . . . "

"Sit down," he said, waving his hand oratorically. She looked down the track. The clock ticked.

"Where were you going?" he asked, stopping chewing, looking at her nearsightedly, seeing her just a blur with her hair untidy.

"Oh, just somewheres," she said. She could never answer straight out.

"Was there someone waiting for you?" he said shyly, screwing up his eyes evilly, "was there someone?"

"Well not that way . . . yes," she said.

"Ho, ho," he said, "so it's that way. Well, I thought the skirts were getting longer."

She looked out the window. She looked down the track. Jenny's ways came into her again like some strange disease and she felt what she would feel, where she would be going. The sense of Jenny going her fatal way made a bright rocketing in her mind almost of envy, thinking: sin, sin. The bright sin and then the washing whiter than wool . . . to be able . . . to be able.

"Aren't you going?" Littlefield said, having forgotten her in the sweet taste of the bread.

"No, I reckon not," she said, sitting down. "Not today . . . I reckon not." She didn't eat.

Littlefield said, "Guess how much I paid for that bread. Two cents a loaf." He laughed noiselessly as if he had outwitted something. She laughed too, not knowing what was outwitted. . . .

On Saturday nights she came to play chess with him because she didn't care if he beat her, and would even go to sleep waiting for him to move as he pondered, hesitated in that vacillation that had lost him his life.

But before beginning, while she cleared off the table, stacking the dishes in the dark lean-to that was the kitchen, he got out a tiny book, bent over to the light, gripped a pencil in hands that came incongruously to him from farmers, men who gripped things of the earth strongly by force, and he never knowing anything to grip, losing what hold he ever had on what he touched, and began to scrawl, chewing the pencil, squinting into the light where gnats fell. In this book Penelope knew he chronicled the minute facts of his going and coming, his spending. In there were the cost of shoes, one pair a year, cost of food, underwear for Winter—thank God it is coming Spring, I can wear my old pants. The cost of stale bread, sardines and jam, as if by these things he could estimate the entire worth of his life. Or perhaps by this he measured something of what he might have been and knew wherein lay loss. Squinting his eyes, half-seeing Penelope carrying out bread and cup and plate, the nearness of her making his eyes smart and tears come out of him, like the only brew he had, the salt brew squeezing out of his dry bundle, following her with pleading eyes that made her feel happy; his loose lips watering, hanging in folds, smacking as she passed near him, as they did at the sight of apples, oranges, fair flesh of girl and woman, splendid contour of young men.

Made these entries, "Up at seven. First day of spring. Will save fuel. Looks like the farmers will do something. Bread 2. Beans 8. Tea 10." Turned a blank and pressed it down with a soiled thumb for a new day, Sunday. Marking days going by to his death, like a man who walks about and sees the maggots in his eyes. Turned back, added, "Penelope as usual for chess." Then folded the tiny book, carefully snapped the rubber close, fumbled, put in in his pocket seeing Penelope coming back into the room, foldin her hands together in front, her long arms which pulled her dress up along her legs lifting the chess box down, turning to smile at him, leaning over, placing it on the table, then sitting opposite him. He let her do everything. As if she were married to him. He was part old man and part boy when she was there. She brought up all the bewilderment, what should have been done and was not, what might have been. "At twenty-three I seemed to be doing pretty good. I seemed all right; I thought I was going to be a great lawyer. What happened? Yes sir, something happened."

He talks to her, making up what he was, what he might have been. She only half listens, seeing the husk of the man blow aside, seeing old powers like stumps, seeing what he spoke of as now dead, being once a living thing, making his body stand straight, making his face a fair mask. "Yes sir, something happened." He speaks of powers he held as a young man to be a speaker that would be heard over the country, listening to such spell binders as abounded then, to Bryan, and to Homer Wilson—"drank right with him in fact." He speaks of winning honors in school, his first case, with a bare table and one law book, of his marriage and the trip to Buffalo on the honeymoon; of things he had accomplished, and his form and face would fill out. She sees this; then his face and body would fall to despair, as if pricked of the wind of their hope; he would look up perplexed, bewildered. "Something happened. I wasn't the success I hoped to be. My wife was dissatisfied, as if I cheated her. Promised her goods I couldn't deliver, so to speak. Well, what was it? You can't blame her. I don't blame her. Look at me. Who could live with me? She was right, the names she used to call me. Who could carry on a life with me? I am covered with mud and dirt . . . ."

She knew he mourned his wife, then, his poverty, the money he never got, the money he had and lost, the education he missed or had too late, the fame he hoped for, and all that grief came from out his pores like a stench.

Over and over every Saturday night he told her about Mrs. Littlefield, how they lived together, quarrelled, how after thirty years they had been divorced . . . . He went over and over it all, how they quarrelled, the poison in each coming out despite them, how they covered each other with mud and abuse. Then his hatred of her would gather in him like a bad spot spreading, corrupting the fruit, and he would become terrible, abusing her for hours. Then, looking up at the frightened girl the tears would stand in his eyes. "I am covered with mud and dirt, that's what. No one could live with me . . . ."

Or it was his childhood that gathered in him again, distilling the bitterness of its brew upon him, showing how poverty had crippled him. "Look at my feet," and there they were, knotted, turned back like a deformation from wearing shoes that were too small when he was ashamed to tell his mother, who was nigh mad with the things to be got, the food, the clothes going out where she could see no end of getting them, and his father squeezed dry of himself long since and his land sucked as dry as himself and the vicious circle leaving them dry and destitute. For when a man had only half enough to eat when that man was boy, it leaves a mark that never comes off. When he's a man he's bound to feel it in his bones still, how they were starved as a boy when the time was to make them bloom big and hold a man well within himself, give him a framework to build himself upon. At the age of eight he had plowed all day on a lean stomach. His father never got on. His mother, stern, angry, belligerent against something she could not touch or fight, taking it out on the men, berating them, going into a hysteria of loss and suffering that never left her, that finally marked her forever heavy with abuse for an unknown thing that had mde her life too spare, too hòrrible. They were always moving from one farm to another, going in wagons, over hill and hill into more poverty, into more poor farms, having more wormy cattle and bad crops. Their own defeat ranked in them worse than disease, for they did not know if it lay within or without, whether it was God, the devil, themselves or fate, not knowing what it really was: that there was barter and trade setting one man against another and the vast multitudes against the wolf perpetually ragging them. The oldest son died, the flower of the family, and he and a puny sister left, a bitter joke along with all the rest. He went to school a spare term, too large for the grade, remembered tittering girls who left a mark and a fear of women deriding him he was never to get over, that left him shy, apologetic, his bony finger hiding his long nose, his eyes frightened or crafty, the odor of him bitter.

One moving left a deep gash in him that opened at night making him weep for the thin boy who sat with his mother and sister waiting for trains that could never take them on. Once in their many migrations they went from town to town on a train, a long way. A relative had died, leaving them a house in Des Moines, so they were going, a windfall of free rent paradisiacal to them. They had felt flush, had used what they got from selling what they had to go by train with their household goods taken by a friend who was taking a load of cattle to the fair at that time, what was left over nailed in boxes, trunks and carried with them.

The mother knew little of such traveling, and sat rigid, her mad accusing eyes expecting the worst which she had been trained to receive. The sister, only one year from her death, cowed as if every sight was a blow, accumulating her future slowly. The father roamed the aisles looking or paced the platforms when the train stopped. They were coming from Texas, and had to make many changes from the cattle range waiting at little stations half the night on benches, not speaking, lost to their own lives not yet gaining another. And the thin lank boy was in torture thinking they would never get to their destination, that the father would be lost or killed, that there would not be money enough. He must suffer for his father and mother who seemed as large and helpless as himself in the unfamiliar world, where there were no fields to plow, no cattle to tend, no earth to tramp; sitting waiting turning, frightened, whispering to each other, their faces gone strange.

It was just as bad when they got on a train at last. He feared it would be the wrong train, because his father and mother had whispered about it before boarding it, because there had been hesitation and fright, and he had felt it, looking at their hesitant faces, feeling the going back and forward of their bodies as if they had become children instead of himself, and his slightness bearing the mature pain and their physical maturity bearing again childish impotence. Getting on trains going nowhere, dragging his aching legs up heights and down, dragging suitcases that knocked him over.

And another station, off the train into that warm room which stood like a small thing at the juncture of two swift rails running together for a moment in the prairie, waiting for a train that would curve down the opposite way and take them again along what was supposed to be a planned way, but which seemed to be only a madness of indecision, of waiting. . . . His mother was wooden now: "Well, do you know where we're going?" He flinched at the lash in her tongue, at the stooped shoulders of the father going off again to wait, to stand like an ox by windows, by stoves, waiting, at last asking, his words hardly forming. Or going to see about their trunks which came apart at one place and had to be nailed up.

He got a hammer and nails from the station master and went away leaving them sitting by the stove with the click of the telegraph connecting again somewhere. The boy watched his mother's face to read there what would happen and read nothing, only that she expected the worst, the most bitter to happen. The father was gone a long time; space disappeared, time fell in like a cavity. He could not remember how many nights had gone, how many meals, how many days. They had eaten all the lunch they had started with and now had only a banana too ripe. No one paid any attention to him except to drag him on and off trains, make him sit still. He slept with his dread beside his mother on benches, through long hours in which his whole life seemed to flow and be with him on the bench like a weight that everyone would notice; the trains shrieking past, gigantic headlights for a moment lighting the dark prairie, piercing his half dreams that would be lost forever; and he hung like a weight from the face of his mother, as if it alone was a lode from madness. Hunger made the wind of the world go through him mercilessly.

He cried out, his mother shook him, and the lights blinked small noises, the click of the operators moved minute inside his head. "See if your father is coming," she said, commanding him always as if not expecting him ever to live up to her expectations. "Hurry . . . Good Lord what did I ever do to be left with you . . . you . . . you . . . Josiah gone, taken by the Lord . . . and *you* left. . . ." And he crept, opening the door looking out at the dark night, the crevasse where the track ran away . . . and he did not look for his father, stood outside the door, wishing he could bring his mother a gift, that he would not be a disappointment to her, that she would say, "Why look what he has brought . . . lovely," and look, her eyes softening a little so he would stand foolish, smiling. . . .

Drawn back inside to her, knowing uneasily every shift of her hard body like a man's for muscle, like a woman's for ills and hysteria, he strained to catch a glimpse of something, heard a knocking down the station which it never occured to him was his father nailing up the trunk, went back into the warm small room, a train man coming in with him which made him think the train might go any minute and his father not on it. As a matter of fact it did not go until morning and he sat there dozing beside her, feeling her bitterness, the odor of disappointment in her making him never expect fullness or greatness except in the dream of himself being a Jefferson, a Lincoln, which was not really his own hope but merely the reflection of what seemed possible from the emotional tirades that seemed the most sure flight from what in his bones he knew to be a fatal limitation. He did not sleep, watching with horror his mother lose consciousness, leaving him with the shifting weight of the broken world coming upon him hunched in the tight Sunday suit he had been proud of two years before, but which now left him sticking out like a scarecrow far grown beyond its limitations, eyes drinking darkness, remembering journeys over dark roads from dawn to dawn, remembering low talk of beaten men who were beaten by all except their own hope, tasting the taste of that defeat when he should have been drinking a good air beneficent on the earth; all remembrance pouring into him until his skin was tight, the world he knew bowing him in terror, making his lips and brows stone. To remember always an anxiety in the great starless universe, smelling the foul wolf's den he was in that kept out the scent of that spinning universe, of that flowering stone, the earth. He sat still until he became the darkness weighted with that black stone of defeat, anxiety.

And when his mother started up away, saying with her wife's lips, "Husband . . . Ellery," reaching too for him she hated but who was husband, and seeing the tiny boy-eyes of her own flesh looking at her in a terror the meaning of which looked from her own eyes and lay like a child she would not spawn in her own flesh: She was moved to him whom she also hated because she grudgingly gave him birth out of a poor bone and a starved flesh, and he was never anything but her own poverty looking out at her with a replica of her own eyes. But now seeing him without sleep starting up, flickering with high cry unusual to him she softened the tense cruelty of the lost night, enfolding him once more before she let him grow into a tall man mostly bone and fear.

Poverty being no sister to tenderness and no soil for a body's blooming, but a dead air where man and woman cannot touch each other except in rebellion.

Penelope, having gone on the journeys of the poor, without enough money, prey to their fear, knew him vaguely as something she too might become, only in women the foulness was bitterness

27

and the sadness was hatred, women brewing an awful mess of frustration. She knew that odor that came off him was the smell of loneliness and sterile grief that had not a movement to make with another, except in cunning, fear and ugly parsimony; knew that he hoarded his pennies, salting many away, depriving himself, never had a moment's enjoyment spending a nickel, had bought his coffin so it would be good and at the same time cheap. That it was the smell of the fine fruit of a man rotten, lying in so rotten a barrel through no fault of his own unless it was a quiescence, the fine bone and flesh of a man rotten, turned back upon its black spreading-filth self, turned back upon itself with a call from no man, no voice calling. And even the apple would not ripen on the tree or the corn on the stalk, she thought, without that call . . . even when the apple is sold in the market and the corn and wheat are bartered in Chicago, the essential call that turns the cheek to red and gives the full round contour is the sun of need, and neither can a man turn in roundly or be of good flesh and cheer where there is barter; one man set against the other like a pack, and the teeth in the throat.

"What time will it be now?" Penelope said.

"The days are getting longer . . . it'll save oil. Lighting the lamps at four makes a difference."

"If you'd make your window hole bigger and wash your curtains, Mr. Littlefield. . . ."

His finger tweaked his nose as he smiled cunningly. "That's what Mr. Littlefield was always doing, scolding me—'Why don't you do this, Littlefield'—she always called me Littlefield, like a man—yes that was the trouble. She was more a man than me, and that's a fact."

"What time is it, Mr. Littlefield?"

"It's almost time for the Five-Fifteen. That shadow moves just that far beyond the chinaberry tree every day, and it'll fall this side, just this side of the picket fence, and then if she's on time she'll come over the trestle just before the shadow moves to the next picket. Pretty smart, ain't that?"

"Yes."

"She's late," Littlefield said. "There, it's all set up. Your move first. . . ."

"What time is it?"

"It's five thirty. She's late."

"Why should she be late?" Penelope thinking, she is standing there now on the platform, and Perkins the ticket man is looking out at her, wondering some dirt to himself about her because she will have it on her where she is going. It'll be on her like a garment of sin, all in scarlet, shining.

"Do you know what sin is?" she said, moving a pawn down without planning, as she did.

"Sin?" Littlefield said, "sin. . . ." He smacked his loose lips, rolling the word on his tongue, saliva coming at the corners. "Now what are you going to do? Say, why did you want to know about the Five-Fifteen? I bet you been sparking Applebaum."

Then the train came rearing up like sin itself over the trestle. She saw it out of the little window as if it would take off and go over them, its black snout pushing a way through as if plunging was its only life, then passing on, hooting for the crossing, stopping, taking on water at the station; and she could see, as if it happened between the moving of the fourth pawn and the next that Jenny would look around flaunting, with it written on her, her leg showing as she stepped up, the five dollars now broken for the ticket to carry her, the many pieces of money broken lying in her new purse, rich now in sin, with money to spend, stepping onto a train.

"There she goes," said Littlefield, speaking of the train.

"Yes," said Penelope, and Jenny came into her like a nauseous odor, a sickness, usurping the way of herself. Jenny, so fleet of haunch to be going those swift ways into hell. And part of it was that Jenny, come summer, could be saved at the camp meetings, could be washed whiter than snow, could be whiter having sinned, if she was not dead, struck down by the wrath of the Lord.

"Play, play," Littlefield said. "Just like my wife . . . women are all alike."

Penelope played. But she was listening to the silence now outside where the train had gone through leaving a torn hole. She felt herself waiting upon him as he leaned over debating what he would do, as if she waited upon that element that had forged him, and that would make him do in the future what he must do.

"Play, play! . . . Women are all alike. . . ."

She waited for him to play, half sleeping in herself, not noticing how long, simply sitting, her golden hair inflamed around her thin face, moving only her cramped legs so her feet wouldn't touch his under the table. She knew every movement of him. He chewed his under lip, scratched his ear, squinting his small eyes, whistling out of loose hanging mouth, twiddling his thumb and finger together, the sound of dry flesh like the scurrying of a mouse. Until at last he placed a soiled thumb on the queen's head, held it there craftily, his nose twitching as if it too could become cunning enough to know how to win, above all things. Then, "No," he says, flipping his long knobular nose. And he puts his thumb on the knight, moves him away from hers slyly, keeps his wide thumb there, brushes down three pawns with his ragged sleeve, retires in confusion and looks at her like a naughty boy. He sets the pawns up in the wrong place, grins beneath his squint eyes, his skin like dirty crumpled gutter paper, twiddles his swollen nose again, sits back and beams derisively. Penelope begins to set up the pawns. "Just like my wife," he says. "I used to knock down the pawns and she'd set them up just like that," he says. "Women are all alike . . . only it's one thing, you don't care how long I take, that's one thing. But SHE . . . she used to walk around the room . . . 'Haven't you moved yet, you dolt, you lummox?' Then she'd pace around so how could a man think decent? 'Now, now, have you moved at last?' she'd say, coming over swift, 'There,' she'd say, just popping off in a move with no sense to it . . . women have no sense. Then it always ended this way . . . she'd just plank her hand down on the board and send everything flying . . . that woman, that woman . . ." and he would dote upon her hatred and his own, creating it again tenderly. "Thirty years we had it. That's the way the chess games always came out with her. . . . Well, well, what a battle that was. No battle in history lasted that long, thirty years, now, did it? My move? Well, well . . . wait now . . . sorry . . . all right. . . ."

He leans over now to watch her, his scraggly brows fluffing out, getting closer to see just where she will move. She waits, smiling at him as if she doesn't see what an exterior gentleman have. The sound of his pursed lips is in the room, she sees them like a hollow wordless mask hole, making a sound. He watches her play, settles back smiling, his legs too long, folded upon him like a jackknife. The kettle she had put on to wash up with begins to sing. They sit a long time, the game terminating, drawing to a close.

"I win . . . I certainly win. . . . Well, I beat you, didn't I?" Littlefield says, eating his satisfaction like a rich tart, smacking his lips, rubbing his hands together, stretching as if he needed badly to win even a chess game from a girl half asleep, whose life had not yet come to the time of winning and losing.

And now he would begin to talk, living over the time when he almost spoke to Bryan. He could have told him a few things; talking from his loss and pain, squeezing it out like sweat coming from him. Then suddenly in the midst of a story he forgets what he had intended its meaning to be, stops, tweaks his nose, paws the air as if for breath, lets his hands drop loose. "Well, where was I? What was I saying?" and she puts him back, remembering a shred for him to clutch. "You were telling about your first law office and when you were going to run for district attorney." "Oh, yes, yes," he says, "yes . . . well, it doesn't matter, does it. Why talk about it. But something happened, I don't know what. . . . How I told my wife, that is, Mrs. Littlefield before she divorced me, I told her she ought to run for it. She always told me she was a better man than I. I always told her that myself in fact. . . . Well, well, let that go, certainly. . . ." He had phrases, words, that at one time may have had some meaning for him, that he may have heard as a young man, and acquiring them in a dearth of speaking made him feel them important beyond their meaning.

Penelope listens, half hearing. Sitting in the chair quite still, her face turned half smiling, because it is his life he is telling and it has passed, and someday she will be sitting saying these things and there will be no choice whether she will go on a train with Jenny Kelly or stay, and what the week of Easter will bring, or what the year of that time will bring. It will be certain, marked in her flesh; it will be going on towards death like Littlefield and there will only be remembrance to brush down the sheen of what is dull. "I was mean to my poor mother. Now what possessed me? Jesus Christ, why didn't I go when she was dying and wanted one of her flesh and blood to stand up for her? But I didn't go, I remember I felt bitter and I didn't go. I thought, 'Let her die' I thought. I really did. How can you account for it?"

He pulls over his coat to hide a spot where he had spilled something, suddenly delicate, not wanting her to see. "I don't know why I never was one of the men who do things. This land is full of opportunity . . . this land is the best place on earth for a man to be born in, and that's a fact. Why look . . ." and he would go over, repeating phrases of all the jingo speeches he had heard since he was eighteen, small opinions moulded like knots on his malady, taking root because of the defeat in him and the poor soil. This hope beyond possibility, deliberately brewed in him by all he heard and saw, made anger and the hatred of frustration a part of him, and almost against his will had hate for its brew.

He is saying, "Listen, Penelope, Reverend Stevens talked last Sunday about the economic situation, and there I was, sitting right in the eighth row on the aisle, you know. There he was, speaking, searching, hunting, and there I was that could have told them just what to do. I have the whole solution to the economic situation. All we need to do is go back to the old ideals, the Jeffersonian ideals of good citizenship . . . and vote . . . no violence. Let them have that in Russia but America is the land of the free . . . I tell you, let them vote. Everyone can vote. He ought to be instilling them with the old duties of citizenship and honor. There I sat and I couldn't get it out of me . . . I couldn't tell him." He blinks, his finger along his nose, his eyes letting brine fall out of them.

And "Look, look," he says with excitement, "I knew that man Rolfe, I knew him twenty years. Once I had a talk with that man.

31

We sat in a saloon and we talked . . . we put our hands around each other's shoulders." "Oh," he leered, "nothing evil, nothing bad . . . that night we really said something to each other. . . . And do you know, ever since, I've met that man every Saturday and we barely speak . . . just as if we were strangers, as if we had never sat like brothers . . . he goes right by me, you see?"

"And once I stood behind a tree, watching a certain house. Now that's funny, you see I fancied I was in love with the woman in that house. I stood there many nights and she never knew it. She never knew anything about it. Well, how do you account for that now?"

"I don't know," Penelope said, "I feel that way too, as if nobody knows about anybody else. Maybe somebody stands in front of your house, Mr. Littlefield, and you don't know it."

His eyes half turned to the darkened window. "Well, I doubt it," he said after a moment of listening, "I doubt it. I wouldn't go to look because ten to one there'd be nobody there. Well, I don't know how it is, something has rejected me, kicked me out . . . that's it, and I don't know what it is. . . ."

"I feel that way," Penelope said in a small voice which he did not hear.

I grew from this thick meaty earth, Mr. Littlefield said to himself, *and I am a ghost. . . .*

And for a long time Penelope watched him hanging over his thin body as if slowly chewing himself off at the breast, knowing that he lived off himself. *Some morning*, she thought, *he will be gone.* He lifts his head, gazes about anxiously just as he did that night in the station as a child, the same look in his eyes.

"You know, I once saved Pfeiffer, loaned him money that saved him at the time, and now he barely speaks to me. You'd never know it now. He's forgotten, you see? My death will be nothing to that man or any man in this Town. I doubt if they'll even come to my funeral. I do. I doubt it. . . ."

"That man doesn't dream," he said suddenly, getting up and waving his arms, "that man doesn't dream I might have been a Webster, a great man; that it was just by a margin like that"—he holds up his bony thumb and forefinger.

Who are you, Mr. Littlefield? Penelope asks herself, looking to see his great dreams and his meanness, his scrimping starving swindling, standing side by side, whispering and shouting in him through his loose and evil mouth.

Saying, "Now, I have a big outlook for humanity. . . . Well, I made a speech once, telling about my outlook. You know the mayor of Keokuk was there and he told me it was a good speech." He stops, embarrassed, grinning, flushing, jerking his shoulders, blinking his tiny red lids, twiddling the end of his swollen nose.

"Well I don't know what has happened. I was getting along all right and then I didn't get any further . . . that's all there is to it."

She listens half hearing, sitting in the chair opposite, listening to her own breast growing, trying to find something on which to grow. But she hears, too, the drone of the old man dying, suddenly looking up to see his mouth in a loose O hanging out of his face, a wound that cannot be sewed up to keep him from talking so much, that cannot be drained either of poisons . . . *Old man, you have had that and that.* She sees something, sees him riding with his mother, beside her, then growing to be an old man sitting in a sack of flesh. *I'll be an old woman too. . . .*

Who are you, Littlefield?

"Well, there's this Town. No one knows my qualifications here. Do you think Perkins would even let me take an examination for postmaster? They don't appreciate me. . . ."

O Town, Penelope thought, seeing the square, the library, the post office. *Where am I? Where was I? Where am I?*

"Now it's the path of Bunyan," he says, but she is asleep, saying *O Town, O Town. . . .*

He stands quite still seeing her asleep, her head falling back against the high chair where he sees her dimly. He sits for a moment, his head dropped forward on his chest, his eyes looking up at her queerly. Then he looks about as if he might find something under the table or hanging from the ceiling. He looks then straight at Penelope and a crafty pursing embitters his face. He gets up, standing tall in the room, pulls the curtain softly and begins to go toward her, putting out his hands as if to warm himself.

She moves, her head falling forward, and he stops. She looks now as if listening to something happening inside the earth, or inside her own body.

He stood before her a long time, rubbing his hands together like a man who has come in out of the cold. He leaned over in close scrutiny, as if to take her apart and find something, his face holding at once an evil and an anxiety, as if he knew the evil and was anxious about it, about what it would produce, dreading what would erupt from himself.

He put out his hands, over her breast but not touching her. Excitement made his long legs shake, the excitement of wanting to participate, even in lust, of wanting to be part, to merge, to act in the heat from which he was always being thrown.

She opened her eyes, not moving, looking straight at him. He paled, reared back, covered his face. "I was just waking you . . . I think you better go. It's late, Penelope. . . . You better be on your way. It's a dark piece into Town, you know that. . . ."

Penelope did not move, looking at him, still feeling what she had felt before awaking.

"Yes," she said.

"Well, I think you better," he said in confusion, wiping his eyes, shaking his long bony hands together, "I think you better go now. . . ."

"Yes," Penelope said.

"Come, come," he began to giggle, "I'll get your jacket. Hee, hee . . . I'll be your beau, shall I . . . ."

"No," said Penelope, "I can put it on." She pulled her old jacket quickly around her, wriggling up, standing beside the lamp.

"You didn't put the chessmen away, and I didn't do dishes yet."

"Never mind . . . heavens, would I have a beautiful lady wash my dishes?" Littlefield kept brushing her shoulder down with his hand.

"Goodbye, Penelope," he said, trying to kiss her, masking it under fatherliness, patting her shoulder, leaning down his mouth. She evaded, passing toward the door.

"It'll soon be Easter," she said, passing out of his reach.

"Little Penelope," he said weeping. "Well I do smell bad. I'm an old man, I eat stale meats, perhaps to a young girl like you . . . you girls are squeamish, eh? Well, I'm covered with mud, I know that . . . I'm covered with mud all right. . . ."

Chapter Four

Outside Penelope began to run into the darkness that rose cold and damp around her, with the croaking of frogs, her legs moving swift, crisscross, carrying her long and strong, changing her, putting her along the path of her own strange and lovely ways, passing the fields, the young orchards sleeping, moving toward the coming fruit, passing the fields that stood, holding the stalks of last Winter up to the stars, freighted with white seed of the future about to ripen up into the air, to fall back again to another Winter and another darkness, but now ready to stand up in mid-region, ready to go in that direction between earth and sky in an old light.

Passing quickly she smelled the night smell, not going back the way she had come over the trestle but cutting through one of the paths she knew. She knew many oblique ways, cutting across the Town, not liking roads and sidewalks, climbing fences, skirting down alleys, going through yards, liking to go near the warm houses where people rose, moved, where lights burned, from which the smell of cooking came, the clatter of dishes, the crying of children. Then swift into the Town streets, Saturday night loosened, the dogs sounding on the edge now, the Town uneasy, striding the streets, girls and boys coupled, wagons passing, cars passing, going back to the farms, cattle going back, unsold or bought. Penelope went swiftly thinking whether to go down Main Street, excited to see the crowd coming from the Gem Theater, to see the people milling around, for this was the first warm day and the wind had now gone down, protected in the Town; even the scurrying wind outside Littlefield's was unfelt.

Like a plunger into a sea she started down Main Street. It was just ten o'clock. The time amazed and consoled her, as if she had come back into a measurement she had slipped away from. The street was bright and the sounds were the first sounds of the Spring and Summer that would' make a fanfare in the Town, shaking people together again. . . . Clots of slender, quick boys stood on sidewalks, couples strolled through toward the tracks, toward Pershing Park where trees made a rising darkness arching above. She was awkward and lost in herself, raised her hand thinking to speak, made a word with her mouth that never came out, walked with neck stiff, hugging herself, feeling her body like a stalk or a bone, without grace, having none of the ease of Sally Carter who was giggling, walking entwined with three others down the street—Louise Tanner, Millie Shields, Ellen Haughty. They seemed so light and their mouths taking to a smile with ease and color on them, their skirts frilling down and a smell of violet coming out of them, passing.

"Hello Pen," they said, nudging each other as if holding back something only until she passed, then she heard it, a shrill laughter, knowing they were leaning on each other, saying funny things, calling attention to her skirt, her shoes, the way she walked, and it would not be in anything said, but in how funny these things would become to them because they said them, how the words would stand up at the moment, funny, so she wished she could lean with them and laugh, too.

She heard their laughter mingle then with sound of man talk, cars starting, hearing a snatch, a phrase swiftly passing. Saw the way men were standing close in together, with some unnamable excitement on them, saw that something had happened, came in close to them, stood under the low swinging stars hearing them say:

"Well anyhow, it was something, it was a try . . . "

"I told you that's the way it would come out all right . . . "

"Sheriff Anderson had no business coming in like that, with arms . . . "•

"Well, what did the farmers do? Scattered in the cornfields, that's what . . . "

"Well, this time. But that corn can hide a man, too, when it grows tall . . . "

"Wait and see, the price of milk will go up . . . you wait and see . . . it ain't lost . . ."

"We'll. wait and see . . . "

"You'll see what'll happen next, goin' against law and order, taking things into your own hands . . . "

"We'll see what we will see . . . that's a fact . . . "

"Well, I see 'em settin' there, all those fellows, with a fire burning to keep 'em warm. Now boys that was somethin', them all waitin' for the milk trucks to come through. They didn't just expect that kind of a greetin' . . . "

Men had lingered later than usual in the Town, talking in groups, one who had been on Highway Twenty telling how it was to the others, who listened, weighing it all slowly, jumping at nothing. The townspeople were in other groups.

"We're going to stop this," Swillman's secretary said. "We're not going to have our Town discriminated against. I'll see that pressure is brought . . . they'll see more than that if thcy keep this up . . . Mr. Swillman'll go to the governor."

But the boys, the young fellows were still saying:

"I says to her . . ."

"Boy, did I make a hit . . ."

"Is she? I'll say she is . . ."

The crowds were breaking up now, the older men moving slowly away, saying:

"Well, he didn't wait for the hay to cure . . . dried it green and salted it down. A stand of timothy on that land . . . heavy . . . heavy . . ."

"Us farmers ain't goin' to suck a hind teat . . ."

"What's the matter Butch, ain't they even buying meat?"

"Well, everybody's living on pig snouts and neck bones . . ."

Laughter all together, cracking the ribs.

"That's prosperity. . . . That's Hoover prosperity . . . sucking us dry, the railroads, the milk companies . . ."

Penelope going past in the dark: "I hear men talking . . . in Utah, in Montana, from Texas to Illinois, men are talking. . . ."

A bevy of matrons came from the Gem, so certain of what they had and knew, buttoning their coats snugly, seeing the men down Main Street out of the corner of their eyes. They passed her, glancing back at her, nodding, speaking low and knowing, seeming to know, too, what she was, measuring and putting her exactly, so she felt diminished, a thing smaller than she was, made so by their askance looks backward, putting her in a place forever as they were, knowing her too small.

The ice cream parlors of the Greeks were teeming. She went past the hardware, the grocery, the book store, dark now. Thinking, Mr. McEvan is home, Mr. Pfeiffer is watching his wife putting her hair on curlers now [she giggled thinking it], Mr. Haughty of the book store doesn't know his daughter is fishing for a beau with that naughty Millie Shields and the others. . . .

Then like a trap, a snare, Bac was straddling her way, a little drunk, swaggering, blocking her going like a quick rock, his quick legs staunch before her. "Hello Pen," he said, smiling that smile he had, like a hunter who has found something in his snare. "Listen, where is Jen?"

"Jenny?" She remembered again. Like a rocket it went through her. "Jenny? Why?"

"Oh, c'mon," Bac said, "where's the gal gone? I know she's been up to something."

"I don't know. I got to be on my way, Bac Kelly."

"You do too know," he said, taking her arm, and his touch made her go swift, resisting as she couldn't do when he only stood, and he pulled her back to him against a sign board, so she couldn't get away, and she saw the letters of the sign saying: RED GOOSE SHOES.

"C'mon, tell me where she's gone. You and her's been up to something lately. I know you have." Then he stepped again behind the signboard, cutting them off from the street where she knew they were saying: two of a kind; birds of a feather, where she knew eyes were estimating them down the street, believing she had gone off with him when she hadn't, giving her sin who couldn't take it. He pulled her up swift against his haunches so she smelled the closeness of his jersey, of sweat and horses and gin, and felt his arms like a darkness enclosing her like a rock leaning over her, pulling her in. Glimpsing too his cruel face grinning down, the set jaw, black hair, the cocky insistence, himself inflaming him now, swaggering with a sap that came up in him, making him drunk of himself.

"You don't need to be doing this, Bac Kelly," Penelope said, "I'll tell your old man."

"What's the matter with you? Don't you like it, ever?"

"I'll be telling your old man," she said, slowly, hanging from his grip, he half shaking her, pulling her to him, flinging her away in anger.

"I don't know nothing about Jenny. I ain't even seen her, Bac, since this morning at the market."

"The hell you ain't. . . . Well, who cares about her? C'mon take a walk with me, Pen . . . take a walk now. . . ."

"I can't. I got to be getting back. My ma is expecting me."

"What for is she expecting you? Don't kid me."

"No, I got to. My ma expects me to wash up this time Saturday nights. I got to be washing up the glasses come this time Saturdays."

"Well, I'll be going along with you then."

"Fine."

"O.K. C'mon."

Nothing to do but launch into the street with him. They came out and she thought no one saw; they began walking and it was an agony to her, so she thought the street would never end. They went into the darkness of H Street, down Maple under the bare trees that seemed ready to bloom. Bac swaggered blindly, pulling her by the arm so he could feel her leg against his, and she couldn't help going beside him.

She felt something pass between Bac and the young men,

turning.

"Well, well Bac. . . . Hello," as if they tasted her, too, along with Bac.

"Hi," Bac said, raising his arm like a victor, as if he had something. She lowered her head, not framing Hello, though she knew the boys by face and name, Harry, Stan, Joe, Shorty, Red . . . all faces and squatness or longness she knew from seeing them along the street, at school . . . boys . . . soon to be talking, like men. . . .

But there was pride in it, too, to be walking alongside, and a new element came and mixed with her being, a hard knowing element, plunging, a swift arrow, through her own vagueness and her own fears. She walked straight down with him, now, not plunging behind trees or stopping to see if others might be looking at her, wondering: What is Pen doing now? What is she thinking? Who is she now? With what is she mixing, and what is mixing with her?

Chapter Five

Bac and Penelope stood outside the wooden house, now heated from within, movements bashing the walls, shadows moving, leaving a blank when they had gone. One window was slightly open because it was so warm, and the sound of men's voices came out very low.

"Are you coming in?" Penelope said.

"I'll say I am," said Bac, walking up the wooden steps that sounded under his quick, willful feet. Penelope half ran behind, feeling it would be a good thing to go in with him, so that Gee and .Mona might see her coming in with a young man at that hour. She came behind his insolent going, feeling broken off from him now, yet necessary to go in his swift, cruel walking, his swift-arrowed being going straight where it aimed, flinging open the door, letting it bang back, and she came in after, shutting it carefully so it made no noise.

Four men were playing poker at a table in the parlor.

"Hit me. Hit me. Another . . . another."

"Go on. O.K. Let her go."

They looked up, nodded, "Hello Bac." He saluted, one finger at his cap. A dim light hung above three tables in the dining room where four or five men sat, thick in smoke. Penelope went into the kitchen where Gee loomed.

"For Christ's sake, Pen, where have you been, leaving your poor old Gee all this work. What do you think I'm made of? Here I am, about dead. Haven't slept a wink, not a wink. Can't eat, my ulcers are botherin' me again. For Christ's sake."

Penelope began wiping glasses, looking towards the door where Bac was. "Give me a glass stiff," she said, "for Bac."

"He ain't paid us. And Mona said . . ."

"Go on Gee, give me one and make it stiff like he likes it."

"Oh for goodness sake," Gee said. "You two . . . *men*. . . . Oh, for heaven's sake.

Someone began singing very low. It went up, fell, died.

Penelope took in the coffee cup with honey liquor. Bac sat tipped back, wisecracking.

Then Mona came thrusting the door back. "Pen, Pen . . . where have you been?" Enveloping her warmly, the door hanging open behind her so the men looked in, seeing her amorous arms over the girl, watching.

"Watch out. . . . Who's the stuff for?"

"For Bac," Penelope said, nodding to the open door. He sat framed, looking at them, smiling.

"For Bac? I'll take it." Mona took it, letting the door fall to behind her full hips.

Gee said, turning her head back from her fat body as she swung the door, "Wash up all them cups, Pen."

The dishes they had eaten off were piled on the table. She heard the talk in the other room, her mother laughing. Slowly Gee came in, letting the door swing back, swing shut, letting sounds ebb in, flow back. Bac talking to Mona, seeing the black hair, the great throat of Mother. Penelope watching. Mother . . . crouching in the room, as if ready to pounce, black eyes wide, feeding upon Penelope, upon men, whose voices were saying,

"Hit me . . . go on, hit me. . . ."

"Another . . . again . . . another. . . ."

"Hit me. . . ."

Penelope washed the white china cups, placed them on the drain. It was so warm the kitchen door stood open, showing the black night. The front door opening and closing, and Mona's voice, a shuttle weaving, a loom, and Penelope hung on the mesh of her love with an ache incessant, with a cry.

Standing in the doorway, looking down she saw a cricket skip across the floor and stop, sensing her. She crouched down on her heels, looking at it; raised her hand above it, swooped, covering it with her palm. She held it in her flesh, slowly turned her hand over, her face close to it, seeing the tiny hard shell body on legs, the antennae, the round hard head alive with eyes. She saw closer, the flat body, the tall upbending legs with the spring in them, so tiny but upspringing in a strength that carried it, its feelings, its soft interior and the hard crust body, the sensitive antennae now waving, feeling what held it, straining with them to find a way. She was so startled, then, she let it move up her finger, for from out it came a long high cry that might have come from a tiny woman, a tremulo out of the hard crust darkness, a thin cry like a stream of mucus. Then it stood in its own darkness, silent. Then again it came, high, as if something broke in it; it trembled and shattered again into that high white scream, leapt a far leap from her hand, into its own flood of darkness without her.

Voices rose from the next room, each rising in its own flow, falling back, as if no object stood to uphold them. A man talked for a long time, as if he talked to himself, nobody listening. Penelope heard the sound of his voice falling down the night like a lost stream, and the dipper slowly moved and turned in the sky above the kitchen door, beyond the apple tree. Mona came into the kitchen, anxious, her eyes roving wildly. "I wonder where Lowell is," she kept saying. "I wonder if they could have arrested him. They ought to be in from Highway Twenty by now . . . they ought."

Gee said, "Oh, a bad penny always turns up."

"Fix something to eat for them when they come," Mona said, going back.

Penelope saw that Bac had gone. The chair where he had sat was empty. She washed more glasses.

The poker players talked in loud voices.

"Hit me. . . . Go on. . . . Hit me. . . ."

Penelope ran around the house to see if Lowell would be coming, looking at all the windows, listening. Nothing was to be heard in the house, and the curtains were drawn down with only a crack showing at the bottom. She stepped up on the porch, but ran around to the side when she saw a clot of men swinging up the street together, moving swiftly, close together as if clotted against the Town, congealed in a swiftflowing mass, for purposes. They came up noisy on the wooden porch, many feet shuffling, stoping, moving again, a smell of man-herd. The door opened letting them flow blackly in, voices, greetings hearty, jovial, waiting on the day and the night, ready to find out what there was, yet speaking low and with purposes. She crouched, hearing the noise of their entrance subside and the night gather round again, the crickets pounding, beating, first one and then another, then joining together in a minute beat.

Lowell was amongst them tall and lean, slowed a little by thought, hesitating in his walk at each step, looking from under his brows at what could change and grow.

She ran around and into the kitchen, hearing Mona letting them in, and the quick steady upstanding talk coming in with them, changing the house. She set out the china cups, hearing snatches of speech. "It was all right. It wasn't a failure."

"The townspeople think so."

"Maybe they do. Wait until next time . . . nobody will run."

The door swung behind Gee, and she saw them, flushed, standing close together. The card players had left off playing, stood in the parlor doorway looking in, cards in their hands, their hats tipped down.

"We showed 'em something . . ."

"The farmer isn't going to take the hind teet all the time . . ."

"You tell 'em. . . ."

"Lord deliver me," Gee said, "My feet are killing me. Hurry Pen. Oh, Lord, what have I ever done to deserve this kind of a life. Oh, God if I could die . . . if I could die tomorrow and go to my heavenly home."

"Here, Gee, slice this sausage," Pen said . . .

"Oh, Lord deliver me. . . ." Gee saying.

And the voices,

"By the time the corn is high . . ."

"Where they ran today they'll be standin' up tomorrow . . ."

And Gee slamming down the cups, "Oh Lord, deliver me from this vale of tears. Oh Lord, deliver me."

The talk in the next room was a low tight sound that gathered around an invisible object, an intention, remote yet gathering, something approaching slowly, like a season, striking down, slowly mounting from the steady flow of their words, out of the shapes of their gestures, out of the intention of their flesh and the toil of their hands, locking now together like the horns of wounded stags gripping and holding.

She stood in the kitchen, holding a cup, hearing the talk, submerged now, wordless, hard and low underneath something that was known, moving like a stone beneath water.

Voices rose again, saying:

"But what now?"

Then Lowell's voice, talking for a long time, seeming to make an assurance grow, slow and persuasive, saying words she did not know, yet making this assurance grow in her until she felt something would be happening, that even if too late for her, there would be a good time growing up in some way, a time different from that time. And the door opening showed her Mona, her hands clenched, leaning on the table looking at Lowell, and the stern faces looking toward what would happen, making it happen.

But much later, when she awoke, she thought she had only dreamed of a good thing.

She came to suddenly, hearing the voices of men downstairs, in some loud altercation. She could not hear the words, only the voices coming up the stairs, strained, shouting. Then Mona's voice lifted, rocking against her fresh from sleep, like something plunging and plunging under her so she could not keep hold. It doesn't mean anything, she doesn't mean anything, she told herself, her hands over her ears; she is beating against something . . . she has eaten something terrible. The voice plunging through, rocking her, hearing that voice rock the house like something gone mad. Penelope knew . . . *She knows everything; my mother knows everything.* She shut her eyes upon that knowledge, holding tightly to the bed.

It sounded like some huge animal threshing in a stagnant pool, with great bellowings, and some man kept shouting back at her, the words were beyond Penelope, the sound simply crashed over her. She held to the bed, burying her head, pressing her stomach into the pillows.

Then abruptly the screaming stopped, as if nothing lay below at all.

Part Two

The smell of the underworld seemed to come up, a fume over her, and above, the sky pressed down, bending her to the earth . . .

Chapter Six

Spring had come on slowly, surely. Penelope felt herself flushing like an apple. Gee felt good, hobbling out in the yard to throw dishwater, calling her four hens to feed, squinting up at the visible sun, foretelling the weather, and as if warmed out of her, reminiscence began to flow like sap, and she told about cousins. Scraps of conversations floated up in her. She stood a long time looking at the grass, the dishpan in her hand, the chickens pecking her old shoes. She was at her sly best, laughing, a good impish mood. A slow past would come up in her, spreading through her breast and arms, enriching her so she looked out at Penelope knowing, and the girl waited for something to be said. Then Gee would shrug, let it go. "I'll be letting the cat out of the bag for sure," she would say slyly, her bad eye watering.

Mona too felt the seasonal change; she was gentler now, with none of her wild sallies, her hysterical scenes and her dramatic sorrow. She let the sun warm her peacefully, lying in the hammock Lowell had got for her and put up on Sunday between the maples.

Penelope missed Jenny. Mrs. Kelly came in often, saying "No word from Jenny?" "No word," Penelope said, but pinned to her underwear was a letter from Jenny, from the first place she had stayed:

Gee, it's swell, you should have came. It sure is swell. Couldn't you come kid? He's got a swell friend you could have. Gee, it's simply swell. I'm having a swell time. Don't tell nobody you heard of me. It's swell kid. So long, yr friend, Jenny Kelly.

Signing her whole name as if she had become more. Not Jenny, friend, girl, but Jenny Kelly, a whole thing, standing out in full knowing. So she pinned the note to her underwear and said, "No, I ain't heard, Mrs. Kelly," seeing it no business of the ugly woman that Jenny should be having a swell time. "A swell time" went in Penelope's head, but gathered nothing to itself. What could it be? Dances, or food in restaurants like in the movies, or ermine furs and long lashes? Jenny had said nothing, only "a swell time," insisting a little: "I'm having a swell time." The letter lay like some undecipherable message from the moon pinned to the top of Penelope's chemise, but she felt she had an ambassador to other regions and it gave a little secret pride to her head and the swing of her legs because there was a stranger, Jenny Kelly, trying it.

She sat in the thicket watching Bac planting the corn, his straight cruel back pulling haw on the lines, or stopping to light a cigarette, one leg curled over the other in that insolent rest he had. She had to go to the thicket and watch him, and mixed with him would be the look of Jenny's mouth, the backward slant of her haunches, making wantonness like a flock of birds whirr through her blood. *Save me from wantonness*, she prayed sitting in the Presbyterian Church on Sunday, when the organ made a great sound filling all her being, the boys perched like hawks in the balcony leering over at the girls who sat prim below.

But the greening world after Easter was a frail loveliness that enveloped her, the birds singing, the slender shadows touching the new grass in the first brilliant Spring sun; all the earth like the young girl and the ghostly delicate planting in the strange gold light. In that golden air the people floated, the Town made tiny like a little carving, heavy and perfect; each blade of grass standing glistening and alone, the fields, now planted, in a dim mist with the coming heat.

Penelope could not leave school as much as she wanted, for fear Mona would be reprimanded should she be absent, so she sat, having her presence marked down but hardly there at all. It depressed her that she was not good in school, but she could not put her mind to it.

As soon after four as she could she walked out of the village onto the wet hills, letting the giant trees along the roads shake their tips in green bright foliage over her; rocketing to the maturity that would make them full, bright bosomed, moving like fresh women across the fields.

And now though she hardly noticed it, her feet were ensnared, turning her toward Bac's house, which was worse now that Jenny was not there for excuse, and Mrs. Kelly always looked at her with some evil suspicion that she harbored a knowledge of the lost girl's whereabouts. Penelope was ill-content to be alone in the fields as in other years, or to lie alone, feeling all her ecstacy in herself. Now she was drawn, terribly, in diverse ways, to see that cruel boy whatever he was doing, to watch him, to hang on every meaning that he had in his swift body that shone and hardened in the Spring labor.

And he, with indifference born of craft, watched her approach, slyly making no move as he knew to watch rabbits, until they sat up, revealing their white under bodies to him, teaching him just the moment to let go at them, to break their swift beings with one shot mowing them down from good running.

She went out there after school, walking a long piece until her legs glowed in her like incandescent stems, and her cheeks were rubbed to a glow by the fertile wind, crisping now with evening. Coming across the fields to the Kelly farm, seeing the white shamble of a house with the chickens walking around the mud ooze, roosting on the porch so you couldn't sit down anywhere. And Mrs. Kelly appearing at the door, her dwarf's face unpleasant as she said, evilly, "You come to see Bac."

"No, I ain't. I just come to see if you had any word from Jenny."

"No word, and you know it. Come on in if you have a mind to."

"Thank you kindly. I will come in before I start back if you don't mind."

She went in and sat down on a broken chair, waiting, and Mrs. Kelly went on cooking supper, frying the salt pork and potatoes, stirring flour and water for gravy.

She could see the darkening prairie outside the windows. "If you don't mind," she said shyly, at the door, "I'll go out and see the cow being milked."

Mrs. Kelly grunted, going on with dinner. "Will ya stay and eat with us?"

"Oh, no," Penelope said, drifting out and once outside, running down, fluttering the hens into the dark, gaining the odorous barns, hearing the squirt of milk into the bucket, seeing Mr. Kelly, his head against a cow's side. "Hi, Pen," he said.

"Hello." She stood in the glooming dark, hearing the cattle move and kick the stalls, their breathing and the sound of droppings, the squirt, squirt of the milk stream into the bucket.

She heard someone moving down the aisle of the barn toward them, still out of sight. She knew it was Bac. A whistling, and the

47

swish of hay. She waited, holding her hand at her neck. It would be Bac. Then he stood before her, like glittering brass, and a kind of dazzle broke before her eyes like a rocket so she could hardly see; it was a confusion of light, like many birds suddenly taking rise and flight inside her, in a confusion so great that she could hardly stand.

"Well, well, well . . . if it ain't Pen herself and not a moving picture."

"Hello," she said.

"Hello there. Well, how did you get here?" His teeth shone in the gloom. Her being tried to gather itself, but he seemed to crash through her and every look he gave her was like something breaking her apart in little bright crashes.

And Mr. Kelly began to grumble, still milking, and Bac stood, preening himself, the pitchfork in his hand, his teeth showing in a smile.

"A fine cornplanter you are," Kelly said.

"Well, what's the matter with me? The best in the country," Bac said.

"You!" Kelly spat, the cow's tail flicking his face, "by mid moon you're done up."

"By mid noon I'm in A-1 shape, old man."

"Like hell you are."

Penelope stood looking at their faces beyond this bantering, seeing it was their way of love.

"You can have a contest, Pa, and I'd be the last one out of the fields. Lay you two to one."

"You haven't got it or you wouldn't be so cocky."

"Is that so . . . is THAT so . . . watch out! you're missin' the bucket. . . ."

"Yer always hankerin', that's what's the matter with you. I never recollect seeing the like of ye, hankerin' after what ye ain't got nor never will have, far as I can see. What business has a laboring man to be hankerin' after what he ain't got?"

"We all got a chance to be President in this country, ain't we Pen?"

"I guess it's so . . . I heard it's so. . . ."

She looked at the goaty faces of the two men, the old one looking twirked up from the cow's belly, not believing, the young one leaning on the pitchfork, overweening, a certainty in the young flesh, in the impudent blood that came up too swift in him.

"I'm going to make my mark in this world, old man, you'll see."

"I'll see what I see," said the old man, bitterly. "I see what I see, young squirt."

"Well, have a look at yours truly, then."

48

"I'm a lookin'."

"Now, this here strike now. That ain't nothin'. That ain't no way to do it."

"Ain't it now?"

Bac half grinning, preening himself, thrusting out his lip, strutting his chest, like a cock. Seeing Pen gone on him, standing no eyes but for him, knowing from the looks of her that he could be cruel as he liked. He began pitching hay over carelessly to the horse whose head rose above the stall, whinneying, just so she could see how well he was made.

"They ain't clever enough," he said. "They don't know their onions. They ain't going to get nowheres that way. Why, that ain't no way. They'll get mowed down, that's all. You got to be foxy to get along nowadays; you got to fool all the people, that's all. Everything's crooked now. You take boxing. . . ."

"You take it," old man Kelly said, getting up and walking out with his bucket slopping white milk like clover.

Before she knew it, Penelope was left in the barn with Bac, and he, swift darting to her, pinning her against the stall, holding her like a rock. She felt the young beard on his cheek and chin. And she thought, he doesn't love with apples or with roses. There isn't any delicate thing in him, just one thing and the rest trifles.

She shut her eyes against seeing him so cruel, like a fox who sees grapes, the sharp glitter on him, reflecting back, keening his haunches, sharpening down his jowls. He tore at her with hands of stone and she fought against him, liking to, as he tore at her. They heard Kelly coming back, the soft slosh of his feet in the mud like an animal makes, his voice speaking to the dog. They heard the low mooing of a cow asking to be milked. The low beseeching moo went into her, softening the stone that had clawed down her, and she fluttered away as Kelly came in, bending her head, her hands at her hair, fearful the old man should see what had happened. Her cheeks were fiery, and the dusky lowing of the cow was like sorrow, like loss, in the high-vaulted shadowy barn. She ran out over the fields as fast as she could, never stopping until she came to Roselawn Cemetery, where she could sit under the tall monument erected to the pioneer dead, and safely enjoy her danger.

Another time she saw Bac and another boy named Elmer Jutts, whose name was all she knew, coming down the road. Before they saw her she hid in the brush, liking best to see him when he could not catch her looking and pin her to his way, down to so small, compact and hard a stone. She hid in the thicket, watching their passing, their feet ringing against stones, their talk high above the ground, standing up in a pride that came from their strutting blood.

They came where she could see them as she crouched down amongst last year's dead leaves.

"Did you see that match last Saturday?"

"Say boy, I can box better than that any old day."

She overheard, crouching, laughing in the thicket, looking out solemn, then laughing, simply because she was hid and was hearing them talking. Their talk went on until she could hear no longer:

"And I hit him . . . say, did I hit him! Why boy, I. . . ."

"I'll say, I seen that. . . ."

"Why say, I could make a million boxing, I could make a million!"

"I'll say you could."

When they were out of hearing she burst out of hiding onto the road. She watched them walking between the little hills, their thin buttocks, their wide strutting shoulders going up to their sun-burned throats saying, I . . . I . . . I . . . like cocks . . . "Men, men, men," she laughed, imitating her Gee. "Men," and she laughed and began running and flinging her arms down the road, shouting *Men* as loud as she could, like her Gee.

And she walked into town knowing this to be upon her, hiding it, walking so they would not know and could not feed themselves upon what happened in the barn, which was something large to her. And she kept it behind her face and breast so they never would know, thinking: this is something even Miss Shelley doesn't know, something she can't smell with her long nose set to smell such things. Even Miss Shelley doesn't know what happened in Kelly's barn.

Chapter Seven

Miss Shelley had tried once to step out of herself and that time had curdled and embittered her, so she peered out now with malice, seeing the doings of the Town, knowing them all to be on the way to death and believing not one thing was let off from that course.

There were many in the Town who thought they knew about that moment when something had happened and then stopped happening to Miss Shelley, so she had to spit upon all who were in the Town, and look askance at what was growing, putting upon it an evil and a disillusionment.

For long afterward she had thrust back her head like one being struck whenever she met Swillman on the street. It was his handsome brother-in-law who had done it to her, and she did not know how much the family knew about what had happened. Only Swillman had found her in the shanty by the railroad track when they had thought she was dead. And he had come once a week, so the Town couldn't talk, and everyone had known it was to see if anything was going to come of what had happened, that is, if she was going to have a child, but no one mentioned it out loud.

Nina Shelley, despite what she knew of what had happened, imagined for a long time that she was going to have a child. Every afternoon she would comb back her hair and lie on her bed feeling that child in her, having all the symptoms she had ever heard about. Even after the time was over when such a thing could possibly be, she still imagined that she had either had the child or was about to have it. The child had even grown with the years, and after her father and mother had died, going to bed at night or lying awake at dawn she carried on conversations with it, deciding whether it should have long curls or short, always having it a girl, never a boy.

People in the Town carried cunning pieces of the design of what had happened, of the Thing, and the worst part of it was, she never knew who carried which pieces. Seeing them, she was in confusion at first between the fact of what had happened and the myth and dream that had grown in herself, and the facts people made up about it; but after a time she simply remembered what she chose, forgot to think about meeting Swillman or Mrs. Littlefield who had been teaching in the same school, or John Flynn, the man she thought always she might have married if that OTHER hadn't happened. The girls she had known were matrons now, with growing children, but she was set apart, that Thing about her like something, the reality of which had long since been consumed by the growing of the myth, and is now half forgotten, told to Penelope by Mona, who took it into herself as a possible thing that might happen to her when things did begin to happen, as a thing that would be better than if nothing happened at all.

What had happened had even in Nina Shelley's mind become confused, vague, mixed new with images of repentance, first with grief, anguish, now only with a sour lust that hunted through all that was, trying to get back in revenge for what had been done to her. Afterwards, of course, she couldn't get a school anywhere. Even if the tale had not followed her, she carried it like guilt, like a child she might have gotten, that would never be born out of her, but would die and rot and eat off her until she was dead. Her family had kept her within itself, a member to whom something dire has fallen. She scarcely went out of the house until her father and mother died, within a year of each other, leaving her enough to live on frugally, along with the house on Maple Street. So she had taken to living off what happened to other people as best she could. And now a morsel, a tidbit had fallen to her lot—Mr. and Mrs. Fearing living next door, and Penelope and Mona—"that outfit" as she called them—right across the street. Now she stayed up most of the night looking out her windows across the street, watching the men come up the walk and turn in the door. In the day she was juicy and full of what she imagined went on behind those drawn shades. She had almost regained some prestige in the Town because of her proximity to "that house."

After her lonely meal at which she only picked, she put her knotted rheumatic fingers on her old upright and sang "Hide me, O my Savior, Hide. . . ." Malice was the cover of pity in her for what she knew to be in the world, and unwitting she passed on what had defiled her, having nothing in her hands but that defilement.

What had happened to her had been more than the Town could imagine, and less than they rolled so glibly on their tongues.

When Miss Shelley was a girl with puff sleeves and an eye out like another for what could be for her, she had been warmhearted, wanting to touch. She hadn't wanted more than to be made to move like wind and fire, with grace, toward what might be rich. Being spare in that sexual genius which immediately conjures a husband, she was put out to teaching, without a mind for it, looking all the time and moved by an obscure ecstacy that came to associate itself with God and Mary after she joined the Church under the auspices of a redheaded evangelist with a silver Irish tongue, who was the idol of the women.

At night she looked at herself in the mirror, letting down her hair, waiting for the fulfillment of a strange ecstacy, and without knowing it, walking amidst that malice that stood ready to ensnare her, and the defeat that was bred more deeply than she knew in the bone. The condition lay without and within her, and she could not escape with her dreams. She could only have taken a lesser fulfillment, losing her desires like so many amongst children that were not born from deeps, homes that sheltered nothing but fear and murder amongst their inhabitants. She came to have a terror of the things she dreamed at night that had no mirror, no reality in the day, imagining some sin on her own part that would make her life fettered and barren; yet examining what was in her, she saw only the goodness of her desires and the beauty of her ways, and continued to hope that she would see these in embodiment, approaching, mating with her.

Then it had come upon her, swift as a fire she had once seen consume a child, leaping to the skirts and quicker than movement lick up, grow upon what it fed, until the hair stood on end, aflame. From the moment in Summer when she saw Watson Hawk standing on the church steps, his wild face had fled down her blood, to be there all her life. When he would not have known her on the street, or standing up amongst old ladies in a parlor, his face would plunge through *her*, a knife cutting her away.

She met him in the square at the Band Concert, amidst the circling summer dresses of girls walking arm in arm, stopping to talk to boys, swishing on, looking back. Watson Hawk did not look after her, but wherever she walked in the park until they had played Home Sweet Home and the goodnight songs, she knew him to be there, looking to see him at every tree, and in the sweetshop where afterward they had crushed strawberries.

Everyone knew after that that she was set on him, even before she knew it. She had her mother give a party and invite him to the house, but he looked only at the more attractive girls, and merely held her hand a moment, murmuring, "a nice party . . . thank you." She couldn't understand why he passed he by when she stood looking toward him, all her ways a magnet, saying Here I am. . . .

She had to go down on the street Summer nights looking for his face, asking for that doom until they all were laughing, winking as she passed. "Well she's smitten, all right," men slapped their thighs, seeing that strained girl's face looking for Hawk, asking it of him, watching her come upon the snare, seeing that she would be entrapped then as they had been, and would be one of them. . . .

She had hounded God in the same way to give up bounty to her and now she hounded Watson Hawk, who had no bounty to give, or to have even for himself.

He had been annoyed at first, but then he was flattered a little, for after all, Mr. Shelley was the hardware merchant in the Town and had a large account at the bank. Such a woman wasn't to be sneezed at. And the boys said, "Why not? She's no spring chicken. She knows what she wants. Easy pickings." He looked at her, and something in her parted lips, her fevered eyes, her hands out toward him, her breath coming so warm and fresh. Perhaps standing before her he felt this was the only time she would hold out hands to touch except in rancor, to tear apart, and was wonder fresh and tender meat to him.

So he asked her to take a buggy ride, knowing a good place out toward old man Mumser's orchard, thinking to have it over with and some good sport in the bargain. But when he asked her to go, she dressed as she had dressed to be baptised. All the Town saw them driving through the streets. Hawk had a spanking pair of sorrels that were worth looking at in themselves, and along with Hawk and Miss Shelley it was a sight, her sitting so prim in her dress with great sleeves, under a tiny pink umbrella, and Hawk, his trousers tight over his swelling legs, his back up, smiling out of the side of his mouth. Women looked out from behind their Sunday curtains and turned their eyes back at their men, who were wisecracking. "You ought to be ashamed," they said, hiding their smiles with their aprons, going out to do the Sunday dishes, thinking how glad they would be when it was Monday and the men and children got out of the house.

Nina Shelley sat beside Hawk, full of fright, her knees shaking under her frilling skirts, her hand holding the new umbrella her papa had brought her from Kansas City.

He took her for a long drive and they talked about happenings in the Town, about history, and politics a little, Hawk holding the reins as they drove through the Summer country, looking at her sitting amidst her starched ruffles, very prim, holding up her little parasol, red spots in her cheeks, not attending to the conversation at all as if she was just waiting, turning her face to him in expectation of something that he had long since ceased to expect.

The sun began to sink low, and he turned the mares down the road toward the orchard, but he felt low and confused. There had been too much talk, too highbrow, he thought, and there she sat, holding the parasol now tilted over, not a ruffle moved, her head bent a little and he could see her handkerchief wadded and wet in the fist lying in her lap, messing her dress a little.

"We might take a walk," he said, pulling the horses up.

"Oh yes," she said, "that would be nice." But he sat still. "Shall we get out?" she said.

He threw the lines over the whip, jumped out and went around, holding up his hand. She let him help her and he smelled the perfume of her dress as it swirled around her, striking the dust, so she caught it up in her hands, showing her ankles, and he followed, his desire growing up seeing her move.

They went a pace down the stream, and now she began to run, in fright. He followed, coming swift upon her, catching her hands, pressing to her so her dress swirled back from her limbs showing where she stood. And this was in no wise what she had expected, and she held out her hands, her head thrown back, crying without making a sound.

"Holy Jesus," he said afterwards, "these virgins . . . these women in love with Christ himself. . . ."

He remembered for a week after how he got up from her, seeing her mouth gasp, trying to breathe an air that was not there. "Jesus Christ," he said and beat it, not even taking her back to Town, leaving her to walk back alone.

Mrs. Littlefield had met her coming along at dusk, her hands thrown out as if feeling through some sightless world, her head thrown back, her mouth parted. Mrs. Pfeiffer had seen her from her upstairs window, too, thinking something must have happened, forgetting until later when she heard part of the story and saw the goings on of Nina . . . saying later, when she was found half dead, that it served her right, such goings on.

But Mrs. Littlefield had touched her, had seen her eyes come open wide, wide as if they were stretched to take in something she could not. Mrs. Littlefield for a moment had touched her, but she had long ago forgotten about it. And so had Nina. And they were back in time like two women touching, flowering for a moment in pity for what was, and then forgetting it.

But Mrs. Littlefield never told that she took Nina home, never bragged about it. It meant that much to her at least. Nina had opened her eyes and then "Oh" she had said, as if all the world were in her, putting her hands over her body; "Oh," she said, looking at Mrs. Littlefield so she could almost see what had happened, and then Nina began sobbing, clinging to her and sobbing, and they walked along Maple Street. She had taken Nina into the porch, saying: Don't let anyone see, wiping her eyes, saying: You mustn't let your folks know, blowing her nose for her, and they clung together—Mrs. Littlefield then just beginning to feel that hatred for men and all their doings that was to send her marching

55

like a warrior in sufragette parades.

Afterwards Watson Hawk was frightened out of his wits, fearing what she might tell, seeing her eyes, her hands wanting what it was not in his nature to give. He was angry, too, as if she were making him a sinner and it hadn't turned out the way he had expected.

"Go on, mind your own business," he said to her when they talked on the street, keeping their mouths low over their words, their eyes out in fright for fear others would hear.

"Aren't you going to marry. . .?" she asked, wringing her hands.

"Not me."

"I'll tell," she said, not wishing to say it, in anguish at his face turning against her.

"You haven't got anything to tell, you got nothing . . ."

"I'll tell your brother-in-law . . ."

"You got nothing . . ."

"You know everybody saw us that Sunday, saw us leave . . . I'll say that . . ."

"You can't prove anything, you can't do anything . . ."

"I love you . . . I want to be a wife. . . ." Oh, the Spouse of the Church, the Bride of Christ.

"Not me . . . not me . . ."

Against her will, to her humiliation, she had to follow him wherever he went. Her mother said, "Haven't you any pride? To think that a girl of mine. . . ." The girls would have nothing to do with her, thinking her marked by some excess that was indecent. She was no longer a teacher, her class drifted out from beyond her control or caring. The Board had already discussed letting her go, but her father being such a good citizen and a pillar of the church they hesitated . . . until after it happened.

By accident she overheard two boys talking about Hawk, whom they admired because he sometimes took Swillman's race horses to the fair; they were saying Hawk would be in Des Moines Saturday, ready for the races. "Gee, I'd like to go there," one of the boys said. He would be staying, they said, at Wolfkills boarding house, just outside the fairgrounds, he always stayed there.

As if bewitched she shut her desk never to go back to it. Went home, and magically walked through what was necessary in order to be in Des Moines Saturday, saying she would visit an uncle, saying she was tired . . . and everything aided her, as if she had to go, her mother saying it would do her good to get away, hoping she would meet a man who was in the hardware business, like her father, and marry.

She got on the train not remembering anything she saw, getting off and going straight as a die, at nine-thirty, seeing a clock, knowing all her life it had said nine-thirty (sometimes now when it came nine-thirty she remembered that this was a time to her). She went to his boarding house, saying calmly: I am his wife . . . being let in as if nothing could dislodge her ways, going up the stairs, knocking at the door, going in, seeing him in bed, smiling, holding out her hands, her head thrown back as if ready to take whatever he had to give, smiling as she touched him.

Hawk got up, gripping her arms, shaking her. He was frightened, having her turn up like this, frightened the Town would find out about it. She had begun to cry and he had pushed her on the bed, grabbed his clothes and dressed in the bathroom, swearing to himself. What if Swillman found out? They'd never believe she had come like this, and he had a new girl he was crazy about.

In the morning he had come, thinking to put her on a train, tell her for good and all that he would not marry her. Going out of the boarding houte he had to pull her back in, seeing Mr. and Mrs. Pfeiffer walking by as big as life, having come up to the fair with Mr. Pfeiffer's cows which he bred on the farm that was a hobby to him.

Then Hawk was afraid, having her there not knowing what to do and she wouldn't leave, just smiled and clung to him. He was afraid to get a ticket, afraid to have her near him at all, nervous as a horse thinking someone would recognize them. He was afraid even to get on a streetcar. They took a taxi and got out on the outskirts of the town. He didn't have any plan, only to get out where no one would see them. "We'll take a walk out in the country," he said, "We'll take our lunch." She smiled at him, her head thrown back, willing now for whatever he had to give. The hat she wore was trimmed on the top with two large bows of very bright red ribbon, and she had a new umbrella which she carried, with a head of a hawk on the handle, which she had got because his name was Hawk, not taking that to mean anything, as if his name might have been benificent to her.

They walked all morning, and Hawk didn't say a word. He was mad as hops now, and wanted to hurt her. She kept saying, "Will we be married?" "No," he said. "Life isn't worth living," she said, "won't you marry me?" Then his anger got the better of him, and he began to abuse her, vilely. He had to be back at the fair grounds at five when his horses were coming in, besides it was getting pretty absurd, wandering with this half-mad dame over the country, but he was afraid to go back, not knowing what to do with her, how to get her eyes off him. Then it occured to him to get her a ride into some small town, pay a farmer to take her there, where she could get a train home. But he was stumped when it came to telling her his plan.

In the afternoon they came to a shed a little way from the railroad that had been built by sectionhands, with a dirt floor and a roof of timbers, open at one end. There they ate their lunch, and she had said, "So this is our home." This made him so mad he forgot about his plan, and said, "I'm going to walk up the track now. I'm going back. You can do whatever you want. I didn't ask you to go following me around, like any moll . . ."

"Oh," she cried, "Oh what is it?" holding out her hands for that touch, yet dreading it, sensing now how men gave it, a bright blade that bore disaster for women, and she began to cry again, at the same time taking off her hat, putting it carefully down beside her umbrella, then her new skirt, her embroidered underskirt, spreading them on the ground at one end of the shed. He watched her, stopped from his going. She was in such frenzy it did not seem strange to her to stand before him in her shift. "You can put your coat over us," she said.

"I know your kind," he said, "not me. I'm not in for any trouble. You won't pay for it . . ."

She stood, her hands out, crying, not saying a word, reaching toward him and him backing away. Then she ran toward him, and without thinking, just to scare her he pulled out his revolver and she had cried in the same tone she might have cried out in love, "Kill me . . . kill me." Enjoying even this with him, tasting what could be between one person and another. Then he threw the revolver at her, laughing, and she flew at him, seeing the laughter on his mouth, and his very structure to her a menace, something she would never break to her knowing.

He threw her off, hating her, and the way she ensnared him, making his strength uneasy on him. He strode away, she shouting, "I'll kill myself," he looking back in a moment's fright thinking, suppose they find her dead, seeing himself being tried for murder. He knew there could be a trial for the body's murder.

But he went on, thinking: She won't do it, not knowing that the moment was her real death, the death of that wonder in her that would sour, just as lightning curdles the milk. So he went on down the track, and then he heard a shot, and without looking back he began to run, thinking: *She has shot me*—then, feeling himself running, *she has shot herself*—then laughing, not believing it, thinking she had shot into the air . . . *women!* And he ran on, feeling his running swift, the dirt of women getting off him as he ran, forgetting her—except in his later fear, when it wasn't certain to the Town whether or not to say to him: Murderer!

When she saw his impervious back turned upon her, moving away, giving her the madness and the hatred which men can give women, and women men, the life and the death they held in them for each other, moving toward, moving away, she did turn the gun on herself, thinking: *He will come back in love seeing me penetrated by hate . . . he will come back.*

When the Four-Thirty express came through, the engineer saw her lying there, the red hat on the ground . . . he saw the red and thought it was blood, so he reported at the next station.

They found her near death, and she was so for many days.

The village wrapped itself warmly in what had happened; its tongues clacked, striking flint on flint like a pack of starved wolves hearing of food, smelling blood; they tore what they could get their teeth in, tore it beyond any shred of its truth. They gathered information together, in case she should die; they held it against her that she didn't die, for then she would have been in their teeth, she would have ravished them wholly, they could have tasted the thing she had tasted, the bared thing.

It stood in the Town. Men enjoyed their wives more because of what had happened to Miss Shelley, and their own loss lay in the self-wounded girl, and the mutilations they gave each other.

Penelope heard conflicting rumors even yet about whether Hawk had shot her or whether she had wounded herself, but it was generally agreed, at least by the men, that she had shot herself. Miss Shelley never said right out which. No one had heard her say much about it at all when it came right down to it. Everyone knew that at the time Hawk had been at large for a couple of weeks, been caught, brought back, held on bail in case she should die. Then there had been a great deal of talk that some remembered and some forgot about how her jacket was lying south of her head, that she had only her last petticoat on, that her skirt had been spread on the ground, as if for a bed, that her umbrella with the hawk's head had been lying west of the cross timber, or was it east, near the front of the shed, and it had been blood the engineer had seen, or had it been that red ribbon on her hat? Some of the women had wanted a piece of that ribbon at the time. It was rumored that Miss Shelley had the hat now, and the umbrella.

The men said she had shot herself. The women thought Hawks had done it, feeling themselves attracted to him, wanting to put him under a shadow. Nina Shelley didn't say. She wished that Hawk had shot her, if the truth were known; then she would have said so, treasuring it as much as love, but as he had done nothing but laugh, she said no word for one thing or the other, letting the Town think what it liked.

Penelope heard this story bit by bit, piecing it together for herself and watching Nina Shelley as she moved to her windows spying back upon the Town, that had set her like a fly in amber, ossifying in her own aborted dream.

After her recovery, when for the first time she came to church there was a hush and a withdrawing around and away from her. She was like the visible sign of something that had filled them all with strange lust. She had now come into the Town's dreams, with her urgency that had lasted so short a time, and they congealed and flowed around her in their bitterness, she being the embodiment of all their lusts and grievances, a sign and a symbol, set up for all to see on a market day, in tight black, coming gruesomely for vegetables to feed the corpse they had buried for her, saying: Well, you see what happens . . . it serves her right . . . satisfied that she had been given her death, glad that she has now gotten what they have gotten, only resenting that she may have had some pleasure denied to them, some illicit joy unknown to them. So the women never embraced or touched her, held her off from their children, from their warm hearths, glad that she by her sparsity made them feel abundant and rich, turning their dissatisfaction into triumph of a sort.

So she looked out of her windows, spying what foulness might feed her, her urgency for that now equal to what it had been for that other. She saw Penelope coming out the back door, looking up at the tree that grew from the roof, saw her slim, gawky figure. "What a gawk of a girl," she thought, bitterly scolding, her hands over the pod of her stomach, drawing a chair up to the window to watch Maple Street. Penelope stood a long time looking at the tree. "What's she doing?" Miss Shelley said, putting on her glasses, "Land, she stands there a spell. I've heard she's a moony girl." She looked at Penelope as if she might at herself at that age. "I was a tall gangly one like that," she said. "Well, she'll fill, and then she better watch out."

She sat looking at the girl a long time, wanting to get in to her, wanting to break her down. "What I could tell her," she said, "What I could tell her. . . . If she knew what it was she wouldn't be looking at trees. . . . What I could tell her. . . ."

Suddenly she went to the phone. "Is Penelope there?" she said, and peering, she saw the girl go into the house.

Then the young voice, questioning, so low she could hardly hear. "Hello, hello . . . talk louder, dearie. . . . This is Miss Shelley, Miss Nina Shelley . . . I'm making some candy this afternoon, and I saw you kind of lonesome-like in the yard and thought: Well here we are neighbors and don't see a mite of each other, and I thought: Well I'll call her up and ask her to come over this afternoon and we'll make some candy. All right, dearie . . . all right." She hung up. She still did such things as she was doing before it had happened, the things young girls and young schoolteachers used to do.

Then she thought cunningly, "I'll ask Mrs. Fearing, too. I'll ask her, too," and she shook with excitement running out in the bright sun across the light, knocking at the back door of the house where that man and woman lived, taking sleep from her nightly.

Chapter Eight

Penelope saw Miss Shelley a vague shape at the window, knowing she was always there, night and day. When does she sleep? Or perhaps she is sleeping all the time. Perhaps she is really asleep and has never wakened since that shot, that must have broken through something in her flesh, so that it would rot.

It made her uneasy, the woman at the window, the greedy sense of her watching. She felt she was being nibbled at, that some caustic acid was eating her as those eyes bored into her, trying to tell her something, standing for something she might have in her own flesh, someday.

She felt Nina Shelley a witch, brewing a poison let off from the Town, all their qualities caught in her, and pointed terribly.

She turned, and saw, or imagined she saw, the woman's eyes looking out of the house. Then they went away, but the house bore them still, seeming like a house that did not enfold or enshrine, but a house that carried a burden it could not name. It was written now on all the gables, gathering about Nina, gathering about her bitterly, sinking into her wrath.

Penelope had always to taste that evil, bitterly, like an old apple that has never been sweet, not come to that time, had to taste what had happened to the woman, which lay in that house like a sour thing, like an old biscuit or a rotting piece of food lain a long time in a cupboard and giving out a smell over the house until gradually everything comes to smell musty because of it, it letting out more of a being in its decay than it ever had in its wholeness.

Penelope went around that odor, seeing the way it went, disaster then change, one way or another. Beauty has two ways to go.

Seeing, too, the house next door to Miss Shelley's, a yellow house the sun shone on, where Mrs. Fearing came to the door, looking out another way, seeing the world a place where she would drop a child, and the sun a thing to shine on her own flesh. The round full curves of her body behind the screen door would be waiting for Mr. Fearing to come back, and yet around her, too, accruing a fear of what the Town was saying: "It's too soon. . . . Mark my words and you'll see it was a shotgun marriage. . . . It'll be born before the corn is up, and that'll be three months too soon. Married in December, we all know the day they was married, they's no getting round it." Waiting for that moment when they could pounce upon the actuality, letting loose their malice.

Penelope too waited for that time between the two things, the lust of the hate and the hope of the flesh; between the Town's grim coiling and the body's fruit. The Fearings, she felt, moved to some consummation in a world of sun and flesh, yet she feared the usurpation of the other, drawing around, like a net that would catch them from the world they were in and pull them up, withering the round flesh and dulling the eye.

Standing in the yard looking at the tree she saw the buds gathering at the stems, throwing themselves out, like a tide that would leave the tree further unfurled all about itself when the season was over. A window opened and Mona called, "Penelope . . . Penelope."

"Mother," Penelope lifted her face, the sky bedazzling her, and Mona leaning out amongst the boughs of the fruit tree that touched the window. Her black hair hung down in thick live masses. The sun was gold and warm, coming straight down for miles and miles, pouring down around them, ready to crack open the seeds that had been planted, drawing up the wheat stalks white from the ground. There was the sound of the prairies cracking under it. Light seemed to come from Mona's bright arms, too, as she called to her daughter below.

Gee was moving in the kitchen, fixing a lunch. Mona was struck from the spring light, the look cruel and living in her eyes.

"What are you doing Pen?" she said in her vital derision, "Mooning?"

"Yes," Penelope answered, smiling up, her neck stretched back.

"Heavens, what a grand day," Mona said, stretching up her arms so her wrapper fell back along them, showing the pits naked. "Why aren't you out with some young man, Pen?" she asked, not watching the girl, moving only in herself.

Penelope looked up happily.

"Is lunch ready? I'm starving, just starving."

"Lunch is ready, Mona. Let me bring it to you," Penelope said, seeing if she could bring her a gift.

"Heavens no. It's noon if it's a minute. Penelope, get into the house and change that awful dress you've got on."

"Yes," Penelope began jumping up and down, pulling down her apron, "What shall I wear? What shall I wear?"

"Wear anything. You would think I didn't buy you dresses, that I didn't spend my hard-earned money buying you dresses."

"I'll wear anything you say, Mona. Only tell me what I should wear . . ."

"Well, come in, darling, and we'll see. Come upstairs, Penelope, and we'll do something nice . . . nice. Come darling."

Penelope was beside herself, hopping on her long legs, shaken, Mona's voice going through her body like a bell.

She heard the phone ringing, waited, not wanting to spoil that moment with Mona, but then Gee said, "Hello . . . yes," and shouting, "It's for you, Pen . . ."

"For me?"

"Well, don't look so struck. I said for you," Gee said, going back to baking cookies. "Here I am, up to my elbows," she began mumbling, "baking cookies to take out to that highway, and you out looking up at the sky like a calf and Mona sleeping and preening herself like a peacock."

"A calf and a peacock," Mona shouted from upstairs, "a calf and a peacock! Oh God." Penelope walking slowly to the phone saw all the curves of her mother's body from that laughter, her strong throat, the black Medusa hair.

"Hello," she said into the telephone.

The dismembered frightening voice of Miss Shelley sprang out and into her like a snake uncoiled from a box.

"Hello dearie . . ."

"Hello," said Penelope again, tucking one foot under her, standing high to the phone. She didn't know what else to say, stood listening, feeling all that had happened to Miss Shelley uncoil out of the darkness springing in that voice as if it rang in the body of that disaster still.

"Yes, thank you," Penelope said, "Yes, I'll come over, and thank you very much . . . I'm much obliged; thank you kindly. Yes . . . Alright . . . and thank you very much."

"Thank you very much," shouted Mona from above stairs. "Thank you kindly . . . oh yes . . . Penelope you're a bootlicker . . . . Thank you very much."

Penelope hung up the phone, stood with her head lowered.

"Yes," Gee shouted from the kitchen, between banging the oven door and slamming down a pan. "Thank you very much, thank you very much, kiss my—"

Penelope stood between the great shouting voices, half grinning. "Well, well . . .," she said, her mouth drawn in a grin and sickening waves moving over her of fear of those two voices, her mind like a hound darting out of the house, into every house, past Mrs. Fearing's, turning away from what would happen there; past Miss Shelley's where it lay coiled and smelling; around the town, out past Littlefield's and back, with Gee and Mona still laughing and shouting pleasantries.

"Lunch is about ready."

"Yes, thank you very much."

"What shall I wear?" Penelope began to scream, jumping up and down. "What do you want me to wear? Say what I should wear, Mona." She leapt up the stairs two at a time, her skirt going over her thin legs, pounced into Mona's room, screaming, "What shall I wear, Mona? Tell me what I should have on?"

And Mona standing in her night gown turned, laughing, her arms out; and Penelope fell into a confusion of black hair that choked her, twining on her face, and the strong arms, the full breast, the lighted flesh. So the girl threw herself about, her eyes stretched back, laughing, shouting, "What shall I wear, Mona?" The black eyes, moving upon her quick, like teeth biting her life to bits, feeding upon that daughter love, sensing the thin shoulders, the thin waist, the scent of a young green thing, and Penelope let her head fall on that naked shoulder with the hair falling over her like tendrils moving over her face that would plant their sensitive tips in her flesh and grow from her always. Mona let her hands go over the good green body. . . . Daughter, daughter. Closing her eyes knowing, Daughter.

The knowing hand feeling in the darkness of the womb, over the flesh that would be her own flesh, giving a sharp pang for that swift and flighting man, one who planted a seed then forgot where it had grown or what it might imply, and going into a void, not knowing. That image coming in her suddenly when she thought she had forgotten it, covered its eyes with Kansas soil. Now here, her closed eyes finding him in the tall body of Penelope, as if she had felt the image that was in the girl, encountered that cry Father, Father, felt something in that flesh unknown to either of them, so that they threw back their heads, looking then eye to eye, and Mona pulled off the girl's apron, doting on her.

"Now I'll dress you up. Who was phoning?"

Penelope was smiling her pleasure in her mother. "It was Miss Shelley."

Mona's dark brows lifted. "Her?"

"Yes, Mona?" Penelope like a dog hung on her word.

"Well stupid, what did she want?" Mona was smiling too, gone in lover for her daughter, getting a dress out of the closet, the two standing entranced in each other for a moment, coming up to that moment from some long past, so it was like a drawing of sap straight up in a long draught that fed them and bound them together for a time.

Penelope said, "Mona, it isn't anything. I won't go if you say so . . ."

"Why certainly you'll go. Of course. Now how is this? You'll look nice in this today if it *is* last Summer's. Look darling, I'll just let down the hem and it will fit. Why, you've grown a foot; it's a good thing Gee put in so much of a hem . . ."

"You see, she's going to make some candy . . ."

"Candy?"

"Sure, that's what she said. Is that silly?"

"Why, sure not . . ."

Penelope stood close to her mother who sat at the window ripping the hem out. Penelope stood close, looking down at the fine head set thick with the loose wild hair, Mona's hands, sewing.

"You sew good," Penelope said.

"Sure," Mona said, now easy, smiling.

"I can't sew worth a damn," Penelope said.

"No, that's a fact," Mona said, wetting the thread between her lips.

"Will I ever?"

"Sure when you have to . . . when you have a youngun. . . ."

Penelope blushed, "Well, then I won't. . . ."

"Won't what?" Mona said smiling, drawing the thread out, her arm touching Penelople.

"Won't learn to sew," Penelope said giggling, hiding her face, now stooping down beside Mona.

"Goose!" said Mona, laughing, shaking back her hair, shaking out the dress, biting off the thread. "There you are, lummox. Let's see how it does. It won't be too big in the chest this year, will it?"

"Lunch is ready," Gee called from below.

Penelope had a moment's fear, sinking into her, that the dress wouldn't fit, would disappoint Mona. She drew in her chest, pulled in her shoulders.

Mona put it over her head and pulled it down, Penelope in an agony of shrinking, wishing to fit what her mother's present desire was.

"Why," Mona said, "it's . . ."

"What is it?" Penelope said in agony, "Won't it . . . won't it?"

"Well for heaven's sake," Mona cried. "Why Penelope!"

"I can't help it," Penelope mumbled, "I don't know what to do."

Around her chest a tight band of cloth was wound, at least three times around, drawing her breasts down tight.

"Why, Penelope!"

"Don't tell Gee," Penelope said, "I wear this so's she won't notice, so nobody will notice."

"But you shouldn't, you know . . ." Mona unwound the cloth, baring the naked breasts, touching them, moved by the small mounds.

"Why, Penelope, I hadn't noticed . . ."

"Don't tell Gee, will you Mona? Don't tell her anything. I scrootch in as much as I can when she's looking at me . . . you see . . . I . . ."

"My darling!" Mona said, seeing the reiteration of herself in her daughter's body, and what that would mean and no one able to tell what it might mean. "My darling . . . my darling . . ."

And Penelope snuggled under that hair, into those arms.

"I won't be able to rock you much longer."

"No, Mona. . . . No."

She drew Penelope on her lap, close to her, in the chair.

Chapter Nine

Going to Miss Shelley's that afternoon Penelope thought: She wants to read something in my face. She stood a long time before the mirror seeing that what was in her could not be told on her face. It was blank, showing nothing of what could happen or what had happened.

Knocking on the wooden door, she smoothed down her face, holding a look for Miss Shelley, who opened to a crack so she saw a long bony nose and one eye; then the door opened. The shadows of the house reared back as Penelope came into the musty dark, seeing the empty chairs, trying not to see the hand-tinted pictures of Mr. and Mrs. Shelley leaning from the walls, frowning at what had happened to their only child. She sat down primly on the sofa and Miss Shelley said, "I'm just going to run over to get Mrs. Fearing. We'll make some fudge. Now you just make yourself comfortable and I'll be right back."

"Thank you kindly. Thank you . . . I will," Penelope said.

Penelope sat still, but alone she felt more at ease. She looked about at the chairs, the curtains. Inside the house she had so often looked at from without, she was emboldened, and she began to smile saying: "Bac . . . Bac," feeling the evil strength of his presence. Bac Kelly, she whispered, leaning over a little with her eyes closed, Bac Kelly I love you, did you know that? I love you. And as long as I'm a-living I'll never love another, she said, listening to the fine sounding words, letting them come to her lips but knowing that they left the confusion in her a sickening thing, untouched, stirring in its own chaos. I'm so lonely, Bac Kelly — and that was real enough — I'm a lonely girl, Bac Kelly, and she stopped, for looking into herself she saw that he did not touch her loneliness, nor ever would. He stood apart as a knife from her loneliness that could not be cut by him, and she left off any saying, sitting with her eyes closed, giving way then to that chaos that rose in her breast, wondering: What am I? What is happening? What will happen? and feeling the menace in what loomed about her, starting up from its own evil, each standing alone, each a menace to another, so that she cried out and started up from the couch.

The back door slammed, and Cora Fearing and Miss Shelley came from the bright sunlight into the dead house.

"Well, here we are," said Miss Shelley, laughing girlishly and looking at the fresh faces of Penelope and Cora. All the fatigue of being shut in her own self alone was gone, and she now fed like a vulture from the bud of the girl, from the fate that lay in the heavy woman, that disaster that she herself held, having been dealt it.

Penelope and Cora stood in the kitchen watching the thin, bustling woman set out sugar, cocoa, slamming them, making a vindictive ring on the wooden table. "Now I'll put out the mixings," she said, "and you all can do the work. Ain't that cunning of me to put on my guests now?" She giggled, tapping about the neat kitchen.

Cora, silent, as if she spoke enough with her body, poured out sugar, measuring two cups. "Want I should do it?" she said shyly.

"Sure, go ahead," Miss Shelley said brightly.

"I ain't much hand to do things about a kitchen," Penelope said, feeling her own awkwardness acutely beside the heavy preoccupation of the pregnant woman and not daring to look at what she carried now before her with such pride, having it so close. The young girl saw even the bare arms as different from another woman's, as they lifted and mixed, and the full tide of the breast and shoulders partook, too, of the tide below.

"Well for land's sake," Miss Shelley said with a little scream and cluck, "tut, tut . . . Cora Fearing and you that way," she leered, "Why it clean went out of my mind. Why you ought to be settin' down off your feet; it's pretty near your time if it's a minute. For land's sake . . . and your time so near," she said with a grin that made everything in the kitchen seem to stand still and wait upon that leer. And Cora stood, pausing a moment as if lifting the whole meaning, as if hearing not only Miss Shelley, but the whole Town whispering: Well, well . . . three months too early and not an incubator . . . quite a chap too, — hearing it already moving toward that saying without any stopping. And Miss Shelley smiled and nodded, mixing with her spoon, turning it around in the cup.

"We mustn't talk like this before Penelope," she said, "I know how careful she's raised," she kept mixing, that dark shadow across her mouth. "It's a wonder your folks don't entertain any time except at night . . . everyone is saying that no one is ever there when they go to call. Our deacon, Mr. Swillman, even brought it up in church, he says it's his opinion the ladies should call on you people, and I says, They surely should, and I, speaking as the nearest neighbor, would certainly be in favor of it, and a committee of us, Miss Krum and myself, we went there one afternoon in our best bib and tucker, but the house was dead as a tomb . . . I reckon everyone must've been gone, or else was sleeping. It's my opinion they was sleepin'. . . . My, my I says to Miss Krum, I says, it's certainly late hours they do keep! It ain't a mite of wonder to me if they're sleepin', I says." Penelope kept smiling, her bones wooden.

"How much butter?"

"Your recipe is different from mine," Cora Fearing said, standing before them as if walking behind her child. Penelope looking down at the butter in the crock felt warmth come from her.

"There we are girls . . . I call us girls," Miss Shelley said, "we can set right here by the window and have a good chat. My, since this strike, as they call it, has been goin' on, you don't get to talk to no one." She went on, in a confusion of speech, a circumference of meaning, ferreting out evilly the meat of her meaning from underneath, making a play to lead them on.

"You all come from Topeka, I hear," she asked Penelope.

"Yes, ma'am. We come from Topeka after my father died."

"Oh, your father is dead?" Miss Shelley said.

"Yes ma'am."

"So you and your grandmother and your mother come on here alone?"

"Yes ma'am."

"My, that's a far piece," Cora said, smiling at the girl, her shoulders drooping over her burden, her hands falling at her sides because there was no lap left now. "I never been very far from my dad's farm in Cook county. That is, until . . ."

"Until you married Mr. Fearing so fast . . . my, my that was a fast one!" Miss Shelley said, dropping her eyes, laughing slyly. "Well, marry in haste . . . you know the sayin."

She felt more sure with these two who hadn't quick tongues, one absorbed in what had already happened, and the other in what might happen. She was on easy ground with them, fancying that they did not know what disaster she stood in, as the townspeople did.

"Yes," Cora said.

"Some people said . . . you know. But of course, well, people are always quick, ain't they? My, they're quick."

Miss Shelley looked up first at Penelope, then at Cora Fearing, and she had a moment of terrible excitement, feeling she could tell them one thing or another, whatever she liked. Her red tongue licked out over her dry lips.

"My, I seen a sight in this Town during MY time," she said. Cora didn't look up at all.

Miss Shelley's hands gripped the sides of the kitchen chair, her body rigid with some curious vindictive power that came out of her, as vigor or beauty might come from another. "I seen a sight, all right," she said, licking her lips.

Penelope clutched her hands together. "What you seen?" she

said.

Nina Shelley opened her eyes full upon the girl, so they showed green in the center. "I seen what was happening to everybody in this Town. I know a heap I don't tell . . . I tell what I want when the time comes."

"Why do you have to do it?" Penelope stammered, as if trying to stop what Miss Shelley might tell.

"Why do I have to do it?" Nina Shelley kind of lifted her sharp shoulders and said "Ha!" in a way that made it wrench the cords of her neck out and stretch her mouth and dilate her nose. "Ha!" she said, "I got plenty on this Town. I been sittin' here a sight more years than you been livin', storin' it up. I got a sight."

Penelope cracked her knuckles.

"I better test that fudge," Cora said in a calm voice, as if she hadn't heard any of it, and she got up heavily moving towards the stove with a cup of cold water. Penelope watched her let the brown candy drip into the cup.

Penelope said, "Why *do* you, Miss Shelley?"

"I got my reasons." Miss Shelley was sitting forward in her chair as if she had been waiting for this moment. Penelope saw how her arms were rigid, how no part of her flowed together with any ease, but every articulation spoke a tension of hate that made it a wonder she was ever taken into any rest, Penelope thinking sleep would reject her too.

"I got plenty reasons," Miss Shelley said, drumming on the table, looking blindly towards the window, and Penelope knew suddenly that probably Nina Shelley had not really seen anything out that window since the THING had happened. A child struck to the roots of her hair knowing it.

"Oh, Miss Shelley," she said, gripping her hands in her lap, "I heard . . . what was it? . . . I heard . . ." then she startled herself, so her feet got cold and her hands sweated like ice. "You almost . . . you almost married once . . . that is . . . didn't you?"

The question, uncoiled from any malice, coming from hunger, so amazed them all that they sat quite still a moment, the light falling on them. Miss Shelley for a moment felt the sun, heard the step of a man passing, as if she had stopped suddenly amidst a desperate hunt that had been marked by wild cries and blood, and for a moment heard a leaf unfurl in a Spring she hadn't known was budding. No one had said anything to HER directly since IT had happened. The word marriage had not been spoken in her mind, except in malice, since she had said it to Hawk in the shed and he had turned his back going down the track leaving the word thereafter unsaid.

"What I mean . . .," they could hardly hear Penelope's voice,

"What I mean is . . . I mean. . . ." She lifted her face, her mouth open, her eyes looking from one to the other in fear. "What I mean, nobody tells you anything . . . what people say isn't so. . . . Do you think it's wrong to tell a lie, Miss Cora? Do you think a person will go to hell? Nobody tells anything . . . nobody says what happens," she said, wringing her icy hands together, looking at the miserable Miss Shelley, who sat quiet a moment before she let her anger boomerang upon her and felt it strike again in her own body as it had done that afternoon when Hawk had turned his back. Not since that time had it come upon her, flaming in that hatred that was the nearest an embrace with another she had ever known. She looked at Penelope, half rising, spitting words out of her yellow teeth, "It'd do well for some folks to mind their own business . . . and that goes for all . . . all in the Town . . . all. . . ."

The candy rose and boiled, hissing on the fire.

They were in the back yard waiting for the fudge to get hard, Miss Shelley sitting like a young, coquettish teacher with her legs pulled up under her skirt, and Penelope seeing that time upon her when her body was long and young, when she would be sitting looking with pleasure at what was happening at a picnic or a party. Penelope could see it upon her, just as plain. But the ruthless Spring sun made her look like a caricature of that time and that perfection.

Miss Shelley had something to say, excited in a curious way by Penelope's question and by her own flare of hate.

"You know," she said, "what was you speakin' of? You know I almost did get married, one time. . . . Well, I guess you may've heard things . . . and then again, maybe you haven't. . . ."

Penelope set her lips, feeling sick, her pity for the woman coming over her, "Yes, Miss Shelley . . ."

"Oh, it ain't much," she said, raising her hand stiffly, "it ain't much . . ."

"I wouldn't think on it, Miss Shelley," Penelope said. But Miss Shelley had her bright eyes fastened on them,

"It's this way, ladies . . . you see I don't speak of it much, I don't think such things should be spoken of. They're too sacred . . . there are some things too sacred."

Cora Fearing kept letting the green blade cut between her full red lips. Occasionally a car went by the front of the house, but they sat in the sun on the back slope, Penelope with pity ready to flow over what they were about to hear, and she waited so that it could fall in a space of quiet and be muted.

"Yes, Miss Shelley," she said, knowing it could not be stopped.

"Well, I feel my life has been very very beautiful," Miss Shelley said, letting her head fall to one side, the big rats of twenty years ago dead as old mattress stuffing. "Very beautiful," she said softly, letting her dead voice fall, speaking like a ghost so she put upon the immediate air a stillness, as if she did not live in that Spring, but was simply echoing something from a lost time that, like stale food, she kept in the house and could not part with until it slowly spread its fermentation through, rose from the past, filling every moment, its fumes usurping the present.

"Very beautiful," she said, letting her eyes close dramatically.

Penelope looked away.

"You see, I was engaged to marry Hawk. Yes, he was Mr. Swillman's brother-in-law, and as you know, the Swillmans are the best family in town, and they were then, that's a fact. Well, we had a lovely courtship. Nobody in this town can say different." She waited. The maple above shook. Cora was listening to her child moving.

Penelope had to listen to everything, having nothing to listen to.

"Yes, it was one of the most beautiful things, our courtship. He was so tender, so courteous. A woman couldn't want a more tender courtship, I often say. It was too perfect, I say, yes . . . too perfect."

Penelope lowered her head, remembering what she had heard men saying, women saying . . . seeing then three things: what had happened, what had been said about it, and what it had become in Miss Shelley's mind, fusing together, lapping over.

Miss Shelley, with her lisping voice, now shadowed so that you might have been fooled into thinking it was the voice of the young Miss Shelley before it had happened, her eyes lowered in proper modesty, told how they had decided their love was too pure, too perfect for this world . . . more like the love of Christ for the Church . . . and that it must not be spoiled by mundane things . . . the poor life they saw about them; that it must remain that high pure thing unsullied by passion. "You understand, I trust," she said, as if she were reading from an invisible book she held in her hand, "You understand, I trust," she said, looking at Cora Fearing's live round stomach and at Penelope's long hungering body with contempt. She flung up her head, and Penelope knew that she felt the line of her neck, hanging in dead pouches, to be slim and lovely as a swan's; that her lips fouled by that shadow were once again fair and parted. Saw her for a moment, resurrected by this fantasy as if it could last.

"Yes, well, I remember that Summer day," she said, her smile ghastly. "Mr. Hawk came and we drove right through the Town, a proud couple we were. I remember the very dress I wore, and the new parasol papa brought from Kansas City that matched. It was on that day Mr. Hawk proposed to me, I remember it as if it was yesterday. Yes . . . yes. We stopped down by the creek . . . he was a romantic one, you know, and going down on his knee he says. . . ." She stopped.

"Yes, Miss Shelley?" Penelope said. Cora kept threading the green blade through her lips.

"Oh yes," Miss Shelley continued, "Yes, yes. Well, I remember it like it was yesterday, I do for a fact. . . . And I said no. Loving him like I did, girls, I said no because I didn't want such a love sullied. That's just the word I used, sullied. . . . We drove back in the gloaming, very slowly . . . it was beautiful. . . ."

There was a stillness as if Miss Shelley had stepped off into a vacuum where they could not follow. she had her head tilted, that idiotic smile was stretching her lips; as if she sat now, her bones showing, the skin raveled, under that tiny umbrella amidst her ruffles, beside Hawk, who had known all the time they were going only to Mumser's Orchard and no further and for but one thing. To Penelope it was like some magic that Miss Shelley had aged and shrivelled but still sat in that afternoon of twenty years ago, under an absurd umbrella, expecting something.

Cora got up slowly, pushing herself up from the ground. "I expect the candy is ready to cut now," she said as if she had heard nothing, and slowly she went in the house and they heard the screen door slam. Penelope and Miss Shelley sat on the grass, quite still.

"What happened to Hawk?" Penelope said, her head lowered, picking a clover deep from the grass.

"Hawk? My dear," said Miss Shelley like a great lady, "he has become a great financier. Yes . . . he changed his name. No one knows it but myself. And once a year I receive a gorgeous present from him. Yes, simply gorgeous . . . but I trust all this will be held in strict confidence. . ."

Cora brought out the fudge. "It came out very nice," she said, holding the plate down to them and they each took a piece, Miss Shelley with delicate fingers and nibbling at the fudge as if it was merely a concession on her part to partake of anything since what had happened to her.

"Wouldn't you girls like to sing something?" she said. "I feel it's such a spiritual uplift to sing together, don't you?" Her gentleness was now from her imagined world, gentleness for a world lost in sin, unwilling to be saved, doomed to its own evil.

Cora said, "I've got to get my dinner on. You see, my husband will be coming home. I've got to get started . . . I'm not so fast now. Please excuse me . . . goodbye," she said, with that shyness which was only because she could not give her attention to what she saw.

"Goodbye," Miss Shelley said, "Is there anything I can do?"

Cora Fearing looked at her a moment. "No, thank you, Miss Shelley, I'm all right, thank you. Well goodbye. . . ."

"Goodbye," said Penelope, clearing her throat, standing, holding the screen door open.

They watched her go heavily across between the houses moving sideways in support of her child. Suddenly Cora called, "Come here, Penelope." Penelope, surprised, ran across the sunlit grass, eager to be near the woman, to do something for her. She stood close, and Cora leaned over whispering so that at first Penelope could not catch what she said.

"What?" said Penelope.

Again the woman whispered, laughing a little, "Ask Miss Shelley if it was her loving suitor that shot her." Laughing as she went into her house.

Penelope stood a moment looking at the grass. Miss Shelley called and she went back slowly.

"What did she have to say?" Miss Shelley asked, uneasy.

"Why . . . I don't know," Penelope said, "I couldn't hear. I didn't hear her."

"Well, that's a funny thing," Miss Shelley said.

Penelope went with Miss Shelley into the house, where the dead seemed to lean down from the close walls. They went through into the front room and Miss Shelley put up the shade a mite. She sat down at the upright, opening her hymnal with her wooden fingers, playing the chords, singing with a long howl from her decayed throat. Penelope stood beside the shoulders of the woman, sensing painfully what had happened, letting it flow into her now they were alone, so she was no longer herself, having to take the body of that tortured woman through her throat, stringing through her breast like a slick wire that hummed and moved in her flesh.

In the sweet by and by . . .
We shall meet on that beautiful shore . . .

Penelope sang very low, feeling her voice merge and become lost in the voice of Miss Shelley raising itself, howling, not knowing the betrayal it gave her of all that had happened.

Suddenly Penelope went cold. "Why . . . why!" she stammered, backing away from the piano bench. Miss Shelley's hands lifted, she turned her head on her shoulders, looking around like a fugitive.

"What's the matter, Penelope," she said, her eyes showing her fright, the fright that was always in her that the Town would find out, know more, find out what she herself did not know. "What is it Penelope? What?"

"Why," Penelope said, gasping for breath in the fetid air.

"You look as if you were going to faint. . . . Do you have fits?" Miss Shelley said, getting up, wheeling like a black dervish.

"No . . . no," Penelope backed away.

"Whatever . . ."

"I'm sorry . . . It's just . . . sometimes I can't stand. I better go. Goodbye goodbye."

She backed to the door, felt the knob, opened and skitted out across the street, with Miss Shelley calling at the door, "You must take some fudge home to your mother . . . here's your fudge."

Penelope ran into her own house. Gee was sitting sewing, the room full of her great obscene quiet. She looked up, her eyes not focusing, looking at Penelope's breasts, so the girl jerked her hand over them, turning away.

"Don't scare me like that, Pen," she scolded. "Is the devil after you?"

Penelope took the stairs two at a time, ran into her room and slammed the door, stood then, turned, facing it — IT — what had been coiling around the thought of Miss Shelley, what had been approaching, almost seen, then gone; what had stood behind all the facts, everything men and women had said, working into the fabric of the Town, making what had happened large as vent to their poisons. Now it came from behind what had stood before it. In that moment when she had let Miss Shelley come in her through pity, she had known it as if that woman's breasts had been her own, cracked the meaning in her teeth, and the bitterness of it lay in her now, whole and complete. It was with horror now she had to say it, had to let her lips come over it and know this, along with what she had found out about other things:

That Miss Shelley had never been able —*she wasn't able . . . she wasn't able. She had a hunger just like me, . . . and that day they talk about, when she was a-going after Hawk and they saw her on the street a-going and a-going after him . . . then she couldn't do it. She couldn't do it. She couldn't know . . . she couldn't risk. . . . She wasn't able, that's what. . . . What nobody is knowing, what is standing in this Town over Miss Shelley's house there is that NOTHING HAPPENED! Nothing happened . . . except what she done herself with that gun, taking a shot at herself, God knows . . . God knows. . . ."*

And suddenly she began to weep, as if for her own lost life.

I Hear Men Talking

Chapter Ten

The Summer was coming in at full tide. Penelope wandered the open fields. The orchards bloomed like clouds hanging low. The heat settled deeper. Penelope wandering saw surfaces, knowing a being lay dead in the earth, while up from it came that dark, senseless root into stalk and flower and from underneath came that incessant beating, and she looked for her own enchantment, asking where?

It seemed to the girl that the body of the earth lay silent, visible and naked before her but without word or myth. She saw it, sinews and muscles of the fields sleek along the articulations that were made with precision and joy, the hard firm strands of the earth's flesh like hempen ropes along the loins, field's muscles, smooth with strength, fastening into the horizon.

She lay on the deep breast of the earth asking, *Where?* Touching the mounds that rose above the dead and above the seeds of the future living. She saw the green flat land, trees, corn, ugly houses for use and the stubborn industry; the interminable fences showing what one man owned against another . . . and the immense and tranquil sky, the wide laxness of prairie as if everything might slip off, with no tension and no climax, and the defenseless houses helpless in the onslaught of heat and light and space.

The Summer rains came with pollen of wheat and grasses, the fertile blowing grain warm, and sweet thunder, distant along with the sound of a team and wagon rattling down the rainpocked dust, hurrying to get home before the shower. The elms moved rich with wind and rain, in heavy tremor, rain obscuring the grain elevators, falling aslant for miles, threading the prairie with grain and corn, misting all the familiar sweep of river bed and road and fields, so alike for miles and miles that it was only the most obscure and subtle sense that made one farmer know his own horizon from another.

Looking at the earth, at faces on Saturday in the market, there was no thing spoke to her, saying: Go this way, turn here, believe this. Close to the ground she heard that unspeakable dark moving below, and saw above her the unspeaking stars and heard only the boiling movement in the closed flesh of Mother and saw only the

77

stark face of lost Man in the face of Father looking up from out the summering earth.

The talk went on in the market that so and so had such a stand of wheat, or timothy, that the corn was so high, that the hogs were cramming their insides until they had drums of bellies from the mash that couldn't be sold anyway, that there was a butchering at so and so's, and the way they talked you could see the fat juicy hogs hacked with cleavers and hanging from hooks by the hind legs; talk of threshing crews, of farm boys driving steers to the railroad cattle pens. And at night men talked in the front parlor, Penelope hearing as she rinsed the cups the low incessant murmur, voices that did not separate, no words standing out, but only the covert blended voices of men, speaking beneath what was happening in a low incessant hum like bees gathering for a flight.

She stood in the doorway seeing Lowell, sitting amidst the men leaning toward him; heard words and saw faces and bodies at such a strain it seemed they might be lifting some heavy invisible stone that stood over them, or like men in a quarry hefting new rock; speaking serious words: produce without market, spill the milk, picket the highways. Saying: we are burdened, burdened. We carry burdens: taxes, loans, mortgages, deficiency judgments. And the cry: How can we save our land? Seventeen thousand farms foreclosed, lost . . . land gone that held the dead and the living.

Lowell saying: "The townspeople are against us. . . . The townspeople should be with us and they are against us."

"They give me the bellyache, always talking that we are spendthrifts wearing silk shirts . . ."

"Yeah, the bellyache . . ."

"The corn is growing tall . . . the corn is growing tall . . ."

"It'll be nigh as tall as a man now . . . a little while . . ."

"If there's no high wind, or hail . . ."

"Tall's a man in a small space . . ."

"We've won now for this much. Milk has gone up three cents, and they say it ain't no use us to do nothin' . . ."

"We've won now for a space, for a small time . . ."

"We'll use spiked telephones again, we will . . ."

"Four governors and four representatives can't do nothing for us . . ."

"This ain't no different than the Boston Tea Party . . ."

"We won on Bunker Hill . . ."

"We'll have thirty thousand crowding these here streets when the corn is tall . . . tall to hide a man . . . we'll have a market for this wheat that's a comin' out of the ground now. . . ."

Mona went with Lowell to the highways and at night Penelope

sat at the table half sleeping, leaning her cheeks in her hands, wishing school would let out so she could spend all her time in the country. She heard Mona and Lowell talk about what had happened, Mona saying it best, giving a sense of how they waited in the dark beside the highway, their camp fires burning, and when they'd hear a truck the men would run out, stand across the road behind the barricade, challenging the passer by. Mona made it all stand up plain, the sunburned faces shining red in the glow, the slow speech stern, puzzling out what would be just; how a young man named Davidson, in blue shirt and overalls and high boots, stopped a man who had tried to bootleg his milk through, saying, "We ought to learn him something, turn him back on the dirt road and learn him a lesson"; how then they would go back to the tent and sit around the rough table with the coal oil lamp on it, talking some more, or eating hot snacks brought out from town, the poplars standing above them in the moonlight. How then there would be a cry of "Trucks!" from the Jones boy at watch on the road, and out they would all come again behind the barricade arguing with the driver, putting it to a vote whether to let him through.

Lowell at night telling how many men were being added, the numbers mounting rapidly from two thousand. Lowell saying, "We can get a hundred farmers in a few minutes by phone if we need 'em." Mona saying, "We don't need so many now, on the road. The farmers aren't coming over the highways any more; they're staying at home, now they know what it's about. . . ."

Lowell eating slowly, watching Mona, lifting his eager eyes, smiling or flashing quick in anger, saying, "In a little while the corn will be tall enough. . . ."

In a little while the corn will be high and a thousand men could hide in that corn and you couldn't see them, a thousand men in the corn. And Penelope saw the corn growing up and the thousand men like the corn growing tall and murmuring in the wind, standing together rooted in the soil of Kansas, Iowa, Nebraska, the Dakotas, Minnesota, Illinois. She saw them waving like good soil planted with fat ripe corn, marching corn, all moving together.

Penelope saw the wheat turning white at the seed as plumes. On that day she danced amidst the corn unseen by any but the wind that walked between earth and sky. School let out early because the school funds were low, and she was glad to roam the country, because of late boys had been telephoning, and her Gee would come, smiling, her eye slyly closed, "Someone for you, Pen. A young man, heehee." And Penelope would step with legs like a cricket, knowing that Gee and Mona were listening to what she said when God knows it was hard enough anyway to say anything. "Hello" . . . and some boy's voice, changing from low to high so she closed her eyes in pain, "Hello Penelope. Is that the way you say it? I told the guys so. . . . Say, I bet you don't know who this is now, do you? Do you? Well, this is Red, see, and I want to have a date with you. I wonder if you'd have a date with me . . . no kiddin' now, gee, I think you're the prettiest kid in twenty counties . . . that's the opinion of yours truly all right . . . what do you say?"

And she, standing with one leg wrapped around the other, "Well, thank you but I don't think I can. You see I have . . . well, I have something else to do you see. . . ."

And at church on Sundays, where she had to go since she had teased her Gee to make her a dress with ribbon sash, she saw young men like hawks, sitting on fences, standing on the street, lined against the church steps before and after the service. With Spring bodies, too, such a fine thrust of being in them, standing like birds with their keen faces, seeming to fly around her as she had to walk with Ellen Haughty, Millie Shields, Louise Tanner, Sally Carter, down through an aisle made by young men. Then out into the downpour of sun and these keen hawk boys on each side of the walk, always getting out first from the balcony to stand quite still as you passed and then seem like a menace at your back as you walked, feeling how long your legs were, swinging from your waist. Bac didn't go to church at all, but she knew he came and stood with the others just to see her come out. She would never look at them, and never knew which ones telephoned her. Some never gave their names, merely saying, "Meet me out by the bridge tonight, won't you? . . . take a walk with me . . . go to the Gem with me . . . come with me. . . ." And she always stood on tiptoe at the phone saying, "No, thank you. No, I thank you very much. You see my mamma won't let me," with Mona shouting at her from above stairs and Gee giggling, taking in every word from the other room.

Bac would be there, standing, dressed up, looking different, as if his mother had washed his ears, a clean shirt on, and a suit from Sears Roebuck instead of his blue overalls, only his body always swiftly shaped the cloth to its own ways, so it cleaved clean to his haunches, curving with his insolent back.

"Hi, Pen," he would say, touching his cap, never taking it off. The other girls would giggle because they weren't allowed to have anything to do with Bac, not the nice girls, so Penelope felt a sort of pride as if she had something a bit wilder and more dangerous than they could touch.

Since her mother or Gee didn't go to church, she could walk down the street with him. While the other girls had to get into family cars with sisters and brothers, she could walk very slowly down the Sunday streets with Bac, knowing that the Town would have to see her, inviting something to happen that could be eaten by herself and by them.

They would walk slowly, Bac gentle, as if Sunday had flowed over him too, and made him different, with no fields to plow. He always rode in now that they didn't have a car anymore, and he looked fine with a horse, tethering it in their yard, sometimes staying to dinner, talking then to Lowell and Mona, very serious, so Penelope rested her cheeks in her hands, listening, wondering that Bac moved in that world full of speech and argumentations clever and quick, so she was proud again, seeing Mona looking at him, admitting him as a fine man to her, quickening her flesh a pace.

Evenings perhaps they would go to a meeting of the men, Penelope sitting beside Bac who got up sometimes to speak. Penelope knotting her handkerchief, the words flying out above her, going over the turning heads, the labor-bent shoulders; or sometimes they would go to Christian Endeavor, just to be seen. Penelope went to whatever church gave most pleasure—the best picnics, the best ice cream socials; that had the handsomest preacher or the finest windows; or because of some person or other she was interested in at the time, so that she could sit near them, looking at their hands, the backs of their necks, trying to crack them to her knowing.

And these young men seemed to grow up in that Spring, so she knew them wherever they were, moving or standing, speaking with their swaggering voices that made her see the whole way their bodies went, the full hard lips, the nostrils curved, breathing desire, and the sheer sheen of will, up-pounding in the sap of them, and their huge hands thrusting out like tree spears, and she must walk between this thrusting, holding her skirts close in.

Something was being drawn to a fine point between herself and Bac, and Bac stood as the pivot and the summit of all that Spring to her, as something she had to move toward, whether she wanted to or not, and she could not stop herself, unless a hand or a look should be in her way saying *don't*, or *wait*.

Committees met in the parlor, every night a group of closewalking men came down the street, turned in the door. Standing behind the curtains Penelope heard them talking. One night Casey, who hadn't believed farmers could stand together, came up, jumped out of his dusty Ford, having come ninety miles for help because his goods were being sold for a hundred dollar note. "I'll be put on the road," he said, "if you don't help." The morning the sale was to be she saw the men leave, piling into cars, standing on the

81

running boards. Heard afterward that they gathered farmers along the way, calling them from the corn, and many unhitched their teams and went along with them. Some came a hundred miles, Lowell said, and they forced the bank to renew Casey's note. The men talked about it afterward with grim satisfaction.

Slow afternoons men came in laying papers on the table, leaning their heads close, Mona bringing them something to eat, hovering there, wondering if at last men might be planting a seed in the future and remembering what it was, not going a wild way.

One Friday night there was a meeting in the parlor and this time the doors were closed off. Penelope sat inside by Bac, listening, hearing Lowell tell them that on Saturday afternoon at two-thirty there would be a sale of Peterson's one hundred and sixty acre farm for the mortgage Swillman had foreclosed, which represented the sole fruit of a half-century's work. The men had made their demands, the cost of the sale at Swillman's expense and the note reduced, and Swillman had said he wouldn't have any truck with them.

Peterson sat forward in his chair, his hands locked together like antlers, his eyes feverish with fear of the devil and the deep blue sea, crying now and then: "We can't do it! It's against the law. We'll get in trouble! . . ."

Lowell saying gently, "It hasn't hurt us yet, has it, to be together?"

Peterson subsiding, "No . . . no. All right. Can I take my wife and boys away in case there is any . . . any . . ."

"No," Lowell said, his look unholding the man. "No, they've got to be there, Peterson, or there'll be suspicion. Seeing all of us there, you see . . . and Sheriff Anderson may know us pretty well by this time," the other men laughed, looking towards Lowell.

"Now you two, Flynn and Tansel, you're to be there early and cut the telephone wires so they won't be able to get the sheriff. That's before the auctioneer gets there, see?" They nodded, taking more upon themselves than the small incident, looks locking with the looks of the other men.

"Now you, Beggs, have about ten men in the corn, see, just in case . . ."

Beggs moved his hands together, nodded. Penelope let the "just in case" go into her, not daring to look at it too closely. They all let it go by.

"We won't do anything unless we have to . . . you see," Lowell spoke slowly, letting his words sink into them as if he were teaching them something beyond his words, speaking as if he were in some way weaving them together in confidence.

"We'll be there. You men spread it amongst the people who we want to come. You and Pendleton will stop everyone down the highway and let nobody in except the ones who know about it, you see."

Yes . . . they all looked slowly at each other, knitting their looks together seeing that each one would be sure and steady doing, upholding them all, and not one going against it or dropping the stitch.

"It ought to all go off handy," Lowell said, "and nobody'll know what's happened until Monday, and then you'll see what a laugh they'll get. We'll just bid about ten dollars for the whole place. They won't even move out your furniture, Peterson. The auctioneer will just give over his papers. We'll see to that. Every one of you has got an important thing to do. If one man is there that'll bid more, it won't work. The roads got to be watched, the wires cut, every man knowing what he's doing, each man protecting the other, you see?"

The men, tense, knotted together, nodded. "Now Bac here is going to make sure that the sheriff isn't tipped off by anybody. He knows the sheriff."

Penelope stood back against the wall as they all charged by her out the door, backing away not to have them brush against her. They emptied out of the room together like one substance, and she stood alone, hearing them shuffle along the hall, flow out into the street, walking swift down the walk.

Bac came back, startling her, standing close in the dark.

"I'll see you tomorrow. I'll meet you at two . . . at two," he said, standing near her, a fire standing up at her side.

She nodded, looking down at her feet that would go wherever he said.

"In front of the library at two," he said, "and we'll take a walk past Littlefields. How about Mumser's Orchard?"

She nodded, startled, knowing instantly how Miss Shelley had said: Yes, we got out at Mumser's Orchard . . . yes, yes. . . ."

"Yes," Penelope said.

Chapter Eleven

Early Saturday Lowell and Mona started in Lowell's Ford, telling Gee not to answer the phone that day, and not to let anyone in until they returned that evening from Peterson's, a hundred mile drive. Gee stood in the door, nodding, her apron over her arm, not liking very well to be left, wanting to be where the excitement was, wanting to go with them to Peterson's farm to see how it would come out, to be in on it if there was any shooting from the corn. "Let me stay in the corn," she said, "that'll hide a woman as well as a man."

Lowell smiled and shook his head. "Need you here, Gee," he said, "see that nobody asks you any questions and you answer none. . . ."

"All right . . . I suppose so. All right."

Mona looked at Lowell, moving where he did, listening to what he said, her head lowered a little, a smile on her face, taking all that was happening into her body, making it a thing that shone on her so Penelope thought it would be a menace, riding through the town like that beside Lowell, the way her head sat, with such boldness, bespeaking the sleeping woman striding in her flesh, from violence to violence, like one in a colossal dream.

There were four hours between watching them leave and seeing Bac, with nothing to do at the house. Gee went back to bed. "Might as well get my sleep," she grumbled, "can't answer the phone or the door. Why they don't bury me is more than I can see. Your poor old Gee, Pen, nobody cares much for her anymore. I wisht I'd a died when poor cousin Antoinette passed away, that was my time, if I'd only a knowed it, but thinks I, Mona needs me . . . yes sir, that's what I thinks. But it turns out nobody loves an old lady like me. I done the best I could all my life, the best I knowed how, and that's all a body can do. But nobody appreciates it a mite. Just walk over me without so much as a by your leave." She began to sniffle, her head sinking into her heavy shoulders, "Now you'll be a leavin' your poor old Gee, she said from the stairs, sobbing, keeping one eye back on Penelope who stood below making a design with the toe of her scuffed shoe.

"You better rest afore tonight," Penelope said, "They'll be

something popping tonight."

"Yes, they'll need me then, like enough, to trot and tote for 'em, ... the bastards."

"You better rest. . . ."

"I'll rest. You rest a long time in the grave. Well, my heavenly Father will give me my reward and that's all I ask. When Gabriel blows his horn . . ." she cocked one eye around her immense shoulders to see if Penelope was still there. Her thick legs hung over her slippers. Penelope was counting the red roses on the hall wallpaper.

"Can I get you anything, Gee?" Pen said, between one hundred and ten roses and one hundred and twenty.

"You could bring me my foot powder off the kitchen shelf."

Penelope strode down the hall, came back with the can, took the stairs two steps at a time.

"You better rest afore tonight," she said, "It's a goin' to be different tonight."

"I expect," Gee said sarcastically, "I expect."

"Better rest," Penelope said, "better rest."

"Yes, in my grave. . . ."

Penelope began to kiss Gee, her arms flailing the big woman, her face coming at her, receding, coming back. Gee pushed her away, laughing.

"Get along with you. Are you crazy? Crazy as your dad, that's what. He was one for kissin'. And where does it get you? Get out . . . get along out. Don't you tickle me! Hey, get along!", and Gee banged the door of her room.

Stopping on the sidewalk outdoors, Penelope saw Miss Shelley running out of the back door of her house, across the lawn and into Mrs. Fearing's door with a dish in her hand. "It's happening," Penelope said, "It's happening. . . ."

She stood still, looking at the yellow house as though it had changed. She saw Miss Shelley in her mind still running across as if she took some importance from Mrs. Fearing having a baby, and some excitement, more than if it were her own. Penelope listened. I wonder if they make great cries, she thought, and sat down on the steps until she saw Miss Shelley come out the door, calling something back, carrying the empty dish hanging down from her hand.

"Hi, Hi," Pen began running across the street. "Miss Shelley," she waved her arms. Miss Shelley stopped in the bright sunlight.

"It's beginning," Miss Shelley called, secretly, "I think it's beginning; you know she doesn't feel very good. Wouldn't surprise me none if it happened tonight or before, wouldn't surprise me at all. . . ."

They both looked at the yellow house. Penelope said, "Have you called Dr. Starry?"

"Not yet. Mr. Fearing is gone somewhere today, ain't that just like a man, to be gone? He's gone looking for work. You know," she leaned over whispering, rolling her eyes toward the house like an owl, "he hasn't had any work for I don't know how long. If it wasn't for me I don't know how they'd live. You know, don't tell anybody, but I take practically all their meals to them. You can't tell me, though, that a man who wants work can't get it."

"It's so," Penelope said, "it's so. Lots of men, I don't know how many."

They looked at the quiet house where this was about to happen. "But he ought to be here now," Miss Shelley said. Men . . . they ought to have their necks cracked. This world would be a better place if every one of them was dead."

"Well," Penelope said, mimicking Mona's voice, "if there is anything I can do you let me know." She went off a few steps. "I got to be going. If there's anything I could get you in town you know. I could get anything . . ."

"No," Miss Shelley said, "No, I guess this is going to be my job, I can see that."

"Goodbye," Penelope said, going down the street, hearing Miss Shelley's screen door slam. Thinking, I could get her some flowers if I had a speck of money, but I ain't got a nickel. I could get her some flowers in the country, but they ain't so much at this time. And she set her mind with excitement on what gifts she might bring, wanting to add something to that happening and have a part in it.

All the things of that day were flowing toward her, flowing back, so that she did not know which way to go, meeting, rejecting, knowing that by the end of the day many things would be made clear.

She hurried, turning in a wild riot of movement towards Bac, thinking something might have brought him to Town at an earlier hour, so she went down Main Street, looking into the library, a knot gathering in her that would not loosen until his sharp being would cut it in two. But not a face was his; she hurried on.

Giving up, then, she turned towards Littlefield's. He had twitted her, of late, for not coming. "Where have you been? No chess games." His rebuke lay in her like shame she could do nothing about. "I got things to do now," she would say, "I can't be coming out, I got things to do." He had cornered her at the market on Saturday, as he looked into his purse, inserting his dirty fingers to pull out small coins. "Is it because . . . well, what people say about it?" he asked.

"No," she said, not knowing at all that anyone said anything.

"Yes, I think that's it," he said, "Well, if you want to listen to the dirty mouths of people . . ."

"It ain't that, Mr. Littlefield. Honest, I promise it ain't that. I'll be a coming. I promise," but she had not gone, staying on Saturday nights to listen to the men in the front parlor, not wanting to listen to Mr. Littlefield's lonely speech that seemed to go on and on like the talk of a man buried in a cave.

"I expect you're just bored with the old man," he had said, his eyes watering, tucking his carrots under his arm, the green tails hanging out, "I expect that's it. Well that's no more than I expect, Penelope. I've had such treatment all my life. I've never been understood . . . Mrs. Littlefield didn't understand me," and his red eyes brimmed with tears, a poor juice, and he went on through the market so lean and dog-eaten, as if an unseen cold wind flapped his coat tails.

Penelope looking after thinking: someday I'll go and look in the window and nothing will be there but his watchchain. He will just chew himself up and there won't be nothing in the shack, only his watchchain lying on the floor showing where he's taken the last bite of himself.

Now she walked across the trestle and the sun was hot. The corn is growing today, she thought, and the men will be in the corn, thinking of the men hidden there while the auctioneer lifted his gavel and the farmers stood about waiting to bid ten dollars for the whole farm. Waiting to bid in money; fox them at their own game. Money. It will be a laugh tomorrow, Lowell had said; she could hear Lowell's voice talking on, patiently like a spinner at a loom whose thread was men.

"Are there others," she had asked him once, "in other towns, in cities?"

"Yes," he had said, "all over the world."

Spinning . . . all over the world. . . .

She opened the wooden gate at Littlefield's and went up the path he had marked with whitewashed stones. She looked in the window, but all she could see was a pair of empty shoes and part of his rocker. She stood straining against the window but she could see nothing more, so she went around in back, seeing the heaped empty cans. She felt she was spying on his life some way, so she went noiselessly back out the gate. On the trestle she stopped, looking back with a sort of fear. Perhaps he is dead . . . perhaps something has happened to him. . . .

She went on, drawing near again to the necessity to see Bac's face. She went into the town to look again. There didn't seem to be so many farmers in town that day, and their absence was an excitement in her, as if she had some part in what was being done, and could tell no one. Speaking to Mr. Pfeiffer gave her a pleasure, so she no longer skitted by in fright, but walked slowly, boldly.

She didn't see Bac because, going by Smeitzer's Pool Hall, she always turned her face another direction and walked stiffly, knowing boys and men would be looking out, gawking at the girls. So she didn't see him deep inside, saying to Bill Nye and Red Davis, "Well, it's today, boys. I'm laying it's today. Three to one."

"Well, how're we going to know? How we going to know you ain't cheatin' on us?"

"Why, ain't I a gentleman and a scholar?"

"Not so's you'd notice. We got to be sure . . ."

"You got to be sure, have you?"

"Yeah! And how!"

"Well, tell you what I'll do with youse guys . . . tell you what I'll do. It'll be in Mumser's Orchard, see, along the creek there. I figure that'll be as good a place as any, and you fellows can cut down across the trestle, see? You come just about the point where the bend is, see?"

"O.K." they said, grinning, "Five bucks don't grow on trees these days. We gotta be sure, ain't we boys?"

"All right, you be there. . . ."

"You ain't set no time."

"Well say, I can't go by the clock, can I? Around dark, around eight thirty."

"We'll be there with bells on, kid."

"O.K."

"Play ye a game."

"Can't. Got to see a fellow."

"It ain't no fellow you got to see."

"Sure . . . got to see the sheriff."

"Are you in bad?"

"I've got important business."

"O.K. We'll be seein' you."

"O.K." "O.K."

He hitched up his pants, lit a cigarette, seeing his own face in the mirror, straightening back his black hair of which he was very vain. He strolled into the street and saw Penelope cutting across the library yard as if she walked blindfolded, searching for something. He threw away his cigarette and began to approach her swiftly, watching to see she didn't get away, calculating what he could do. He came up swiftly behind her.

"Bac," she cried.

"It's me, and not a motion picture."

"Oh," she said, her hand at her throat, her eyes widening upon him.

"Well, you seem surprised, all right."

"I am."

"Now don't tell me you been looking for me."

She smiled, shaking her head.

"Will you have a sundae, Penelope?"

"Why, yes," she said, "but I ain't got a sou."

"Well, what's that to yours truly," he said, jangling in his pockets the money he had already borrowed on the bet. "C'mon, and don't never say I was stingy with you."

"Oh," Penelope walked in delight. "Oh no, Bac," she said, "you ain't stingy." He took her arm, propelling her in front of him.

There was hardly anyone in Kris's, so they sat down in a booth towards the back and Donald Krum who worked at the fountain took their order.

"Two banana splits," he repeated, winking at Bac. He was a pimply youth with a long neck. Penelope was smoothing her dress over her knees. She had on her Sunday one because it was so special a day. Bac leaned over, as if his black head thrust close to her breast held her on a pivot so she could not get away from his look.

"You look at me like a rabbit; is it somebody else you like better?"

"No," she said, leaning back, turning her eyes away.

"Well, then, what's the trouble, you act as if I was poison ivy."

"I don't, either."

"You do."

"I don't."

"Well, there ain't anybody in this town suits you better than me? Ain't that so?"

"Yes," she said, lowering her eyes.

"Well then!"

"Here ya are," said Donald Krum, setting the banana splits on the table, "Anything else?"

"That's all from you." Bac said, laughing so his teeth hung white in his lips.

"C'mon, give us your hand," he said, to Penelope. She put it out on the table. He turned the palm over. "Your hand's like a sick person's," he said, "are you scared?"

"Of what?" she said, hardly knowing what she was saying.

"I don't know. Don't ask me. Your hands are wet. What's the matter with you, staring at me like that? When I meet you on the street you're staring at me from head to foot."

"I do not," she said.

"You do too. And that time in the barn, getting as red as a beet like that and then running off and leaving me when the old man didn't come in at all and we might've stayed in the barn a long time. I went out looking for you behind all the hay stacks. What's the matter? Ain't I good enough for ya?"

"Oh, you're good," she said, taking a nibble of banana and cream.

"Well, you don't live forever, do you?" he said, dipping up a great mound of cream and cherry, "You don't live forever, now. You can't afford to waste too much time. At least I can't. I got to have my fun, y'know."

"Oh sure," she said, "sure."

"All right then," he said, "we understand each other then, don't we? Don't we?"

She hesitated, "Well . . . I guess so."

"You guess so? Don't you know nothin'? Are you just plain dumb?"

"I guess so," she said, startled, and he laughed, and then she laughed.

"What about this afternoon?" she said very low, looking around the booth to the front of the store which was empty, "Is everything all right?"

"Oh sure," he said, laughing, "I got that fixed O.K. But I got to leave you. I can't go walking like we said. I got to see a fellow in about an hour, about one o'clock. It's very important. But I aim to meet ya say about five. I got to do a little errand, see? But you can have dinner with me down town, see? And then we'll walk about sunset, see? Won't that be keen?"

"You mean have dinner with you right down town at a restaurant?"

"Sure. Certainly. Why not? Let 'em all see we're engaged to be married?"

"Are we?"

"Aren't we?"

They both laughed and began eating.

"Just between you and me," Bac said, his mouth dripping white cream, "Lowell's got it all wrong. Just between you and me and the gate post, you can't buck the game, see? And no matter how you say it they're goin' straight against the law. You got to do it crafty like. You got to be inside the law, see? I'm going to be worth a million dollars some day, amongst the big guys. This stuff is all wrong . . . that's just between you and me Pen, see? Don't say a word about it."

"But Bac," Penelope said, "You're supposed to be one. They're depending on you. . . ."

"Oh, I'm doin' it all right. I'm doin' it up brown. . . . But I know which side my bread is buttered on, that's all. I ain't no dumb sister."

She didn't say anything. She was set upon some hard brilliance in him like a gem, and she could not hear his words or know their meaning. He went on talking, swaggering, bragging, which made her laugh, knowing it in men, taking it for granted. And it made her think of her father, what a great man he was, what he did in the world, what a cock he was. She heard him murmur now along with Bac, "I'll show them. I'll show you. I wasn't born for small things. I been buried out there behind the plow but now I've got my chance. I'll be sheriff first, then congressman, then there's no stopping . . . all you got to do is play with the big boys, that's all."

She lowered her eyes, pushing at the ice cream, stirring it with her spoon tip, hearing the voices of men below ground and above, speaking alone, and together.

"But Bac," she said, "It's one thirty!"

"One thirty! Well why didn't you tell me?" He jumped up, "There you sit facing the clock, just wanting me to be late."

She stood up guiltily. "I didn't see. . . . Honest, Bac."

"Well, I got to beat it. I don't know exactly what time I'll be through," he said, "I don't exactly know, so maybe you better wait awhile at your house and I'll call for ya. I don't know what I'll have to do. You see, I have to go home and take care of the stock while Dad's gone with Lowell."

"Oh," she said, "Where's your ma?"

"You trust me," he said, "I got to go," pushing her swiftly along with him.

"All right, I will, Bac, I will."

"So long," and Bac started running down the street before her. She saw his fleet legs knowing she would never know which way or where he ran. When he had disappeared she wondered what would be in the day until that hour when she would see him approach again to touch her, not knowing where he had been or where he would be after.

She began to run. The day was a giant apple sliced in parts; she took one piece then another and forgot each piece as she took up another. Now she had thought suddenly of Mrs. Fearing, of Miss Shelley running back and forth across the yard, in the sun. It was hot on the street, and beads of sweat stood on her and trickled down her legs but she kept running. The Town seemed ominously deserted. She sprinted down Maple Street, under full trees that moved like green bells above her. Coming within sight, she stopped and looked at the yellow house, but it told her nothing. Her own house still had the shades drawn so her Gee was still sleeping in the upper story. Penelope stood in the heat, wondering what to do. She heard a door shut in the Fearing house, so she skirted around Miss Shelley's house, going into the back yard where the three of them had sat on the slope waiting for the day which had now come.

She stood under the maple tree looking at the back door. Miss Shelley came out on the porch to put something in the icebox.

"Miss Shelley," she whispered, "Miss Shelley."

The thin woman turned and saw her, beckoned, rolling her eyes like an owl. Penelope tiptoed over the grass, stood at the screen.

"It's the beginning," Miss Shelley said, rolling her eyes back towards the door, "It's beginning. And Penelope, do you want to come in and help? You could heat the water. There ain't going to be anybody here but me." Miss Shelley's hair was slid over her head, her eyes were bright as if she had a fever; she was frightening.

"Why sure," Penelope said. *Why this is birth*, she kept knowing, her feet walking differently, knowing what it was. *"Why this is birth,"* she kept telling herself as if she couldn't believe it. "When is it going to happen?" Penelope said in the kitchen, which seemed very silent, as if Cora Fearing had just left it for good, even the pots and pans seeming changed, knowing there was birth in the house, standing above the threshold.

Miss Shelley stood like a mad dervish in the center of the room.

"Land sakes, Penelope, how should I know? I never been at one of these afore, I never have." Sweat stood on her temples.

"I've sent for Dr. Starry, but he wasn't in. Gone to lunch I guess, but he hadn't gone home. Mrs. Starry said she'd get in touch with him soon as she could and send him over. And she said to have these cloths ready," she pointed to a great pile of white sheets on the kitchen table, "and plenty of hot water she said," and she pointed to the stove, where every kettle sat filled with water. "Now you should keep 'em hot, Penelope, and I'll carry 'em in and help the doctor. They can't afford to have no nurse. God knows when Dr. Starry'll ever get anything, but I guess doctors are used to that."

"What's she doing now?" Penelope leaned to Miss Shelley, whispering. "What happens? What's she doing? I don't hear nothing."

"She's sleepin' now, sort of, she kind of sleeps," Miss Shelley whispered, wringing her hands together so that her mother's old ring marked into her palms, "then she starts up and moans and then goes to sleep again like it sort of passes over then passes off, sort of."

"Oh," Penelope said, seeing something approaching that made a grip of fire and then a grip of peace. She leaned back in her chair her eyes closed saying *birth, birth, birth* . . . but it made no sound in her, no echo.

The doorbell sounded through the house, ringing in the kitchen right at their heads.

"It's him," Miss Shelley said, taking off her checked apron, dropping it, for the first time in her life, on the floor. Penelope stood at the door hearing Miss Shelley say, "Yes, Doctor . . . come in, Doctor," heard the door slam and the doctor's voice,

"All right, Miss Shelley. I'm glad to see you here. We'll need some help. How is she resting?"

Then they passed out of hearing into the bedroom and Penelope peeking, saw the doctor's hat hanging on the hat rack in the hall, having in it what the doctor would have to do, knowing more about it than she knew.

The afternoon then seemed like a thing that gained in momentum towards a moment that would not come, as if something pressed from outer space, unable to find entrance. Penelope waited in the kitchen where she soon forgot to look out the door, out the windows, and looked only toward the hall through which voices might come asking swiftly for this, for that, and through which cries came with swifter momentum at first gathering from the woman, then stopping in a silence that was heavy and then breaking again in a moan that became a cry that became a scream, like an animal. Towards five o'clock, knowing it was that time, hearing Dr. Starry in the hall saying, "Five o'clock. . . . too long . . . it's dropped too far. . . ." The words lay without meaning like a black dread in her stomach. "It's dropped too far" lay in her like a fatal thing. Then she stopped looking out of doors or windows and the house became a confinement that was too close for this outward pressure and this outward knocking, as if it would not be the instrument to hold what was trying to be held in it.

"Where is my husband?" Cora Fearing cried in a voice that was now the voice of birth, too. "Where is my husband?"

Dr. Starry went away in his car for something that boded no good, for an extreme measure that would mean it went one way or another, and Miss Shelley stood in the door looking at the bed. Penelope crouching in the hall not even looking into that fatal door that had become now tall and dark, the Entrance that would not give way.

"Where is my husband, Nina Shelley? Are you keeping him away? What have you done with him?"

"Why," Miss Shelley said in fear of that voice, "I . . . you know he's lookin' for work . . . I suppose you believe he's doin' the best he can, Cora Fearing."

Then a fearful thing happened. Penelope stepping behind Miss Shelley saw Cora rise from behind her awful stomach, her face stretched beyond its human contours, the mouth open, screaming:

"You get out of here, Nina Shelley. I know all about you, you damned ————." Penelope saw the obscene words strike and scar Miss Shelley's face.

"You get out of here," the woman who was not Cora now, but a terrible sibyl, screamed, "You find my husband and get out of here."

Miss Shelley started towards the bed. "Why you . . ." Cora rose towards her, but both women were stopped by something unseen in the room. A blank look crossed Cora's face, before she doubled in a groan that became a series of short and awful grunts, as if someone were striking her one blow after another. Miss Shelley stopped, whirled in the middle of the room, a look which might have been a passing fright rigid on her face.

The front door opened and shut, and Penelope turned to see Dr. Starry come in the door, his face anxious.

"Get that woman out of my room!" Cora cried.

Miss Shelley ran to the door, "You hear what she's saying?" she said to the doctor, "You hear that, when I've done all I could. When I've done everything, kept them in food . . . took care of her and all . . ."

"You liar!" Cora said, in a guttural that changed to a cry.

Dr. Starry started toward her, "I think, Miss Shelley," he said, over his shoulder, "I think perhaps you'd better stay in the kitchen. You can see how ill the woman is. . . ."

Penelope stood in the doorway, those cries threading her pores.

"What about Miss . . . er," the doctor said, pointing to her.

"I'm Penelope," she said, feeling her body striking up to the circumstance, standing tall and ready.

"Well, you look like a good strong one," Dr. Starry said, as if he had heard nothing about her, looking at her with his steady eyes that knew how to meet something more extreme than anger or passion.

"Ha!" Miss Shelley said, flouncing into the kitchen where she began to weep, the dry sobs giving birth to nothing, scraping her out.

Penelope stood in front of Dr. Starry as he opened his bag, not looking at the bed from where that animal grunt still came, not seeing the mound writhing like the earth, tearing out of itself another.

She kept her eyes on Dr. Starry. His hands moved exact and real. He looked at her, holding her rigid to what would be expected of her. She felt something striking in her, leaving no loose ends, catching her up so she moved like the instruments he took from his bag, moved under his hands direct and keen, with joy, her movements held within the time of what was happening, cutting through, waiting upon it as if something passed from an unknown world beyond them into their hands, and they took it, threading it through them precisely and nakedly, passing it on to death if it should be, to birth if it should be.

The doctor stood a moment by the bed looking at her. "You'll do, I believe," he said, "I believe you're a pretty good soldier," he said, seeing that she was keener metal than perhaps an older woman. "Sure the sight of blood doesn't hurt you?"

"No sir," she said, "I've seen blood aplenty," and her face lifted, pale but stern, with no giving way in it, meeting whatever was.

"All right," he said, "bring some hot water in here."

She went swiftly, lifted to an important moment. Miss Shelley sat in a chair by the window, crying.

"Some water," she said.

"There it is," Miss Shelley waved bitterly in the direction of the stove. Penelope got a towel, picked up the kettle. Miss Shelley sat sniffing, watching with one eye out of her kerchief. She felt very bad being robbed of this moment.

"You could bring the water to the door, Miss Shelley," Penelope said, "It's a shame. You'd be more good than I am."

Miss Shelley sniffed and wiped her eyes, pleased.

"I expect it's more important," Penelope said, "to have the water just right." A very meek and eager Miss Shelley got up, drying her eyes, and took the pot of water and came to the door, handing it to Penelope. "Bring some more and have it ready," Penelope whispered, turning into the room, not looking at the bed, not being able.

Out of the corner of her eye she couldn't help seeing that Dr. Starry had turned the huge form across the bed, and was working at the other side. The groans had stopped, the woman lay still. Penelope suddenly saw her face half hanging over the edge. "She's dead," she thought. As if in answer Dr. Starry said, "I've given her ether. Take my watch," he said, "count the pulse."

Penelope took the heavy gold watch from him. Without looking she reached for the limp hand of Cora that was not Cora's hand now, as if out of it came birth, too. "Count, Penelope," Dr. Starry said, smiling at her above the raised knees of the woman, "Don't forget to count . . . you know how to count don't you?" he said, smiling above the bed to her.

"Yes," she said, catching in her lips and feeling then the steady unseen beat in her hand, counting. "Tell me what it is," he said, "after each count." She looked at the watch putting the beat together with the time, thinking, this watch won't stop but this unseen thing can stop, maybe is near stopping now. And she looked down at the face hanging back with the mouth open, the brows knitting, in pain like a shadow passing above her.

"How much?"

"Sixty-two," she said.

"All right," he said.

She counted again. The lips moved on the face below her.

Dr. Starry left the bed then. "She can't do it," he said. "We'll have to take it."

Penelope stopped counting, waiting upon the word: *We'll have to take it*, waiting upon what it would mean.

"You get that blanket ready," he said, pointing. She saw then for the first time on the dresser the clothes spread out, strange at that hard moment, as if they would never be filled by anything.

She found a blanket with rabbits on it, and birds, and blocks of letters saying:

<blockquote>
Rock a bye baby
On the tree top
</blockquote>

She turned, hearing the bed slide over the floor. She saw he was moving it toward the wall. "Get a basin of water . . . something to bathe it in. Also one of cold water, just in case . . ."

It was coming. It would be there. She had a feeling of excitement and elation then as if someone were coming from a far country and she would look upon a beloved creature she had known before.

She hurried out into the kitchen. "It's coming," she said, then stopped, seeing Miss Shelley apparently fighting with a large dishevelled man and saying, "You keep out! You keep out of here. You'd only mess everything up, you drunken beast." She seemed to be in embrace with the huge man who leaned over loose from the shoulders like a bear, and she under him, shoving him up from the chest with all her weight.

"It's Mr. Fearing," she said to Penelope. His eyes were glazed, his face flushed and heated. "I want to see my wife," he said to Penelope and began to sob, sinking into the chair by the table. Miss Shelley's dress was unhooked, and she had lost one of her rats. Her face was flushed and shaken strangely.

"Two basins of water," Penelope said, "one hot, one cold. It's a coming!" Miss Shelley's eyes opened on the word straight upon Penelope, dilating so they were green in the center, then she dove for the basins, her hands quick towards what was there. Penelope took the hot water and went quickly out of the room. The drunken man began to shout as she left the door, his cries filling the now quiet house. They came from the kitchen without stopping, the bellowings and moanings.

Penelope stood in the bedroom door, and the basin became like a feather in her hands and her whole body weightless for what she now saw.

Dr. Starry sat on the floor, his back against the wall, his feet braced against the bed edge, his hands gripped on the steel forceps which held in them what looked like a piece of coal, half emerged. She saw his face against the wall, stern, as if he were looking past everything in the room, forging a moment with a vulcan heat. She set the basin down on the dresser beside the blanket, and only then realized that he was pulling as hard as he could. She gave a cry which he didn't hear.

"Will you stand over and put your hands under her armpits?" he said to Penelope, although she thought he hadn't seen her come in, and it made her think: he is seeing more and hearing more than I know. She went over, now light and unfeeling like an instrument herself. Dr. Starry had a light on his head which shone as he moved in the darkening room, as if they were all turned away from the world, opening a door from another.

She put her hands under the arms of the woman who gave a sense of being conscious in all her body and not in her mind, as if her eyes were simply closed but her great body was below, a growing thing. Penelope lifted the heavy shoulders against her and then she felt the tearing stricture, the pressure, the weight away from her, taut, then falling back lax against her, repeated and repeated, until she was swaying with a rhythm transmitted to her and she felt a compassion go through her bowels, and she thought: she's crying! but saw it was her own tears dropping on the face under her, as Dr. Starry released the pull and the head struck back against her.

She forgot what they were doing in the stress of doing it until she felt the body go limp as if its use were over, as if something had finished with it. She herself dropped the head and shoulders then, and stood her eyes wide open upon what she saw, the tears coming out of them without grief or sorrow or joy, like any excrescence of the body sweetly bringing it to fruit.

In his hands lay a body, round belly, budding head, budding thighs, hanging down from the heels as he held it by the feet, patting its back, its round shining buttocks. It was black and inert like a fruit too ripe. Then she saw him begin swinging it around his head by the heels.

"Bring me that cold water," he said, his voice unrecognizable.

She ran to the door where Miss Shelley had left the water and in the hall, she saw Miss Shelley fighting with Fearing, standing under him so he dropped drunkenly over her, and they fell against one wall and then the other, she, pushing him back, just keeping him out of the door which he couldn't see. Penelope paid no attention, as if it was quite natural, a small thing, came back with the basin of cold water. Dr. Starry was breathing into the still mouth that had not yet uttered a sound. He splashed water into the black face that hung in interrogation between one thing and another.

Then, like a suffusion of heat with the entrance of the earth's air into it, the black skin began to glow, the ribs moved out in a spasm, the mouth opened, the negroid nostrils dilated; then from out of it came a high protesting cry. The air of the earth made this cry, generated it in the closed belly, striking in the lungs for the first time. His tight closed fists beat the air, the eyes crinkled, the mouth opened with each breath, one following another, the belly like a bellows thrusting it through the sleeping throat: wah, wah, wah!

Dr. Starry breathed easily now, too, and smiled. "There you are," he said, "Alive!"

And naked and slippery he handed it to her. She stood crying, holding the naked new baby, flushing and flushing now from darkness to the earth's light, becoming rosy as she watched.

"Don't stand there," he said. "Bathe it. Just bathe it. Don't drop it. Don't be frightened. I've got work to do here. I'll have to let you take care of that fellow, soldier," he said. And with the slippery, rosying flesh in her hands she laid it in the water. Being in water soothed the weakened child, and it lay under her hands, which she was afraid to take away to wash it.

"Don't get the cord wet," he said, from behind her, but she could only nod, looking at the knotted bud in her hands, the closed, screwed face now relaxing in a sleep, like something under a dream, so she thought: He's born now, but not out of a dream yet. Her hands growing more used washed the slime from his head, from his body, and she saw that it was "a little boy!" she said to herself, the tears falling on him without her knowing. "That's the way they all come, is it? Men . . . men. . . ."

"Wipe him off," the doctor was keeping an eye on her. "We'll put on this dressing," he said, putting it on, "and this band," he turned him over for her on the dresser top. "Now I guess you must be a woman, aren't you? Although you stand up better than many. You dress him and wrap him up warm and put him over there in that crib and let him rest. He's had a hard voyage."

"All right," she said, doing it all, terrified at the loose head falling from her hands. Putting him there where he slept, the bud of a man. Saying: *Men . . . men. . . .*

Chapter Twelve

At six the house was quiet. Dr. Starry had put Fearing to bed, and Cora Fearing's sister had come in from the country to stay a couple of weeks. Miss Shelley had lost her touching meekness now and added this to her store of abuses. She would set out to get some revenge, what little she could, for always being thrust out from the final moment, robbed of what was crucial. She went away, across the back yard, sniffing, the flaunt of her skirts boding no good.

Dr. Starry said, "I thank you, Penelope." He looked very small and lean and tired, and Penelope felt that she would always know him now, seeing him on the streets, not knowing how such a crevasse made by violence can be closed by the drifting of days. "Drop in and see me sometime at my office," he said, "we might make a nurse of you." He thought her face too stern and drained; she might have some inner malady.

"Thank you very much," she said, "I'll be glad to. Only I'm never sick."

"Well, that's the time to see a doctor," he said, "when you're never sick." She was walking to the sidewalk with him seeing him put on the hat on the hall tree, seeing him carry the black bag of instruments whose meaning she now knew. She watched him get into his car and drive away without looking around.

She saw her own house standing as usual under the elm behind its rickety wooden porch. No one was on the street. Everything looked strange, as if something had happened. Some foreboding came into her, seeing the sun had passed over without her knowing; the robins hopped on the lawns; the day had gone without her, as if birth were as remote as death, and set you as much apart.

"Bac," she said, "Bac." Letting him come back into her who had been gone without a thought since she had whispered to Miss Shelley early afternoon. Fearfully she crossed the street, tiptoed up the steps, opened the door, not knowing what she would see, as if they all might be enchanted, gone, so she would never see them again.

She stood in the door hearing a woman's voice speaking a long monologue, then she saw Gee and Bac through the hall door, sitting over the dining room table, waiting. Bac was drumming his fingers on the table. Gee was talking. He looked up and saw her, tilted his chair back.

"Well for God's sake," he said, "Where you been? Double crossing me. Got your own friends, I expect." He got up and took her arms as she came toward him.

"Leave me be," she said.

Gee was crying now. "All gone away and left me. Poor old Gee . . . gone away and left me here . . . not a soul all day."

A fear came over her. "Where are they? Haven't Mona and Lowell come back?"

"No," Bac said, "They ain't come back."

"What's happened?" she said, pulling loose. "You tell me, Bac Kelly, what's happened? What's happened?"

They ain't nothing happened. It's a good hundred miles out there, that's all," he said. She stood still, wondering what had happened.

"You better go up to bed, Gee, and get some rest," she said.

"Bed!" screamed Gee, lifting her fat neck up from her shoulders, "I been in bed all day!"

"All right. You stay here. Bac and I'll go out."

"Now you leave me, Pen. Penny, don't leave me. . . ."

"Well, we'll go out and see if we can find out anything; if anything's happened, we'll find out about it in town."

Looking back she saw her Gee sitting weeping at the table. "Goodbye, Gee," she said, "We'll be back . . . you'll have company soon."

They went out the door. Penelope stopped on the porch, seeing Miss Shelley bustle out of her door, putting on her gloves. Anyone could tell she had intentions, that she was not just going to the Gem. She had on her Sunday hat, too, and seemed dressed for some festival. Penelope watched her pull down her corset, step onto the walk and turn toward Town, walking very fast and furtive, still with an excitement, like a woman who might be going to meet a lover.

"You know where I been?" Penelope said, letting Miss Shelley get far ahead of them down the street.

"Where you been?"

"I been over there. I been helping a chap get borned."

"You have?"

"Sure. I been helping, that's what I been doing. I was a help. I helped clean through it."

"Well, I guess that ain't nothing so smart."

"It is something. It's more than I ever knew it was afore," she said. "It's something's got a lot to do with women."

"Well, I guess I won't ever have no baby," he laughed.

100

She walked along now, feeling her legs striding with their bold-ness that took her own way, always.

"Ain't we goin' to take our walk along Mumser's Orchard?"

"Sure we are," she said, "It's a grand evening." She felt good, knowing how it was to get into the world.

"It's a right lot of trouble," she said, laughing, "to get yourself borned. You know it is?"

"It ain't no trouble to the men," he said, laughing.

"I suppose it ain't," she said, contemptuously. "I suppose it ain't. I suppose it's a pleasure to the men."

Bac laughed, taking her arm. "Let's cut across here; we ain't got no need to go through Town. You won't hear nothin'. It's a good hundred mile back from Peterson's. It's too early."

"Is it?" she said. "I expect . . ."

"Why you walkin' so fast?" Bac said.

"Ain't we going for a walk," she said, letting him follow. "Well, you gotta walk, then . . ."

They held hands across the trestle.

"I heard you used to always go to Littlefield's on Saturday," Bac said. "What did you and him do all the time?"

"Play chess," she said.

"Chess . . . don't tell me. Others say different."

"Let 'em," she said.

"Well, you ain't goin' there tonight."

"Maybe I will," she said, "and maybe I won't. It's time for having tea now, like I used to, but I can get back in time to have a game of chess. He's pretty powerful lonely, I reckon."

"So is a lot a people."

Just as they were passing, Littlefield's face pressed the window pane, then he opened the door, waving his long arms. "Penelope," he called, "Penelope."

They stopped.

"Hello, Mr. Littlefield," Penelope said. Mr. Littlefield saw Bac and stopped. "Well, I see you ain't coming here," he said, "I see you've got other things to do."

"We're only taking a little walk . . . it's an evening, Mr. Little-field . . . and did you know the Fearing chap was born this after-noon? And I helped."

"You!"

"Yes, sir. I helped."

"Well, well."

"I thought I might stop in when we come back this way and have a game of chess."

"Well, I think you won't be wanting to," he said evilly, "when you come back this way. . ."

She hesitated, then without speaking she went on, following Bac. Littlefield stood in the door, his eyes filling with tears. "Penelope . . . Penelope," he said, holding out his hand as if to stop her but not stopping her.

Later, when he saw Bill Nye and Red Davis come across the trestle around seven-thirty he stood at the window watching, in some way half knowing what they were about, sitting in the dark, weeping for himself.

Bac was in some way disturbed by Penelope who walked so boldly, not now like a rabbit scurrying before his look. He was uneasy, thinking everything could be going awry; uneasy, too, for what he had done in the afternoon, feeling that something was going on that he couldn't gauge, with elements that were beyond the power of his muscles to bend or reap.

They came to the heavy fruiting orchard and walked under the trees, Penelope touching the bodies, touching the fruit tips, hanging low, not yet ripe.

They came to the stream and followed along, Penelope queer and withdrawn as if he could not touch her. Well, he would wait for darkness, and he knew the power in his arms and back and the power in his loins.

"We don't want to go too far," he said.

"Why not?" she said, "Are you weak?"

"Well no, but you know I been working all day, don't forget that."

"Well, I been working too," she said proudly, "I been a laboring, too."

"Well, hell, I want to take a look at you, and you race along like a filly. . . ."

"Well, weakness, let's sit down here," she said, sitting down by the stream, folding up her legs under her. The evening was settling, darkening; the birds were feathering themselves in amongst the trees, making a sweet twittering in the Summer twilight.

"Evenings are long," Bac said, "They're getting longer."

"Whose a tending to the cattle? Who's doing the milking?"

"My ma will. She'll get back in time."

"How will she get back if your pa hasn't got back yet, to go get her?"

"Well you see . . . her sister is goin' to bring her back and stay over night."

"I didn't know she had a sister."

"Well, she has, all right. I ought to know. What makes you so questioning?"

"Oh, I don't know. I wish I knew where Mona was, if everything is all right."

"So you don't believe me there, either. I told you it was O.K. Don't you believe me?"

"Yes."

"All right then, what's the fuss?"

"I don't know . . ." she said.

"Oh, Pen. Ain't we engaged? Can't I kiss you?"

"I don't want you to none."

"What's the matter? Ain't I a good looker?"

"Yes. Yes, you look good."

"Well then, give us a kiss."

"Not right now, not right this moment, this instant . . ."

"Sure," he said.

She turned her face so he kissed her cheek, then he caught her.

"I gotta do it," she said to herself, *"I gotta do it. You gotta do it, be carried with it. A man's got to go swift together with other men, and woman's got to go swift with this, that comes in to carry her, and with the other too,"* knowing birth, but not saying it.

She let him come upon her with his rock grip, close in, kissing her; but she was not there on her own lips, because of knowing there the taste of wolfish hunger, not with roses, not with apples.

"It's getting mighty dark," she said, pulling away, "I think we better be starting back. . . ."

"We ain't startin' nowhere," he said, his arm holding her half-sitting, half-reclining to him, gripping her with insolence. It was like a dream of stone to her; strange that when she was away from him, he was fire and she must find him, but when he was upon her, he was stone and she must run. His thick lips were on her neck when there was a crackling in the brush, just a sound, and then it was still. Bac listened, looking over her shoulders into the close briars. She felt him stop, listening. It was quite dark. She listened, too, heard the stream go over rock, being broken, dropping into parts.

"What are you listening for?" she asked.

"Nothing," he said, still listening.

"Did you hear somebody?" she said, sitting up, smoothing down her dress.

"Just a minute," he said, "I'll see . . . I'll be right back."

She saw him move away from her, saw the straight back going up to the hard block head. She got up, crouching on her knees, seeing the way he walked, so cruel and stealthy moving down the creek, not knowing upon what errand he would be going, but smelling that errand a wolf one. She crouched down, seeing him go down the bend of the creek.

The minute he went out of sight, Penelope got up and began running in the opposite direction, through the orchard in the dark.

Bac met the boys a hundred yards around the bend under the orchard. It was dark, but the dipper hung to the left.

"It's all O.K.," he said, "you can cut across that bend there and have grandstand seats."

"O.K.," they said, starting to step through the orchard grasses.

Bac went back by the creek and saw where she had been sitting. A flame of wrath went licking up his sides; then he thought he would see her hiding. He stood waiting, knowing she was gone. He should have known, the way she had always run . . . the time she ran away right across the fields from the barn when he almost had her.

He began to swear. Then he saw the boys looking through the leaves.

"Come on, you," he swore at them, "run around that way . . . cut her off! She must've cut across there . . . go on! You help get her and we'll divide. Go on! you can have her, too. Only help me get the ————!"

The boys with yells started running around a circle in the direction she had gone.

"Shut up, damn you. Let me call her. Maybe she's just hiding. Shut up, don't make any noise. Find the ————!" Bac like a mad goat was running through the grasses, hitting his face against the low swinging branches, knocking off the green apples so they fell in the dark on the ground.

Penelope ran through the orchard in the silent dark; then she heard, fanwise behind her, the sharp cries of Bac and then two others, on one side, then on the other, as if they were closing in. She doubled over, cutting across so she would come out in the cornfield on the other side, running swiftly, bending low under the branches, feeling the fruit strike against her, and birds rising frightened from the trees.

The orchard seemed to peer at her with a great unearthly face out of every limb, as she ran low and secret underneath. She would hear the running of feet and double back; then the shouts that her silence baffled. And she knew now that her blooming would not be for the running feet of wolves, was not to be dogged down by shout and cry. She ran, low and swift!

The yells became fainter and she stopped, looking into the darkness, the sweat standing out on her. All around her stood the trees; she felt them coming up to her as if they were walking in a progression of likenesses. Speech went out of her mouth, her legs trembled.

In the Spring she had thought that the most terrible thing could be an orchard in blossom, like the first day of creation lying in mist and the waxen hold of the virgin bloom; but now, standing by the old trees, moving eyeless, soundless, shaking, opening in the dark, a terror crawled into the roots of her hair. But now, the orchard seemed to have an old power of procreation, burning in a conflagration of growth, fruiting in the night, the dark leaves flung skywards, the round fruit drooping groundward, revealing something that spoke and yet whose speech was lost in the round fruiting. An eye seemed to be looking at her, a presence approaching her. She began to run, and almost instantly fell out into the wide fields, in the earthlight that swung low, darkening toward the sky. The stars clustered warmly. It was the Summer sky.

She began to walk along the low lying fields, folded in night sleep, night rolling in upon their secrets. In little waves the wind moved against her.

Walking across the fields in the white interspace between the upper night and the earth night, blackness rising like a vapor and the star luster falling richly downward to illumine strangely the corn with a white uncanny radiance, like a mirage, like a light that might be coming from the stalks, corn and wheat kernels and star kernels intermingling. She stepped out of the orchard into the dark, lustrous country night, the corn murmuring, moving dreamily at its tips towards a ripening moment, the black earth cooling, breathing up, black and cool after heat.

Through the delicate vast night she went running, treading the dark with her bright feet. And the earth turned to speak to her flowering step, surface to surface, and she thought she saw blooming inward all the light of the minerals reflecting those stars that hund above imbedded in that night that lay above her and below her . — stars above her head, stars beneath her feet.

She did not even look back, knowing they would not find her now, hid in the corn. She came in sight of the lights of the Town and stood still, knowing she saw it differently now, as if she held it naked, as she had held the Fearing chap, convulsed and blind in her hands, held it to the stars above the corn. . . . . *O Men!*

Chapter Thirteen

She got back to the house on Maple Street, the cold sweat drying on her. Cars were parked in front along the street. She ran into the house and saw Mona standing in the dining room.

"Mona!" she called to her as if she had been parted from her for a long time. She ran in past all the men to get to her.

Mona looked as if she did not know her. "Hello, Pen," she said coldly.

"Mother, what?"

Lowell sat at the table.

"What's happened?" All she had been full of went out of her. Had there been shooting in the corn? The men in the room were quiet.

Mona said, "Where's Bac?"

They all looked at her. "I don't know."

"You've been with him, haven't you?"

"Yes. . . . I. . . ."

"Were you with him this afternoon?" Lowell suddenly asked, lifting his eyes to her.

"No," she said.

"Come here, Penelope," he said. She came and stood beside him, and he took her hands looking up at her. "Somebody tipped the sheriff off this afternoon," he said.

"Oh!" she said, her hand grasping her throat. Mona was looking at her in anger, putting the guilt on her.

"Do you know anything about it?"

They all waited.

"No," she said, "No, Lowell, I don't know anything about it." Mona sprang at her, shaking her.

"You liar! It was that whelp of yours. I never trusted him around here . . . come on, tell what happened."

"Leave her alone, Mona," Lowell said. Mona let her hands drop. The other men watched.

"It's this way, Penelope. We don't know that Bac did it. But somebody tipped the sheriff off. Only they did it half an hour too late. He was half an hour late . . ."

"Half an hour?" Penelope said, trying to think where that half hour had figured in the day.

"Yes . . . so it had been done and we were gone. But something serious might have happened. The point is that one of us," the others stirred uneasily, "one of us squealed. You see . . ."

"Yes," Penelope said, the color hot in her cheeks.

"Where were you?" he asked, kindly.

"I was over to Mrs. Fearing's all the afternoon. She had her baby . . ." she said in a low voice, and it sounded now different, not like what had been at all, very small.

"She had her baby?" Mona said, "What were you doing?"

"I was helping."

Mona began to laugh. "Oh, God, you were helping! Well, for heaven's sake. Well, no harm has been done this time."

Penelope felt it was somehow her fault; she was under a shadow. "Could I wash the cups, Mona?" she said. She ran to the kitchen and began washing the cups that were piled high in the sink. Gee had gone to bed.

She stood in the tide of all that happened, in the dark kitchen. Lowell came in for a drink of water, touched her arm, smiled at her.

"Did you help? Really?" he said.

"Yes I did Lowell, I did pretty good . . ."

"That's all right," he said. "We met Fearing today, getting drunk, and tried to get him to go with us. A man like that when he loses his job thinks he's all alone. He ought to come with us. We all ought to be together. The grass doesn't grow separate, stand alone, does it? Or the trees?"

"No," she said, smiling at him as he stood drinking the water.

"Goodnight, girl," he said. "Don't keep too late hours. You have to grow. Goodnight."

It's about done, this day, she thought drowsily, wiping the heavy white cups, setting them out where Mona got them. But it wasn't done yet. There was time to wash back in the tide the wreckage of the day.

A man came in saying, "What's this I hear about Fearing?"

"What do you hear?"

"I hear he cut up something terrible this afternoon when his brat was comin'."

"You heard that? Fearing always seemed a decent man."

"Well, that's what I hear . . ."

There was a commotion at the front door, then, and Penelope looked and saw the lurching back of Fearing, looking as if something had snapped him in the middle.

"I want a drink," he bellowed.

Mona said, "We don't have any here, Fearing. You better sit

down."

"I want a drink and I'm going to get it."

Davidson took him by the arm, and Fearing began to weep. "I suppose you fellows all heard what an ass I was . . . what I done . . ." The men all looked away.

"We ain't heard nothing," Beggs said.

"You all heard it. You all heard, and that's a fact." Davidson was holding him up, as Miss Shelley had done.

Mona said, "You all better take him over and put him to bed, quiet . . . or one of you take him home with you." Nobody said they would. They all looked at him.

"I guess my wife thinks I'm a bum husband, what with all," he said, weeping, and Davidson and Beggs started across the street with him. He began to shout, and they struggled with him, so it looked like all three were drunk. At the same time, Penelope, standing at the back door, saw Miss Shelley coming down the walk, stop to watch him, her best alpaca shining under the street lamp.

The other men stood in the door, watching. "My wife says Miss Shelley was the one helped out at the birth, did everything for them, fed 'em for months before . . . they ain't had a thing."

"You don't say."

"Yes, and she says Fearing tried to attack her this afternoon, right when his poor wife was near death's door with the kid."

"Well the low down. . . ."

"Who'd of thought it?"

"Women's talk, most likely. . . ."

"No, that's a fact. I hear it all over Town how it happened."

"Guess Fearing won't stick his nose around here quite so cocky when this gets around. . . ."

Littlefield came in, stopping to watch the three men struggling up Fearing's steps. He went in to talk to Mona, and Penelope ducked into the kitchen, looking around the door, thinking of Bac too, not thinking he would come here, though. Something that had glittered brightly between them had been cut, but she could not tell if it was gone from her until she could withstand the sight of him again.

"What's all this I hear?" Littlefield said, "What is happening? I hear men talking. . . ."

"Do you hear something?" Mona asked.

"I hear something is going on . . . I been hearing something . . ."

"You have?"

"Yes, I been hearing. . . ."

Just then, in the house, in the street, somewhere, there was a shot.

Littlefield stopped with his hand upraised, Mona with her shawl half lifted to her shoulders, Lowell, who was just going upstairs, with his foot on the first stair. Men stopped talking, words were broken. Then all of one movement they went towards the door as if it was known beforehand, and the place known and planned and the time known. They flowed into the street. Lights flashed on in the superintendent's house, in Miss Shelley's house, and instantly she ran into the street.

On the sidewalk for a second a man was standing; then he whirled as if he was spun from the head, with his feet like a puppet's, drawn upwards. The men ran across, a quiet drove, and Miss Shelley was running all alone down the walk. She got there first, saw the blood come out of Fearing's head, and just stood there as if something had been paid her and she held it in her hand; and the men, leaning over, found out he was dead.

Lowell called to them in a low voice, "Is he dead?"

"Yes," the men said, "Dead. . . ."

Then they lifted their heads although there had been no sound, and saw Cora Fearing standing on the porch in her night gown looking at the walk, hearing what they had said. Shamefaced the men stood in front of what was on the walk, flowed together like something filling a gap that has been made.

Then, as if something slashed a whip over them all, Cora Fearing began to scream, high, long, sharp. "Nina Shelley . . . Nina Shelley . . . Nina Shelley!" and Miss Shelley started to run like charred paper scuttling under the light.

Penelope stood by Lowell. . . . "That's what happens. A man can't be alone. He should've come with us . . . a man can't stand out alone, now, can he? . . . not alone . . ."

The men standing around the thing on the sidewalk broke away, drifted over, waiting. Mona had telephoned for the coroner.

They came across, standing in clots.

"A man can't stand out alone when a tide comes up, now, can he?"

And Penelope, feeling the surge of men's black bodies in the night, trembled as she had in the orchard at some movement coming in, a changing, a turning, stirring an old pool, rousing an old passion, moving over ancient hills; as if something was looking out at her that would have to be when men began to move, that would have to be, like what happens when whales start coming together, when migrations of bees or men or beasts start and no one can say why or know a reason, but all must go. And she saw the look of that going in the eyes of furtive, lonely men, turning together, moving from out sourness, turning upon each other again with an old sensuous dream beyond the dream that had been too

109

little for a man to dream, or a woman to follow.

They came up quietly in a car, and picked up something off the walk, and drove away.

Part Three

*". . . there is a song deep as the falltime redhaws,
long as the layer of black loam we go to, the shine
of the morning star over the corn belt, the wave
line of dawn up a wheat valley."*

Chapter Fourteen

After that the hot days came upon them. The harvest was approaching, the dust wind came in off the prairies, settling over the Town.

"Cyclone weather," men said to each other, watching their wheat and corn standing still, hardly ruffled by a wind in the fields for miles and miles standing silent on the prairies.

Penelope could hardly move going slowly through the Town hearing men talk of what had happened.

"That was pretty smart. For ten dollars ninety cents they bought old Peterson's farm"

"Never moved a stick or a stone from the house. His old lady never took off her apron . . ."

"You don't say!"

And the merchants, Mr. Pfeiffer and such, clacking their tongues, "What's the country coming to. Going against law and order like that, going against it. A mortgage is a mortgage."

Lowell saying, "Of course that's where their bread is buttered. They probably hold mortgages on half the farms around here, one way or another."

Hearing them then saying, their hands in their pockets:

"The farmers always was a lot you never could tell which way they was going. Not in any election. Never. Go one way today and another tomorrow. Like a weather vane."

"Showing which way the wind's blowing maybe, eh Pfeiffer?"

"Hell!" Suddenly anger flaring for no reason stood on the sidewalk with them.

"Who done it? Who was there?"

"Why, Beggs was there . . ."

"And some say Tamsun was there, and Mumser . . ."

"Why, they're good citizens!"

"Why sure, as good as we got, support the community chest."

"They ain't foreigners . . ."

"No, not by a darn sight."

"Well then . . ."

"Who was there?"

". . . and Gerhardt, and Rooney and Marner . . ."

"Them?"

"Yes, them."

And then looks flowing around Lowell, down the street. "He ain't one of us . . . Lowell ain't. Come from a far place. And those three women . . ." And looks coming to pry around their house. On Sunday cars driving by real slow, like they had not done since Miss Shelley lay across the street and it was a question whether she would live or die, going by very slowly, people looking at the house as if to find out something. And Mona and Gee and Penelope, the three of them standing inside the windows, looking out at the Town.

The Fearing house was very quiet, Cora Fearing's sister came in and out with her shopping bag during the day, but no word came from there except that at night you could sometimes hear the squalling of the baby, crying and crying as if the earth's air hurt him.

Penelope lay at night listening to the Town and its hate slowly congeal, so she knew it would come to some point and burst, changing what was there, and she lay crouched in her bed, listening, waiting now for what was already on the way.

A guilt lay in her, too, for the part she had had in that Saturday's business, although it hadn't been her fault even if Bac had left her and gone to the sheriff, a half hour late. She knew now that it was that half hour when he had sat bragging, ice cream dripping from his jaws, that branded him. Said nothing yet, not liking to say until there was a sureness over his head. But she felt that the men looked at her, let her pass in a silence that wrapped her single; that Lowell followed her with his eyes, asking a question; that Mona shut her away, turning on her her own fierceness.

She washed cups in the kitchen with Gee, or made sandwiches for the men, many of whom came hungry, ate what they could get, and took sacks of flour home to their families, coming in, saying to Lowell, "There's my kids out there, and my goats and my pigs ain't had nothing much for two days. . . ." So that sacks of flour began to stand up in the front room now instead of card players, and men came in bringing what they had, giving out to the ones among them who hadn't. They brought vegetables and exchanged for wheat, or wheat and exchanged for meat when one of them had butchered a hog. So a commissary stood in the front room, and Lowell let her keep a book which made a kind of record when one man took more than he left, saying he would bring something when he had it. And this she wrote down besides names that were German, Irish, English, feeling proud of the book, keeping its records as clean as she might.

But when she stopped with her pencil poised she heard the Town, heard what was gathering, ready to break.

Bac came to the meetings, but the men put a lariat of silence around him, saying nothing, accusing in no way, but putting around him a question which snared his feet and gave him an uneasiness that sent him on his way. She saw him at church standing outside on hot Sunday mornings, waiting to watch the girls. But she did not walk with him, yet nothing was spoken or came to any head, only it had changed from what it was before, and hung heavy and silent, like everything else in the Town under a pressure and a heat that would in no way be relieved until it was threshed down by the harvester, winnowed and sacked for their usage.

She said to Lowell, having to say it, feeling it gather in her throat, "Lowell, I don't know whether Bac did it or not. I don't know . . . I don't stand in any way of knowing."

He looked at her, then went on eating. "I know. All right."

"But Mona thinks I do. She thinks I do . . ."

"No," he said, "I don't think that . . ."

"Thank you," she said. "I wouldn't."

"No, I know you wouldn't. But just the same, maybe he did, you see? We can't take chances."

"No."

"Well, then. I'll tell you what you can do, Penelope. You can kind of go around with him, you see, like you did before and then perhaps you'll find out something."

"You mean, go with him like before?"

"Sure. We'll know how it is, you see, and I'll tell the boys how it is."

"Oh," she said, fingering the cloth.

"Will you do that, Penelope?"

"Oh, all right," she said, not seeing how she would be able to go back to the way it was before that Saturday and be able to hang upon that glitter as she had, but still an excitement rose in her because it was something that gave her strong pain and bitter pleasure and was better than nothing at all.

"I'll do it," she said, "I'll do it," but she trembled seeing Bac's look hot upon her again and his heat turning her on a spit of itself, warming her, but at what awful fire, what awful price. "I'll do it," she said.

She went out trembling with fright at what would now surely happen, seeing Bac's wolf look softly burning, gripping her with grip of fire.

Everything bore upon its face some change she could not name, but the Town walked close and silent in the heat, and its approach was in the air, in the stillness, in the corn that now topped a man, in the wheat that waited for the harvester to come down the road, The anxious eyes of men watched the crops grow to big size that they would not be able to sell, that would not feed them, that stood sterile in the fields, unable to yield them in flesh what they had sowed in flesh.

She went softly, approaching Bac, a smile on her face, though her teeth froze under it, letting her ways flaunt a little, letting her looks go backward drawing him, so he came. She felt in her own softness now some power she had not known, seeing him follow, and having of herself a reason as great and hot as his own. They circled upon each other in a silence that had no breaking point, in day after day of corn-growing heat, and wheat-ripening sun, that made them all seem to crawl and sleep like an enchanted Town, but the talk going on in all the stores, behind every window, wherever two men met on the street, or with a counter between them, the talk went on.

"Well, what's agoin' to happen?"

"What now?"

"The Lord only knows."

"Anything might happen now . . . with all them farmers forgetting the sacred rights of property."

"Well, a man who tills and drops his sweat has some rights, too . . ."

"I dropped my sweat along my fields, and my sons give their thighs and their shoulder power to it . . ."

"There she stands up as good a crop as man and God can sow . . ."

"And what'll it get us?"

"They was a Boston Tea Party once too . . ."

"We ain't got nary a thing to lose now, have we?"

"The shirts off our backs, that's about what's left . . ."

"Our barns hanging crazy, our houses peeling . . ."

"I can hear the paint drop right off my house in this heat, I can."

"Mine's peeling down like a ripe banana, yes sir . . ."

"And our fields standing a full crop . . ."

"And not a sou for it . . . not worth putting the machine to . . ."

"It's gotten so a man can't have a kid. . . ."

"It's got so they ain't no crop you can have. . . ."

"It's that some people hold all the money . . ."

and they could say the words "international bankers," tasting them brackish on the tongue.

She walked in the market, seeing men clotting, talking, spitting, swearing, and women listening, standing with their market bags with spare patience, their eyes turning from one face to another, their mouths grim and closed. She sat a ways off, too, listening.

To make the time more strange, and seem to be floating static in a space that was like dream, one day Jenny . . . with tight short skirt, with bright cheeks so you hardly could see and say: Jenny, Girl, Friend . . . again stood on the streets of the Town, her sharp flanks turned back impudently, her dress tight showing now breasts and shoulders speaking of what had happened . . .

"Hi kid," she said, and Penelope's eyes looked and stayed on a beaded handbag swinging on her arm . . .

"Well for heaven's sake," Jenny said, "you ain't changed much. Gee whiz, I ain't a ghost, am I? C'mon, we'll step into Kris's and have a little something, what say?"

Penelope walked beside her, looking another way.

Jenny talked, laughing too much, Penelope making her feel how she had been changed, setting it upon her, so it happened more in that moment than when it was happening. She was uneasy and talked too much, wanting to make Penelope believe that something had happened that would be as bright as what should have been, and having strong pleasure, making of it, now it was over, something curiously mixed of what she had known and what she had hoped. . . .

Penelope tried to see what it was, to find a meaning beyond even Jenny's knowing. Despite what Jenny kept saying, the words rolling out of her bright cheeks like something that formed no deeper than her lips, her body saying that another thing had turned in its flesh, setting it upon decay. . . . She heard Jenny saying she had been sent home instead of to the reformatory, and held that in her hands but could not know what there would be in Jenny leaving with excitement, stepping on that train, wanting what surely would not be a vicious thing, wanting only to be what she was, beyond yearning, and have what stirred in her seen in the world like any stalk of wheat or shining leaf of corn . . .

"What did you do? Did you steal?" Penelope asked in wonder.

"No, for Pete's sake . . . why should I steal? I was sittin' pretty . . . I never done nothin'; I wasn't doin' nothin'. Gee, I was sittin' pretty. I had an apartment of my own, kid. . . ." She went into the wonders that she had, spinning them out of her as a spider spins a web, and Penelope took every part, piercing it together to see what it was . . . men . . . parties . . . but knowing only the words that hung above their ice cream sodas, standing for what had been a margin between life and death for Jenny, who made a mask to cover whatever had been beyond that margin, which would now harden until she would have forgotten when it was a question . . . Penelope had a sense of swift movement of men from the moment Jenny had gotten on that train and men had started a migration towards her, feeding on the small flame that could have no other vice but tawdriness . . .

The words intimated a glamor that was beyond any single thing she had gotten from men, saying: She had met a man at a restaurant and they had gone to the Family Theater, where they had stayed until it closed . . . then they had gone to the hotel and the cops had followed, so they had left and gone down the railroad track, but the cop had followed and got her . . .

"Yes, yes," Penelope said, her mouth stiff, her eyes lowered, "Yes . . . yes . . . yes." Wanting to say: Yes, but what was it? What has it been? Saying, "Yes, yes. I gotta go," getting up, "I'll see you again. Goodbye." Goodbye Jenny Kelly . . . knowing she would see her on the street after that and not know her; that she would be gone as Friend, her ways would now be known and marked without secrecy; that the letter would have to be taken from where it was pinned in her shift and put away as something that was ended without being finished. That Mrs. Kelly would not ask now, "Where is Jenny?" "Have you heard from Jenny?" Jenny stood now known, and there was nothing more to be heard and no letter could be expected.

"Goodbye Jenny . . . goodbye."

Chapter Fifteen

There was to be a meeting at the Dance Hall on Friday night, and the hall took on an air of being not the same place that on Saturday night was rocking with lights and hot music and girls and boys spilling out the door into parked cars to take a nip before the next dance.

Penelope went with Mona and sat in the balcony, which was full of farm women looking down. Lowell and Beggs and Peterson stood at the door as the men came in, passing through a double file of men, so that no one would come in and have a vote who was not one of them. Each man who was unknown to any of them was stopped at the door and they would look at him and call people from the hall, saying "Do you know him? He says he was on Highway Twelve at the picketing last Spring. . . ."

"He says he was at Bunker Twenty."

"Well he wasn't. We ain't laid eyes on his face afore."

"Sorry, no one seems to know you," and he would be backed out and another would pass through the line of men all carved alike by the same labor, shoulders, backs, thighs all pulling downward in the same way. Many young men came in too, and their age and the number of years of their labor were marked on them as on a tree.

Then the hall was full and men standing shuffling along the sides, used to standing up in fields, on their own land, thinking of themselves as quite alone, now a little uneasy, but dogged, standing together in the barnlike hall, making a sea below Mona and Penelope. Penelope looked, heard, felt them surge below and the talk swing, not to her mind, understanding little, but the intent swinging upon her steady, like a man cutting a great swath with a hand sickle; like an army of men approaching rhythmically making a swath through what was before them, cutting down to the root quick. Mona sat looking, her full cheeks on her hands, her body stretched, waiting upon what men would do and ready to do it in bitterness herself, if they failed or fumbled, holding both hate and love, the flesh warm and the power quick, showing in her neck and forearms, in her knees spread wide apart under her skirt, in the coiled lithe back.

Words rose out of one throat then poured together, in a thundering, stamping that made Penelope cover her ears.... They spoke again and again, listening to each other, one rising, one breaking off a moment, stepping back again. Lowell spoke of produce witheld from market, of what had been done in the Spring, of what had to be done in the Summer. He spoke of what they already knew, simply adding it up, how they were burdened with taxes, liens, feed and seed loans. "You can't muddle along by yourselves any more," he said, "You join hands with the worker. You can't muddle along."

There were cries; there was silence; then speech again. A farmer got up in the back of the room, all heads turned. "We stand together," he said. "The first day we ran in the corn. Now it's tall to cover a man. . . ."

"Now boys . . ." they began to each other, with a slow courtesy. "Now boys, it's this way . . ." taking a swath, making something plainer. "Now boys . . ." taking a slow yankee cut into what they meant.

And Beggs crying: "But what are we going to do NOW, NOW . . ." and you saw his land was sliding out from under him, a thing he thought would never move but would hold his seed forever.

"Let's see how big a hog CAN grow," bitter laughter cackled. "I got eighteen hundred pounds now eating their heads off. The big men eat all they want, they don't pop. Let's see if the hogs will. . . ." Laughter again through them sparely. Then talk which made them look backward to see who was at the door, but not in fear, each one rising, speaking, sitting again.

Someone came up speaking to Mona. "The townspeople," the woman said, her cheeks flushed, "are millin' around outside, mad as hops. The sheriff says he's got a right to get in here, and the boys at the door won't let him, they say if he gets in he'll have to make it hisself."

Mona put her hand up pushing her hair back; "Sit down and listen," she said.

"We're the heart, we're the heart here in the Midwest."

"What about the governor calling out the militia?"

A silence fell around the question, rose, went around it and went on.

A vote of thanks was passed to the women for bringing the picketers their food.

The talk turned to a leader, and someone saying, "No salaries for farm lenders. Let 'em come out of us." Saying over again that they stood for "no eviction of any farmer."

"They're going to sell out Refen's farm in the next county," Davidson said, "what's to do?"

118

"The committee will handle that," Lowell said.

"Adjourn then."

The women were rising in the balcony, waking children.

The men now massed close together, rose, flowed out, parted slowly, moving now but bound to each other, waiting upon the next move.

The committee for that district, two young men and two older, slower men, came with them to the house, riding in Lowell's Ford.

Penelope made sandwiches, setting them before the men, and waiting to hear what would come of the plan, until she saw it stand up, ready to move when the day came that would force it.

Two days later men gathered at Penelope's and they heard what the committee had done, young Davidson telling about it, the others saying their say, Refen saying, his eyes shining, that his farm had been saved at the foreclosure sale. "There were five hundred farmers there," he said.

"There was a thousand," Davidson said, "the paper said five hundred."

Beggs said, "If the papers said five hundred they was a thousand."

"O.K., a thousand . . ."

They told about how they held the judge at the courthouse not letting him call for aid and his explaining to them that the law set forth his duty and it was clear to him that he was compelled to sign the mortgage decree, that he could not do otherwise, then telling them about some law that was in Kentucky after the Civil War.

"But I told him," Refen said, "What's goin to come of my farm right now!"

They all laughed, "Yes sir, we told 'em."

"We held the courthouse."

"Yes sir, why even the telephone operators was with us."

Looking with fresh eyes at each other, feeling a power beyond their own thigh and shoulder power, "We could rouse the countryside in fifteen minutes."

"We could, like Minute Men . . ."

Chapter Sixteen

The heat did not let up, but stood over the Town, slowly penetrating everything. The chickens drooped under the barn floors, the leaves hung heavy on the trees not stirring, a man could not plow his corn except late afternoons. Everything was sickening ripe, and whatever you touched, harness or machine-head, was burning. In Town a rocking chair contest kept up, and they were having a Revival.

The spinning hot earth was obscured by heat mist, the fields of corn stood wilted. The thresher had started on Begg's farm, and men looked at the sky, wishing it would hurry and get around to their fields.

Everything looked strange, isolated in the heat, in a meaning beyond their use, as if they reflected, before its coming, a disaster that would mark them all.

Penelope that day went out to Bac Kelly's because she had to find out if what stood above Bac's head as suspicion would show itself as true. She had wandered the Town, found Littlefield sleeping, and she remembered afterward that he seemed to have disaster on him already, as if he had been coming towards it for a long time, so she closed the door quietly and seemed to feel everything in his shack looking after her. She went on out the Kelly road. It was around four o'clock. Penelope passed Bill Nye and Red Davis, who had shotguns and said that since it was too hot for the birds to move, they thought they might kill some. She could hear them shooting down by the creek, the sound of the "ping" making a hollow steel hole in the unmoving air. It was four o'clock, but it was more like noon.

She came into the Kelly yard. The chickens sat under the house looking at her. She sat down on the porch in the shade, her body cooling, out of the sun.

Bac came around the corner of the house, stopped, seeing her, stood looking at her.

"Well," he said bitterly.

"Hello," she said, pushing back her wet hair. Suddenly, so she did not know how he covered the ground, he was upon her, the length of his body like rock against her, his lips upon hers.

She looked into the house. "Don't," she said, "someone will see

120

us. . . ." She looked at him, the sweat coming down his temple. He stood like some awful bright fire that she must take.

"Come on with me," he said, taking her hand and walking so they might have been holding hands but he had a grip on her so the muscles of his forearm showed. "Come on," he said, giving her jerks that threw her against him. They went down the road cutting off through the thicket that stood still, the sun coming hot through the leaves. Her eyes were open as upon fire. And when she had thought it was all over, the sight and grip of him again was something that did not ask a by your leave, more than a tide or a season. She could hear nothing but the sound of their feet and the soft far "ping" of the shots making a metal hole in the still air that was like a thickness you could touch.

Then a shot came from the bush, soft and penetrating. She felt each time that it penetrated softly through her flesh, a soft "ping, ping." The sky lay flat and hot, the earth still beneath and the soft "ping, ping" as if it entered her skin and echoed inside her. Her eyes closed, feeling the sun, the hot pressure all around, the terrible day, and the sweating face and the black hound hair of Bac, the soft "ping" in the thicket and the cry of birds taking off from their sleep into the air.

There was a sharp close shot, a rustle in the leaves and a bird dropped at their feet; Penelope looked down at it, the beak open, the wings parted, and saw its swift movement dim before her eyes and silence spin over it a new habit of memories uninhabited by wind or space, saw it dropping into a tiny void of its own death.

Bill Nye and Red Davis crashed through the thicket, hunting the bird.

"Better be careful," Bac said, "you could shoot a man with that gun."

"Oh, we're just shootin' birds," Bill Nye said, looking at them knowingly.

"Well, happy days," he said, bagging the bird.

"Better luck this time, Bac," Red guffawed.

"Tend your own business," Bac said, sullen. "Damn fool," he said, when the two boys were out of hearing.

Penelope looked at him in fright. "I can't do it," she said, "I can't do it, Bac. Let me go."

"What's the matter?"

"I don't know. I can't do anything. I don't know. I'm sick."

"I guess what they say is true," he said.

"What do they say," she asked. Oh Penelope, how beautiful you are . . . with flowers. Oh Penelope, going down the streets, so tall and swift!

"They say you're an idiot," Bac said, "that you haven't got sense to come out of the rain. They say . . ."

"Let me go. I can't do it. I gotta go," she said, wrenching her arm around in his hand . . . let me go to the bed of death, dark and wild.

"Not this time. I've bagged you this time and you don't get away like you done in the orchard . . . not this time."

She fought him silently, feeling his rocklike sides against her. Once he lifted her off the ground so she was upon him in horror, feeling him so ruthless, sharp stone beneath her, kicking his shins till he dropped her, then went for her again to cleave her to him. She didn't cry out, not wanting Bill Nye any more to see this than she wanted it to be; and fiercely she scratched and tore at him, yet weeping that his beauty could not burn her and his strength be a staff.

Then quite suddenly she seemed to be free. She had gouged his eye and he had stepped back blinded, pain running down his face. She took off, running very fleet back the way she had come, the sun pressing upon her, the day going in a terrible golden crash that turned the world dark before her eyes, even the blooming, piling clouds and the thundering heaviness of tree and field, running, crying: Turn my eyes another way, then . . . Death . . . Death . . .

She went to the cemetery and sat beside the stone for the pioneer dead, angels flying at the top of the tree of life, carved in stone, as if she had to wait there until a certain time.

Bac started for home, seeing Bill Nye and Red Davis going across the field. Just then a flock of blackbirds flew out, startled as he came through the stillness, and Bill Nye turned and began shooting. Bac ran out, waving his arms, and fell forward on his face without a sound.

Bill and Red started running toward him over the cow pasture, turned him over and saw he was dead, struck in the temple. In a panic, at first they thought of running, and then, knowing Penelope had seen them, they thought why not say she did it, so they left one of their guns beside Bac and caught a ride into Town, growing big as they went with what they concealed and what they told.

It was five-thirty, and the cyclone stood on the horizon five miles out of Town at about seven forty-five, according to Applebaum who ought to know since he had nothing to do that evening but look at his watch until that happened.

The boys came into town, saying to whomever they met that Penelope had killed Bac Kelly in the Kelly thicket and everyone started up as if the news meant joy to them, not caring for Bac Kelly living, but valuing him strangely when dead.

The news spread faster than the sixty mile wind of the cyclone that would later sweep them down. Sheriff Anderson was let loose by this happening and was out to the Kelly thicket in less time than it takes to tell it. He looked at the body, at the gun, and went back to look for Penelope.

Gee let them in the house, and looking through it, they did not find her, only her other pair of shoes under her bed and her Sunday dress in the chintz built-in closet of her room and the apples ripening outside the window.

Nina Shelley watched from her front porch. "Go to Mr. Littlefield's," she shrieked, "that's where you'll find her."

The men piled into their cars, the sheriff's car going first. They went out the road to Littlefield's, eyes watching from every open door. They went under the tree where the owls were, Sheriff Anderson standing on the running board.

Pfeiffer said, "It's muggy weather."

"It is that. Cyclone weather, I say."

Pfeiffer replied, "You could hear a pin drop; the air feels uncanny. You can taste it."

"They say they's more currents of air in the Middle West coming from all direction and sort of makes a whirlpool, like a cauldron, so to speak," said Anderson.

"Is that so? You better go over the bridge this side of the railroad trestle. I hope we find her."

Penelope sitting on the cemetery hill saw the cars crawling over the railroad bridge, but they were hidden from her as they stopped at Littlefield's. She did not see them emerge beside the road along Mumser's Orchard, and wondered where they could have gone, not thinking anyone would stop at Littlefield's.

The Sheriff knocked on Littlefield's door with the butt of his gun. Presently it opened slowly, Littlefield blinking, having been shut in his dark house. "Good evening, gentlemen," he said, bowing a little, his arm out.

Sheriff Anderson butted open the door, thrusting his leg through, pushing into the house. The other men, about seven, came into the house, filling the small room. The chess box fell off the shelf.

"Please don't step on my chess men, gentlemen," Littlefield said, "they were my father's."

"Listen, Littlefield," Sheriff Anderson said, "we want to know where Penelope is."

Littlefield looked at all the men, excited, seeing them standing in his house where not a man had stood since he built it ten years before.

"Why gentlemen," he said, rubbing his hands together, "won't you be seated? I'm afraid . . . no, not enough chairs, but then . . . we can talk this over better."

"Now listen, Littlefield, none of your gabbing, see? We're looking for this girl Penelope."

"Why yes," he said, looking idiotic at the men, his hands out as he shook like a leaf in that excitement, wanting to say to them what he had wanted all his life to say in the presence of men, "Why gentlemen," he said, "I wish you would sit down. I am glad you've come at last. I knew this town would come to me sooner or later. Better late than never," he said, smiling, spreading out his hands, the sweat starting from his forehead.

The sheriff grabbed his arm, "We want this here Penelope. She's wanted for murder."

Littlefield stood still, looking from one man to another. "For murdering who?" he said at last.

"Bac Kelly was found dead in the Kelly thicket and we're looking for her. And you know where she is, most likely . . ."

Tears of excitement and weakness came to his eyes, being suddenly within the presence of men. "She's not here," he said, his hands going out toward them. "If I could do anything for you," he said, "if I could be of any service now . . ."

"Well, you certainly could, Littlefield," the sheriff said, letting go his arm. "Here, have a cigar."

"Why thank you, sheriff. Thank you very much." He put the cigar in his mouth. Pfeiffer gave him a light. He looked at the men, smoking.

"Come now, professor! Where does she hang out? Where would she be?"

"Well, let me see," he said, "you might remember me, you know, for that post office job. I'm the most capable man you can get. . . . This Town never appreciated me."

"Certainly not, professor," Anderson said, winking at the men. "I'll certainly remember you," he thumped him on the back.

"Well, most likely at this time of the day she's most likely up the hill at the cemetery. She likes to go up there, I've heard," he said, laughing amongst the men as they went near and around him, out the door.

"Good day, gentlemen," he said, coming after them, the cigar in his hand.

"Good day, professor," they shouted. "Toodle do . . . ta ta."

The cars turned toward Mumser's Orchard.

"It's seven-forty," Sheriff Anderson said, standing on the side of the car. "Holy God!" he said then, seeing it stand above the horizon ahead, over the cornfield, back of the cemetery.

The men looked. The cars stopped.

Penelope saw the cars come around the orchard, then she saw them stop.

Applebaum had started to take a walk before he knew about Bac Kelly's death, and was just skirting back on the other side of the cemetery, not having seen Penelope more than three times in his life, and not seeing her now. He was starting back to Town thinking he would go to a picture show since he couldn't be with Alice until the next night anyway.

He turned as if catching the thought of the men a mile on the other side of the orchard, and saw the cyclone standing like a genie beyond the hill of the cemetery, on the level horizon.

A few seconds later the Town saw it, and had something to look at.

At the same time a rain of hail and wind came down black over the Town.

Penelope turned, started to run, and the people running together in the Town, a black tide running one way, turning back on itself, running another, and the lights wavered before the wind flaming black like women's hair, then snuffed out, as if the village had gone in the black wind.

When the Bear at midnight wheeled westward over against Orion, the Town lay broken, a swath like a scythe had cut down Main Street. The trees lay athwart the streets, windows were broken. It had mowed through the country, downed Mumser's corn, torn up the cemetery, sucked up Littlefield's house, cut a swath down Main Street from the Gem to Sweitzer's meatmarket; then it had risen, divided, and passed beyond their knowing.

Lowell and Mona had driven in from the other side of Town because of what happened to Bac Kelly. They got to the house soon after the others had gone. Lowell started after them, just to see the thing standing over on the horizon, and went back with Mona and Gee to the cellar.

The wind had passed, and through the darkness the Town felt itself to see who was dead and who was living. The farmers began to come in with the wounded, saying how the country was laid waste. The Town stood revealed in its own darkness. Pete Swillman's wife was brought in, a car from Kansas City having picked her up. She had been coming from her mother's house, having had supper there. She was dead, and the four months' child of Swillman that she carried was dead, too.

Miss Shelley volunteered as nurse when the hospital was full and the wounded were being brought to the library. Her eyes were bright and she kept saying, "Land sakes, it's a sight. You could have knocked me over with a feather when I seen it. It only goes to show. . . ." What it went to show she didn't say and didn't know.

Mona and Lowell looked at everyone that came, searching for Penelope. At one o'clock she hadn't been brought in yet. Wagon and car were searched and she was not seen dead or alive. Mona got wild, saying she would go out in the country and look herself. "She wanders around so," she said, "she might be anywheres . . . Penelope!" she cried, as if she had never seen her wildness, and it was blowing over now giving a bitter hunger.

Bill Nye came limping in; a tree had fallen on his foot. He still carried his bag of dead birds, having forgotten he had them. "I saw her around four, I recollect," he said, "I saw her then, going to Bac Kelly's."

Red Davis stood in the corner watching the dead and wounded come in, with frightened eyes, tearing his cap up in his hands.

Sheriff Anderson and his men had left their cars and laid flat in the road when they had seen the cyclone, and had escaped with only a soaking and the buttons torn from their coats. The wind had jumped clean over then, leapt from Mumser's corn and sucked up Littlefield's house beyond.

Eyes searched each other over bodies, to know what had been. It was talked of in whispers, the wonders and the horrors, hands leaned together, nodding and shaking:

"I smelled sulfur and there she stood . . ."

"Where is my wife?"

"Came and was gone before you could say Jack Robinson."

"It was a sight!"

Bac Kelly lay in the morgue, having found his place first.

Littlefield was brought in. They found him lying half way into Town, dead, without a mark on him. Mrs. Littlefield came to the morgue that very night, a strange lust prompting her, and saw him lying like a foreigner, his face severe, as if it had been carved back to its youth when she knew him first.

"Where is Penelope?" the question began to move amongst them.

"She always was a queer one . . ."

"She was . . ."

"Where is she now?"

"Blessed if I know . . ."

"Who's seen her?"

"Nobody's seen her since four o'clock unless it'd be Bac, and he's dead."

And they looked at each other trying to know who had killed him in the thicket, opinion going for and against her, not now liking to believe ill, seeing her lost, feeling that for a moment they all ran together, calling each other, feeling the flesh a boon and not a barb; and there was a curious love in them for the violence, for the disaster as if it brought them close where love could not, and was a good thing lacking a better, so that when Red Davis got hysterical and, tearing his cap in his hands, walked up between the rows of bandaged victims, saying, saying, "It was an accident. That's what it was. He run right out of the thicket, right into our shot. It was an accident, I tell you . . ." they accepted that, too, looking, repeating what he had said, accepting it along with the other, patching it all together with what they knew of that day's happenings and what went on all the days from the beginning of their lives.

At one-ten a wagon drew up by thelibrary and there was a murmur traveling rapidly, "There she is!" "That's her, all right!"

Mona ran to see and there was Applebaum, with his head tied up, sitting in the back of a wagon with Penelope on the floor, he holding her head against the wagon's movement.

Applebaum's teeth were chattering, he was soaked and the blood trickled from his head. "That big stone fell on her legs. . . . That big stone with the angels on the top fell across her, right across her, and I couldn't get it off . . ." he said, his fat hands helping them to lift her.

"Penelope!" Mona cried, and she was not answered.

Chapter Seventeen

Three days later Penelope opened her eyes, saw the apples outside the window hanging red and heavy. Awakening, she looked a long time at the apples now on the bough ... *Spring and dawn ... night and death.*

She heard someone breathing near her and slowly, turning her eyes, without moving her head or her body, she saw a woman sleeping in a chair, her head fallen over the ample breast, the black hair hiding the face, the knees fallen open in sleep.

Mother! Mother.

The women loomed in a sleep that stood on her like time, immobile, carving her great body in silence and peace.

Up from below, through what must be an open door, there came a murmur of voices, steady, tidal, rising in volume receding down the stillness, rising again.

"It strikes. It strikes. They's no gettin' away from it . . ."

"No matter where you go . . ."

"No matter where you go. . . ."

"It levels a man down all right . . . puts him in his place . . ."

"Don't know no difference in men at a time like that. . . ."

"No sir!"

Saying in an excitement that would not abate:

"Hail the size of a crabapple!" Saying:

"Yes, sir, that size, with prickers on them like a gooseberry and that's a fact. . . ."

Voices lifting under her, rocking, flowing together, saying:

"My wheat looked like it had been sered, as if there'd been a heavy frost in late October and that's a fact. . . ."

"Blamedest durn thing I ever see . . . the leaves were turned on the top. . . ."

"Yes sir, and the trees and the grass the same . . ."

"The trees on my place looked as if they have been struck by lightning. They had a dead look exactly as if they had been struck, split clean open, clean as a whistle . . . you could see the fibers right through, split down and the bark stripped off as if a hand had done it . . . blamedest thing . . ."

"Vegetables in my garden looked burned, yes sir, just plain burned."

"You knew I went out yesterday and I could trace the way it went just by the color of the leaves burnt brown, see the track right past the cemetery down cutting Mumser's corn clean down there past the brewery. . . ."

"They was a flash of lightning when it was a happening, that took my eyesight nigh unto three minutes."

"I saw that, too. Man, there was a lightning stood in our garden striking right down perpendicular like, striking right down as if it was going to cut the earth right off and it scared me so I darsen't stop. . . ."

"No sir. What I see was a flash from the south. I got into the woodshed and I thought it would fly off and that's a fact. I sat there a little and there came such a flash of lightning I never saw in my life, never. And when the flash came the woodshed was gone, just like that . . . quick as that . . . I fell down someway and it took my hat right off with it. . . . Yes sir, you can laugh but I looked up and the woodshed was gone, gone right away like the hand of the Lord. . . ."

Penelope's eyes moved, her body not moving.

"There was a cloud on either side and this one appeared to be coming in the center of the storm. These other ones on either side came together and they appeared to make a whirling motion right there as it rolled nearer, standing up right up before me just a mite above the earth, that was . . . I supposed then from the way the lightning was flashing that it was something. . . . It must be a cyclone, I says to myself. As it drew nearer I saw in the center of this cloud a fiery luminous light, I supposed it was a fire something like a headlight on a locomotive and from that flashes of lightning and some flashes stood up half a minute, I'll swear . . ."

"On the book . . ."

"Yes, on the book . . . I was standing on the earth and it came near me and the light was more bright. I could see plainer, and I could see the light in the center. It rushed by, and the house was gone in an instant. Yes sir, just like a wave of my hand and the house was gone. Dead gone. I saw the storm when it struck the Town. I could see it. I said then to myself, it looks like it's goin' right down Main Street. It's lucky it's when everybody's gone home, I says . . . that's what I said as God is my witness. I saw the light from behind then, and flashes of light continual . . . and a roar of thunder that didn't stop . . ."

"I noticed just afore it came up to my house a ball of fire came right down and tore up some ground close to me."

"I saw it too, it was like a rolling cloud of smoke about one third of a mile high."

"Yes sir, I saw it too. Fire and smoke and smell of sulfur . . ."

"I saw fire, too . . ."

"Before God, I saw fire standing in the storm . . ."

"That ain't no lie . . ."

"That's a fact sure enough, that was about seven-forty."

"Seven-forty if it was a minute. I says to my old woman . . ."

"I saw the fire and was burned on the side of my neck . . ."

"The smell of sulfur too was powerful. I smelt it first and then it kind of went away like a battle. . . ."

"That's true, I smelled it too. . . ."

"One side of my hair was all singed off. . . ."

Voices fused together, talking, of what they had seen and would see, of a tide they knew now carried them and did not separate them doing battle against each other.

She turned her eyes, her body lying lost and unknown to her consciousness below her as if it had been caught in a bad season, and would not know, now . . .

Her eyes moved slowly. She could not see the door, but knowing a door stood open, hearing the voices rolling up so she rode them like a tide: *In Iowa, Dakota and Tennessee, in Kentucky, in Illinois, in Mississippi, in Georgia . . . I hear men talking.*

"I saw a fire. . . ."

"Before God I saw a fire standing in the storm . . ."

"I saw a fire and it was bright and it was all around. . . ."

The Bird

He stood impatiently on the deck of the Salvor waiting for her to put out to sea. On one side of him rose the city, swarming in the noon heat, on the other rocked the sea, fantastic and real.

The Salvor was an old boat that used, in far years, to ply between San Francisco and Alaska, but now it went rather desultorily between Los Angeles and San Francisco carrying assorted cargoes of rice and soap, and an ill-assorted one of human beings. Sometimes it took only two days to make the voyage, and sometimes as much as four. But no one on her was ever in much of a hurry.

The boy, standing impatiently on the deck watching her being loaded, thought they would never pull away from the sight of the land whose odor he could endure no longer. He had to get off the swarming earth, away from that threshing floor on which nothing was threshed. The whistles blew a long blast announcing noon and from the buildings along the wharf came tiny figures, a black swarm, and a faint hum came from them. The boy turned away, his nose quivering in pain and disgust.

When someone spoke to him he cleared his throat, blushed and spoke in a stilted way and then he would walk away feeling miserable, as if he had failed. He wanted to meet a brother or a priest. "I am Floyd Young," he wanted to say, announcing himself, but when he was spoken to he broke out in a cold sweat.

He kept hearing something going on inside himself that he did not hear in the outside world, something he could not locate or connect, a whispering, like voices talking in the night in the next room, audible but meaningless. So he heard the clear enunciation in the outside world, real and yet wraithlike.

He went down the deck, past the saloon window. His tall frame stooped a little, his large hands hung useless from him as if they did not know what in the world to touch. His face was delicate and somber and when he was listening and looking he had a sullen look, heavy and baffled, his childish eyes pouted, and his eyes were wild and hurt.

He stood on the deck looking and looking. The harbor was full of little boats, topping the waves, darting up, pennants flying, decks shining, striking in the dazzle of sunlight. On the decks of

131

the Salvor men were lifting lumber into the hold; the crane creaked as the lumber swung in the air, was lowered. It was a man's world, acrid, tangy. He tasted the life, heavy, nauseating, strong. He saw the little hard upright male bodies, the soft loins, compact breasts. What did it take to make a man compact and sure moving, what welding in tangy man heat? A tattooed man, wiry and obscene, directed the loading. He stood like a monkey dodging the crates, swearing, cracking jokes with the stevedores. Some laborers came and sat on the wharf, watching, opening their pails of lunch, shouting to the men, laughing. Their quick male persiflage was below Floyd as he stood looking from the upper deck, listening, leaning over, watching the body of the tattooed man, moving swiftly in a visible pattern, a known destiny. He knew his own body with its sweats, its sudden disproportion like a pain. When would it be that he would be swift, all of a piece, when would his chest house the world, and his loins be swift with knowing?

The single compact body seemed made for lifting. He had a pockmarked wizened face and he spat clear over the side of the boat into the water. The Salvor rocked gently lifting on the great floor of the thick sea. The men shouted, laughed. The boy listened as if they had been talking another language.

"Used to come up here to see my girl, must have been thirty years ago."

"I riveted that bridge myself, longest span of bridge in the world by God."

"The Doctor said I'd die...." "Die?" "But I'm still living by God."

"It's carrots, that's what I say."

"Carrots hell. Lima beans."

"It's women."

"And I said to her, what about a little game tonight? O.K. You're on."

He could make nothing of it. The boat rocked under him in the thick port swell. The gulls wheeled in a cloud crying, and the sea flashed like a signal. He wished they might be gone away from the earth.

He looked and looked at the pockmarked man standing with wide stance in the flashing sun, the water reflecting, flashing up on him in a ripple of light over him. In a city you never actually **see** a man stoop or walk or sing or talk. There he is always part of a swarm. You never really hear a sound or see a sight. It is always removed, taking place far away, nightmarishly, so it does not strike straight on the senses and resound to the darkest fiber. He watched the single man lifted up on the bales, cursing, shouting, and laughing. What did the man know that made his body beautiful and swift, and his face black, knotted in obscure pain and evil?

132

The laborers on the wharf laughed, called back. Their voices, their banter struck straight upon him; the bodies of the unknown men gave him confidence he was in the world, that it would in time reveal its secrets. He leaned over and the boat rocked and lifted under him.

He thought he would have to be released from the outside. He could not do it for himself. His own world was fanstatic. Some violence would have to pierce him. He wanted to run against it, to have it done. But he did not know how it could be done. A cocoon must have a body to cling to while it slowly cracks open at the back and crawls out of the dead corpse of its life, and then it must hang in a benevolent world while the juices of the new creation pour down and it takes off at last in a new element.

There seemed nothing for him to hold to, no leverage that he might use to break out of himself. He thought he might stay forever in this awful state of half-death with his hands sweating from fear of exposure. Suppose he should never be born in the world but remain in that awful pupa stage in the mechanical world, shut up forever in that green state. Such a thought made the sweat stand out on his forehead. He felt grotesque and ill.

There were sailboats in the water and fishing smacks with bright sails; and men looking from the decks of foreign ships, straight at the boy. Their many unknown eyes gave him a fright, looking and passing from a strange world. He could feel his heart pound against his chest but he lifted his hand in salute at a passing ship, and some sailors lounging on the deck halloed and lifted their hands as if he were known to them.

A fisherman with a pipe in his mouth came close to the hull and looked up at him with ancient eyes peering, looking straight and nodding as if affirming something, lifting his pipe in salute. Floyd's hand moved. He could lift it in salute with ease. There was a cold thing in his brain, a weight of fear and guilt whose source he could not know.

The gulls flashed in the sun, wheeling to show their sudden white breasts, soaring, dipping in the water. Small overalled figures moved amid the yellow piles of lumber. Sailors lounged, loose, slim. The docks swarmed. The passing boats wailed, hooted. The wharves even in the sunlight had the odor of night and crime. A woman came down the deck swinging her tight hips. In a panic Floyd pressed himself against the rail, trying to be invisible. He looked out to the open sea until he went easy again in himself.

Out as far as he could see toward the horizon the light speared into the sea, struck and struck back towards the sky, white, dazzling, a sea of moving light flashing from the sky, striking up from the water.

The images of his life in the city were barren to him, the hot swarming streets, the endless walking and hunting, the welter of raw houses, people walking past him dimly near in the dusk, their voices muffled, the looking in windows, asking for jobs, sleeping in hall bedrooms like a corpse on a slab, eating food that only made him thinner, breathing air that made him tired, in the ennui and terror of sheer nothingness, the taste of ash in the mouth, and the fear of being dead, too, in the dead city. And he suffered bitterly, wanting to lift the weight and substance of a visible and embodied world.

He watched the contours of the men's bodies, the bend of a single man, the lift of lumber in the air, the scent of the cargo, the weight and immediate pressure of sight.

Then amid a commotion the boat lifted, a fear shot through his belly, and the boat broke away from the land. A fear like a sword went through him as he felt the bodiless lift of water beneath and the boat took off like a bird over another element. Where was he going? When he saw land again something would have happened. A dark weightless fear struck like bells in him as they left the womanearth, her fecundity, dusts, heats, swarming. He was struck in his body with fear, waves of it going up his loins as if he were being struck and struck with some thong. He held to the rail, dizzy with the bodiless light below, above, and the swiftly moving land. He could hardly stand up. His blood lifted and fell with the slightly moving ship, his hands were icy.

He made himself walk along the shifting, falling boat to the other side where the fresh air from the open sea struck him straight on the face and along the front of his body, so strong a wind like a body so he could almost lean against it. They seemed to be coming upon the sea as upon some element. He felt exultant as if something at last was about to happen. He pressed close to the bow, feeling himself borne swiftly over a dangerous element. Perhaps one came upon life as they were now coming upon the sea; and then looking, it seemed that they not only bore down upon the sea but that the sea rushed in upon them, so they met at the moment of their moving, and the ship rode upon the sea and the sea rushed under their mutual movement, upholding.

The Salvor crashed through, between the fast-rushing water and the swift-plunging clouds so that it seemed everything was in movement, clashing, moving, passing on. The birds wheeled and cried, casting swift light and shadow upon the deck. The light itself was like a crashing, a flying, passing in swiftness over the visible bodies.

He stood all afternoon watching the horizon. He could not go away from the prow. He had the feeling of people stirring behind him, of voices, of human speech, even of people stopping to peer at him.

He stood looking ahead at the crash of light and the wide running sea, and the ship plunging further out. He thought that life came upon the virgin self as they were coming upon the sea. There was something to be risked. His virgin self must break open and be known and in turn know. It must come to pass. Once he looked behind and saw gimlet eyes looking at him. He knew there were men on the ship with him and women. He looked uneasily behind him. He heard their movements, their speech, knew them to be on the ship with him.

The light from the sky and water at last began to diminish. The water ceased to flash and run, slackened, the long waves darkened as they turned around the bow. The horizon began to deepen. The sun went down naked and round and then the dusk fell swiftly like something falling from the sky, and met darkness rising noiselessly from the water. The sky came closer down and the dusk closed in like grief.

The ship plowed on between night and day in the rich plumy dusk. Then he heard something coming from the ship. At first he did not know what it was. Then he knew it was someone singing in the hold. It came up like the first male voice in the world, clear, lovely, startling. He knew it came from the breast, thorax, throat of a man. He felt as if he had never known a man before. The voice rose clear as if resounding in the body of water and sky, a single clear singing, stinging clear, with a lonely drifting note. It came so simply out of the body of the unseen man in the hold of the ship, as if the fiber of his male body being struck resounded of its own substance into music, a lone voice sounding in the face of the vast sea.

It struck deep in him. His hands were warm. He looked at them on the rail. They seemed near him. He raised them near his face. He put one hand on the other, feeling his own human warmth. He held his own hands together. The man kept singing, the pure single singing coming from the hold . . .

Or where was it coming from? From the bottom of the ocean, from the sky, from the substance of the visible world? The water turned gently against the moving ship and from somewhere came this singing of a single man. Perhaps it came from his own male breast. He gripped his hands hard, feeling their warmth. He felt as if the singing came from his own body. He was set virbating delicately, almost painfully. He felt everything, the air upon him, the singing plunging through him, the night like a plum against his body. He felt it on his tongue, he tasted it.

The singing ceased. He saw the ship was lighted. Two girls were looking at him. He saw men standing at the rail. He heard talking again. There were gimlet eyes peering into him, and the sound of human scurryings along the deck. . . . "Have you got a light, kid?" "Sure as shootin'." "What's he standing there so long for?" "Is he . . . ?" "Let's speak to him, what say?" "Aw, leave him alone." "He's just a kid." "Well . . ." "God am I hungry."

He could not get by them. He wanted to find his cabin but he could not get by. "What's your hurry?" "Say it's getting cold." "When is that lousy dinner goin' to be ready?" "Shut your trap honey, don't you always eat?" "I'll say so, in this world." "Could I get by please? Excuse me, I'm sorry." "O.K." "Ha ha ha"

He tried not to run down the deck away from them.

2

The night came swiftly and the wind blew cold. The passengers went into the hot saloon. Floyd kept walking around and around the boat, past the doors of the saloon, looking in from each side. A light swung from the center of the room so he saw the painted faces of the girls and their shining legs. He stood on tiptoe looking in the small window. It was closed so he could not hear what was being said.

He saw two girls who kept laughing and laughing. They sat close below the window, he looked half down on them, and saw their faces when they threw back their heads, as if they were lying down. One was fat with her round cheeks painted, the other was thin with thick cropped hair that hung on her pipestem neck. She Might have been a Mexican. Her neck looked dirty, a different color from her face which was powdered over. He looked down, seeing her thin shoulders.

A man was standing under the swinging light, talking. He was thin and gaunt, with a mouth that went in an O. The light kept swinging over him, and his hand stuck out stiff, gesticulating as if he were wound up. Saliva ran out of his mouth on his chin. The girls kept laughing at him.

The room under the swinging light was unstable, in a breathing motion, the light kept distorting the faces of the perpetually laughing people and threw their shadows huge behind them. The room seemed full of people all laughing at the lanky man who kept his arm out stiff. Floyd looked at them a long time, the light swinging over them so they looked as if they were under water, changing under the flux of light.

He left the window and ran around on the other side and looked in the window opposite. From there he looked directly on the crossed legs of the girls as they sat on a plush seat that ran in a half moon around one end of the saloon. The dark girl who might have been a Mexican leaned forward, her chin on her hand, looking at the old man who was talking. Once her ox eyes lifted to the window and he had to duck. There was hardly any expression on her face, only a monkish curiosity, but when it was expressionless it had a certain beauty, like an old mask that has been dug up out of the ground, and a touch of dissoluteness. The other was fat with little eyes. She was colored brightly and kept laughing. He stood in the darkness with the wind at his back looking at the faces of the two girls. The fat girl laughed and laughed. He could hear the faint ring of it where he stood as if someone had dropped a spurious coin. The dark girl laughed quickly, her face breaking in a flame of evil, and one of her teeth was gone or black. A flush went over him when he saw her face suddenly break up in that evil laugh and the black tooth flashing and the cords standing out on her thin neck. He waited to see her laugh again but she leaned back as if tired and watched with that shriven monkish look on her dark face.

An upright piano stood at one end and a thin man sat leaning against the keys. His clothes fit him too neatly. His face looked as if nothing had ever made a mark on it. He kept lifting his hands up to take the cigarette out of his mouth. Nothing in the room meant anything to him. Then he let his hands hang down between his legs. Behind him half sleeping against the piano was a frowsy woman. She looked as if she were drunk. In the other corner half-dozed a large man whose head converged upward from puffy cheeks to a small black cropped head. The man kept talking, his mouth in a loose O, and the girls kept laughing, embracing each other, throwing back their heads.

Floyd stood looking. He must go in. He must find out what they were. In fright he opened the door and moved towards them. The room seemed to shake, curdling and flowing upon him. They all stopped and looked at him, the man with his stiff arm out, his mouth open, the girls in the midst of laughing, the man at the piano with his cigarette in his hand. He thought he could never get to the plush seat and sit down. He got into a corner. He crossed his legs, then uncrossed them and put his shoes far under him. He watched the faces of the girls to see if they were laughing. But they looked solemnly at him, the fat girl squinting her eyes, the other one with her monkish curiosity. They wondered why he had stood so long on the boat that afternoon, so still, without moving.

The tall man held out his stiff arm moving towards him. "Hello young feller" he said like a professional talker, "It was you standing there all afternoon, meditating as it were." He turned his eye over in a wink. The fat girl giggled. Floyd tried to laugh. "Oh, that

137

was nothing." The tall man collapsed beside him and put a long, bony hand on his shoulder. "My name's Fletcher," he said. "We want you to be one of us." Making his voice go into a deep intonation as if he were reading Scripture.

The man sitting on the piano stool ground his cigarette out with his heel. "Now, pastor," he said, sneering, and the fat girl rolled back laughing, her legs flashing up, her garters showing. The dark girl laughed suddenly. Floyd saw the black place where a tooth was gone.

"Well, Hackman, I was pastor for many years and the youth are dear to my heart," Fletcher said, and the fat man sat up, leaned forward and started to laugh soundlessly, his belly shaking.

Hackman got off the piano stool. "Oh, for God's sake," he said, and picked up a magazine from a chair and sat down, looking nervously through the pages.

The fat girl was looking into a mirror, powdering her nose. The dark girl sat looking at Floyd, her sharp chin in her hand. Her eyes were wide open and her face flickered slightly at him. "What's your name?" she asked. "Uh huh, look out," said the man from behind the magazine, his eye peering over lewdly. "Shut up," the girl said without looking at him. "You fathead," said the girl, powdering her nose.

"My name's Floyd Young," said the boy stiltedly, flushing.

Fletcher leaned over talking into his face, his loose mouth falling around the words. Floyd pressed back away from him. The thin girl sat leaning forward, never moving her ox eyes from Floyd's face. Fletcher kept talking, leaning over, peering, as if from a great distance at the boy. He was telling how he came up this route years before, to go to the Klondike. He made great stiff gestures, he made everything seem grand as if in memory things had a special life.

The sleeping woman by the piano seemed to waken. She got up and started out for someplace, swaying with the boat. She fell against Hackman and he looked at her and went back to his ·magazine, flipping the pages over. She swayed and fell against the girls. "Look out, Fannie," the fat girl screamed, pushing her away with all her might. The ship lunged and the woman careened straight across the room, down the floor. Floyd saw her as if from above as the ship listed and she came down the room, reaching upward, grasping nothing. She fell against him and lay there making no effort to move, lost a moment. She smelled of moon and stale sweat and lay like a dead weight. One of her hands lay against his knee and he saw it was shriveled. He shrank against the wall at his back, his hands pressing behind him. Everyone was laughing and he could not move. "Where am I? Where am I?" she kept saying, looking around, and they all screamed with laughter seeing her. She kept turning her ruined face towards him with her blind white eyes, and saying "Where am I? Where am I?" He was looking close into her awful face that was like a mask of life horror. Her old hat hung over, her little eyes white and blind looked at him. What had she seen to make her face go in that life horror? She had looked on worse things than soldiers knew, she had suffered worse things. He wanted to cry out in one long scream, "What is it? What has she seen?" She kept mumbling in his face with her rancid breath, "Where am I?"

At last the two girls got her between them and all three struggled away on the upward slant of the floor, lurching with the boat, the light swung back and forth over them. The man Fletcher kept talking. Someone said, "When will that ———— dinner be ready?" "Always late on this boat." "I'll say...." The fat man slept and woke and looked at his watch. Hackman looked into the magazine, flipping the pages. Fletcher kept leaning over, talking with that mesmerized smile of a man who is always remembering. The light swung making the shadows swing and rise from the human forms until they looked bigger than the bodies and swung from them like some exudation, filling the room swinging, fastened to the figures but swinging like some huge evil into the upper air.

Floyd sat pressed back away from the foul breath of the old man who leaned over as if he could not see clearly from the past in which he perpetually lived. He leaned far back looking into the room that swung under the pendulum light. The three women sat passive on the seat, huddled together. The light swung over them so that they seemed curled in shadow at one moment, the light passive over them, bedding them in like angels, and again a great shadow grew from them rising, mounting upward awfully like the substance of all their darkness.

The thin girl's face was lighted in an antique beauty and then the shadow falling made her face evil and dissolute, as if beauty had fallen to swift decay in her. Under the light all their faces swung from momentary beauty to momentary evil. Fannie had fallen on the plush bench and sprawled sleeping, and the mounds of her body had sometimes a fleeting remembrance of some past grace. It was as if they existed in a changing element, something outside their own power, that made them prey to good and evil. The mixture of corruption and purity so visible made him a little sick. He saw the changing world, the malleability of all form, and he was frightened. He saw some quality in the world that would mix and change his own purity as it had in these people sitting quiescent waiting for their dinner. He was frightened. He thought he could go no further.

The door opened, the lamp dimmed and flared as the door closed again. The Captain came in, eating an apple. He held the apple in a hand that had nails like a hawk's. He clutched the red flushed apple and carried it to his mouth biting into it with his huge yellow teeth. His face like a walrus' was overhung with brows, mustache and beard; and he was gray except for his red-veined cheeks and his nose. He walked with that enchanted assurance of a man who is always drunk.

He now stood stock still looking at his passengers. They all looked at him. The fat man leaned forward rubbing his knees. "Well Cap, when do you think the eats will be ready?" The Captain grunted, "Soon enough for you." He looked at the apple as if he preferred it to the man. But he saw everyone in the room, especially the dark girl who got up and came to him, swinging her thin shanks. "Hello," she said, brushing up to him, her black tooth showing in a grin. "Hello," he said, stopping and looking down on her, fixing himself on her. He had a boil on his neck so he had to turn his head down stiffly. "You're a nice one," she said, and he grunted. "I hope we're not going to have hamburger all this trip," she said, "like we had before." "What's the matter with hamburger?" he grunted, looking down at her. She came just to his chin. He began to stroke her shoulder. She wriggled upwards towards him. "You're a pretty good buzzard," she said, "even if you have got a boil on your neck." She writhed her body up from the hips.

Hackman had put his magazine down and was watching. The Captain gave her a shove, laughing in his beard. She grinned, showing her black tooth, and pushed him. He reached out and gripped her shoulder and she screamed, half laughing, wriggling under his hand, her evil face turned up full in the light. He shook her and she laughed and he laughed silently. Hackman grinned. The fat man half closed his eyes. Fletcher was breathing heavily. Their faces all had the same leer. Floyd looked from one to the other, then back at the girl. Her face had that fascinating expression he had first noticed, that flash of evil burning up her wizened flesh. They all watched her as if with one expression, one face. Floyd looked nervously at that one multiple face in the room. And then back at the girl. They were all as if mesmerized, looking at the girl as she seemed to hang limp from the hawk hands of the Captain as he shook her back and forth, and her body shaking as she laughed, her teeth bared, and the Captain laughed noiselessly. He let her go suddenly and she stood sullen in the room pulling her close sweater tightly over her thin lascivious body. She stood biting her nails looking up out of her monkish face. The Captain paid no more attention to her. He stood by the piano biting his apple.

"See how the fight came out?" Hackman said, getting up and lighting a cigarette with his shaking fingers. "What's the matter with your neck, Cap? All the meanness coming out, eh?"

"Oh, I don't know," the Captain said deliberately.

Hackman, nervous and crafty, wanted to get at the other man. "I don't know," he said, sneering and wriggling. He wanted to pry into the other man, eat through him in some way, corrupt the power he had. "I guess you couldn't get another ship, eh Cap? They leave you on this old boat. I guess this is about done for, eh?"

The Captain flushed. He stood chewing his apple.

Hackman came up then like a bantam. "You wouldn't have no chance now for another boat. This here's a great age. It's a great age. They ain't no place in it for birds like you. It's the smart guy that gets it now, the smart guy." He seemed to be prancing, he blew the smoke straight out of his mouth into the Captain's face. He was half mad with his lust to wound the other man. Why do you allow that jane on this boat? This is the second time I seen her. Is she your mother, or somethin'?" He pointed at Fannie. She slept on the bench, her shrunken arm folded over like a bird's claw, as if she had shriveled it in some ancient fire and had become half witch, half evil bird. "Look at her. Ain't she pretty now, I ask you."

"Aw, leave her alone," the fat girl said. "Say, when do we eat?"

"I'll say, when do we eat."

The Captain stood a moment looking at all of them, looking from his massive bulk at the little nervous man. Then he walked straight away from all of them, and opened the door. The lamp dimmed and flared.

Fletcher got up. "You're sort of tough on the old boy, ain't you now?" he said vaguely, standing up then sitting down again.

"All right, Hackman. Good for you," said the fat man. "I guess you give it to him then all right, all right."

Hackman grinned. "I guess I give it to him now, didn't I, say?" "Well, I'll say you did." "I'll say." "I'll say you did." "Sure, you put him in his place." "Pretty good for you oldtimer." "Where's dinner?" "I'm empty, I am." Fletcher said, "But I remember him when this boat was new and used to go from San Francisco to Alaska, a fine boat she was then, too, only the best rode on her." "Who cares about that, anyway. Sit down, you old buzzard." "Say, didn't I give it to him though?" "Put him in his place, all right." "Old men ought to be chloroformed, eh Fletcher?" "Shut up." Hackman winked his little dry eye.

The light swung over them so they seemed as if under changing water flowing over them. Fletcher got up to make a speech. A Negro stuck his head in. "Dinner," he said. "Dinner!"

141

There was the sound of eating. A fly buzzed over the table. The meal was good. The first day out it was always good. Bowls of hot soup, pork chops, potatoes, gravy, peas and rice pudding. They all tried to grab the best chop.

Floyd sat next to the Captain and he could see the strong taloned hands with the big nails moving on the table. On the other side sat Fletcher. He ate as if he munched a memory and not real food. Floyd smiled and smiled. He could hardly say anything. He could hardly eat. The light seemed enormously bright, the sounds gargantuan. A player piano stood at the door. Someone got up now and then and put in a nickel. He was unable to cope with anything he saw.

Fletcher kept chewing the cud of his life as if all food were a memory. He smelled like a sick man. Hackman sat across the table. "When I can't eat I want to die," he said. The dark girl laughed. The fat girl laughed, putting her handkerchief over her mouth. The drunken woman laughed after they had all stopped. "Boy, you'll never die, the way you eat." "I'll never die of consumption unless it's consumption of food. . . . "Ha ha" "Edith, you're choking." "Pound her on the back." "Hey, what's the idea, knocking me out like that."

A man with a clown's head hovered over the Captain. He had a shaggy head like a wig, on a quick seaman's body. His brows were thick. He kept bowing between Floyd and the Captain, his heavy bulbous nose coming between them as he bent over. Because of the boil on the Captain's neck he couldn't turn his head, so the comic man had to bow between them. "Yes, sir. Yes, sir." "A plate, a plate." "Here you are, sir." The Captain chewed up his food, then spat it out on the plate.

Fletcher smacked his loose lips and chewed looking up at the ceiling. "Yes, sir," he said, "That was the administration of McKinley. I used to make speeches. If I do say it, people used to say I had the tongue of Jefferson." He gazed about anxiously. No one was listening. Floyd smiled, he kept smiling. "My wife was a wonderful woman. So was my mother. I'm a worm, a worm; always been a worm." His little eyes watered. He stopped chewing. He seemed rotted with loneliness.

Floyd could see through a window into the kitchen. A Negro peered back into the dining room. He moved without legs, only the upper half of him showing. He held a knife in his hand. The women were laughing. The piano kept playing. Hackman got up and put in a quarter so it would play five pieces without stopping. "Getting generous in your old age." "You don't know me, baby." "With that mug?"

Fannie got up reaching for the pepper. They pushed her down. "Sit down, sit down." "What the . . ." Say, where does she get it?" "Leave me alone, leave me alone," she cried. "She wants the salt, that's all." "Please pass the chops dearieee." They passed her the empty platter, winking, laughing. She saw the empty platter and began to cry. They leaned on each other, laughing. Fannie sat without covering her face holding the empty meat platter that was mottled with blood and juice. Floyd tried to laugh.

"Hey, big boy down there . . . I mean you . . ." "Me? Me?" "Sure I mean you. Who else? Why don't you come down here and sit?" "I'm all right."

The Captain kept spitting his food, chewing up the meat and spitting it out.

Floyd could hardly see along the table, then suddenly he would see everything, a hand, a face, hair, nose, torso, a plate passing along. He would go into a trance, seeing.

"Say, Captain." Fletcher leaned across. Floyd reared back from the odor of loneliness. The Captain leaned over, poising his knife. "Say, what's the dark one's name?"

The Captain just leaned his ear over without looking into the long face of Fletcher. He looked at the table cloth. "Her name's Mamie," she said.

"Mamie, Mamie." Fletcher smacked his loose lips.

"Mamie" flashed in Floyd's mind. "Mamie."

Hackman was passing cigars. Fletcher smoked, turning the cigar around in his mouth. The Captain put it in his pocket and took out an apple. Floyd took his but didn't light it. "Light it." "Hey, aren't you going to smoke?" Hackman leaned across the table grinning at him. "Sure, sure I am. A match." "Here." "O.K." They all watched him. His hand shook. "Don't get sick." "Leave the kid alone." "He's mine already." "Yours . . . say." "You're going with me, ain't you, kid?" Hackman said, "Oh I guess so. Sure." "Sure." "Sure, he knows a good thing when he sees it. He ain't passing up nothing." "Oh, you would be something to pass up." "Shut up."

Floyd looked at them all, wanting to touch a friend, an evil, a good. To touch something and be touched.

"I'll be good to you, honey," Mamie smiled. Fletcher patted him on the shoulder. "Her name's Mamie." "Mamie, that's the label." "Here, Mamie." "Mamie, Mamie, Mamie."

The plates were greasy and empty. The fat man kept belching. Fletcher leaned forward, flourishing the cigar now. "Watch out," Hackman said, "Old Pop Fletcher's rumbling. He's going to talk." "Oh for God's sake."

"Well, son, when you've lived as long as I have . . ."

"Old men should be chloroformed at forty."

"The age of wisdom, my boy."

"Oh hell. Oh hell, what do you know."

"You should read the Bible."

"Oh, for God's sake . . ."

"Pick on somebody your age," Mamie said.

"All right, Floyd."

"Oh, he's in diapers yet." The fat girl shrieked. "That's right, honey."

"Honey . . . honey." The word kept going in him. He saw his own frightened face ahead of him. Where was it? He was startled. He kept looking, seeing himself. It was in a sideboard mirror ahead of him. His frightened close face like a green husk, unformed. He could not even keep an expression on it. It was distorted in the mirror, but he saw it for his own. What risk had these taken he had not? What is there that I can touch? Where is the friend? Where is the woman coming from dreams? Where is the body of a brother?

"Listen, dearie, have you heard this one?" . . . "Not in the smoking car?" "No, the hotel." The fat girl giggled, shrieked, her voice trailing up lasciviously.

The distance to the kitchen became a distance, the Negro glared over as if in a mirror far away. The confusion became almost a stillness around him, like a fabric so thick you could cut it, sound with colossal slothfulness, deadly indifference, ennui thick as butter. The fly buzzed around the room. The Captain bit and chewed his apple and spat out the chewed skins into his hand and put them on the plate beside the meat.

He was surrounded by gimlet eyes, by sounds whose meaning came from the intricate flesh. His muscles began to twitch. He was drugged. Something in the essence of the scene was like an opiate because so much of it was inert, dead to him. The bright words broke like a surf around him. The light swung above. The ship kept its steady tossing.

Somebody shouted. One of the women shouted, "Hello boy, snap out of it . . ."

The place was like an inferno now. He felt he could never, never leave the room as he could never leave the world, as if he were hideously confined in this hell of sound and flesh, as if all these people were inextricably bound to him by virtue of their mutual living.

They all went back to the saloon. Hackman began to work the player piano. Mamie sat on the arm of the Captain's chair, and Floyd sat across, watching her. Her body was thin and pointed, and terribly alive with a raw terrible kind of vivacity as if she were skinned. She sat swinging her thin sharp leg, grinning at the other men, rolling her eyes. Floyd had to look.

She lifted her blouse and set it on her shoulders. She leaned her sharp body over towards the Captain whispering. He kept paring his nails and leaning his ear toward her, but his face flushed and his brows were raised so his eyes shone out, startling. She had her tongue in her cheek, her thin lips baring her sharp teeth. She began to laugh, lifting her sharp bladed shoulders. She put her long nose in her cupped hands. Her shoulders shook. Then she suddenly flung her head up gasping a little, her burnt-out eyes looking straight at Floyd, solemnly.

To his horror she got up and came towards him. "Will ya dance?" she said, in her hoarse, pleasant voice. She pushed back her hair nervously, waiting for him to get up. "Say, come on and dance." She jerked her thin shoulders. Hackman pumped, his back moving to the music. She took Floyd's hands and pulled him up. "Oh no, no," he cried unable to touch her, his large hands flying out. "Don't be crazy," she said, pulling him. No one else was dancing. Hackman turned and looked at them, still pumping with his feet. He kept on looking while he lit a cigarette.

She pulled him around. "Let yourself go," she kept saying, pulling him. He saw down on her hair, on her back where his hand was. She came in close to him. He could not dance. He saw the way her hair grew down her neck. He followed her around painfully. She pushed him playfully down where he had been sitting beside Fletcher. "You'd learn," she said, "You'd learn if you wanted to." She stood in front of him pushing her hair back, staring solemnly at him. "Don't be afraid," she said. "You're a kid, don't be afraid," she kept saying as if sensing something in him, then seeing him so timid she could not resist giving him pain. "Say, look at this, willya? The kid is shaking. He's all wet." She put her hard warm hand on his head, "Look at that, willya?" She pretended to wring out his hand. "Look, Edith," she said to the fat girl, "look at that, willya? This baby should be with his ma, he should."

Hackman looked from the piano and suddenly guffawed. "Lay off the kid, Mamie. Lay off," he said. "Don't rob the cradle."

"Say," she said behind her hand, ogling the Captain.

Floyd could think of nothing to say. He sat feeling huge, grinning.

"Come on," Edith said. "Lay off the kid."

Fletcher peered at them. "Why don't you dance with Edith?" he said, moving his head on his thin neck like a turtle. Then he leaned over putting his moist hand on Floyd's. "Let's take a round on the deck," he said. Floyd saw his face with the moist mouth in an O, the watery eyes and the sentimental smile of a man always remembering.

"All right," he said, glad to be gone, dreading the walk to the door.

"Don't go. Don't be a wet blanket," Mamie said, letting go Edith, standing in front of the door. She put her arms around him. "I like you." He did not know what to say. He kept looking at Hackman who had stopped playing and sat looking at them, turning his head like some emaciated bird, watching them, his eyes narrowed as if they fed him some foul food he needed. Mamie put her arms around Floyd, clinging in close to him. He reared back carrying her against him. Fletcher took hold of him. "He's going out with me," he said, half-pulling him. Mamie stretched up against him. He could feel her bones in her thin body. "I want to go out and get some air," he said. "Stay and dance. I'll be good to you," she kept saying, keeping her eye on the Captain too, who sat paring his nails. "Come on honey," she said. Suddenly at the word "honey" he could stand it no longer, he lifted his arm awkwardly, lay it across her body and shoved her away from him so she spun across the room. He heard her swearing as he got out the door.

The wind struck them after the hot cabin. The Salvor was riding the black waves, lifting and falling dreamily. It was like another world. The light shone out of the cabins and the Salvor went peacefully plying her way over what menacing deep he did not know. A pale moon shone beneath the rapid flying clouds. He walked with Fletcher in the black wind. Fletcher kept talking and talking about McKinley, about the old days. They walked clear around the ship, passing the saloon windows where they caught snatches of old records, Ain't We Got Fun? Momma Loves Papa! Floyd had to look in the bright windows seeing the faces of the girls. Then out at the black lifting waves and the sky where the stars burned. Fletcher talked, gesticulating with his stiff arm. One minute he was excessive and idealistic, the next petty, repeating some prattle. In his top mechanical mind he seemed to carry the greatest optimism and in his essential deep self the most appalling decay.

He talked about his wife, he was obsessed by his own promise and his failure. He had been stunted everywhere, by idealism, by poverty. He had thought that circumstances would lift him to greatness, that greatness lay in the democratic structure of society and now he was dying of loneliness and rancor, his feet crippled, his eyes haunted.

They kept walking around looking in the windows. In one cabin four men were playing cards, sitting around the square table, looking down. They seemed not to know the black night swept around them, the black sea below. Terrestrial magnetism pulls bird from migration to migration. Even the common little shrew is moved to restlessness by the earth magnetism. But these men seemed to be isolated from the elements that supported them. They had cut themselves off and played a game.

"I don't know what happened, I don't know what it is," Fletcher stood still craning his long neck, "I don't know where I slipped up. I was headed for the biggest success this country has ever seen. I would have been one of the big men now. Some place, probably just one place, something slipped. Things happen like that. I can't understand what it was. I can't understand it." He forgot himself and left his arm going stiff from his body.

Hackman came out of the saloon, the opening door throwing a bright light over the water. "Run along Pop, I got something to say to this bozo," Hackman said. Floyd felt sorry for the old man. "I was walking with him," he ventured. "Never mind, never mind," Hackman said, taking Floyd's arm.

As they went along the prow the wind came stinging against them, blinding, swift. They turned back down the deck on the other side. Floyd was uneasy because of the neat hard body of Hackman walking close beside him, holding familiarly to his arm. He tried to pull away but the other man had his nervous fingers in his flesh.

"Say, what's your racket?" Hackman said, stopping to light a cigarette. The match flared, showing his dried face. It looked like the inside of a dried nut, a little rotten.

"What's your racket?" he said.

"Oh, I don't know " Floyd said, trying to light his cigarette against the wind. "What's yours?" he said desperately. Hackman walked with his nervous body close to Floyd, half caressing his arm. It made his own body feel huge and loose. He gripped his hands together trying to confine himself.

"I've got a damn good racket and don't you forget it," Hackman said in his metallic voice. Floyd didn't answer. "I'm pulling a big deal," Hackman lowered his voice. "There's a lot of jack in it. When you know me better kid you'll find out that I don't go in for nothing small. Hell I usually travel on the Harvard on this trip. Took this lousy tub just for the fun of it. See?

"No sir. No small racket for mine. This country's a big racket, that's all. Everybody might as well get in on it. That's what I say."

Floyd nodded. "I guess so," he said senselessly.

"Say, what's your game?" said Hackman.

"Oh, I don't know," Floyd began.

"With that face of yours you'd make a good blind. Are you looking for some easy money? Easy money's what I said."

"Well, I guess we all have to have some money," Floyd said.

"Money makes the mare go." Hackman laughed and threw his cigarette into the water where it fizzed out. "Every kind of mare." They stopped, leaning on the rail. The confines of the man were so sharp, so cutting.

"What kind of a racket you got?" Floyd asked.

"Well, I ain't saying. But there's money in it and how! And it's money, what I mean!" He came up close under Floyd's arm, who reared himself back as if Hackman had been a snake.

"Oh, yes?" he laughed uneasily.

The saloon door opened. Mamie and the Capta n came out. "Ain't it a grand night?" Mamie said, walking close to the Captain who walked solemnly as if he were drunk. She veered toward Floyd and Hackman but the Captain had her arm in his claw and pulled her up sharply. He seemed not to see the two men or the night, only the girl. He smiled looking at her, swinging her around him, holding firmly to her arm. They went down the deck the Captain half dragging her. Mamie kept laughing, throwing her dark frowsy head wildly. They stopped at the end of the deck. Floyd could hear their low voices as they stood together. The waves lapped against the boat sides and their voices struck on the boy's nerves. He could not hear what they were saying; he could not listen to Hackman but listened to the dull heavy male voice of the Captain, the husky voluptuous voice of the girl and the slap of the water against the ship's sides.

Hackman kept talking, confining the world in his hard nut-like consciousness as if he had got it all in his little mind, reduced it until he confined it proudly in his small consciousness. There was a kind of boastfulness in his so reducing it, as if he had cracked open everything, exposed it, revealed its innate nothingness with his own nothingness.

"Oh, that ain't nothing. There ain't nothing to that. Say, do you know the inside dope about that? Say I'll put you wise to that. Aw, that's baloney, that's a lot of hooey." He exposed everything and was satisfied, as if it were a final exposure. He could explain everything, he stopped at nothing. He had cracked the nut of the world and found it hollow and rotten and minute, and he was gratified to find it so, that it was no better, no more infinite or mysterious than himself. There was the world in his obscene skeleton-ed head; he had cracked it wide open and found nothing. . . . It was a racket, a hoax. He kept cracking it between his yellow rotten teeth, dropping the shells over the side of the boat that went from mystery to mystery in the night.

The Salvor road between the unknown sky and the unknown sea. The unknown stars flashed and burned, and Orion sent a ray clear into the water of the earth upon which they rode.

Hackman spat over the ship. "You travel with me, big boy, and we'll go places and see things."

"I think I'll go to bed," said Floyd.

"Hell, it's early."

Floyd said, "I think I'm beginning to feel a little sick."

He ran down the deck but before he could find his cabin Mamie came running up to him. He didn't want to see her. He couldn't remember the number of his cabin. He thought it was eight. He couldn't remember.

"Hello," she said. "I'm going to bed," he said. He wouldn't look at her thought she wiggled in front of him. He wouldn't look, yet he remembered her voice as she had talked to the Captain. She took his arm walking close in against him. "Gee, it's a swell night," she said. "Yes," he said. "Say, don't you love this? Ain't it swell? Can you imagine it, that old Captain wanted me to go with him. Say, what does he think I am?"

Floyd looked at her. "Did he? That was pretty rotten."

"I'll say." He was walking with her, now. "It's wonderful. I think you're wonderful, too. Honest. A girl like me doesn't come up against a boy like you much." She wormed into his loneliness. "Where you from? What do you do?" He told her. He talked more and more. She seemed to listen to every word, looking at him. His loneliness poured out. He told her about the city, about following that woman. "You know . . ." he said. "Sure," she said, snuggling close to him.

"But I'm talking about myself. Where do you live?" She played a pure role. He touched her hand. They stopped, leaning over the water. The stars were burning as if from a conflagration, falling in sparks along the horizon as they watched.

"We're both lonely," he said; "we're both lonely."

She turned swiftly to him, pressing up against him, her face shining below him lifted up evilly. He looked down at her. She wriggled up to him so he could feel her bones, and he reared back away from her. "Gee, you're nice. You're nice. You ain't going to push me away like you did before. You ain't going to knock me away again. Come into my bunk. Nobody'll see us." And she murmured all those words he had covertly known; he heard them as she stretched up against him, her face invisible to him, and her words bursting like rockets.

He kept taking her hands away from him, plucking them off. He could not get her off him. She clung like some hideous prehensile animal. He plucked off her hands and they were on him again. It was hideous. He took her at last, lifting her off him, pulling her dress in back, lifting her off by the scruff of the neck. He held her out away from him, half lifting her from her feet. She fought. She tried to regain her feet. Her hands groped for him. She had extraordinary pleasure corrupting him. "Somebody's coming," he said. "Stand up, somebody's coming." He let her go. "Go away," he said, feeling that someone was coming down the deck. "I'm sorry," he said. "Go away."

"Oh you're sorry are you," she said, "all right, all right." And she struck him with her flat hand full on the cheek. She struck him as hard as she could. Then she went down the deck, swaying, falling against the wall.

Floyd stood stock still, his eyes dilated, his face stinging. He struck a match as if to see something and let it burn out. He began to prowl the deck in a kind of physical anguish. Everyone had gone in, for the wind was becoming bitter. He looked in where the lights shone out and saw people moving inside. He prowled the decks. He could not go in. He went round and round. Then it startled him to realize that he was trying to find which cabin was Mamie's, that he was looking in all of them. But he did not see her. There were Fletcher and Hackman and two others playing cards. They looked almost comic, sitting so still and serence, playing a game while the boat went through the bitter wind and the stars burned so far away. He stopped at what he thought was Mamie's cabin and listened but he heard nothing.

Those words kept breaking in him like rockets. He kept beating his hands together making a little sound of his own flesh beating upon itself. He stood back against the wall. He could not tell the boundaries of the real. He had no way of knowing what was happening to him. He thought that he and all the people inside the boat must have heard that far cry, that hail of some dream for which they had lost their part of a single being, to gain—what?

A terror of fear and loss came in him. He half ran around the deck over to the other side as if something might be there to instruct him. But there was not a soul, not a sound. He leaned against the wall, pressing close back against it. He wanted to make no further encounters.

He began to feel the boat rock under him, lifting in the long swells. In the stillness he heard someone breathing close beside him. He was startled. He distinctly heard regular breathing as if a sleeping person lay near him. Then he saw there was a stair near, leading to the upper deck. It seemed to come from there. He stood listening, afraid to look. It was regular and soft, near him, strange regular breathing of a nearby human life, separate from his, moving in the same element and separate.

He looked around the side of the stairs. It was a woman half sitting, half lying against the steps. It was Fannie, sleeping. Her face was turned up in the dim starlight, her mouth open. Cautiously he leaned over her, looking. She might have been some strange beast so cautiously he looked at her, not touching even her skirts.

He looked at her carefully. Her hand hung down limp and the one that seemed paralyzed as if she had taken hold of some searing thing lay across her body and the little finger fell over the palm, dead looking. Her powdered face looked green in the light, and sleeping, lost some of its horror. She looked as if she had once expected something and had now forgotten what it was she had expected.

He could not imagine what she had seen that had violated her so. Not being able to imagine it, he suffered mysteriously from ills more colossal perhaps than could be. But he knew that nothing in this world could wipe out the memory of what she had seen, just as a soldier can never forget the horror of flesh torn apart. Had she come unsuspecting as he upon this insane horror that lay mysteriously in everything, so that now perhaps only death could annihilate the memory that seared her? Looking at her, he shuddered at the risk of death and putrefaction. But in her sleeping face there was something that could not be imagined when she was awake. It was as if she was listening, listening as he was to something going on in an inner room.

Suddenly as he leaned over her one eye opened in her green face, one huge knowing eye looked at him. He could not move. It rolled, closed again as if in a convulsion, and then opened on him, a wide unseeing Horror. His blood froze. What was looking at him? What did she know? He encountered the wide eye a long time, then the withered hand moved toward him suddenly, striking him, and he fell back in horror close to the railing. Then he turned and ran down the deck.

He tiptoed past the saloon where the light still shone. He listened at the door and could hear nothing. Everything was still. He tiptoed on, watching, fearful someone would come around the corner. His heart beat in fear he would meet someone. Then he began to run down towards his cabin. Wildly he pulled on the door, shook it. It would not open. He shook it with all his strength. To his horror it opened suddenly, with ease, and Fletcher reached out a long arm, pulling him in.

5

He was pulled into the close warm cabin. Hackman and Fletcher had been playing chess. Hackman squinted through the smoke he blew from his nostrils. "Hello boy. Come in." "Mighty glad you've come." "A game, a game." Fletcher made Floyd sit down, pulling up a chair. "You referee, eh Hackman?" "The old buzzard is a crook." Fletcher sat down, tweaking his long nose in his fingers. Hackman leaned over the board. They began to play. They seemed set on each other, each bound to win. Fletcher tweaked his nose and looked at the board a long time before playing. Hackman fidgeted, threw away his cigarette, lighted another, cleaned his nails, tapped his feet, drummed his fingers.

"Play, damn it, why don't you play!" Fletcher tweaked his long nose in his bony fingers. "Give me time. Give me time." "I can beat you with one eye shut." "Don't be too sure. Don't be too sure." "Play. Play. Move."

Floyd sat huddled in the chair. He did not know how he could leave. He did not know how he could get out the door, how he would get to his cabin. He watched the two men abusing each other over the game, eyeing each other warily, moving, playing, trying to get at each other. "There. Take that. Now I've got you." Fletcher sighing, watching, pulling his long ears at the lobes, scratching his head. "Move. Move!" At last moving. "There." Sitting back, his thumbs in his suspenders, his loose mouth open, his eyes twinkling at the other man. Hackman leaning forward white about the nose, rapping with his white fingers. "Oh, you think you're smart don't you? Well, put that up your nose." Hackman turning his eye over to Floyd in a wink, drawing out a bottle of white moon, passing it around. "Go on take a drink. Go on."

Floyd wiped the bottle mouth with his sleeve, took a drink that burned his throat. He looked at the two men playing a game, leaning over, hating each other, trying to beat one another. He was looking to see men come together, to see something wonderful happening between men.

"Move. Move. What's the matter with you." "Now I've got you." "No you haven't." "Get out of that if you can you old buzzard. Get a move on you. Don't sit there."

Floyd wanted to get to the door but he didn't know how he would leave without offending the men. He didn't know how he could leave. Besides he must see what the two men would do. What did men do in the night together? Did they only try to beat each other? He had to stay and see.

"Move, damn it." Fletcher looked over his glasses, his eyes watering. "You'll never be a success," Hackman said, "you're too damn slow. This is an age of speed, this is."

"Who says I'm not a success? Who says I'm not? I had a silver tongue once. That's what I was called, the silver tongued orator."

"Who cares about that? PLAY."

"They passed the bottle around. Floyd tried to drink. He drank whenever they told him to. Fletcher began to laugh in a long senile wheeze. "I wonder if the Captain went to bed with Mamie . . ."

"Move, you son of a goat."

Floyd wanted to tell them he had walked with Mamie. "I don't think so," he said eagerly. "I was walking with her on the deck . . ."

Hackman stopped playing. "You . . . Well I'll be . . ."

Floyd blushed.

"You innocent little—Well I'll be damned." Hackman laughed dryly.

Floyd kept grinning. Hackman leaned over and put his arm around Floyd's shoulder. "You and me, kid. We'll go places and see things."

He put out his thin fingers and moved his king. "How's that for a play? Pretty smart, eh?" He sat back and watched the old man trembling in fear he would lose, leaning over the board trying to see the wooden men.

"Move, move, why don't you move? Why do you sit there? You old sinner, you old hypocrite, why don't you move?" He laughed soundlessly, tightening his arm around Floyd's shoulder. Floyd tried to laugh. The old man got excited. His eyes watered so he couldn't see. His long hand shook over the miniature battlefield. He leaned back, then forward. He shook all over. He looked up unable to see Floyd and Hackman. Tears began to roll down his cheeks.

"I'm going to trim you, you old goat. Lick the tar out of you. Move. Go on, move. You can't take a thing. You're beat."

"Your queen . . ." the old man was half mad. "You're a crook . . ." his wet fingers left a mark on the table.

"You're beat. Why don't you move? You're beat and don't know it. You're beat. You're beat."

The old man got up screaming, "I'm not. You cheated me. You cheated me. I've been cheat. I've been cheat." He stood sputtering, shaking. Hackman sat looking up laughing, gathering up the pawns, setting them out. "Sit down," he said, reaching his foot under the table. He tripped the old man so he fell bewildered in his chair. Hackman laughed and winked at Floyd. Floyd tried to laugh. Fletcher sat putting his hands over his own body as if trying to find himself. He could not see the two men at all now. He mumbled to himself.

Floyd said, "Don't mind. It doesn't make any difference."

Fletcher didn't hear him. He looked dimly in his direction, moving his head up and down, retreating from them to the past. There had never been any present for him. "I want to die," he mumbled, tweaking his nose, leaning in confusion over the table. "I want to die."

Hackman knocked his head up. "Get off the board. Sit up."

Fletcher sat up, feeling the blow dimly.

153

Hackman grinned. "Well, die. I don't want to die, I'll tell the world. Your move first. Move, hell, why don't you move."

"I want to die," Fletcher said without the least expression on his muddled face.

"Move. Move."

"I don't think he hears you," Floyd said.

"Of course he hears me. Move." Hackman suddenly shouted and began kicking the old man under the table. Fletcher didn't seem to notice until without warning he stood up, his mouth open as if in some terrible cry, but only a faint jabbering sound came from him and the saliva ran out of his mouth down his chin. He lifted his fist shaking it, his whole body shaking in convulsion, his mouth open in that soundless scream.

"I want to live until I die," Hackman said, not looking up. Floyd kept looking at the awful mouth open screaming in the flesh but not a sound from the throat. "Sit down, for Christ's sake," Hackman said.

In confusion Floyd got up.

"Sit down," Hackman yelled. "Sit down," he yelled at Floyd who sat down and then got up again. Hackman got up too, his eyes white and unseeing. He put his hands up over Floyd's shoulder and began caressing him. "You're a nice kid. Don't pay any attention to that old man. He's as good as dead. Just ain't buried yet." He laughed that soundless laugh.

"Don't. Don't touch me," Floyd said, but the man clung to him. He had the impression of trying to shake him off, undo those terrible hands from his flesh. "Take your hands away," he cried. "Don't get excited," Hackman said. "Don't get excited. I like you. See?" "Take your hands away," Floyd kept saying, looking around for the door. He could not see it at all and the walls kept plunging and he felt too tall in the close cabin.

Fletcher stood as if lost under the lamp. He kept peering around as if trying to see some substantial thing. He saw the two men far off, as if they too were in the past, invisible, ghostly, without substance. He kept weeping. Never to have seen a man, only ghosts; never to have loved a woman, only memories. "Where are you? Where are you?" he said. "Where are you?" he cried, tottering backwards, holding out his hands as if he were going forward. He receded swiftly, went back strangely, out of sight as if he were sinking away.

Floyd ran from Hackman, running through the light. It was only a few steps but he thought it a long distance. Where was the deck? Where was the night? Where was the boat? He fell over something and fell flat banging his head. He lay there.

When he opened his eyes he saw Fletcher lying prone on the

floor, his long nose thrust straight up, his mouth sagging down as if something had violated it.

He heard nothing now but the soft beat of the engines in the hold of the ship and the far-off movement through the water. The ship lifted in that strange movement, plunging, lifting, like some movement that took place only when the human cries, the grotesque suffering was over. Again he heard the sound of close breathing. It filled the room, the steady sound of breathing.

He wanted to get out. The air seemed befouled. He got up. There was something foul on his own coat and he clawed at it. He stood up and saw another man in the room. It frightened him at first as if he had stood up on the first horizon and seen another man. He stood looking dully. Then he saw it was Hackman sitting at the table, his glazed eyes seeing absolutely nothing. He seemed content like some viper reduced completely to its own sting, sitting amidst its own poisons. He sat looking with his narrow glazed eyes at nothing.

Floyd began tiptoeing out, falling with the list of the ship. He dreaded rousing Hackman. If he could only get out without rousing him. He dreaded having him stir, having the little mind stirred up.

Hackman sat looking at nothing. Fletcher lay on the floor. Floyd got them placed in his mind so he wouldn't have to touch them. He looked clear around the cabin, searching for the door. Seeing it at last he put forth all his effort to reach it. In a moment that blew to great size he turned the knob of the door, opened it, shut it behind him.

The room disappeared as if it had never been. There was the black night and the bitter wind striking against him. The boat lifted her nose and plunged, soared up like a bird. There was a soft swish of her through the water. The stars burned in the black sky.

He was set on finding his cabin and seeing no other human face. He was canny as any beast amongst danger. Every sense was alert. He heard the sounds below, muffled scurryings, and the throb of the engines. He heard the water rushing softly past them. He heard the sea lifting and moving upon itself, he heard the very deeps. He heard the creakings of the boat, heard her strain and lift. The deck seemed twice as long as it had been. He crept on, looking at the numbers on the doors. He know he would know his cabin when he came to it. He crept on, craftily, making not a sound.

He heard someone coming down the deck. Swiftly he swung himself up the stair leading to the top deck. He hung looking down, suspended in his whole being looking down the deck where the unknown person was approaching. He would see no one. He knew in his soul he could stand no further encounter. He wanted only to conceal himself with a strange alert passion. All his being seemed alarmed, awakened in a passion of protection. He hung in perfect quiet and suspense, his face clear and set in his passion for isolation.

It was a woman. He heard the tapping heels. She was talking to herself, mumbling. He could not hear the words. It was Mamie. She was directly below him, her great head of hair, her thin body falling directly below him. He heard her breathing. She stopped below him. He heard her breathing coming in a hissing sound. She stood for a moment so he could have touched her, then she went on around the deck.

He sprang down and ran around the corner of the stairs and into his cabin and bolted the door. He stood shut in himself again. He listened. He heard only the boat moving through the water. He listened a long time, feeling his own body and the body of the boat and the water. At last he got into bed with all his clothes on. He put his overcoat over him. He covered himself over. He wanted to be completely covered over.

He lay still, his eyes wide on the darkness. Then as if suddenly, he went straight to sleep, plunged straight down, away from the world.

6

The next day they all sat on the flat top deck. The Salvor rocked and dreamed. Floyd was entranced. He sat or walked the top deck directly under the sky. The gulls soared slowly following the ship, turning and coming back, drifting on unseen currents of air, wheeling, crying out, keeping their eerie eyes turned on the Salvor as she rode the waves.

Mamie and Edith sat with their short legs danglings. Fletcher was nervous, not remembering anything of the night before. He had a plaster over his left eye where he had struck a chair falling. Hackman smoked cigarettes, throwing them into the water.

There wasn't much talk. Floyd looked at them all but he was wary, knowing of danger now. Mamie watched him. Whenever his back was turned she looked at him, but she was sullen, refusing to talk.

The Captain came halfway up the steps now and then, poking his walrus head up, standing with just his head showing, peering at Mamie, looking at Floyd. He ate an apple.

Floyd strode the deck under the broad sky, peering under his cap at the others. He had a secret exultation in his breast, a kind of shock of fear and ecstacy. He watched them all from under his cap, knowing at last something about them. He received some impact straight upon his own substance. No matter if it menaced destruction, at least it was something, striking him with a knowing sting. Hearing their speech it had some meaning for him. "Do you know how far we are from land?" "Can I use your binoculars?" "Well, did you sleep?" "I say I couldn't live except for rice." "You're a fine guzzler, you are." "Don't tell me you don't remember what happened." "When will we get there?" "Where?"

He couldn't talk to them though. He wanted to speak to them. He would dash down stairs, run to his cabin. Inside he would stand breathing, smiling to himself. He felt strong, powerful, knowing, the juices of a new life and knowledge were running down him, and his muscles had a delicacy and fiber they had never had.

Then he would dash out and run up the stairs to the upper deck and there would be the sky and Mamie examining her stocking and Edith reading True Confessions and Hackman spitting into the running sea. And he would feel awkward, green. He would walk again looking at them, swinging around them.

"Oh for God's sake, Young, why don't you light someplace?" Hackman said.

Fletcher came over, peering half-blind at them. "A fine day" he said, looking anxiously as if he thought they might remember something of the night before. Floyd had tried to mention the night but they had looked as if they remembered nothing.

"Look at my hat—those damn sea gulls. One cinch they don't get on you," he said to Floyd. "You move too much."

Floyd had to keep the whole deck under his eye. He was afraid to be watched, to be off his guard. He saw everything, accepted the impact. His eyes were wide open in hunger, and he thought he was actually accepting something in the things he encountered beside their fantastic convexity that hitherto his own ignorance had given them.

The water lay around them like some volatile intermediary, unformed and chaotic as himself. There was a mysterious and exhilarating stirring of light and form. The ocean would stir as if some invisible thing were passing over it, all the light would writhe and shift in mid-air, change, move; then the upper sky would convulse and move swiftly, the clouds racing so that everything seemed in frightening movement, the water lifting, shifting, running ahead, running behind, lifting at the sides, swift and slow, changing as he looked like a great volume of visible sound upon which they moved, making a counter-movement; then the high racing clouds, running across, slashing another movement in speed; and the mid air striking cold and then warm, and the sun coming through a straight flash speeding all the myriad movements, giving them point and lift and flash.

Then the sun would go under again and the sky and water would become a curving lifting mass again, heaving, as if some force curved beneath, invisibly. This sense of an invisible world wafting against him, moving beneath, shafting above, gave him a sense of some elemental thing in which they all moved.

The others sat relaxed, arms dropping down. They looked out a wide way. The sun cast a broad pale light. There seemed to be different thicknesses of light, the upper sky rising tenuously but falling to the thick coiled light of the ocean.

They all half dozed, the wide horizon putting them into a sleep.

At lunch everyone was quiet. Fletcher kept telling stories that seemed unreal, about his youth, about American history. No one bothered to listen. Floyd couldn't wait to get up on the top deck again.

In the afternoon the Captain came up and stood looking ahead. He was steady, drunk and easy. Fletcher and Hackman wanted to talk. He looked down at them or didn't look at them at all. He paid no attention to what they said. Then he said, "This is my ship. I've had this ship for twenty years . . . been on her. We used to sail to Alaska. We had a good cargo then, in the hold and on the decks . .

"To Alaska, eh?" Floyd said, trying to look cocky.

"Yes, Alaska," barked the Captain.

The three men stood there, Floyd stood nervously by. The Captain looked down at them all turning his head stiffly because of the boil on his neck. He looked at them silently.

Then he called to the man at the wheel, talking differently, saying there was going to be a fog, then a storm. Then he went below.

Floyd thought, his feet have worn down the steps. He could not tell how many times he must have gone up and down. Before I was born, he thought, the Captain went down that stairway just as he did this moment . . . before I was born . . .

The afternoon got very pale and time seemed to have stopped. Mamie kept following him around, edging close to him. He was afraid of her sullenness, the way she didn't talk, just touched him, and lifted her sharp body. The image of her dark wizened face, her blank eyes troubled him. "Gee, you're young," she said. "I guess so . . . yes, I guess so." "Well, for cryin' out loud!"

An opaque light, thick at the top, lay above the moving ship. The sun rarely came through. Hackman went to sleep in a deck chair, looking like a husk. Mamie slept in a chair next to Floyd's. He watched her face for a while, feeling as if he shouldn't. She looked exposed. The powder and rouge looked blue. The wind was blowing on her. He gingerly covered her with his coat. But he had to look at her face. He had to look at her, as if some answer lay in her. He looked at them all. Fannie came up but she looked away. She sat down and covered herself up. He felt they were all obscured but he was wary even of the sleeping forms.

He looked at Mamie's dark monkey's face slumped in the chair, her eyes closed, that antique look of a dissolute beauty on her features. Her face troubled him—those words she had whispered to him broke like rockets—mixing with the purity of his longing and the corruption of his mind. Her face was like a wound. It had upon it all the marks of that risk and of that danger.

But looking out at the sea, at the sky, he forgot them, feeling an alliance with the natural world that made him delicate and sentient in himself. He felt some strong meditation swaying deep in him like sea weed at the bottom of the ocean, and from this ovement there came a wave of peace up his loins, surging up softly like the lapping of water in sleep.

In this pale abstraction he fell asleep. In his half sleep he felt the tides of air, the mid air alive and sentient, striking against him from another world. It laved over him, bedding him deeper in sleep.

He woke suddenly as if there was danger near him, and saw Mamie looking at him, resting her chin on her hand as he had seen her in the saloon, looking at him solemnly. She made no move, even when he wakened and looked back at her. She kept looking solemnly at him like a child. He was embarrassed.

He got up and rudely walked away, feeling ghostly and unnerved. It was late afternoon and a fog obscured the sun, the gulls moving slowly in the under air. The horizon was invisible behind the fog. It made them seem lost.

He thought the others looked at him strangely. They all seemed nervous, and green, colored in the light. They seemed cut off, each knowing and crafty.

The girls went with Hackman. They stood huddled together laughing, looking sideways out of their eyes, telling stories to each other. Floyd felt out of it. Perhaps they were talking about him. The fog was lowering over the Salvor. He kept walking past Hackman and the girls but he could hear nothing, only the higher words and the laughter. He wanted to break in, hear what they were saying. He caught them watching him. He walked as close to them as he dared. He had to lower his eyes when they looked at him. He became confused. He felt he could never leave them, that he must join himself to them forever; a torture of love came in him for the three of them, standing together in the fog.

He looked at their terrible bodies, at the faces of the girls, aslant, laughing in a confusion of angelic and evil qualities; and a luminosity shone in them, an outline of something he could not grasp.

There was mystery and horror in their bodies. Who could know the vivid and sumptuous life in a human body no matter how vile? How did he know what gorgeous manifestations of life they concealed, like the fairy tales of lepers and dwarfs? He walked past them again and again. The fog was coming in thick.

They concealed something standing there. He could not hear their words, only the sounds of their voices. He could see the turn of their heads, the forms of their bodies, the lines of the faces. They concealed more than they revealed. There was something lost. Some risk had been taken, some menace and some glory.

He turned away a moment, unable to bear the sight of them. He head Edith scream. When he turned Mamie was crouching her eerie face between her hands that were clapped over her ears. Hackman was laughing and pointing a gun up. Edith was screaming and laughing.

"Are you crazy?"

"I'll show you what an A-1 shot I am, baby."

"Stop it!"

"Watch out. He's been drinking."

Edith ran screaming. Fannie got up from her deck chair, with both hands raised she let out a scream of filthy curses.

And Hackman shot into the sky three times. The sky ripped apart. The ocean to its depths ripped open. It reverberated clear around, rolling like thunder over them as if the boat would be submerged, then there was silence, then the thud of a body falling plumb out of the obscure sky and a gull fell two feet away from Floyd.

Hackman was grinning, somewhat abashed by the intonation reverberating so unexpectedly around the sky, through the water. It still quivered in the sensitive air. Floyd felt all the fibers of his being torn out. The girls were chattering with excitement. Fannie in a rage was trying to get the gun out of Hackman's hands.

"Look at that . . . get the hell out of here, Fannie, I'll use it on you. How was that for a shot?"

Edith came back looking at the dead bird in excitement. "A dead ringer," she said, looking at Hackman almost with love.

"I'm some shot, baby," Hackman said.

The excitement was very strange, the girls chattering, Hackman beside himself with the luck of bringing down a bird. There was something strange about it, as if there were some illicit satisfaction in the violence. Floyd looked at the dead eyes of the bird, half closed, a mist coming over them. A mist seemed to be coming over the whole bird, the eyes were moist and half open, looking voluptuously at the sky.

Edith was kneeling down touching the breast of the dead bird almost with fright, her eyes rolling back in fright. "I never saw one close before."

"Get away from it," Mamie said shivering.

"It's dead all right," Edith said in wonder, still kneeling.

Hackman kept walking around, the pistol in his hand. "How's that for a shot? A dead ringer." Edith put a finger on the feathers. There was a still wind upon them, the bill was open, the feet still spread. The moment was so spare between the bright winging bird and death.

The Captain stuck his head up, following the eyes of the others, seeing the dead bird. The other gulls crying shrilly circled above them. Hackman brandished the gun. "Better look out, you fellows." Fannie still cursed at him, lunging for the gun when she could. The Captain came up slowly. Hackman stopped, watching him appear above the steps. He came up and looked at the dead bird, then at the grinning man, then again at the dead bird that lay stretched in a still flying.

Hackman grinned impudently. The two looked at each other.

"Why did you do that?" the Captain said.

"Oh, just practicing up," Hackman said impudently, shining his gun on his handkerchief.

"I don't see why you had to do that," Floyd said, suddenly going over to him. "I don't see why . . . I don't see why." He was shaken badly. They all looked at him. Edith looked up where she crouched by the dead bird. Mamie looked at him and put her hand on his arm as if he were a child. He flung away from her. "I don't see why," he said wildly. They all looked at him and he stood impotent, his great hands hanging down.

The Captain then put out his taloned hand and laid it on the chest of the boy, gently pushing him back. It was half a caress. He stood a moment, his hand on the boy's breast, looking down at the dead bird. Still with his hand on the boy he told Hackman he would allow no more shooting, then he went downstairs.

They were still excited by the violence, the girls laughing, embracing each other, crying high.

The fog came thickly as if the intonation had loosened, sent it drifting down.

Floyd ran downstairs. He gained his cabin and threw himself on the bunk, lifting his shoulders, sobbing.

The boat rocked him as if in the womb of some terrible birth. He sobbed, trying to understand. The sweat stood out on him. He held his hands together.

He thought he could never go on deck again. He heard the Negro calling dinner, twice around the decks. But he could not go out. He burrowed his head in the bunk. He covered himself over;

161

the boat rocked and swelled. He wanted never to see any of them again. He kept seeing the voluptuous eyes of the dead bird looking in that strange love at death.

There was a knock at the door. Someone tried the knob. He didn't move. "Hey," someone said He could not answer.

Mamie came whimpering at the door. Then Hackman. He lay still. When he thought they would all be eating dinner he got up and looked out and saw the moon, unreal, muffled in the fog.

Mamie came back, whispering through the lattice. He stood still behind the door, hearing her through the thin partition. He felt he could almost touch her. How could he know the life in her body that stood a few feet from him? She was whispering close to him. O, if he could open to her, let her in, know her. But he was paralyzed. He could not move, because of that danger, that menace obscure and awful that lay in them all, that would lie in him too.

He let her go away.

7

As he lay obscure in the cabin his mind fell open like a rich fruit at its time, rooted delicately and deep, swaying upwards, through spaces, towards a far surface light, with a million tactile surfaces, feeling about in the unknown spectral world; swaying and swaying in many unknown directions, sensitive and alert.

Hackman came knocking at the door. "Say, Floyd, are you there? What's matter, are you sick?" Fletcher came whispering, "Come to dinner. Anything I can do?" Then they stood silently listening. He knew they were standing silently wondering who he was, what he would be doing.

In unbearable horror he heard them breathing outside his door, coming to call him; the girls came rustling, whispering to him through the door, unbearably attracted to defile him, to initiate him into the unutterable secrets they knew.

He lay, moved subtly from below, stirring at the loam, his being shifting and shaking in its fiber, shaking out.

And he was aware of menace. He felt a little sick and knew that the ship was plunging heavily. He remembered what the Captain had said about there being a fog and a storm. A physical fear shot through him.

"Floyd, Floyd," Mamie called throug the door.

"Who is it?" Floyd answered, knowing.

"It's me," he said. "Come out. There's going to be a storm. I'm scared."

"I don't want to come out. I don't feel good."

"Floyd," said Hackman. His voice made his throat and mouth

visible to Floyd. "I want to talk to you. You ain't going to go back on a buddy, are you?" And Fletcher whining through, "What's up?" He wouldn't answer them. He listened and listened, heard them approach and creep away.

He wanted to go out. He knew he must. He looked out and saw the frightening darkness and the black clouds lowering, moving across counter to the boat. He opened the window and heard the wind. The waves rose and did not break. There was something eerie and wild and sinister in the blackness through which they plunged. The Salvor had begun to rock.

Someone was coming. He shut the port window and ran back to bed. Mamie tried the door knob. "Let me in. Let me come in." Her hoarse voice made him see her whole thin body, her pipestem neck with the black hair growing down it.

"I'm sick," he said. "I'm sick. . . ." He felt sick for saying it. Why didn't he go out? There was nothing to be afraid of. But he thought that when he should see land again he would be different, something would have been done, it would never be the same again. "I'm sick, Mamie," he said. He shivered, pronouncing the name.

"Gee, everybody's sick," she said. "There's a storm coming up. It looks terrible. I'm scared. Let me come in."

"No. I'm sick."

"That's all right. Fannie's sick. She thinks she's the Queen of Sheba. Let me come in." She shook the door. The fog horn sounded, a long doleful sound. It startled him. "Gee, what's that?" Mamie said. "Gee, it's the horn. We're going to have a terrible night. Let me in."

He got up and crept to the door to be near her, and stood not a foot away with the door between them. He could hear her moving her hands. He listened to the small sounds of her body moving, her breathing. She stood still clinging to the door as the ship tilted and lunged. What was she? What knowledge and menace lay in her body? What had she and Hackman and Edith been saying to each other, and laughing about?

"Go away. Go away," he said. He hoped she would not go. He clung to the door too, to keep from being thrown back into the room. Sometimes the slant of the ship was incredible, frightening. "Go away. Go away," he said.

What did she want of him? Who was she, standing so close to him? A terror and hopelessness came upon his delicate opened heart, for all the things that would not happen, the things that would be lost, all that would fail. These unknown people were passing his door, knocking, begging access and he was shut up in fear. He felt the horror of life lost, without word or gesture taking place in the void, vile and unfettered and barren.

"Mamie," he called. He opened the door on the black wind. She had gone. No one was out there. He looked up and down the slanting darkened deck and saw no one, as if he were on the boat alone.

The Salvor lifted her nose high and plunged down so he was thrown against the door hurting his thigh. The deck was wet and slippery. The waves lifted and washed over when the boat tilted to the side. Where was everyone? He felt his way along, clinging to the walls. Above him raced the dark clouds counter to the movement of the boat so it made him dizzy. He went clear around the deck. He saw no one. The light was turned low in the saloon, it was empty. He became frightened. Where were they all? What had happened?

The boat careened wildly almost as if it were unmanned. It rose to the top of the mountainous waves, skidded off, fell down its side. The water struck it, slapping the sides. She staggered under these blows, rose again and was lifted, spanked down, so Floyd had to stop and cling to the doors.

He looked in that saloon again. The light was turned down. The seats were all empty. The piano was closed. He rounded the stern and saw the Captain standing watching the dark sea. The water hissed up the prow, ran in white froth along the sides. The waves rose against her, and broke in white hissing flowers as if in contact the water bloomed. It lifted up to that light, up to the pointed swirl and broke in light from its own abysmal darkness.

Floyd stood beside the Captain, glad to see him. The wind rose in the upper air. He had no cap. He looked as if he had lost it. He kept looking straight ahead.

"Is it going to be a bad storm?" Floyd asked. The Captain didn't look at him. "Is it going to be a bad storm, sir?" There was a long silence. The Captain turned his head slowly above his stiff neck. Floyd saw that he was drunk. He backed away. He went down the deck.

It seemed to him the ship must be derelict, without a Captain. The roll made it difficult to walk. The steady lift and plunge made him ill. The water hissed like a nest of snakes. It rose and broke around the bow or lifted myriads of shining heads over the stern, breaking, crawling on the deck, running swiftly off back into the sea again. The spray went through his clothes. It seemed to him they were adrift.

He tried to find his way below. He didn't know what time it was. The Captain still stood wooden, looking ahead, dead drunk. Floyd found the way below. The dining room was empty. He saw the Negro washing dishes. He saw just the upper half of him as if he were cut in two. He stood watching him over the length of the dining room but the Negro did not look up. He decided he didn't want anything to eat.

He found another stair, leaned over looking down below. He thought he heard voices. He let himself down. It was dark except for a dim light. He had to cling close to the wall as the Salvor tipped crazily. He came to a door and looked in. There were some men sitting at a table playing cards. They had their shirts off. He thought he recognized some of them as the men he had seen helping to load the Salvor the day they sailed. They were drunk. They sat playing cards. There was the tattooed man. He was the only man with a shirt on, so only his scarred face showed. He was afraid they would see him. He stole up again.

On the middle deck the nose of the storm struck him. He had the impression that the Salvor was running wild. She tipped so crazily he thought she would go over. Sometimes he had to cling along her sides while she rode a mountainous wave. He was wet. His hair clung wet over his eyes. He thought he must get to the upper deck to see if anyone was steering her. He was trying to find the stairway but he had to stop for whole minutes clinging with all his might to the doors to keep from being washed overboard. The water hissed along the deck, clung around his feet, and then ran hissing over the sides again.

A door opened and Mamie and Edith came out supporting each other. He ran to help them. He was glad to see them. They both looked ghastly. Mamie was swearing, "I shouldn't have drunk that gin." Edith was crying, "Gee, are we going to go down? I don't want to die." She blubbered off. He tried to hold her but she pulled away insanely and fell towards the rail where she clung. Mamie leaned against him. "Say kid, where is everybody? Is it all right?"

Floyd was scared too. "It's all right," he said, feeling Mamie leaning against him. He grew bold and touched her side with his hand. She was sick, leaning over the rail. All three of them clung together as the boat tossed. They had to shout. "Say," he said, trying to joke as Hackman would have, "You're not much of a toper are you?" The storm made him bold.

Edith was screaming. "Oh, we're lost. This is awful." Floyd tried to hold her but she pulled away and clung to the rail. Mamie leaned against him and he boldly touched her body. It made him feel sick and dizzy but he made himself touch her. The cold spray flew from the breaking sea and blew on them. Mamie leaned heavily against him so he felt her whole body. A terrible retching shook her thin form. While she was sick he touched her breasts. He was intent upon it. He felt sick doing it while she was ill. "Gee, gee," she kept saying, and when he saw she didn't notice what he was doing he touched her again.

She clung to him with her hard little hands. He felt guilty and humiliated, touching her. He watched both corners fearful someone would come. "You'd better lie down," he said. The Salvor nosed into a wave. They all clung together. He kept his hand on her. The water hissed over their feet. The Salvor climbed up, righted herself. They could see the door again. "You better lie down," Floyd mumbled. They tried to get in the door bumping against each other. "You better lie down," he said to Mamie. Touching her had made him feel tender towards her. He helped her to lie down in the bunk. She looked ghastly. He kept touching her as he covered her. He felt humiliated and at the same time exultant. He kept touching her.

"I better go," he said. Edith sat, her head in her hands, moaning.

"O, I'm scared. Don't leave us alone."

"I'll come back," he said. He backed out mumbling, watching Mamie on the lower bunk. Outside he ran straight down the deck shouting, raising his arms shouting against the storm. He felt gross, alive. He had touched her ignobly, when she was sick. He had been crafty. He was amazed and horror-stricken and at the same time exultant. He ran around the deck careening, gasping, being thrown against the doors, against the wall. He was going to find out if the boat was derelict. He dashed up the stairs to the top deck. He stuck his head up the stairway as the Captain had done and he saw there was a man in the pilot room. It looked like the clownish man who had waited on the Captain. He could only see the clownish wig. He watched a long time; the man didn't move but he thought he must be piloting the ship.

He crept down again. It was pitch dark. The Salvor plunged and pitched through a frightened darkness. The water swished over his ankles. He did not notice.

He wanted to find Mamie again. He was set on finding her. His baseness seemed vile but he was exultant. He started around and saw the Captain still standing bareheaded just where he had been before. He was soaking wet. Floyd tiptoed around him. He felt full of laughter. He kept shouting and it was as if he had not uttered a sound. He lifted his face and the spray struck straight against him.

He saw a frightened face against a window. It was Fletcher. Then quickly there was Hackman's beside it. The door opened. They pulled him in. "Lord, what is it?" Fletcher said, his eyes rolling. "This is the worst storm I've seen on this trip. . . ." "Oh hell, it ain't nothin," said Hackman. Floyd patted him on the back. "It's OK," he said, surprised to hear his own voice that sounded loud in the room shut in from the howling wind. Hackman looked at him. "Have you been drinking?" he said. "No," Floyd said. "No, I feel better though." "Why man, you're wet clean through," Fletcher said, "You'll catch your death."

Floyd stetched up his arms toward the ceiling. "Look at that height," Hackman said, "You ain't no dwarf." Floyd laughed. Fletcher leaned close to him. "You missed your supper," he said. "I snitched a sandwich for you." "Oh say," said Floyd, "that's great. I'm as hungry as a beast." And without self-consciousness he bit into the meat.

They were drinking. The bottle was on the table. Floyd took several swigs. Fletcher kept knocking against the chair, looking out the window. He was scared. "Say I bet the crew is drunk. They always are." Floyd felt important as if he had knowledge of the ship unknown to them. "The crew is roaring drunk, playing cards." "How do you know that?" Hackman said. "I been down there," Floyd said, munching. "I been down there. I saw them sitting without their shirts on playing cards."

"What's going to become of us? Fletcher said, taking a long draught from the bottle. "We're lost. Repent ye . . ." he said.

"Oh shut up," Hackman said.

Hackman pushed Floyd down at the table. "Let's have a game, you and me," he said. Floyd looked at him, wondering if he could play against him. Hackman pushed him into the seat and sat down and began shuffling the cards. Fletcher looked out the porthole, wandered around, falling against the chairs. The fog horn began to sound at regular intervals, about two minutes apart. The table tipped. They had to lean against the tip, put their hands over the cards to keep them from sliding off. Hackman dealt and kept looking at Floyd. Floyd tried to return it, but he began to be afraid. Hackman was hard and cold. The drunker he got the more diminished he became.

"Say," Floyd said, his own voice sounding far away. The sea made a strange thunder, the Salvor rocked and creaked. She seemed to be full of inward noises, rumblings, creakings. The fog horn sounded its long weird note.

"This ain't nothin'," Hackman shouted. "You ain't seen nothin'. I been in worse storms than this."

"Oh, we're lost," Fletcher moaned. "It's the day of judgment. Repent of your sins . . ."

"Listen to the old buzzard."

"Leave him alone," Floyd shouted, holding to his chair.

"What?" said Hackman.

"Say," Floyd said, "Say, Mamie and Edith are sure sick."

Hackman flipped over the cards and grinned, "So that's where you've been, Mama's angel." Floyd grinned back. He felt sick suddenly. "Our little boy ain't so pure after all," Hackman shouted. "Well," he said, leaning over, his tight evil face close, "Maybe you was laying down. . . ." His face cracked in a grin, his eye turned over in a wink, then his bloodshot eyes opened wide.

Floyd lifted his hands and put them on the table to steady himself. "I think I'm going to be sick," he said, but Hackman couldn't hear him. A huge report sounded, bringing them both to their feet. Fletcher went down on his knees.

"It ain't nothing," Hackman said. They sat down again. Hackman dealt the cards.

"I don't want to play," said Floyd.

"What," said Hackman. Floyd picked up the cards. The boat cracked and groaned under them.

"The Captain is stewed," said Floyd, shouting.

"Stewed," repeated Hackman. Floyd gripped his large hands on the table. He giggled. His tongue was dry. Every lurch of the boat sent a fear through him and a sickness. "The Captain is stewed. He's stewed. He's been standing for hours looking out. He's probably been washed over . . ."

"Not that bozo. Play," shouted Hackman.

"We're all going to die," Fletcher said, peering down at them trying to see.

"Go sit on your thumb," shouted Hackman. "Play. Your play."

"Repent . . ."

"Hell, for God's sake . . ."

Floyd got up screaming. "I don't want to play cards. I don't want to play. I don't want to play," he cried hysterically.

"Sit down," Hackman shouted. "This ain't nothin'. Don't lose your nerve. Sit down. It's your deal." He put the cards down with a flip.

Floyd picked them up and threw them. They parted and came down in a shower.

"It's getting your goat too," Hackman said sneering. The fog horn sounded so they could not speak. Hackman started picking up the cards.

Floyd sat down and buried his head in his arms. Hackman started playing solitaire. Fletcher was praying, kneeling on the floor. They could see his lips move but they couldn't hear a sound. Hackman kept putting his cards down with that little flip, flinging them down expertly.

"Say, Mamie is some girl, ain't she?" he said in a lull. He flipped Floyd's head playfully. Floyd sat up. "I expect you know, eh?" said Hackman, and Floyd had to watch that small red eye that reduced everything in the world, roll over in that obscene wink, in that terrible minute knowingness that made the world nothing.

Floyd laughed shrilly. "Yes, she is," he laughed. He couldn't stop.

"She's some jane," Hackman said. There was a terrible crash

again and the fog horn, then the thunder against them and the Salvor cracking, moaning, lifting again. The minute crack of the cards as Hackman slung them down sounded too. He snapped them down between his thumb and finger.

"I'm winning," he shouted. "I'm beating," he grinned.

"Who over?" shouted Floyd, laughing.

"I'm beating. I'm coming out on top. I'm winning."

"Who're you beating?" Floyd began to laugh crazily.

Hackman stopped playing and looked at him, then handed him the bottle. "This is getting on your nerves," he said.

Floyd drank. He felt better. "Say," he shouted, clinging to the table. He felt an awful boldness. "Say, let's go and find Mamie," he said. "They're scared. Let's bring 'em in here." He pushed himself up. The storm was howling, a long strange howl, and the thunder cracked as if under them. He got up.

"Sit down," said Hackman, and got up and pushed him straight down into the chair again.

"Don't do that," Floyd sputtered. "See? Don't do that."

"Don't get excited. You can't go anyplace in this ..." Hackman said.

"I want to see Mamie," Floyd said, flinging his arms out in a raw kind of boldness.

Hackman laughed. "Go easy . . ."

"Listen, Hackman," said Floyd, a terrible loud desire in him. "Listen, I bet you know a lot about women."

Hackman looked at him. "Well . . ."

"I bet you know a lot about women," Floyd said. He wanted to hear something violent, awful. He didn't know what he wanted to hear.

Hackman dealt out the cards again. The boat was lunging but the wind had gone down for the moment. They had to stop talking when the horn blew, Floyd felt sick, great waves of sickness went up him. Hackman began talking. Floyd listened to every word. A terrible lust came in Hackman to blast the boy's world, to belittle, reveal everything. Floyd broke out in a sweat listening. Sometimes Hackman was talking low, sometimes he had to shout over the storm. The foghorn kept blowing.

Hackman forgot the cards and leaned to the boy, almost touching his hands. He was opening everything and Floyd had to look in. They leaned towards each other. Sometimes the movement of the boat thrust them together, or apart. They drank from the same bottle, were rocked in the same world. Hackman moved around talking, talking, talking; cracking the world open showing its rottenness, leaving it spoiled, ravaged, violated. He put his arm over Floyd's shoulder, he shouted, he whispered. Floyd had never heard those words.

"I had a big hat on. The most gin I ever saw." The walls slanted weirdly. Hackman's face seemed to have been close before him for eons of time. Fletcher listened too. "I was sure embarrassed. Can you imagine?" Then he had to shout. Floyd listened, his eyes riveted on the evil, reduced face. He felt his face grow hot at the words.

"Let's go find Mamie," Hackman said. Floyd was looking at the man, laughing, looking up at him as he stood up. "I'll go get her. You're too unsteady."

"No, I'll go." Floyd got up.

"You stay . . ." Hackman said. They half-embraced each other.

Hackman opened the door. The darkness outside was thick, a cold swift wind blew in. All the cards flew off the table. Hackman closed the door behind him. Floyd peered out the window but could not see him. He might have gone out of the world completely.

8

Floyd and Fletcher sat in the close cabin. Fletcher sat quiet, still. Floyd watched him. It seemed a long time since Hackman had gone out the door. Perhaps he had stayed with Mamie, perhaps they weren't coming back. Floyd got up and went to the door. Fletcher, mumbling, came after, plucking at his sleeve. Floyd without knowing it struck out at the old man, knocking him back against the table. He opened the door. The wind struck him. Mountains rose on all sides, breaking against the ship. It was raining, a torrent of rain coming straight down, striking the water.

The thunder rolled round the sky, and down into the water. He clung to the door. The sound of the thunder sprang skyward in a shaft and fell down again, shafting down into the soundless water. A man seemed to be hallooing from some place under the water, it must have been at the end of the boat. There was a terrible scream that rang around them and ran, piercing the water, echoed from right, then left in the blackness, that rang far off, diminishing. It sounded again and again. Floyd clung to the door. He tried to get down the deck, but he had to creep and the force of the rain bent him low. The Salvor pitched and he clung to the wall hearing the screams, one right after another, pierce the fog, echo down and up. The Salvor went on and the scream shattered the storm again.

Then he heard words screaming. "Where am I? Where am I?" It was Fannie. "Oh God, where am I?" And the long piercing scream that seemed to be disembodied, coming from the sky, from the water, from the deeps on all sides, from the fog, from every throat on the boat.

Floyd saw no one. He clung to the window while the boat seemed about to turn over, to go under the mountainous wave. The water struck him. He clung with all his might and the scream of pain and terror went through him, echoing, resounding, struck in his own flesh.

Then he saw Mamie and Hackman crouching against the rain, running when the boat righted, stopping, clinging together and to the wall as she listed, then running. He tried to get back, to hold the door open. The water washed over them. The screaming and the fog horn and the sound of the rain striking all around made a terrible confusion.

At last they got inside the cabin and Floyd could hardly force the door closed against the wind. The rain drove straight in on them. Hackman helped and they got it closed. They could still hear the beat of the rain and the scream but it was muffled.

Mamie took off her coat. She was sopping wet. Her face was ghastly pale in her wet hair. "Hello," she said. Hackman was grinning. His clothes stuck to him. "Well I got her like I said I would," he said. Fletcher was sleeping with his head on the table.

Mamie came over to Floyd as if nothing had separated them. She put her arm around his neck and leaned against him. What had Hackman told her? "I need more gin," he thought. The screaming of Fannie had unnerved him. "Gee, that was awful," he said. "Fannie . . ." "Oh it's nothing," Mamie said, "She'll be all right by morning. She'll be all right." He looked at Hackman and tried to feel like he looked. He tried to pat the girl's hand that was on his breast. "Hello, Mamie," he said.

Hackman was grinning. He sat down. "Come here, Mamie," he said. Mamie went and sat on his knee and he began touching her. If made Floyd a little sick to have to watch them. The bottle of moon had been knocked off the table. He stooped down to get it. He took a drink, not looking at them. He passed them the bottle.

"Why don't you take off your blouse?" Hackman said. "Say," she said laughing. "Watch, I'm going to sit on *his* knee," she said, nodding towards Floyd. Floyd clutched his hands together. The boat slanted over and she had to steady herself and wait until it righted. A crack of thunder rolled around the sky. He could not hear what she said. Hackman was watching them, tilting his body toward them. Floyd clutched his hands together. Mamie sat down on his knee. He leaned away from her. He was smiling but he didn't know it.

She leaned back laughing against him, her face looking up below his, her eyes back. She took his large hand. She bent his fingers out, laughing. They were stiff; she could hardly bend them

171

out. Hackman was watching, his face tilted, lifting; sometimes he seemed below them, sometimes far above. And the face of the girl laughing below his shoulder turned, tilted, the black tooth showing, her eyes rolled back.

She unbent his hand and put it on her. His hand was stiff. He withdrew himself from it. He was smiling. She was convulsed with laughter. Hackman was laughing far above them now, looking down laughing. There was a crash of thunder and then a long scream. Mamie seemed to be saying something but he couldn't hear her even though he saw her mouth with the black tooth close to his face, slightly below on his breast. Hackman got up and stood beside them, laughing. They were both laughing.

Floyd thought he was laughing too. He tried to laugh. He couldn't hear what they were saying. The sweat stood out on him.

The boat lurched half over. Mamie was thrown from his lap and he sprawled out on the floor. He heard that laughter now. He could not tell from where. He was confused. The walls were slanting. He did not know for a moment how to get up. He tried to get up. Something terrible was happening. . . . Then he saw Mamie and Hackman, what they were doing. He looked at them because he could see nothing else in the room. He stood against the wall, wringing his hands together, his mouth open. He saw what they were doing. He saw them distinctly, as if something had exploded sharply. He stood looking at them. He saw them clearly, what they were doing. It seared into his mind. He stood leaning toward them. He felt the flesh of his own hands, one on the other. He saw them clearly.

He did not know he was sobbing. He did not know that he went out of the room. He did not know he was on the deck with the water washing over him, knocking him down. He was still seeing them seared on his brain colossally. He got up and the water and wind struck him down, blow after blow. He began to cry wildly, feeling along the darkened deck. It rose abrupt before him so he had to crawl up and then it sank, so in terror he had to crawl back.

The thunder sounded straight around the sky. A man hallooed from somewhere, the sound flew up then as if shot, fell waterwards and a muffled echo came up like a man drowning far below on the bottom. The pilot bell rang and bells out of the storm answered and rang faintly as if an unseen pilot were answering. The horn bellowed as it shot like a cannon through the sky, forward and above. The vast shell seemed alive with bellowings.

The whole world seemed answering in anguish, struck in anguish on a million surfaces, that shook and bloomed on strange convexities. He could see nothing. He clung to the floor of the deck on his hands and knees, sobbing. There was this shock and echo in a terrible elemental world. He felt danger and death and horror. Everything that was spoken, of every image of action, seemed to resound endlessly, echo and reecho in endless reverberations. He saw the awful image of the man and woman reechoing in all his fibers.

He clung to the bare floor while the water rose mountainous falling over him. He clung with his huge head hanging down.

Crawling, climbing up the deck, digging in his nails he got to his cabin. He got in. He crawled dressed into his bunk.

9

He slept exhausted. He wept in his sleep. He saw the boat going through the storm with its drunken, lost crew. He saw Mamie and Edith and Hackman and Fletcher and he wept sleeping.

Then it seemed he rode an invisible steed whose movement was familiar to him, spray came from the nostrils and for hoofs there was the vital form and compulsion of water. All night the steel lifted him and surged him until his blood was rocked and roused.

He saw the foul crew, the sick girls, Hackman suffering his own reduction, and Fletcher touching only ghosts and wraiths. And a dream was cast over it all. The body of water seemed in his dream to be the unformed stuff of the world, its invisible body, and they were all lifted upon it. It plunged beneath, lifting all that was broken and foul with that great muscular thrust, lifting them all upon its great whorls into a splendid dream.

And the boat went on and their dreams reflected and surrounded them as the water reflected and carried the Salvor, and their own forms were reflected in convexity and concavity and echoed and reechoed until there was an intricacy of meaning, and a profundity in the image that was amazing. What had been flat and stale only seemed so then, for the dream repeated it endlessly, reechoing and deepening what had been flat, repeating and enriching what had been stale.

In his dream he was enamored of it all, and had courage for undreamed of voyages. The boat went on through a mythical sea, fantastic and real.

10

The next morning the sun struck out of the cloud, the sea ran swiftly dark, then there was the swift striking of light over the swooning underworld darkness. Floyd stood on the upper deck watching the swift stroke of light, and then the quick swooning darkness passing over.

No one came on deck. He had it all to himself. To his surprise he found they were only a few hours from San Francisco. He had eaten breakfast with the Captain and that is all they talked about, how they had almost miraculously kept their course in the storm. The Captain looked quite hale as if he would not even know the man who had stood entranced on the deck throughout the night.

Floyd stood on the deck ready to land. Nothing would ever be the same again. Something had happened. There was a certain faint form and ease to his body as he stood watching, hearing the Captain say, "We haven't been ten miles from shore the whole voyage. . . ."

The land lay to the right—static, visible.

The Horse

They were driving down from San Francisco to the ranch, below the Sierras, for the birth of a horse. The big "Twelve" went swiftly through the countryside. It was early Spring and the fields past which they sped were sprouting.

Mercedes rode in the front seat with her brother. The mother and grandmother sat in the back. They had crossed on the ferry and were driving through the rich lowlands that had just been planted. The almonds were in bloom. Soon they would be through the lowlands, and then would come the hills which rolled gently toward the Sierras. This land everywhere bore the mark of the early monks, of Sutter, of the rush for gold.

"We'll make it by eight," Eugene shouted back to his mother. "That's faster than Dad's ever done!"

"Good. Good, Eugene," Mrs. Willit called. The two seemed to get a certain pleasure from the speeding car, but Mercedes hated it, and the grandmother prayed to the saints that the ride would soon be over.

"Better enjoy yourself, Mercedes," Eugene said with an evil grin. "This is your last play day. You'll soon be married."

"I won't be," she said sullenly, her hate gleaming from her as she looked at his sleak head, his bland face. "Mama, make him quit."

"Eugene, Eugene!" Mrs. Willit called laughingly, "don't tease your sister." But she was really pleased, amused.

"Tch. Tch," clucked the grandmother, wrapped in her shawl, her thin shoulders coming to a point. "I hope we aren't too late," she said in her thin, sudden voice.

"We won't be," Eugene said patronizingly over his shoulder. "Don't worry, Granny. . . ."

"What do you know about it," shouted the old lady shrilly. "Be still!" she cried at him in a fury. That always made him nervous, suddenly shrilling from her dark world, or reaching out dry electric hands to touch him. She went on talking. "That Mallard, that groom knows nothing of horses. The old goat. Nothing. I hope we're not too late. She's *my* mare. Your father must remember that she's my mare and I prize her." No one paid any attention.

Mrs. Willit sat up, feeling very lovely. It was a pity there was no one to see her. These expeditions to her husband's breeding ranch annoyed her. She felt uneasy outside her social world—and a bit terrified. She felt like just nothing when she was unseen, uncreated by the swift mechanical pressure of her world. It was Saturday. She determined that she and Eugene would come back Sunday anyway.

Her rouged, mask-like dollface was unchanged by any meditation or reflection from the Spring country through which they traveled with such speed. It maintained itself in its rigidity. She would not have come at all without her son Eugene, who unceasingly held up the mirror to her vanity. Within her setting she felt very secure, with a distinction of blood from her mother— the old line of D'Harencourts—and of money from her husband. The D'Harencourts had, very early in the history of California, settled just north of San Francisco. The land had been bountiful and they had lived in abundance. She, the only daughter, had married a promising engineer who now, by his canniness and Yankee wit, with the aid of her dowry, had more than tripled her fortune. In one generation they had become fabulously rich, and she had been swiftly lifted from the earth that bred the old lady her mother into an artificial, rapidly changing world ornate with speed and power.

From the marriage had come Eugene and Mercedes, but Mrs. Willit had never quite believed they were her children. She was always a little terrified to think of birth. In Eugene, however, she found an ally in her world. He was like a leading man, echoing and enlarging her whims, playing to her caprices. But Mercedes was a stranger, fractious, willful and impossible. The problem of Mercedes made Mrs. Willit feel very wistful, very helpless, "nervous." "My nerves are being wrecked by that child," she would say, going dramatically off to bed. But the girl, adamant, flew into rages and swore roundly at them all.

The trouble was that she would not marry. She was at the proper age. It was time, there was a man approved by the family and their set. But she would not do it.

Mrs. Willit craftily watched her sitting in the front seat, her face, one side of it, set firmly. The mother determined that she would come back with a docile daughter. It irritated her beyond anything to see the absurd way Mercedes wore her hat. And the way the girl refused to fill out was maddening: her long slim legs, the mannish walk, the gangliness that persisted although she was eighteen. "She doesn't take after me," Mrs. Willit would say, remembering herself as a young girl, round and desirable.

She would feel much younger when Mercedes was off her hands. She had gotten so she could not bear the girl's eyes on her, nor her presence in a room. She would fly at her, "Why don't you put on some rouge? What do you want to do? What haven't I done for you. I went down into the valley of the shadow to give you birth. I was sick for years after. I am still frail. Look at my poor body. You have no gratitude, no love. This is for your own good." Then she would put on her wolf tenderness, "I want only the best for my baby. This marriage is for your good, my darling. Trust your mother who loves you." Then the girl standing there would be too much and Mrs. Willit would fly into a tantrum, and the slim awkward pale girl would stand without moving, without seeing, until the mother had exhausted herself and her son would support her wilting body to the couch.

"It's the way she looks at me that makes me nervous," Mrs. Willit decided, keeping her eye furtively on the back of the girl and on the side face.

Mercedes was very Latin in appearance, with wide dark eyes that were always keen and wide on the surface but at the back unseeing. The grandmother had such a look, too. It made people uneasy as if they were being spied upon, discovered.

Looking at her, Mrs. Willit itched with a terrible rage to have at her; she could not help it. "I wish you would tell me, Mercedes, what there is about Michael you object to."

"Yes," said Eugene, slowing down as they passed through a village, "you might at least say when we've taken all the trouble to interest him in you. I don't know why the devil he wants to marry you, the way you insult him."

Mercedes fidgeted as if she were being cruelly prodded and could not escape. Eugene looked brightly down at her. She was his prey. He could not have lived without her to prey upon.

"Won't you tell mama what it is?" Mrs. Willi said. She could wear away anything.

"Are you in love with someone else?" asked Eugene. "Have you a secret romance? Maybe she has a secret romance," he shouted to the back seat, jutting the car around a curve. Mrs. Willit laughed.

They decided to stop at a tea room for a bite to eat. It was still too chilly to eat outside, so they went in. Mercedes sat down beside her grandmother. The old lady reached out and suddenly patted the girl's hand with her thin one that was like a monkey's, full of queer vitality.

"Well, this is your last vacation," Eugene said, sitting down, moving up his chair, thrusting his bland, grinning face close to her, "my little sister." He ironically stroked her arm, winking at his mother, who laughed. Mercedes went a little white. She often flew into a passion and struck out at him.

Mrs. Willit fluttered the menu, laughing, looking about for admiration, but the tea room was almost empty. Only two women sat at the far corner, and a woman and child near by. Eugene kept chattering, looking at his mother brightly. Mrs. D'Harencourt sat tight in her shawl looking as if she had been hewn out of seasoned wood. "Don't you want to take off your shawl, Mama?" said Mrs. Willit as if moved by her own thoughtfulness. She couldn't bear going around with the old lady in that shawl. At the ranch house she was rather proud of her mother and the old world atmosphere, the mystery of old days, the Spanish life, but in *her* world the old lady with her shawl was impossible. "No, I don't want to take off my shawl," the old lady mimicked.

Mercedes sat unseeing, looking out for barbs, willful. The old lady touched her again delicately as if calling her back, her seared hand like a dying leaf that scraped on the girl's hand.

"What are you going to eat?" she said, smiling into the startled face uplifted at her touch.

"I don't want anything to eat," said Mercedes, sullenly sinking away again.

"Tch. Tch," clucked the old lady, her mouth puckered like a scar.

"Oh, I suppose not," Mrs. Willit said petulantly. "Nothing suits her. She wants something special—don't you?"

"Yes," Mercedes answered looking down stubbornly at her hands. "Yes, I do."

"Of course," her mother sneered. "You're too good for this world." Then suddenly, in a torrent, "I'll be glad when you're married. When the marriage is over and you're off my hands forever, I'll be glad."

Mercedes flinched as if she had been struck. "I'll be glad too," Eugene said looking at her, knowing how she squirmed under his look, how it was a torture to her. He would be glad to see her broken in.

"I'll be glad," Mrs. Willit continued cruelly. Her devouring little eyes narrowed. She sighed for herself. "Mama, do you know what is the matter with the girl?"

"Leave her alone," the old lady replied cryptically. "Leave her alone."

But Eugene could not. He had a nervous lust for scenes and emotional violence, as if he could not feel anything but the sharpest cruelty. "Michael is going to be the biggest architect in the city. You mark my words."

"Is he a builder?" the grandmother asked.

"Yes, an architect, builder—makes buildings," Eugene said elaborately. He loved to explain things to the old lady as if she were growing childish.

"I understand," she said ironically, "I wasn't born yesterday."

But he must go on explaining. "He built the big Exchange

178

building. It's going to mean something. . . ."

"Think of that, Mercedes. You will travel. You will have fame. You will go with the best people."

The girl sat white-lipped, turning her head as if trying to escape from them, but they were upon her like flies upon a wound.

Her mother ordered a salad for her but she would not eat. Eugene ironically passed her the crackers. "Will my lady have a cracker?" he said. Mrs. Willit giggled like a girl.

Mercedes suddenly hit the dish with her upflung hand and it crashed to the floor.

"Mercedes!" cried Mrs. Willit, half-rising in her chair.

"I'll be damned," Eugene was red with rage. "You ought to be spanked for that."

She sat looking at her plate, all the color draining from her face. Her grandmother kept right on eating as if nothing had happened.

"An accident," Mrs. Willit was saying to the waitress. "So stupid."

Mrs. D'Harencourt looked up comically, her sharp eyes shifting brightly from one to the other as if she knew all about them.

"I'll not have it," Mrs. Willit was saying in an undertone, pretending to eat, while the two women in the corner were looking at them. "This is too much."

"Be your age," said Eugene. "What the devil. She ought to be spanked, Mama."

The girl sat, refusing to eat.

"Everyone is noticing," her mother said nervously and began to talk brightly. The old lady's eyes glistened as if she were secretly laughing.

"Eat!" Mrs. Willit said savagely, going slightly mad against the silence of the girl. "Eat!" she hissed.

"I won't," Mercedes said. "I won't," she said without moving, looking down at her hands folded in her lap. And her mother, infuriated, kicked her as hard as she could under the table with her sharp, smart little shoe. The girl paled but did not move. For a moment she felt as if the sap of her life were running from her; all her blood went low in her like a swoon, as if she had suddenly been killed. She could not see the room at all but she did not move. Automatically, she even picked up her fork, but the tears welled suddenly and she got up, bumping blindly against the chairs, and went out.

She wanted to go away, but there was no place to go, so she stood by the car. She felt stupid standing there but she did not know what else to do; she stood there waiting for her own capture. They came out very soon, the old lady first, coming sharply out the door, her quick eyes searching for the girl, seeing her and marking her.

Mrs. Willit came out in a fine rage, her bracelets clanking as she pulled her gloves over her ringed fingers. She would not speak. She got into the car, looking very injured, very martyred. The old lady, like a marmoset, scrambled into the car, her thin shank showing as she mounted. Mercedes got in beside her instead of in the front seat. She wanted to be close to her grandmother. They did not touch each other, there was not even much speech between them, but the grandmother had a sharp way of contacting things outside herself, of suddenly becoming aware. She astonished and bewildered them with this sharp contact she could magically make with them all through the terrible crusts of their little deaths, her sharp-edged hands suddenly on their shoulders, on their hands; her penetrating voice poignant in the air, touching them with some gnarled mystery of her personality.

She kept sniffing as she did when she was angry, sitting between the mother and daughter, sniffing crazily. Mrs. Willit sat very straight and injured, pouting.

Eugene came out, scowling, ready to conciliate his mother. "You better come and sit with me, Mama," he said.

"No," she said. "No, I guess I'm not wanted anywhere," and she began to weep very delicately.

The old lady simply snorted, astonishing them all, then she turned to look intimately at Mercedes, and she seemed to be laughing and nodding to her, her thin satiric brows turned up. The old lady and the young girl were somehow alike, the same thinly lifted brows, the same skeleton, and a gangliness and strength as if the girl had been thrown forward with some ancient thrust, with a vitality and a hunger hard to fulfill.

As they got out into the road and picked up speed, Mrs. Willit began one of her long nervous harangues. They were like a madness, going on endlessly; the words went on and on. "Mercedes, you have no right . . . I've done everything, everything . . . why aren't you like other girls?" Followed a list of nice girls. She spoke rapidly, her fine, blasted, nervous face rather frail and lovely, her slightly whining voice lifting and falling. The evening came down and the swift car shot through the twilight and the voice went on and on, and the mask-like dollface in the gloaming light was a bitter thing. Mercedes was afraid to look. Her mother was like a corpse with the meaningless face floating on the twilight.

Now they had reached the hills and the car shot along, over the gradual rise and fall in the ground. Trees stood unexpectedly sharp against the darkening sky. "Why, why? What have I done to deserve such a daughter? Why? Why?" The voice went on.

The grandmother, like an old bird with one eye closed, was winking and ironically watching her daughter out of her open eye. She seemed at one moment to be sleeping like a bird, and then again in the tricky light she looked forever awake, winking slyly, nodding, wrinkling with laughter.

"I've done everything for you. Everything. You won't dress properly. I've done everything. No one can blame me. What more could I have done? What?"

No one answered. But she would not have heard if all the undone things had chorused at once.

They left Sacramento and went through the flatlands and then suddenly into the hills, through the orchards, coming upon the wild mountainous night. Eugene drove recklessly, plunging the car along the road with his deft skill that had something vicious in it. They had left the sea-tanged air, the phosphorescent dusk of the lowlands, and were entering the somewhat frightening night of the low mountains.

Mercedes could not see her mother now, but heard the low whine beating against her, trying to edge into her, beat away her resistance, to make an opening so that she might be destroyed. She pressed away against the window. She looked out into the country. She felt her grandmother might be an intimate of the country, that within the old lady might be stored vast knowledge and intimacy of which she only dreamed. But she knew she could never ferret that knowingness out from the hard nut-like shell of the old lady, They were removed from each other with only this swift contact that was more intimate than speech. She saw her grandmother look out at the dark country, and felt she would know what the darkened orchards would bear in their time, know the labor, how the asparagus was planted, and the rice; that she came out of this land dream and grew from some might and definite soil.

She stole a glance at her brother, his sleek head rounding on itself, his bland face turned straight ahead, blank, mesmerized with speed; and her mother, turning in upon herself, rootless, derelict and frightened, exhausted with her own activity that knew no source, admitted none, and had no renewal in mystery. What nourished one like the grandmother so that the sap came up in her gnarled limbs from a deep source, rooting her in peace?

She thought she could not bear to go so swiftly and insentiently over the country. She wanted to scream for them to stop, to let her out. But she knew they would not stop and that she could not be let out. "I won't come back with them," she thought cunningly. "Now I've got away, I'll stay away. I won't come back." It had only suddenly occured to her, but she was set in that determination instantly. She did not know what she would do, but she would not go back to the city. she would stay at the ranch.

She set herself in that determination and lapsed away, letting them go through the night-drenched country. The movement was soothing, too, lulling the terrible anxiety that sat like a disease in her body in the city. She saw the mountains of the Sierras range along the sky. The land rose and rocked like a crystallized sea around them. Looking out, the thickness of the night sometimes rose into the thickness of the land—close, frightening, and there seemed to be ghosts of men long dead, ghosts of dreams forgotten, hopes violated, lost.

The car swerved sharply away from the highway and Mercedes opened her eyes wide, feeling that they were coming back again to the world of little things. Her mother had long ceased her wail. There had been nothing but the sound of the car as it sped through the darkness, thrusting its way through its own projected light. Now they turned off the highway, into the grove of live oaks; the sky disappeared as the branches closed thick above them. The headlight fell weirdly on ancient trunks and intertwined boughs. And now the road turned again, into the ranch road, palms flanking it, the sky open above. And then the lights fell on the low ranch house of rough hewn logs that had been designed by Michael. The car stopped.

They could scarcely move, or regain themselves. Only the grandmother came instantly out of her sleep, like an animal, alert at the stopping of the car. And she prodded them, trying to get out. She hated cars and always got out as soon as she could. She prodded Mercedes with her sharp knees and hands, trying to get past her. The lights went on along the porches and Mallard and McClaren, the head grooms, came from the stable. The houses for the help were lighted up and people stood in the dark, unseen, but their presences vivid in the mountain night. The horses could be heard in the stable, stamping, whinnying as they sensed the excitement of the arrival. Under the porch lights, Wizzy, the old woman who cooked and had been with Mrs. D'Harencourt for many years, stood peering from under her hand. Mercedes quickly followed her grandmother out of the car. She didn't look, but she knew the mountains were near. The sharp cutting air was against her and in her nostrils. The luminous night that carried the sound of voices clearly, and the scent of the sleeping orchards, was all about them. She walked along beside her grandmother and they went into the house, the old lady speaking in Spanish to Wizzy, the two speaking clearly together. Mrs. Willit came behind, talking to Mallard. McClaren did not come into the house. Mallard was the head groom, he bullied everyone on the place, but he was a good trainer—or so Mr. Willit believed.

Mercedes could hear her mother talking steadily, laughing, enjoying her own arrival. Eugene, too, was joking, laughing, flinging up his head nervously as he followed his mother, echoing her words.

A fire burned in the long low room that was the heart of the house. Mrs. Willit went to the couch, laying off her wraps in flattering fatigue. Mallard stood back away from the lamps, half in darkness, watching her. She knew he watched her. He was very attractive to her, the only reason she could bear being at the ranch. She was flattered by the subtle, insinuating, half-bullying way he looked at her. Mercedes and the grandmother hated the man. He was a mechanic really, without the delicate, sensuous contact of the men Mrs. D'Harencourt had at the old place. She held her skirts away from him and refused to sit down at all in the room. She and Mercedes stood, accepting a little of the heat from the fireplace. But they ignored Mallard, and he detested them powerfully, feeling the bitterly aristocratic old lady ignoring him so completely, and the vague girl shying away from him. Mrs. D'Harencourt considered him an insolent, democratic bully, with that "I'm as good as you are" air that she couldn't stand.

But he was saying that the mare's time had not come yet.

"I hope you are taking the best of care of her," the old lady said. "She's one of my best horses."

"She's getting the best of care," Mallard said.

Mrs. D'Harencourt's eyes glistened, thinking of her mare, but she shrugged and said in Spanish, "The old goat knows nothing. The devil have him."

Mallard flushed, not understanding, but knowing she spoke of him. Mrs. Willit was lying down on the couch. Mallard always tempted her to be frail. She liked his gross, bullying desire beneath his words as he answered her questions about the horses and the ranch. Mallard gave attention, but he also looked at Mercedes. He hated her with a fine pang that went through him. "She thinks she's better than I am," he thought, "she and the grandmother," and he would have liked to bring them down.

"Well, good night," he said. "I'll take you around and show you the horses in the morning."

"Good night, Mallard," Mrs. Willit said, looking up at him with her nervous coyness. He grinned down at her boldly. Eugene followed him to the door.

"I'm going to bed," said the old lady, and started out, her thin-shawled body holding out against everything in the room, not mixing, but single and almost awful. She seemed fierce as she walked through the fireglow. Mercedes followed her, not wanting her to be out of sight, yearning toward the wizened old lady who was so rooted, with such a terrible identity.

"I'm going too, mother," she said.

Mrs. Willit's hands went out, trying to lay hold of her. "But my dear, I wanted to talk to you. I never get to see you. No one pays any attention to my ideas, to my wants. I never get to talk to anyone. You all avoid me. I'm only your mother."

183

Mercedes stopped in the doorway. The old lady plodded on into the hall, up the stairs, as if she walked in another time and place. Mercedes watched, listening to her mother.

"I wanted to talk to you, advise you. I am older, Mercedes, whatever you may think. I am older, and your mother, and I can advise you from my experience."

Mercedes looked at the massaged face in the firelight. She knew her mother had nothing that she would want. She stood waiting to be released. Her mother began to cry. "I don't see why you want to be so difficult, why you want to oppose everything. We are living in the world; there are things we have to do. You can't ignore the world."

Mercedes didn't speak. She waited. She wanted to be gone forever from them.

Eugene came back into the room. Then Mrs. Willit forgot Mercedes and felt how delicate, how abused she was. A sensuous feeling of self-pity was on her like the fireglow, and the tears ran luxuriously down her face.

Then the girl knew that she was released. When her mother turned inward in self-pity, Mercedes knew that she was no longer remembered.

Eugene gave a cry, "Oh, Mama," and he knelt beside her, turning a dramatic eye on Mercedes. "See what you do to poor Mama," he said.

Mercedes could see her grandmother just turning around the curve of the stairs going slowly but without fatigue or weakness, so she followed. She never wanted to see them again.

Eugene knelt beside his weeping mother, soothing her as if he were her lover. His mother's scenes and tears moved him voluptuously. He loved her almost passionately because of her erotic sense of herself, so precious, so fragile, never opening to any word or gesture. She always kept him in a nervous state of excitement that had become necessary to him like a drug. He stroked her hand, feeling her white nervous flesh that seemed to crinkle like an electrified substance. He almost wept with her. They forgot what they were weeping about.

Mercedes undressed slowly. She could hear her grandmother moving in the next room. She leaned against the wall, hearing the old lady walk about in the room talking to herself in a patois no one understood. She heard the low mutter of the Ave Marias, then a low spinning sound that rose, slowly, until there was a kind of hum not like a human voice, but like some chant of an insect coming from the body in some peculiar way. The girl leaned against the wall, listening. She heard the bed creak as the old lady got into it.

When she opened her window, she saw the night standing out like a presence. For a moment she stood, gazing out, then she spun around and jumped into bed, covering her head, and she went to sleep instantly.

She wakened in a fright, a shock of terror going through her as if the fright had entered her before it had vibrated through her sleep and wakened her. It was a terrible bellow, a cry that struck her and went in a ripple through her body. At first she was so absorbed in that scream in her body that it did not occur to her that it came from without, then she realized that it came from outside the house, and at the same time she heard running on the stairs.

Fearfully she looked out and could at first see nothing but the darkness, the crystal dark between the sky and earth, growing denser toward the earth, lifting toward the stars that let a faint eerie light fall downward. It was from the earth darkness that the high whinnying came. She heard it now, the scream of a horse in pain.

She heard her mother's voice down in the yard, excited, taking on importance from the very event. She felt them hurry across the yard through the dark. Then a floodlight was turned on over the stable, making a pool of light below the door. She saw her grandmother moving swiftly, straight into the heart of the scene, going like a meteor of darkness across the light. Then she saw her mother, talking to Mallard, the hard, bright voice coming up. Mrs. Willit did not go into the stable, but stood looking into the black, gaping door, peering in. Eugene ran in and out of the light, terribly excited. Mallard came and went, Mrs. Willit always looking at him, waiting for him to look at her.

The bright spot of light made the darkness impenetrable outside, and Mrs. Willit seemed to stand within that hard kernel, shut up tight. Mercedes stood at the window looking down on the brightly lit pool, seeing them all move in their own image, only the grandmother moving straight to the birth, contacting it almost fiercely. The girl brooded above, looking out the window, pressed close, looking down at all she knew of the visible world, looking through the glass of herself she could not break. She felt that she could shout and they would not hear, that she could die there behind the glass and they would not know it.

The cries of the horse continued, going straight through her body, making her shudder. "Birth," she kept saying, and she could not get beyond it. What it was she could not tell, but the shudders kept going down her body with each cry and she pressed against the closed window, looking down at the bright forms moving suddenly in the circle, disappearing off the edge, and her mother going into no darkness, standing distraught always in the hard kernel of light.

At last the crying ceased and then she saw her grandmother come out, walk directly through the light, past Mrs. Willit, and into the house. Then she heard her coming up the stairs and she ran to the door, looking out, frightened.

"Is it all over, Granny?" she asked, seeing the old lady as she appeared above the stairs.

"Yes," she answered, chuckling. "Yes, a fine birth. Oh, a beauty. He's a beauty. Beautiful. Beautiful," she said. "Go back to bed my girl. What do you know yet of birth? Go back to bed." And in passing, she slapped her roundly on the thigh. "A beauty," she repeated, going past, into her own room. "A beauty, a fine birth. A beauty. . . ."

Mercedes went back to the window. The light was still on. Mallard stood talking to Mrs. Willit who looked at him coquettishly in a way that seemed ridiculous beside the black maw of the night and the stable that held birth.

She went back to bed. All she wanted was sleep. The thought of her mother wearied her; the thought of the house, of the world, wearied her beyond endurance. She went to sleep hearing the thin penetrating sound of her mother's voice spinning out brittle in the darkness.

The next morning a stillness hung over the ranch. Mrs. Willit and Eugene did not get up. Mrs. D'Harencourt sometimes slept half the day when she did not care for what was being done. She had gotten up early and gone to look at her mare and the new colt, then she had gone back to bed. So Mercedes ate breakfast alone, Wizzy silently setting it out for her. Afterward, she stepped out the door into the early pale sunlight. The ranch lay just below the Sierras where the land curved, protecting the ancient orchards. The almond blooming was about over and the prunes were a froth of blossom. The land lay in a breaking sea over the horizon and the air was heady with perfume. It was like a madness, the wave of breaking blossom that rose and surged and broke all about her in blinding light. The ground was damp from the February rains and she knew what flowers would be close to the ground, those small blossoms of Persephone coming out of the black tomb of the earth. She started across the yard with the thought of finding them, but Mallard came from the stable and boldly accosted her, standing in front of her so that she had to stop.

"Well," he said in that obnoxious heartiness he had, which he thought was irresistible to women, "how are you this morning? You seem to be the only one up yet."

She looked at him rather insolently. "Let me by," she said.

He frowned; it was incomprehensible to him that he would not

186

be attractive to a woman. Yet he was slightly afraid of her.

"Say," he said, "can't we be friends?"

She looked at his clean-shaven face, so hearty and empty, so convinced of its desirable maleness. She wanted to strike him as she wanted to strike everything. They both started to walk toward the stable.

"We had a new arrival last night," he said. "Want to see him?"

She did not answer, but went with him automatically into the dark interior of the stable. They went between the stalls. The horses moved nervously, watching them. Then they stopped in the darkness and it was a moment before she saw the newborn colt lying on the hay. She stood looking down at the still curled form with that sullen expression she habitually had; then her face brightened, her lips parted. She leaned over, but she did not put her hands on him, she just bent over in wonder, seeing the shining, curling form.

Mallard kept snapping his suspenders and looking at her.

She saw the newborn colt, fresh from the womb, curled on the new hay. His coat was a flame, close curled over him, and he lay with his nose on his long forelegs, his thin serpent-like neck curved down. He was so weirdly proportioned and so new; she looked and looked at him as if he had come out of another world. She forgot her hatred for Mallard, turning to him, her eyes wide, startled. "When was he born?" she asked, just to be told, for she had not forgotten the cries in the night wrenching through her. She wanted to lie down beside him and curl up in the curve of sleep, in that fiery tenderness that was on him.

"Can I touch him?" she said.

Mallard was looking at her. She was, suddenly, like a woman in love. He thought any excitement in a woman was amorous. He watched her, half laughing desire on his face.

"Can I touch him?" she cried in her husky, foreign voice. "Can I touch him, really?" she said, with her hands out, still looking at Mallard.

"Sure," he said, laughing, looking down at her possessively, seeing her so suddenly vulnerable.

She squatted down like a child on her long haunches, close to the hairy body. She put out her hands and touched his neck. Mallard had expected her to fondle the colt as he had seen women do newly born things, but she touched him only with her finger tips, almost fearfully, and he could hear her breathing and feel the palpitant wonder of her body squatting there so strangely back on her haunches like a child.

She was in pure wonder touching the rounding long curve of the haunches, and the down curving neck and the rear legs where they stuck out, as if the colt had not got the location yet of all his body and had left his legs out. She saw the little ebony hooves so miraculous, and only part of his head—for he lay with it down on his forelegs. She could not see if his nose had a mark of lightning like his mother. She put her palm then on his side quite firmly, the flat of her hand, and a shiver went through him and he lifted his long head to look at her with his huge startled eyes. She gazed straight into them, trembling, and felt the gigantic heart striking against her hand. He struggled, trying to rise, and Mercedes started back at his quick strangeness and the sudden movement of the alien animal body. A pang of fear went through her. But the colt could not locate his gangly legs, and so sank down, half turning and lifting his neck to look at her. She was startled by his eyes so large and soft, looking at her and not knowing what she was. They were like eyes within herself, looking and not knowing. There was a touch of wildness in them too, and in his testy body a touch-me-not wildness so that he shied and trembled even at her light touch, and his skin rippled along and drew away from her hand.

But Mallard put his blunt red hand on the colt, holding him down insensible and firmly. The colt trembled and reared back his head, and his lip trembled up in a snarl, his ludicrous big ears turning back.

The girl saw his whole naive disproportion, and of what a ludicrous assortment of parts he was made. She couldn't bear to leave him.

"Don't put your hand on him like that," she said to Mallard.

"Oh, that's all right. He'll have to get used to it," Mallard laughed.

"He doesn't have to," she said, the old sullenness shadowing her face. "He doesn't have to like it."

"Colts have to be broken—like everything else," Mallard said. He was idly beating the stall wall with a mop stick.

"Then everything has to be broken?"

"Well, colts do," he said. "Your father wants this colt to be something, and his schooling will start right away."

"Right away?" she said. "How will it start?"

"Well, we'll just lead him to his mother for the first meal so that he'll think leading is just as natural as eating."

"Oh. And what else?"

"There's a lot to it," Mallard said. He was glad to have her asking questions of him. "Then we'll break him in, depending on whether your father wants him for a racer or a saddle horse. But he's got to do what he's told."

"Oh," she said. "What else?'

"Well," answered Mallard, in an off-hand way, "I guess he'll have about the same education you had—with all the trimmings."

"What?" Her eyes widened, thinking of him being trained for

188

certain reasons, apparently as she was. "What? Tell me what they do."

Mallard was amused and flattered, thinking she did not really want to know, but only to flatter and draw him out.

"When it comes to its mother," he said expansively, "we'll put a soft bandage around his rumps, below the tail, and run the loose ends between his legs so they can be held at his neck. If he shows any kick about being led, we pull the bandage and he thinks he's being pushed from the rear. Pretty clever, isn't it?"

She shivered. "And then?"

"Then he has a heavier bandage around the middle; a make-believe saddle girth, when he gets to scampering around. Then when he's used to that, he's fitted with a lightweight halter. This is his kindergarten. Then he's put in an enclosure, especially built with rounded planks so that he can't hurt himself, and a real saddle—light, of course—is put on him. After that he's given a rider, a stableboy at first, and then the halter is replaced by a bridle. He graduates from high school, you might say! Then he's breezed."

"Breezed?" she repeated.

"That means we give him a real sprint to see how fast he can go."

"Oh, I see," she said.

"We know then just what he can do; whether he'll be a racer or a breeder. You might call this his coming-out party," he said laughing.

Mercedes laughed bitterly.

"You can see if they're paddlers or climbers; what kind of stride and action they've got."

"If they're good, they go to college, I suppose," she said ironically. "And if they're breeders, they marry." There was a bitter darkness on her face.

"Sure, that's it. Then the racers are taken and trained at the post; hour after hour they're taken to the barrier until they get used to it."

"Don't any of them ever rebel?" she asked.

"Sure they do. Horses are just like people. There's every kind. Some of them break clean at the barrier the first time and keep it up the rest of their careers. Others always cut up. Sometimes they even run the wrong way of the track and there's nothing you can do about it."

"They run the wrong way of the track?"

"Sure."

"Have you got any here that run the wrong way?"

"No. Your father doesn't keep them. Sometimes he sends one who has good form to the city for the women—for a saddle horse."

My father doesn't keep them," she repeated. "No, I suppose he doesn't. He was the kind who broke clean the first time at the barrier—and has been winning races ever since. Thanks a lot," she said, saluting him with an odd, mannish gesture.

He stood watching her go toward the light that came in the stable door. She strode with a peculiar gangliness, a boyish swing, and yet with a strength and wildness to her. Seeing her, he was perplexed. Men did not know how to covet her wildness nor prize her strangeness.

She sat down behind the pump, where she would not be seen, to watch for Mallard to leave the stable so that she could go in and look at the colt again. But he did not come out, and she got cold sitting on the ground.

She got up and went slowly toward the house. She heard the clatter of dishes and knew that Wizzy must be cooking her mother's breakfast.

Eugene and Mrs. Willit were sitting by the fire. Mercedes stood unseen in the doorway looking in at them.

Mrs. Willit was making one of her long, inconsequential speeches that were a litany of her many activities. Such speeches usually went on until she had exhausted herself.

Eugene got up nervously, thinking of breakfast.

Mercedes looked at her mother. She could see only the back of her head and her lifting, falling, ringed hands. She entered the room, watching her mother, until she stood just behind her and could look down at her as she lay on the couch. The girl wondered how it would be if she should put out her hand and touch her mother as she had touched the colt, and why there would not be that instant lovely contact. She saw the white taut neck, the short bob clipped to the skull, giving her mother a kind of smart, garish femininity. And she saw the wiry body that suffered continual ravishment and violence, the thin breasts, the flesh made repulsive by rapacious hungers. But she did put out her hand and touched her mother at the nape of the neck with her cold fingers.

Mrs. Willit screamed, sprang up wildly, her hands at her breasts. She turned, her eyes filled with a mad light, as if a spring in her body wound tight had been released by the chill touch and now rebounded in extreme madness.

Eugene whirled to face Mercedes. "What have you done to Mama?" There was a wild gleam in his eyes and in his mother's as they gazed at the girl.

"My God!" Mrs. Willit gasped. "Mercedes! My God! you frightened me. What possessed you to do that? What possessed you?" Seeing the girl standing as if in ambush, so impregnable, drove her to madness. She half screamed. "What is the matter with you? You

190

will kill me! You know my heart. Oh, I wish you were married and off my hands. My God, what have I done to deserve this?" She wrung her hands. "Did you hear her come in, Eugene? Did you? I heard nothing." She did look quite white. It had been startling to her. She never liked to be touched. She hated anyone really touching her.

And now it maddened her to see the girl still standing there with her hand out.

"You wanted to hurt me. You wanted to! I will do what I can for you—and I never want to see you again. I want to do my duty—that's all." She went suddenly to the girl and shook her by the shoulders. "What do you want to do? What do you want? Why don't you say? No, you stand there with that look on your face. Eugene! Eugene!" She held out her arms as if about to fall. "Eugene—speak to her. Speak to her."

Mercedes drew back from her mother's clutching hands, striking them from her. "Leave me alone. You might as well stop those hysterics. . . ."

"Hysterics!" Mrs. Willit leaned on Eugene. "She calls it hysterics! You had better not be too high-handed, my girl," she said in a sudden, cold fury. "You'd better remember where your living comes from, the clothes on your back, every mouthful of food you eat."

"Mama. Mama. You'll make yourself sick," Eugene said, half holding her up. He led her back to the couch.

"Oh, what difference does it make," she said, lying back, sighing. Then she held out her hand to Mercedes with a coy tenderness, her voice welling up. "Oh, my dear little girl," she said. "Come here and talk to mother. Come, sit down right here beside me."

Reluctantly Mercedes sat on the couch, drawing away from her mother's rapacious hands.

"Let's talk it over now. We have to get back. This thing has to be settled. Everyone is expecting to hear about it. People will think it's awfully funny." She seemed to think herself irresistible.

"Marrying Michael isn't so terrible, is it?" Eugene asked. "I can't see why she has to be begged! He's one of the most important men in San Francisco." He was standing by the mantel smoking, bland and certain.

"Not to me," Mercedes said. "I won't marry him."

"Mrs. Willit burst into tears. She could not keep from weeping when she was balked. "We won't talk any longer," she moaned. "You will go back with us tonight."

"No," said Mercedes. "I'm going to stay here. Father is going to give me that new colt that was born last night and I'm going to stay here."

Eugene laughed. "And what are you going to do here—with a colt?"

"I'm not going to do anything."

Mrs. Willit was aghast. "What will people say? What will Michael say?"

Mercedes did not answer.

Mrs. Willit and Eugene were dismayed with their own hatred, as if their crusts were broken only by hatred.

Just then Wizzy called them to breakfast.

"Oh, what have I ever done," Mrs. Willit moaned as she went in to breakfast on the arm of her son.

Mercedes fled in a fury of rage and sorrow, up the stairs and into her grandmother's room. She threw herself on the floor and sobbed, kicking her feet. Mrs. D'Harencourt looked at her for a moment, then she got down on the floor beside the girl, making clucking noises, caressing and stroking the girl with her bony hands in long swoops until the convulsive sobbing stopped and the girl lay mindless under those strong strokes as if some vitality of the old lady's, some vital knowledge, were going into her body.

Her head in the darkness, pillowed on her arms, the old woman squatting down like a gnome stroking her, Mercedes said, "I'm going against the barrier. I'm running the wrong way on the track. I've been breezed and I'm no good."

The grandmother began to chuckle. First she stood far down in her dry body and the laughter sounded like peas rattling in a dried pod. The girl opened her eyes and listened. She began to smile, her wide mouth in a satyric grin.

The old lady shook with laughter as if all her life had gone into ripe seed inside her and now she was moving with laughter. The girl smiled her mouth stretching in that smile that went darkly over her flesh.

Then the old lady began to laugh harder; it came up in her throat and sounded like a castanet in her body, and she tickled Mercedes, putting her sharp dry fingers in the girl's ribs until she doubled over with laughter and rolled on the floor under the dry, quick hands, and the old lady rolled her in her hands as if she were rolling her out of her dry husk, rolling her out tender and alive. And the girl saw the old face of the woman, cracked with laughter. They were both gasping and the old lady rolled her right out of the pod of dryness she dreaded so, and the girl fell out of the husk and lay looking up, laughing.

They quite forgot where they were; what they were supposed to do.

Eugene and Mrs. Willit stayed three days trying to get Mercedes to consent to the marriage, but she would not. She shut herself up in her room and would not even listen to their arguments, entreaties, threats. "I am not going back. I am not going back," was all she would say.

Mrs. Willit wrung her hands, raged, walked, went to bed, but Mercedes would only say, "I'm not going back. Daddy will give me the colt and I am going to stay here." And that was the end.

Mercedes went into the stable to be near the colt. It was midafternoon. There was no one about and the colt went knocking about the stall, hitting the sides as if he did not know distance. The girl leaned over the gate, watching him, and he kept eyeing her. Then he trotted off to eye her again from a distance. The door to the corral was open, but he did not go out.

Mercedes stood perfectly still, hardly breathing, looking at his wonderful form, the testy lift and throw of his long, snakelike neck, his gangly legs with the knobs at the joints as big as those of a mature horse; the ludicrous short body, the whole pelt burning alive, burnished by light as he moved. His black nostrils kept sniffing at everything and he came so near once as to blow his large breath on her.

She stood perfectly still, her heart set on him.

He turned around, his breast toward her, his knees knocking together loobily. They looked at each other. He started at last to come up close to her, taking a wide stance, picking up his feet at the end of the long legs, walking widely, balancing his high body like a young girl, and slowly setting his feet down on the unfamiliar earth. He came toward her and she was afraid to close her eyes, that were strained with looking at him. He came over and stood for a moment facing her, then he looked at the light that came up from the darkened funnel of the stable at the door. She could have put out her hand and touched his fiery coat that looked uneven as if it too grew unaccustomed, but she did not move. He moved nearer to her, butting up against her, but still looking away, and so she leaned against him a little, touching his neck with her head.

She heard the sound of her mother's voice talking to Mallard and she moved away quickly. They came down the shaft of light toward her, coming to see the colt. Mercedes hovered near in terror lest they molest the tender thing. Mrs. Willit went into ecstacy, looking at Mallard half the time.

"Isn't he sweet . . . sweet," she said, her hands fluttering over him in possession.

The colt trotted off to the rear of the stall and with some difficulty curled himself up and lay down. But Mrs. Willit would go into the stall to touch him.

"Better not go in," Mallard said, but she was not afraid, thinking perhaps to charm and bully the colt too.

"Sweet . . . sweet," she chirped at him, and seeing her descend on him, the colt stood up uncertainly, scrambling up on his tall legs, setting his little body far up in the air. "Oh, he is too, too sweet," she cried, putting her handkerchief delicately over her nostrils.

The colt stood in a delirium of balance looking at her, his eyes wide and startled, not knowing what she was.

"Oh, I must touch the darling thing," she said, holding out her veined hands with the cruel shining nails.

Mallard had stepped in with her and he now held the nose of the little horse. "Steady there," he said. Mrs. Willit put her white, dead-looking hand on the flush of the colt's pelt. He shied away, lifting his head, but Mallard held him firmly by the nose. So Mrs. Willit came nearer and put her arms around the colt's neck and he went wild with terror, squirming and bucking, his long heels flying out striking the stall side. His quick flash of life made them both lose their hold of him and he careened, his long neck rippling and lifting, and he bucked and kicked wildly, knocking the stall sides with his flying black hoofs, barely missing Mrs. Willit who was screaming. Mallard pulled her to safety outside the stall door and the colt trotted testily, still bucking.

"Oh, he is awful," Mrs. Willit sobbed. Eugene supported her on one side, Mallard on the other. "Oh, I'm so upset."

"It's all right, Mama," Eugene said, enjoying the excitement with his peculiar lust for violence.

Mercedes had stood quite still, looking on. Now she watched them go out into the sunlight, the light glinting through the sheer dress her mother wore as she walked, supported by the two men. They passed out into the brilliant sunlight and Mercedes stood in the tunneled darkness looking at them as they moved through the light to the far side where they looked black and their voices were distant. They seemed to have passed out of her life as if they had never been anything but flat shadows. She had a bewildered pain, wondering how she could be born of a woman who had neither dimension nor thickness, how she could have been born of a flat space. A man passed over the sunlight carrying a bucket. The others were out of sight. She could hear the man scrubbing, but she could not see him, and the colt kept going round and round the stall, nervously knocking his body against it, because he did not know the distance very well.

That evening Mrs. Willit announced that she and Eugene would go back to the city as soon as dinner was over. Mrs. D'Harencourt said she would go too.

Mrs. Willit was very upset by the episode of the afternoon with

194

the new colt. "I will have Mr. Willit get rid of him," she said.

Mercedes was only waiting for them to go and leave her alone with the colt.

The sun went down early behind the high Sierras and the darkness came up from the under mountains, from the earth and the orchard. They were all ready to leave, but they lingered in the under dusk. The young colt was in the corral with his mother. They could see him trotting around in the dusk, exciting, shying if a bird flew over him.

"This nonsense has got to stop," Mrs. Willit said playfully. She walked out on the lawn. Mrs. D'Harencourt got into the waiting car. But Mrs. Willit could not leave. "We will give you just two months," she said.

Mercedes looked at the colt standing beside his mother. The mare stood still, her nose drooping, and the colt stood at her thigh, his nose against her. They were quite still.

"You must marry," Mrs. Willit said. "We will come for you in two months."

Mercedes leaned against a tree in grief, looking at the colt and hearing her morther's nervous vehemence. The dusk came sifting down around them. She saw the colt standing close to his mother's flank as if warming himself.

"Oh Mother," she cried to herself. "Oh Mother." She went into a swoon of loss and sadness. She wanted her mother; wanted to burrow under the mask-like surface and find the warm sustaining body, the mother flesh. "Oh Mother, Mother," she cried.

"Now Mercedes, my own sweet girl," her mother said, coming nearer her so that Mercedes had to look into the silly, smiling mask. "You must not be sullen and obstinate; your mother knows what's best."

Mercedes felt that she was going to cry. She set her lips against it. But over her mother's shoulder she saw the colt still beside the hot mahogany flank of the great mare, his head lowered mesmerically against her hide that was like a fire sweeping up from her hocks over her shining pelt and his body in the same flesh fire. The uncertain new form, uneasy in a strange world, stood partaking of the mare's burnished, certain form in its full flow of fire and heat and contour.

Mrs. Willit pecked with words, with the unraveling fingers. "Good-bye, my sweet," she said gaily leaning to embrace the girl, but keeping her body away, touching Mercedes just at the shoulders and pecking with her thin lips so that the teeth seemed to come through. The girl shook with chill. "Why you're trembling!" her mother said in surprise. "You're cold. It's too chilly out here in the evening air. Eugene, get her a wrap."

Everything was ghastly in the rapidly falling light.

"Now don't for heaven's sake cry,"Mrs. Willit said, seeing the girl's stricken face. "I'm upset already. That colt upset me so. We must be getting off now." And she whirled out through the dusk in a flurry of leaving, calling, laughing, holding her furs elegantly around her.

Mercedes stood on the lawn in anguish. She could hardly see them as they got into the car, and then her mother pressed against the window laughing hideously, waving, her lips moving, but Mercedes could not hear a word and the face seemed to float on the surface of the dusk like a dead mask whose meaning had been lost. The car began to move.

"Mother, Mother," Mercedes called, but the car turned out of sight.

In the next month the country became bright and green. The sun poured down warming each day, and the green shafts of wheat in the lowland began to spring up. Everything was splendid in its lavish fertility; the orchards flowered, the lemons, figs, and olives.

Mercedes got up at dawn and wandered over the country, through the fruit villages, down into the valley. Her father wrote to Mallard saying that she should have full care of the colt, so he had to let her, even though he was very angry about it and it was unpleasant for her even to go into the stable.

At first the colt stood close to his mother and Mercedes watched him warming himself at the mare's side; the mare's body had given him birth and he had not yet been fully broken off from the giant form. He would stand beside her to assure himself of his mother-presence, then trot out bare in the world, but he could not stay long and must trot back, finding the world-air too wide, blowing about his skinny form. He was so looby, set high on his thin legs with his flicking shabby tail like a jack rabbit's. The girl made friends with him at last so that he followed her about the ranch or through the orchard, cavorting after her like a huge dog, uneasy, quick and uncertain, so high on his legs, keeping one huge eye on her.

Then they went on further adventures, down into the wheat, and he followed her, gamboling, testy, shying away from what was unknown letting his hooves fly out wildly. She showed him everything she knew in the country; squirrels, rabbits, and birds.

She took complete care of him, cleaning his stall, carrying him. No one else so much as touched him and he became very shy of people, very arrogant and irascible. Visitors at the ranch could not come near him. His heels flew out and his lips lifted in a fierce snarl. This delighted Mercedes. She hated these casual contacts herself, these hands that went out to possess—this unclean touching. She was delighted when his heels flew in the air and he went snorting cavorting over the lawn so that everyone took to cover. Mallard was in a passion about it, but she would let him do nothing. She even forgot about him, although she felt his hatred and caught his eye upon her, but she refused him to her consciousness. She went as if in a magic circle—she and the colt.

On their excursions over the countryside, layer after layer of the world she knew seemed to be peeling away from her, stripping her bare and sensitive so that she seemed fresh, without rancor or anger, and she could lie for hours in the sun, feeling it penetrate her body so that she seemed to unfold and become new.

And the colt was always near her, nosing her out of deep sleep; or she lay watching him crop, his long legs wide so that he could reach the ground with his down-sloping neck, the small high buttocks like a young girl's. And as he cropped, he rolled his eyes up at her. Then he would snort and shy away, trotting off so that her heart beat wildly, fearing he would go away from her; but he would not go far. Shyly he would trot back. She felt strange around him, sometimes so gross as if she could not touch his exquisite shyness and sensitivity, that nervous living palpability, sensitively nosing in, then off, testing, like lightning turning back his huge eye on her, suddenly aloof, irascible.

That swift electric thing in him filled her with love and terror, as if he had been poured molten into the form, the curves taut, and his sensitive pelt rippling along the skeleton. When he stood near her in the sun, there was a curious communication between them, wordless, soundless, but potent and electric. She felt then she was changing subtly in her human form. Then suddenly he would trot away into the woods and she would see him indifferent, dappled under the leaves. But he was subtly connected with her and could not go far; he would come back again near her or crop in a circle around her as if binding her inside his magic.

They came through the wheat that was shooting up in the sun and it swished like a sprouting tide at their feet. They stopped under an oak in the center of the field, that was raised a little on an unplowed knoll, where they could see the wheat blowing below them and the mountains rising in the deep distance, and the horse lay down half sleeping, his head resting on his forelegs. But he would open his eye and look at her, marking her presence, then he would close his eye again and seem to sleep. She half drowsed too, but always knowing the body of the little horse there, and thus, half-asleep, she seemed to lapse over into his world. He seemed to create for her a world she could not have maintained without him, as if it were rather in his body than in her own that they existed.

She had been lying down looking into the grasses and the

minute world had become magnified so that she seemed to be in all smallness when she looked up at the gigantic world and at the horse. And he opened his colossal eye with its long lashes and the eye was wide open not *at* but *into* her. That look entered his brain and she was possessed by it and re-created. She saw the soft knowing eye open in the long skull looking into her, not coming against her surfaces but looking straight into her and he seemed to possess her in an enchantment, in the soft beat and pulse of the great will-less animal world.

After that she moved as if bewitched, not seeing at all in the objective human world. She went back to the ranch in a sort of trance. She saw no one. Mallard's grumbling fell on a deaf ear. Wizzy put out her food and she ate. She slept. In the early morning she went out to see the horse.

"It's a wonder you don't sleep in the stable," Mallard said, and she thought, "I would like to."

"Well, he's got to have a name," Mallard said in that sneering tone he used with her now. "What's going to be on his stall?"

She had thought of that but all the names she knew for horses seemed absurd. She had come in her own mind to call him just the Horse. So she said to Mallard, "I call him the Horse."

"Just the Horse?" he asked. "The Horse. Jeez! that's a good name. That would look swell for a race."

"He isn't going to be a racer," she said, currying his thin shanks down the hard slender hip and thin leg.

"Oh, you wait till your father sees him," Mallard said. He was itching to get his hands on the horse.

"He's not going to be a racer," she said.

"What about starting in to give him a little workout?" Mallard said, laughing disagreeably.

"No."

"Oh, don't worry," Mallard said, "I've got my orders. Just the same. . . ."

"No," she said. "Nothing like that."

"All right. All right." Mallard beamed upon her, edging up as close to her as he dared. She moved away, seeing him through the maze of her own life.

"Don't you get tired of eating alone?" he said.

"No," she answered, drawing away, the colt following her and half-nipping at Mallard's sleeve so that the man drew back and slapped at the colt.

But Mallard could not give her control so easily. It irked him that she had the finest colt on the place in her charge. He felt the men doubted his authority because of it. So one morning Mercedes heard the colt whinnying and she ran down in her pajamas, in a fury, into the barn. And there she saw Mallard's big back conceal-ing the whinnying colt. He was trying to put a halter on the Horse.

Mercedes, in a rage, picked up a mop stick that hung on the stall, and began beating Mallard on the back. He turned viciously, caught the stick, held it, laughed at her.

"What are you doing?" she cried in a rage, trying to get the stick away from him.

"I was just going to lead him around a bit," Mallard said, holding the stick tight.

She hated to wrestle with him like that; she felt the resistance of his hand on the stick and she saw the stubble on his chin. She lurched away, gaining the stick, and struck him full across the mouth with it.

The blow dazzled him and without realizing what he was doing, he struck her between the breasts with his hand and she dropped the stick and, gasping, stood looking at him. He fell back from her, the blow still stunning his lips. They both stood looking at each other in wonder. She saw him clearly now as a menace, as if he had just sprung straight on her vision.

Mallard wiped his mouth that was bleeding a little and the girl stood, her hand at her breast where he had struck, gasping for breath, her eyes wild and dark in a hatred that frightened him, cowed him. Suddenly Mercedes began to speak, the words rasping from her.

"You leave that horse alone," she said. "I'll kill you if you lay hands on her again." She walked out of the stable, Mallard's blow still burning in her body, reminding her that she not in paradise, giving her a swift knowledge that there was a menace, and not only the delicate world where she and the colt wandered. She kept for a long time that knowledge in her breast like a tension, the barbed willful evil human contact that she had set herself against.

Mallard wondered if she would report his striking her to her family, but as no word came within the next few day, he breathed easier and he was rather frightened that she did not say anything; it obscured and deepened their antagonism, and he was mortally afraid of what was not obvious and facile. In his top mind he chose to persuade himself that she liked being struck. He had a happy notion anyway that women liked brute men, the kind he imagined himself to be. So he began to wear his silk shirts around the ranch and kept his hair combed.

But she saw none of it. She only felt the blow at her breast continually reminding her that she must be on guard.

A few months later, when she got word that Eugene and her mother would be out over the weekend with Michael, she purposely went away the Saturday they were to arrive and stayed out all day with the Horse. She coiled herself tightly in the world she had gained, pitting herself against the world she resisted.

Mrs. Willit was exasperated when they arrived and Mercedes was not to be found. There was nothing to do but await her return. It was not until dusk that they saw the girl coming up the road to the ranch with the young horse following her, his nose at her shoulder. She came up carelessly, her long gangly legs swinging. Mrs. Willit, in a fury, watched her come up the path. The girl was like a barb to her.

When Michael saw her coming up the road, the half-grown horse following, it seemed that she came out of strangeness, out of myth. And it startled him. He had never really seen her in the city. She had been obscured, and he knew himself to be always away from her, muffled, dim. The war had been a death to him from which he had never recovered. He had managed to pull himself together, so that he looked all right to the outside world, but really he had been buried in the war and had never walked the upper earth since. And when he saw her coming up the road, something stirred unexpectedly in him as if he could be renewed, born of her; as if he recognized suddenly in her the instrument of his birth and he was moved with a strong excitement that he could not conceal.

She came out of the far gloom into the near under half-light that lay close to the ground. She seemed to come reluctantly as if out of another world, walking up the gloom into their faint presences. Her hair had grown rather wildly around her head and the half gloomed light struck up on her face eerily. They all stood up and Michael felt foolish standing and looking at her, so he sat down and did not go to meet her. But Eugene went smartly through the twilight as if he knew what he were doing.

"Mercedes," Mrs. Willit called sharply, like a parrot repeating something meaningless. But the girl did not answer. She stood rather obscured and awkward in the smoky gloaming. The Horse lifted his serpent-like head at the voice and started, seeing the assemblage of unknown forms. Eugene bounded down to them in his white summer suit and his feet were certain.

Mrs. Willit was still calling in her brittle parrot's voice, "Mercedes, where have you been? We would have been worried, but Mallard says you do this every day. You must not have gotten my note."

"Yes, I got it," Mercedes said.

"Don't you see that Michael is here?"

"Yes, I see," Mercedes said, standing quite still by the Horse.

Michael felt like a dummy saying, "Hello, Mercedes."

"Hello," she answered in her husky voice as if she were calling through a dream.

Eugene put his hand on the colt's nose. "I'll take him to the stable," she said. But the Horse snorted, shook his head, lifted his forefeet, and reared back lowering himself on his hind legs so that his belly showed. Mercedes stood by his neck and spoke to quiet him.

"Leave him alone, Eugene," she said. "He might hurt you."

"What the devil's the matter with him?" Eugene said, brushing off his jacket. "Hasn't he been broken?"

"No," she said, still with her hand on the Horse's nose. They started for the stable, the Horse still shying down a little on his rear legs, looking back at Eugene, walking sideways, his flanks quivering.

They disappeared into the gloom of the stable.

Eugene laughed as he went back to the porch where his mother and Michael were sitting. "You'll have some breaking in to do, Michael," he said, forcing a laugh.

Mrs. Willit said quickly, "Oh, I was like that too when I was young. Really, I haven't changed so very much," and she laughed coyly.

Michael said, rather awkwardly, "I like her."

She soon came toward them from the stable. She was very tall as she came up the darkening air toward them.

"Hello, Michael," she said. She let herself lie down on the grass a little way from him. The light seemed to cling to the ground like smoke. The earth, the trees, were in a darkened fume, but Mrs. Willit, Eugene and Michael stood out phosphorescent, their faces like masks. Their words were rejected by the very air, falling brittle like dying leaves in an early winter. But Mercedes looked covertly at Michael who half lay in the lawn chair, his elegant legs stretched out quite near her. In that moment she had stood before him she had seen his lean blond face, the nervous anxiety of a successful man marking it, and his taut body drawn to such a fine line that it seemed to twang in the soft twilight. In that moment she had felt unexpectedly some excitement in him as he lay looking up at her. She was almost frightened by what had been communicated between them. She had been prepared only to resist them all, and in that instant a flicker of some delicate flame had licked up between her and Michael.

"Don't you want something to eat?" her mother said, taking charge of her.

"No. I had things with me."

"Aren't you afraid to go all around the country alone like that?" Eugene asked.

"No," she answered.

Mrs. Willit began nervously to talk since Michael maintained a strange silence. She tried to draw them in. Silence frightened her. Mercedes lay on her back, looking up at the darkening sky, feeling the night come over the under earth. The mountains loomed above and the orchard stood in a sea of gloom, and light lingered in the upper sky a long time until a cone of darkness seemed to fume up from the earth. Eugene and Mrs. Willit were almost invisible to her, but their chatter kept up. They were impervious to the night, nothing affected them. They seemed beyond cataclysm, beyong beauty, or death or fate.

Mrs. Willit chattered about the city gossip, but something had come over Michael's mind and he could not answer. His tongue felt thick, his consciousness numb, struck in wonder. He felt that something was about to happen, something silent, wonderful, and he wished that Mrs. Willit would go away.

Mercedes lay, her mind full of the design of acorns, the sound of wheat growing, the smell of the Horse, the rear and prance of him, the way the hills rolled like a living body. She kept her eyes on Michael. She could see his feet with the expensive shoes, his leg in the expensive trousers. That afternoon she had thought the earth was like a male body, a colossal boy half-covered with grass, bold and nude, a hand jutting from the rock, the powerful juxtapositions of colors. The fields had become like flesh, thighs, strong bended knees. Her mind crept stealthily from the hills she had loved to the body of the man sitting beside her whom she was to marry.

She had thrown herself amorously upon the ground, weeping in grief, wanting something she could not name, and the Horse, bewildered, had trotted around her. Now she sensed the body of the man sitting beside her in the deepening dusk. She felt a sudden inexplicable knowledge of him. She had seen him at parties, at teas, golf tournaments, but he had always been moving—a hard resisting little object—far at the small end of her vision. She sat up abruptly in wonder.

And she began to listen to him. He was talking rather jerkily to Eugene about his work, something he was building. She had never thought of him as a builder. Now she listened carefully to everything he said. He was talking about the new architecture in terms of poetry. "Buildings must go UP," he was saying in his rather subdued but compelling voice. "There is nowhere for them to go but up. A decent architect simply lets it go that way." This interested her. She saw instantly his life and the lives of men in the city, how they poured themselves as into a vat and it took their qualities, their substance, melting it into steel erections, schemes, plans, cities, machines, politics.

At last her mother got up from her chair, saying, "We're going in. I suppose you two have plenty to talk about," and she laughed the small tinkle of her laugh.

When Eugene and Mrs. Willit had gone, a silence fell between the man and the girl.

It had become very dark and still around them. Michael did not know what to say. The social thing sounded rather lame.

"Mercedes," he said, "how are you? The city has been nil without you." He could feel she was looking at him through the maze of her hair.

"There's no use beating around the bush," she said with a boyish movement. "I know why you've come, why they've left us alone."

He laughed uneasily, taken aback by her candor. "Oh, I suppose so," he said. "Your mother said she thought we should be married before the fall."

"I don't want to marry," she said.

"Why?" he asked, letting himself down beside her on the grass, taking her hand. "Why are you so set against it?"

"I hate marrying."

He was bewildered, like a huntsman who has lost the trail. He did not know which way to go, what to say, but he wanted terribly to touch her, to make her turn toward him. "You don't hate love," he said, and she hesitated, hearing something in his voice that struck into her, and yet she was wary.

She drew back and looked at him as he leaned toward her. Then she saw his eyes gleaming at her, and they were devoted, almost frightened, just like the eyes of a dog with not one dangerous glint like the Horse's; just devoted, begging to be loved. She moved away from him, all her desire dying down to the ground.

"I hate this doggy begging for love," she said bitterly. "I won't have it. It's just messy." And she could not bear to see him looking like that. The moment before, sitting in the chair, he had seemed so withdrawn, austere, and attractive. And now she could not bear his dog's eyes begging her to come into the human kennel with him and love. "No. No," she said, moving away from his hands.

He was frantic with love. "But Mercedes you are so beautiful." He knew he was wrong, but he couldn't stop. Since the war there had been something soft begging in him. He wanted a woman to comfort him. He always went a little mad for the comfort of a woman, wanted her to make him feel a man again, and heal all his wounds. He knew this but he could not stop.

"Oh, Mercedes, I need you so."

But she saw all the time his soft begging eyes, and knew what viciousness of one eating another lay behind that wolf tenderness;

what bondage was covered by that soft masquerade. He had her hand though and was softly caressing it, and she felt in his body some taut manhood that attracted her. She let her hand lay passive to see what would happen. She watched him from her own invulnerable wildness. He knew he was not reaching her, that she went untouched by him, softly like an unknown invis ble animal, going softly through the brush, burning up alone, looking out forever invisible, untouched. He became a little crafty then. "You're so beautiful," he said. "Coming up over the road tonight, I thought you were the most beautiful person I had even seen."

He's lying down now, she thought, laughing to herself; he's rolling over. She let him talk.

"Well, now you've said everything you're supposed to," she said. She saw instantly that she had touched him deeply and again she was moved by some magic of his presence that was beyond her reasoning. She saw his hard single crystal body and she put out her hands to his shoulders almost without knowing, attracted. He was too swift in responding, but she let her hands feel his breast through the silken shirt, the hard form of his breast and sides. She was in an ecstacy, touching his body at the quick, feeling the bones and the taut covering of the flesh, but then he was kissing her and she felt the soft possessive probing, and a black pang of revulsion went through her and she was pushing him away with her hands, flinging him from her. She stood up trembling, beside herself with horror. He got up too, knowing how he had bungled, how poorly he had come to her with his self-pity and his hideous death of the outer world.

'I can't. I can't," she kept saying. "Go away. Go on back."

She ran away. He could hear her running but he could not see her. He stood whipped, looking at his own death, and he was glad she had not accepted the body of that death, and a new fresh thing moved in him at last.

Leaving him, Mercedes ran into the lustrous country night. She ran over the ground through the darkness, falling down, striking against the trees. Then she stopped in the dark, hearing the black earth cooling after the heat. She ran into the orchard and she felt as if something peered out at her from the branches; something there that moved delicately in its own life, with no octopus arms reaching out and no hungry mouths demanding sacrifice. The great trees antlered up into the dusky mid-air. The procreating face of the orchard peered out like an identity.

Immediately she left his presence, and the light ceased to reach her from the house, she stepped into this chaste world. She began to walk through the fields under the full sky. She began softly to tread the earth, very sensitively feeling her feet in it, her body

slenderly upright, treading on the dark with the dark around her
head and looming up softly around her sensitive feet. She felt half
in the earth, half above it, softly treading, her feel bright jewels in
the soil, and the earth turned round them in its dreaming,
speaking to her, surface to surface. She uncoiled, the spirit that had
tightened and become rancorous in her breast clicked open like
something budding, like the soft clicking of a flower uncoiling
from the stem.

And the trees seemed to tread beside her as if the solid earth had
begun to move and glow and burn with her, as her breast and feet
had begun to sing and to glow. She felt all the closely designed seed
of that year and every year beneath her budding feet.

"Oh, Lord," she kept saying, half crying, "let me be bride to the
earth. Let me be bride to the sky. Oh, Lord," she kept saying,
walking on the moving darkness. She kept her feet treading
through the dark that seemed itself to be a seed growing in time,
into light. "Oh, Lord," she kept saying, walking and walking in
an ecstacy.

In the morning, Michael said, "I would like to get back today."

"But surely nothing is settled," Mrs. Willit said.

"We won't marry right away," Michael said, and it seemed final.
Mrs. Willit, however, was relieved that the marriage was not
entirely ruined, so she said nothing.

"I'm coming to see you again," Michael said, telling Mercedes
good-bye, and he seemed quite casual. But Mercedes was
distraught, out of her wits, unable to see any of them.

She was glad when the big car disappeared slowly around the
palms and she was alone again.

And she was quite sickened by "lovemaking," the "making" of
love. It disgusted her. She would have none of it.

So she stayed on at the ranch until fall.

One day Michael appeared, walking down the road from the bus.
At first Mercedes was frightened, thinking he had come for some-
thing, but he was quite casual, as if he didn't care at all about her.
She found him attractive again.

He went with her for her walk, the Horse following them. At
first she was shy, awkward, wary, but when it became clear that he
was not there to "make" any love, she found that she was quite
happy with him.

"Do you know," he said as they stood in the orange grove, "that
the orange tree is the only tree that bears its fruit and its blossom at
the same time?"

She did not know and it astonished her. He kept pointing out to her things she had never seen, weaving a kind of positive fact world with her own nebulous emotional one. She knew so little about the real world, her mistrust shut her away. It was amazing how little she knew. She didn't know the names of trees, flowers, birds. She rather turned up her nose at names, at the whole fact world. But now he walked carelessly beside her, talking about what they saw, and it was rather wonderful.

He paid scarcely any attention to her at all. He treated her as if she were a man companion. She watched cannily to see if he was going to try to trick her in some way, but he seemed careless, lax, hardly noticing her.

Yet it cost him a great deal to maintain that indifference. He was like a hunter, set on her, but following her to her lair. He wanted her deeply, he wanted to startle her out from her dense being; and he wanted her unwounded too, uncaught. He wanted her to come freely.

The Horse would not come too near him and he seemed not to care. He wasn't bothered that he couldn't conquer everything. He looked like a fawn, so careless, and at times Mercedes was piqued that he was so remote and inaccessible.

He came out often during the fall days but he never stayed long, only for the day at most, then he would be gone. She was disarmed. For a few hours following his departure she was always a little lonely, bewildered; but then she would sink back into her relationship with the Horse in which she felt more secure and she would forget him so completely that she could not remember what he looked like.

The foggy days came on, closing them in, so that even the mountains were invisible on some days, and the trees dripped. Mercedes let herself go blank as if she were falling through space away from the world into the unknown, and she let herself fall. She was no longer fractious and willful. She matured quickly and rounded out. She was as one bewitched, as in those Irish fairy tales where one leaves a picnic and goes around the corner of a mountain and enters magically into another world, another space and time, and there enacts a whole life and comes back to find the picnic still going on and no more time passed than passes between the laying out of the cloth and the eating of the meal.

One evening she came in very tired after stabling the Horse and found Michael sitting by her fire. She was taken back, seeing him so unexpectedly, coming upon her from her own world so suddenly He saluted her quaintly, just lifting his hand, not getting up.

"This is fine," he said. "Shut up here in the fog."

She stood wide-eyed, her dark face startled, seeing him half-lying in the chair. She saw that he was terribly tired and gray about the mouth and her heart was moved for him. She touched his hand unexpectedly, just brushing it with her fingertips carelessly. His heart pounded but he did not move.

"Don't you like the world?" she asked, her eyes wide, mesmerized above him. "Don't you like what you do? Don't you like your being?"

He shut his eyes and she leaned over looking at him. He was afraid to move and she leaned over looking down at him. Then he felt her finger tips brushing his face. He lay still with his eyes closed. When she felt him so still, waiting under her hands, she was unafraid. She felt him so far, purged of his groveling and self-pity. He did not move and she stood looking at the lean lines of his taut blond face. She squatted down on a stool beside him.

"There is something awfully dead since the war," he said at last.

"Do you think there is something dead?" she said. The flame crackled.

"Yes, there's plenty dead," he said and she looked up quickly, shocked at the ashy anger in his voice, and she saw that his head had fallen back as if he were tired unto death. She was really frightened, seeing how compelled he was to death.

"Oh, what can we do?" she asked.

"There's nothing to do," he said. "There's nothing to do."

She went down on her knees and he let her come between his thighs and put her head on his breast. He just put his hand on her hair. She heard his heart beating against her and she listened, entranced, sensing his fresh live body.

"I don't want to die. I don't want us to die," she said.

"No. No," he said, his hand still resting on her head. "We must not die." She relaxed then. The fire lay on her back and the taut heat of his body under her, and she lay curled in that warmth and there was a strange fertile warming between them. She felt that she was accepting him. She half went to sleep in an alert fertile sleep like an animal, so that she knew his slightest move and woke instantly refreshed as if never before had she been wide awake. She opened her eyes instantly wide as if something were opening from her into an unknown world.

And she was transfixed, seeing a face pressed at the window as if floating in the fog. She did not move, only gasped, so that Michael, more quick in the world than she, turned instantly and saw the face too as it was disappearing, and he got up so quickly that she fell back on the rug, and he ran out of the door.

She knew that it had been the face of Mallard; she had seen him quite clearly.

Michael came back, his face flushed, his eyes wide with a kind of fear she did not like.

"Who was it?" he asked.

She shrugged. "It doesn't matter," she said, looking at him.

"But who?" he insisted, looking out the window.

"Probably one of the men," she said, smiling curiously up at him—and he was almost frightened, seeing her so naked, looking full at him at last. It startled him deeply; he was awake suddenly, like a hunter, his inner will coiled, alert to make the right move.

"But they saw us sitting like that." He was not able to forget the annoyance of the outside world.

"What of it?" she said, smiling.

But he was uneasy again, looking about nervously. "Perhaps I'd better go," he said.

"No. No." She spoke positively. "Sit down." But it was some time before he could forget.

They had dinner and Mercedes seemed like a new person to him and he was rather frightened because she was so suddenly given over. He looked at her and saw her so startled awake and knew she had wakened subtly to him.

Afterward, they sat by the fire again and she sat on the floor and he saw her opened to him almost unbeknownst to herself, so gentle and vulnerable, and he knew he had made her so, that he was responsible for startling her up from the deep marshes of herself. He was wily, treading softly, his heart beating violently, fearful he would not know the crucial moment when to let fly his shaft to touch her in the innermost depths.

They seemed shut off in the tender flickering light, in some kernel of the world, shut away in the flickering kernel alone. Mercedes, laughing, pulled down the shade.

She seemed shaken out, dreaming without fear, stirring, looking up at him not knowing what was on her face, her eyes wide, looking out for the first time. He was afraid to go for her, afraid to trust his own being, really afraid of the vulnerable wonder in her.

"I must leave early in the morning," he said.

"Can't you stay a few days?"

"Not now. I'll come back."

She got up, a brightness over her. "Let's take a walk," she said. "Let's go out and see the Horse—shall we?"

"Yes," he said. "Are you sure it was only one of the men looking in the window?"

"Oh yes," she answered, knowing it was Mallard. "We had better put on wraps. This fog is chilling."

He put his sweater on over his head.

"We'll need a light," she said, "and the flashlight is broken. We'll have to take a lantern."

She went through the dining room to get the lantern. He opened the door and looked out. The fog lay thick, smoking from the earth. She came back and they lit the lantern. She held it high, peering out into the smoking air. It was very still. The fog floated close to the ground, but the sky was invisible. The flame in the lantern hardly moved as they stepped out into the obscure sea. Their eyes were wide, for the ground was uncertain, dropping under them. Mercedes took hold of Michael's arm, holding him close to her, and they walked through the fog. They could hear moisture dripping from the trees like someone murmuring far off.

"Which way is the stable?" Michael asked feeling bewildered— the moving fog shifting around them.

"This way," she said. "I don't know how I know." The light shone against them and made a faint run out from them, not illuminating more than a few feet around them. Michael looked backward uneasily; the fog seemed to close up after them, cutting them off.

"This is a wild thing to do," he said, shivering a little and laughing, holding her closer to him.

Someone spoke to them and Mercedes started, holding the lantern high so that it fell on the disembodied face of Mallard in the fog.

"Well, are you out for a walk?" he said, standing in front of them.

"Let us by, Mallard," Mercedes said. "We're going in the stable."

"Oh, no you're not," Mallard said, standing squarely in front of them. "Visitors aren't allowed at night."

She could not get by him. Michael was bewildered, not understanding the instant hostility between Mercedes and the groom.

"Oh," he said, "we won't be a moment, and we'll be very quiet. Surely there's no harm."

"No?" Mallard sneered. "Well I've had enough interference. I'm the boss here, see? And there's no one going in that barn."

They could not pass him. He stood directly in their path. The light fell up, revealing the stable door back of him. The horses moved uneasily within.

"Then bring him out. We just want to see him. I often get him at night," Mercedes said coldly.

"Well, it's going to be different from now on," Mallard said, looking familiarly at her so that she knew he had seen them when he looked in at the window.

"It doesn't matter, does it, Mercedes?" Michael said, not understanding the hatred between the two. "We can see him in the morning."

"No," Mercedes said. "No, I'm not going to be bullied by him.

You let us by, Mallard."

"Or what?" Mallard said, standing like Gibraltar in front of them.

Mercedes smelled his breath as he came close to her. He had been drinking.

"Or what?" he repeated, and she was frightened as if he had struck her; he was so stupid, so vehement, just standing there so that they could not get by.

She was in a fury. "Michael," she said, "do something. Don't let him stand there like that."

"I think you'd better bring the Horse out for a few minutes," Michael said.

Mallard wavered, then he lurched back angrily. "All right," he said. "But only for a few minutes." He started fumbling with the door.

"Oh, come on," said Mercedes. "Don't bother, Mallard. I'll remember this, don't worry,"

Mallard mumbled something but the words were inaudible.

They started back in the small circle of the lantern light. A chill had come over them. Mercedes was shaking when they got to the house.

"Oh, it's hideous," she cried. "Everything is hideous, spoiled."

"No," he said. "It's all right."

"I hate everyone," she said and began crying. She stood in the hall crying, shaking with sobs. He tried to comfort her, but he felt desolate himself.

Mercedes put ashes on the fire and screened it and they went upstairs.

"Goodnight," Michael said tenderly. "We won't die."

"Oh, everything dies," she said bitterly, in childish grief.

"Never mind. Never mind," was all he could say.

The next morning they were both quiet. The fog was still thick, the water dripping from the trees. They had not the heart to go out to see the Horse. They were distant, withdrawn from each other. She stood in the fog, telling him good-bye.

"I think your father should get rid of Mallard if you're going to stay out here," Michael said.

"Oh, don't think about him." She lifted her chin disdainfully.

"But I do," he said. "He's a petty fellow."

"I hate him," she said simply, smiling in an odd way. "Something will happen to him."

"Because you hate him?" He smiled. "You are a strange child."

She looked at his face, smiling at her through the mist that swung around them.

"Remember," he said, holding her hand, smiling in that delicate way. "Remember, we're not going to die."

"No," she said. "No."

Again he felt the death and the dry dust of the war leave his limbs.

"We can make our world," he said.

She remembered the passionate life she had made of her own; the sensuous pure being of the Horse. "Yes," she said. "Yes, we can."

He felt he must move magically. He put out his hand softly and just touched her breast. Then he turned and started warily through the fog, hearing her call after him as though a dream.

"Michael. Michael."

"Mercedes," he called, and he could not even see the house. He could hear her voice, husky, strangely near him, and yet she was invisible.

"Good-bye, Michael," she said.

He went the wrong way and had to come back. Then there was his car standing close to him and he heard her voice, curiously muffled, "Did you find it?"

"Yes," he called, and felt that he was shouting and wanted to go back, but he hardly knew which direction the house was.

"Good-bye," he called into the fog and he was struck with an unutterable terror when she did not answer. In a kind of horror he started the engine and drove slowly away.

In the Spring the Horse was a splendid animal, simply magnificent. He had filled out, rounded, grown stalwart. Everyone at the stable was deathly afraid of him. He would allow no one in his stall except Mercedes and the boy Pinky who sometimes helped her in the care of him. Mercedes wanted them all to leave him alone. She wanted him all for herself.

"Who's going to ride him?" the stableboys asked.

She didn't know whether she would ride him or not.

One day she put a halter on him and led him out of the barn. He was astonished, but he let her do it, measuring her will.

She began to touch him more. She brooded over mounting him. She thought he would let her if she could gather her power delicate and sheer enough. Then out in the fields, as he stood slightly below her, without contemplating it, quite unexpectedly she slung her leg over his back and gained a seat. He stood stock still a moment, his back shuddering under her, then bounded off, a little in fright. He put down his head and pawed and she felt the shudder ripple through him, the shudder of dominance by another. But she spoke, patting his neck, not wanting to ride him, to make him

211

a beast of burden, but only to share in his splendor and give him of her own in delicate wondrous balance. She felt if that moment that by one thought, one moment she let go of that brilliant power that seemed to shimmer between them, he would kill her. The shudders kept shaking through his back, down his flanks, as he paced wildly, looking back at her. They were held together in that first moment in a balance that was intricate and subtle. Then he stopped, scudding under her. He surged up, meeting her weight, bearing her splendidly, prancing down the field, then he turned and galloped back, shaking his mane. And he let her turn his head by the loose halter. They came up the road into the ranch. Pinky let out a yell and the hands came running to see them. The Horse careened, pacing beautifully, almost with vanity, as the hands exclaimed in wonder.

"My God," Mallard said, seeing the fine action. Everyone came running out.

The Horse capered up and Mercedes felt splendid partaking of his powerful flesh. A flush of pride went over her. She slid off his back. "Don't anybody try to ride him," she said. "He's dangerous. Don't try to ride him," she said to all of the stableboys.

Mallard said, "You mean no one is to ride him but you?"

"That's what I mean, Mallard."

He looked at her, a little sneer on his face. The men listened. "Well, we'll see about that," he said. "I'm managing this place, you know. Remember! Your father will change his mind when he finds out what a beauty he's got there."

"I'll see to that," she said coldly. "You had better leave him alone."

"Well, I won't promise." He grinned wickedly at the men, winking hugely. Some of them laughed uneasily.

"Well, go ahead," she said in disdain, giving the Horse over to Pinky and starting toward the house.

Mallard walked along beside her, looking back suggestively at the men. He felt that he had gotten the best of her.

"What's happened to your friend?" he asked, leaning toward her so that the men would think he was talking intimately. "Don't you get tired eating alone?"

"No," she said. "I'm not lonely." She walked on faster, leaving him, but when she got to the house she was quite weak.

Now she delighted in riding the Horse. They went over the countryside through the mountain villages, even far up into the mountains through old mining camps. She was like a myth on the splendid, touchy horse. Women and children came to the doors to watch them pass. Mercedes seemed to take on assurances and loveliness from the splendor of the Horse.

Michael, when he came out, was astounded. She was like one possessed. He watched her mount and ride the beast almost with fear, and she paced off down the road laughing and waving to him and he stood feeling lost and inadequate on the ground. She was sometimes shy and elusive with him, and sometimes that miracle happened again, and she would open out gently.

One day they started out for a walk. "Why do we have to have that Horse trailing us?" he asked.

She drew back. "Why?" she repeated.

"Yes. You can't live all your life with a horse."

She would not talk. She became sullen. He could not woo her back. So he went back to the city, but he wrote her very rich full letters and she rode into the village every day to get them. Mallard was angry about the sensation she made there. At the store, at the post office, at the barber shop, that was all he heard—stories about the girl and the horse. It riled him.

"Say, Mallard," they said at the barber shop, "we don't see you ridin' into town on the Horse. Are you afraid, or won't she let you?" They kidded him everywhere.

He began to covet the horse monstrously. He felt, besides, that she was managing the ranch too much. The men had a great respect for her since she rode the horse. He could not bear the snickers of the men. He was proud of his bullying dominance over horse and man and he was maddened to be undermined by Mercedes who teemed to be impenetrable, bound away from his wrath by her contempt.

She began to feel that the man was poisoning the very air she breathed. She felt his inflamed eyes on her whenever she turned around. He stood watching her from every angle of the stable. He tried to talk to her. He even wrote to her father about her, for she received a long letter from him begging her to come back to the city, and not to create dissension at the ranch, even threatening her a little. She felt something was about to happen and she did not know which way to look for its approach.

Michael too was urging her to return and she was bewildered and confused by his attack upon the Horse, yet deeply she knew there must be a break, a disaster that would crash upon the closed paradisiacal world.

Then came a wire from her mother begging her to come back for her birthday. "Please come for your birthday my darling," the night letter read. "We miss you so Remember your poor mother." And despite herself she must yearn for that mother flesh, yearn back toward that form. So she consented to go for only two days. She would leave Saturday and be back Monday morning at the latest.

She had to go to Sacramento and buy a complete outfit of new clothes, she had grown so much since she had been to the city. Passing mirrors, she saw with some astonishment that she was a woman as sudden grown as the colt.

She told the stableboys to keep the Horse in the stable until she returned and that no one was to touch him but Pinky. Mallard drove her to Sacramento and they hardly spoke to each other. She went on to San Francisco on the train,

In her deep mind, far below, she knew that Mallard would ride the Horse, but she was surprised, horror-stricken when she got a telegram at her birthday dinner Saturday night saying that Mallard had been killed that afternoon riding the Horse. She sat holding the telegram in her hands and they all were looking at her.

"What is it?" Michael asked. He was sitting next to her.

"Oh, Michael," she said, her eyes stricken with fear and horror.

"What is it?" her father said, getting up.

"Michael," she said, ignoring the others, "the Horse has killed Mallard."

Mrs. Willit moaned. "Oh, I knew nothing good would come of that terrible horse. Oh, I knew you would bring something terrible on us, Mercedes."

"Serves him right," said the grandmother, going on calmly with her dinner. Mercedes looked at her as if trying to understand what she had said.

"This is serious," said her father. "That such a thing should happen on my place. Really, Mercedes, I was afraid of something like this."

They all looked serious and pleased. Except Michael. He surmised something of what it meant to her.

"You know the rule in my stables, Mercedes," her father said. "A horse that kills a man must be killed immediately, within twenty-four hours. I won't have my men imperiled."

"Oh, there are worse perils," she said, crying.

"I don't know what you mean," her father said, looking blank. "Nothing is worse than a fractious horse."

"Lots of things are worse," she cried. "Oh, I'm going. I'm going. He did something to him. He used spurs or a whip. He was a cruel bully."

"Why, Mercedes," Mrs. Willit said, incensed. "Mallard was a splendid man." They all seemed to be letting their hatred coil around her.

"Mallard was a fine man with horses," her father said.

"He was not," she said. "I'm going. You must let me have a car. I want to go now."

"I should go myself," Mr. Willit said.

Michael said, "Let Mercedes go with me. I'll take care of everything."

After consideration, Mr. Willit said, "That will be all right."

"We must go now, Michael," Mercedes insisted.

Mrs. Willit cried, "Oh, what will you bring upon us, Mercedes, what will you do next."

"I'll go too," Eugene said, sensing a tragic scene just to his liking. But they would not have him.

They started immediately.

"Mother, Mother," Mercedes said.

Mrs. Willit bent over from the hips, kissed her grimly, her teeth pressing through. "You're going to ruin us yet, Mercedes," she said primly, as a joke.

"He's not going to be killed. He's not going to be killed," Mercedes kept saying all the way there. Michael tried to soothe her, holding her hand under the wheel. "Oh, Michael, everything is always spoiled."

"No," he said, smiling at her so delicately that she became quiet and huddled close to him.

They got to the ranch at dawn before the sun had topped the Sierras. There was no one in sight. Mercedes kept looking up and down the road to see where Mallard had been killed, but everything looked the same. She could not believe anything had happened. Wizzy came to the door and when she saw Mercedes she gave a cry and put her apron over her head.

"I'm going to see him," Mercedes said, and Michael didn't know whom she meant but she went toward the stables, going rapidly into the gloom between the stalls. Nervous horses looked out at her; their eyes were all turned toward her. She went to the Horse. She saw him far back in the gloom, his eyes looking at her, but he did not come forward. She stood looking at him with horror and he looked out at her. She called him but she did not go into the stall. She was trembling in fear and apprehension and sorrow. At last he began moving slowly toward her, his breast looming up, the full shining sweep of his neck lifted frighteningly above her. She had not realized how big he had grown, and she drew back. He stopped when she drew away, snorting and rearing a little so that he loomed above her, breast now set thickly into the swift legs, the python neck lifting to the long face with the nostrils drawn back and the eyes bloodshot, looking at her obliquely. He kept trembling. He was hurt and uncertain. When she realized this, she was without fear, and reached up and stroked his neck. He lowered his head and the warm breath went in a blast on her body. She clung to the strong neck and he almost lifted her.

She went into the stall and he reared back a little, but she kept

talking to him, stroking his neck. He trotted around once and she
saw his huge frigthening body and she felt she didn't know him, as
if something had happened. He trotted around eyeing her, then he
stopped his nervous gait and stood beside her, his head hanging as
if he were listening, only his ears bent forward, moving slightly.
She knew he had come to her, but she did not touch him. He stood
with the long swoop of his neck, subjugated to her, his eyes rolling
up, in unutterable sadness and lack of memory.

"Oh, what did you do?" she said, and his ears twitched and he
sadly nosed her, moving so close to her that he almost knocked her
over, like a burning wave mounting against her. She stroked his
neck, his body, his full haunches. She knew she would not have
him killed.

McClaren opened the stable door, letting in the first shaft of sun.
"You'd better leave him alone," he said. "This is a bad business."

She liked McClaren, but she was sullen. "Don't let anyone
handle him. I'll feed him myself," she said.

"Is your father coming down?"

"No, he isn't," she answered curtly.

She felt that McClaren eyed her strangely.

She met Pinky as she was going out and he gave a little yell of
fright and skidded past her.

Michael was having coffee in the sun room. Wizzy began mutter-
ing in Spanish and crossed herself when Mercedes came in.
"What's the matter?" she asked. "Am I bewitched?"

"I think you are," Michael said.

"Well I'm not going to have the Horse killed," she said sullenly.
She started into the other room where she knew the body must be.

"Mercedes," Michael said "Don't go in there now."

"Yes, Michael," she said, fingering his jacket, just touching his
breast. "I must see what this is about. What it means."

"All right."

She went into the room and saw the body lying on her mother's
couch. She pulled down the sheet and looked at Mallard's dead
face. It was just the same, death would add no mystery. But still,
looking closer, she could see a certain flight of fear across his
features as if he had seen a breech of horror and mystery that lay
between himself and all men and beasts. As if he had been
reprimanded in death. She knew his body would be crushed at the
chest. She only looked at the face. There was a scar above the eye
making it droop a bit, adding to the impression of astonishment
and fright and the subtle flight of terror that was like a shadow on
his face as if for once he had seen something.

She was satisfied it had happened to him. She was glad he was
dead really. There was a little point of pity in her because he was a

man with the mystery of man-stuff begetting life, but she wasn't sorry that his little form was broken, that the Horse had broken it with his jewel-like feet, crushing the cocky little form open so that Mallard had to accept death at last.

He had mounted the Horse to have dominion over him, to break the beast to his ignoble uses, and he had got what he deserved. She wondered if her mother had had a hand in it, had wired her to come away, had conspired with Mallard to break the Horse in to other hands besides her own. Without any evidence still, she believed that her mother had done that and so her mother was dead also. And Mallard was dead. They had done it to themselves. She was glad. And she also had guilt for she had let them. She should not have gone away through pity, without desire, and conspired with them with death.

She went out of the room, out of the house, and stood in the warm silent sunlight that fell as if nothing had happened. It was midsummer and the wheat was high golden, below, and the mountains clear, rearing above.

The activities of the stable were going on as usual, but the men watched her fearfully, talking in little groups. They were ready now to do what she said, but there was a covert hatred beneath their servility. She heard one man say, "If she doesn't have him killed by nightfall, I'm quitting. I ain't going to let any woman or horse lord it over me." They were expecting the shooting of the horse that morning, so she went over where they could all hear her and called Pinky.

"Pinky, will you send a telegram for me to my father. You know the address." She spoke loudly and everybody stopped to hear. "Simply say that the Horse will not be shot. Just that: the Horse will not be shot."

Pinky ran off for the ranch Ford, his legs twinkling with enjoyment and amazement at what he was doing. She went in, paying no attention to the almost open hostility. She fed the Horse and curried him. She was uneasy amidst all the hostility but she let the Horse out into his own corral and stood watching him.

McClaren came up and stood beside her. He was a quiet Scotsman for whom she had great respect. "It's too bad," he said.

"Yes," she said, not looking at him. "But Mallard shouldn't have done it."

"Perhaps he shouldn't," he said in his preternaturally sad voice so that she looked at him, liking him. "But he's got no right to kill a man . . . a horse has got no right to kill a man."

"A man's got no right to bully a horse," she said.

"No," he agreed, and they both stood watching the Horse.

"It's all right to kill a bully," she said. "A man who tries to bully

217

the spirit of another deserves to be killed."

"Nay," he said sadly.

Then she had to ask the question, "Where was he killed?" She asked it almost in a whisper.

He looked at her. "Right where the ranch road turns into the grove, before you get to the highway. He must have just mounted him."

She looked at the man. "Did he have a whip?"

"Well. . . ."

"Did he start out with a whip?"

"Yes." McClaren shook his head sadly.

She said no more. Surely he had more sense than to be spurred, but she did not know to what lengths his anger would lead him.

"He's a beauty," McClaren said. "But he never should have been raised wild like that. That's to blame for it. I don't think the Horse is mean or vicious."

She was aghast. Then *she* was to blame for it.

"Yes," McClaren said, "he just reared and threw him and then turned and trampled on him."

"Trampled on him. . . ."

"Yes. I was watching from the turn in the road expecting something. I saw the horse over him rearing, trampling on him, coming down on him with his front feet."

She ran away; she ran across the lawn calling "Michael, Michael." She did not care that everyone saw her. Michael ran up from the orchard. "Michael, could it be my fault? Could I have done something? Is my world wrong? Is it wrong? Oh, it seemed so lovely. How could it be wrong?"

"It isn't wrong," he said. "We aren't wrong."

He walked with her down into the wheat.

"What is there, Michael?" she said, and her face was so white that he was frightened. "Where is there to go?" Everything looked strange to her, no longer innocent. Something had happened. The world lay broken around her; even the trees stood differently and the earth was just the earth.

When they went back they stopped in the orchard and saw the men bringing the body of Mallard out of the house on a stretcher, covered up so that they saw only the outline of the man under the cloth. Without a pang, Mercedes saw them carry him to the car. She was glad he was gone with his overweening, bullying consciousness.

When they had driven away, Mercedes and Michael went into the house. But Mercedes was nervous. She must go out and see the Horse. "I must see if he has changed. Could he have become corrupted, Michael? If you once feel that power of a bully then do you have it? Do you want to wield it too?"

"I'm afraid so," Michael said. "I'm afraid it's so."

"No. No. It isn't so," she suddenly shouted. "It isn't so. I won't believe in it. I want to believe in everything impossible, improbable."

She ran out to the stable, into the stall. He seemed gentle and bonny as usual, prancing in that far world, turning his eyes in upon her. She saw him as he had been before. Nothing had happened in the human world. It wasn't true that a horse could get a touch of that violence of vanquishing another that a man had. He hadn't been touched. She saw him there so magnificent and swift in their far delicate world. He could not have that evil bullying of a petty man. He had seen it just once and had reared and struck it down as one would a snake—that was all. He had struck for them both. He harbored not even a remembrance. He would do it again to a snake; there was no evil sense of power in him. She must show them all, articulate by one gesture, all the prehuman gigantic world they had created.

She took him out and put a bridle on him. He stood docilely. She walked him out into the sunlight. He shied, having been shut up, then he seemed to grow in her sight, ripple and unfold and undulate along all his burning form. The stableboys knew she had taken him out. They were watching. She could feel them all watching from the houses, from the orchard. Her heart was beating. She felt they put her outside.

Pinky drove up in the Ford with the answer to her telegram. He ran to her with it and she tore it open. She knew he could see how she was trembling. "We will wait until I can get there," she read, "but don't ride him. It's dangerous." It was signed, "Your father, W.W. Willit." She looked ironically at the full name signed.

"Pinky, get the light saddle," she said.

He ran for it. McClaren came out of the stable.

"Once a killer . . ." he said.

"It isn't true," she said, trying not to cry. "I'm going to ride him into town."

"You shouldn't do it," McClaren said.

"Once a horse gets a taste of it, you never can tell."

"Leave me alone," she said. "I know what I'm doing."

Michael came running out of the house.

Mercedes was cinching the saddle girth.

"Mercedes, you mustn't do this. Don't you see what you are doing?" he said. "You are destroying your own world."

"I'm not," she said, beside herself. "Don't stop me."

"I won't," Michael said.

She mounted, looking down at him standing so frail on the

earth, his fawn face looking up at her, and there was a glint in it that she feared for the moment, but the Horse was taking her away, like a moving wave of flesh, and Michael was saying something that she did not hear until an hour and a half later.

"You're doing violence too," he shouted.

But she was laughing wildly as the Horse capered down the curve of the drive and she saw them all standing agape watching her, and Michael on the lawn with his hand out in remonstrance. Then he seemed to recollect something and he came running after her calling, "Mercedes, Mercedes."

"Go back," she shouted, and the Horse was affrighted and bolted down and around the curve, but he slowed up then and cantered through the oak grove and suddenly without warning she saw the PLACE. She knew it instantly, a confused spot where the turf had been kicked up and then where it had been tramped down on the road. She looked closely as they passed and imagined she saw blood on the grass. But the Horse paid no attention.

They went along the highway. He cantered his best and she felt exonerated, splendid, going toward the mountains under the unbelievable blue sky.

On the outskirts of the village, several little boys gathered, watching her come down the road, and apparently very excited by the sight of the Horse. More gathered quickly and she had a feeling of some kind of menace. One little boy covertly threw a stone that clattered under the Horse's hooves.

Women began to gather at the doors and ran out to the fences watching her go by. She was astonished. Mallard was to be buried from the town the following afternoon and she could feel that they thought it improper for her to ride the Horse into town. She felt for the first time a kind of fear. She went deeper into the town and people gathered to watch her pass, talking about her. It made the Horse nervous too. By the time they got the the main street, he was shying testily, going sideways so that she could hardly control him. She tied him at the post office.

When she came out, people had gathered at a distance watching them, and she saw that the Horse was frantic. The people put an awful fright in her too. Why were they looking at her as if she were somehow outside? It frightened her, these weasly eyes all looking at her. In a confusion she got close to the Horse, half-hiding her head in his side, but she knew she would have to mount.

When she mounted, the Horse reared on his hind legs, stepping sideways so that everyone fell away from him and ran for doorways; he nipped at a man who came too close to him. A buzz of anger rose like wind. And Mercedes had no power over the Horse.

He started galloping down the streets, beyond her control, and she saw people run out with their mouths open and she knew they were shouting but she could hear nothing and not one man dared make an attempt to stop the runaway horse. He ran until he was a mile out of town, then he turned off the highway and galloped slowly down the country road, coming to a stop, his sides distended.

Then he walked slowly and she sat numb on his back. She could not think or feel. The Horse carried her down the secluded road that wound through the orchards and they met no one and were seen by no one. They went through the ghostly green of the olive orchards. His back was powerful and rigid under her and he started, shied from unseen objects. He turned his head and cast his eye back at her and she shivered. He did not follow her guidance but went exactly where he chose, eating as long as he liked, wandering on and she sat quiescent going to what destruction he might embody.

He went down the road alone and she knew that she was being carried and that she could not get off. He had chosen the road. He cantered clear off down a lane into the woods, and it was borne upon her subtly that he was compelling her. She sat frightened, waiting.

He stopped and whinnied, then turned and looked and she saw that he was *watching* her; with a start she saw that he was watching her as he did the others, with that craven fear and craven power in his eyes. She wanted to scream, but not a sound came from her and he stood for some moments with his head turned and his eyes rolled back looking *at* her.

She shivered, but she could not dismount. She had not the will. She felt the quiver of power along his spine as he started galloping. She had to hold to his mane. He reared and cantered and sidestepped willfully. Then he went along gently and she thought for a moment that she must be imagining everything, that he was the same as before. For a moment she saw the mountains, the flowers under his hooves, the meadows again shifting in that pre-world loveliness and innocence, but only for a moment. Then she felt him shiver under her like a ship in a heavy sea.

He jumped, swerved, and she clung to him as if she were drowning, and then suddenly—with terrible awareness—she knew that he had cut back and they were coming out the highway at just the curve in the road that led into the oak grove, going to the ranch road, and that he had come that way purposely and of his own desire.

Instantly she was gripped with fear. She never forgot again that moment in which she knew all that was going to happen and heard the words Michael had shouted. She never again lost that feeling of menace. Trembling, the Horse entered the grove.

Her eyes were wide open, waiting. She felt him give and rise under her, as if he had to do what he was about to do. She saw through the grove as if through a dark tunnel, and coming out at the other side was the palm-lined road that led to the ranch. She knew they would never get that far.

Michael, Michael, she cried, but she did not utter a sound. The Horse shivered under her, then his flesh rose, lifting her up, wonderfully into the air, then she fell swiftly and struck the ground and he turned, rearing, his belly high above, and as she lay curled below, he brought his bright hooves down on her again and again. She did not utter a cry. She accepted it at last, crouching as if in the womb, and he trampled her. She felt as if her eyes were wide open on horror as well as loveliness; on death as well as life.

Then, feeling her under him, the Horse reared back, stepping on his hind legs, almost toppling over. He let his forelegs drop and stood a moment, half crouched down, as if trying to remember what he had done, then as if he remembered nothing, he trotted off, stopped, came back uneasily and ran swiftly around her. He nosed her and snorted at the blood. Then in real anxiety, he began to circle around her, whinnying, shivering like a taut wire in a storm.

She had not lost consciousness in the ordinary sense, she SAW everything; the trees, the minute earth, the Horse outlined in the electric brightness, circling, coming back. She saw him from below looming rocketlike from his slender hocks, but her eye was simply wide open seeing only the physical image.

She lay, her eye wide open, seeing him trot around her from her eye close to the ground. She lay with her hands up over her bleeding head and she could not move them to bring them down. She felt she could not even close her eye. He came close to her again, his breath fanning her hair; he drew away at the smell of blood, then put his nose back and, sensing disaster, gave a cry, a terrible scream and began beating up and down so that she thought he would go over her. He ran back again screaming. Then, turning through the tunnelled darkness toward the pouring sunlight, he galloped past her for the last time, and thundered through the cone of darkness, plunging into the golden light.

At the same time, she saw Michael running through the light. He stopped, just a dark stroke, minute, awaiting the oncoming Horse. The Horse plunged toward that golden sunlight and the man stood, a stroke of a pencil, a black upright splinter in the immense light beyond, and fired.

The explosion split the sunlight, showering, shaking it down with swiftness, and her wide open eye saw the Horse rear up so that he looked like a centaur from his rocket flanks wedged down in darkness, his front feet lifted up. And he stood screaming while Michael fired shot after shot into the exposed shaft of his upreared form; then it thundered down, part falling into part, like a burnished stream falling back into the ground again.

Afterword

Meridel Le Sueur's effort "to claw out of the bourgeois relationships" which threatened to engulf her as a young woman is vividly
reflected in her memory. Though her mother, Marian Wharton,
was a socialist and a feminist, and her stepfather, Arthur Le Sueur,
was the first Socialist mayor of Minot, N.D., and a participant in
the Farmer Labor Party in Minnesota, the young Meridel faced
many of the same pressures to conform to the "safe" roles for
women that young girls without radical parents faced. Her mother
feared for her health, her sexual safety, and her economic stability.
She sent Meridel to a physical culture school in Chicago in her
early teens and later encouraged her to pursue a stage career in
New York. "She was really anxious to get you up in the bourgeois
world. She was afraid of how you would suffer [otherwise]."(1)

As a child, Meridel's home was a stopping place for radicals of
such note as Emma Goldman and Alexander Berkman, and she
learned about socialism through her parents' involvement with
the Socialist Party and its "People's College" at Fort Scott, Kansas.
The world beyond her home, however, taught different lessons.
She remembers going to town or to school as "going into the lion's
mouth." "I thought the townspeople were terrible." In Fort Scott
the town "drove us out with axes and feathers." As she entered
adolescence, sexual harrassment mingled with political attack. "I
was timid, shy, unsexual. I didn't like boys. They were very
dangerous in those villages. If you were a radical, they knocked on
your door—'Gimme some of that free love.' " She took courage
from the radicals who resisted oppression: "It was part of our life
to be attacked by reactionaries. You were proud of it. These people
[the Wobblies, the Socialists] were heroes."

In her late teens, Meridel left the Midwest for New York and a
possible career in the theater. She lived at the anarchist house of
Emma Goldman and Alexander Berkman and she studied drama
for two years. Though sensing it was not the right thing for her,
she signed a contract. Meridel recalls that her mother "was making
me all kinds of clothes. It was like a marriage. I kept fainting in the
skirts." Both in New York and later in Hollywood, she had
opportunities in the entertainment world, and, although both the

theater and the movies offered many attractions, she rejected them. "I just smelled death," she explains. Of herself at the time she now says, "I really honor that girl, whoever she was. They were offering me all the fruits and I was hungry. I just smelled a dead rat. I didn't decide *not* to accept—I just turned away."

Her resistance to the "world of bourgeois culture" was made harder by the seductiveness of the image of a woman as a "delicate victim," an image that offered safety from the threat of male harrassment which she had been taught was the usual lot of women unless they married the "right" man. She remembers the stereotypes of the "delicate, beautiful, victimized girl" as influencing her sexual feelings until she was almost twenty-five years of age. "That's what I wanted to be. I identified with the victim." The image of the Gish sisters and Norma Talmadge was attractive to women because they were "the alternatives to the brutality of sex. It was a 'safe way' to deal with the threat of sex, and you weren't guilty, either. You were doing what you could and remaining pure. . . . Women were taught to be attracted to the conquistador—to marry him before he detroyed you."

Meridel sees her own struggle to free herself from the seductions of the bourgeois world and the fear of sex as especially torturous because the schooling started so young. "My grandmother warned you against [sex]. The corset was your armor." At the same time, any understanding of the realities of female sexuality was suppressed. She was told 'bad things would happen,' but "I don't think they had the words for sexual functions. They could point." The only expression of eroticism she identified in her grandmother was her love of Jesus. "He was the only person she ever loved. She would sing 'Jesus, Lover of My Soul, Let Me To Thy Bosom Fly'—I thought that was pretty radical, to fly to someone's bosom. He was not just an androgenous savior. He was the only loving male they ever knew." The first women she remembers who were not puritanical were the Native American women she knew in Oklahoma. "They had no sexual repression, no guilt, no fear of nature. I went wherever there were any Indian women."

Her mother's warning to her was to "save herself for the great moment." In New York "the corn virgin of the prairies," as she remembers being derisively called by Edna St. Vincent Millay, was challenged and pressured by men and women who were willing to use sex both for casual pleasure and for economic or career advantage. "I had a terrible time. You almost had a choice of being a wanton or a virgin. You could be ruined by either one." She remembers Emma Goldman as the "only woman I knew who controlled her sexual life entirely," and at age 83, Meridel says "I

226

never knew a man who wanted a relationship with a woman equally creative."

The struggle against the repressions of sex, the conventions for women, and the seductions of the bourgeois world which Meridel endured in her young womanhood left her "wounded" and scarred. At times she thought of suicide and at times "I was insane, I think." Her story "Persephone" was one expression of this torture. "I wrote 'Persephone' when my mother was antagonistic and controlling." "At age twelve I saw clearly I could be a wife, a mother, a teacher, a nurse, or a whore, and I couldn't be a teacher or a nurse without money to go to school."

She found lifelines for herself during those years in the world of nature and her reading of D. H. Lawrence. "The first thing that saved me was the earth," she says. "It was something you could have." She started reading Lawrence in 1923-24. She has said that "Lawrence saved my life. I'd never have gotten out of that Puritanism without Lawrence."(2) Feminist readers have sometimes been puzzled that Lawrence, whose portrayal of sexuality focuses on the dominant male as the instrument of female ecstacy, could have been so important to a writer as feminist as Meridel Le Sueur. According to her, at the time she first read Lawrence "you never read anything about sex in a woman. [Lawrence's] mother was the first woman in literature described as a sexual woman." In Lawrence she found a writer who described sexual intercourse as it had not been described before in literature—a fact of stunning significance to a woman seeking to escape her mother's and grandmother's sexual repression and a writer who could find no literary images for the kinds of womanhood she wanted to express.

Equally important was Lawrence's effort to free sexuality from class constrictions and commodity value. "He was trying to break the idea of sex as a commodity. To consider the body as living relationship instead of a commodity was revolutionary." She remembers her own parents telling her they wouldn't love her unless she behaved a certain way. "My love related to pleasing, to serving them. I always felt they were wiping me out." One's sexuality was both repressed and regarded as a commodity. "You have no idea how lonely the object was. The Puritan alienated and put the object outside you."

Lawrence's attempt to suffuse sexuality with mysticism was one way to destroy sexuality as a commodity. Meridel Le Sueur connects sexuality with the mystery of natural instincts and ties it with her sense of the wonder of Nature. She does not, however, turn to Lawrence for the presentation of how women experience sexuality. "Lawrence never understood fully a woman's experience," she says. "I was on the opposite end." Thus Lawrence's importance to her should neither be underestimated nor misunderstood. His work illustrated for her the possibility of writing about female sexuality and denied that women's sexuality should be alienated from its place in the natural world.

The limits of her indebtedness to Lawrence are clear in **I Hear Men Talking**. Her men characters, such as Bac in this novel, possess none of the mystical sexual enchantment of Lawrence's men and women, and her women are usually severely disappointed when the moment of intimacy is more harsh than ecstatic, more isolating than unifying. Sexuality is not a transforming fire but a false promise, an illusion fed the young by bourgeois culture and given credibility by the insistent language of the body. Sexuality is corrupted when it is used to dominate the less powerful.

Though Lawrence and a few other writers offered some guidance to Meridel as a Midwestern radical and feminist, she found little help as a writer in traditional American literature. The writers' community on the American Left presented one alternative. In her girlhood, she was exposed to the Industrial Workers of the World. The IWW believed in people's culture. She recalls, "Everybody wrote. You didn't open an IWW meeting without a poem." Her earliest fascination with language resulted in trying to take down the speech of people in the small Midwestern towns where she grew up. This fascination with the oracle of the people would remain with her throughout her life and become a major technique in her own writing. She took the story of Floyd Young in "The Bird" from talk of ship adventures and war stories by young men whose words she recorded.

The prominent writers of the time, however, were heralded for a different kind of talent. In writing classes she studied Hemingway, Sherwood Anderson, and Chekhov. "I studied Hemingway and Anderson. I really studied that structure—I wish I hadn't. I did admire the structure, the frugality of language, the singleness of the narrative." Many of the women writers she knew faced a similar problem of how to write the truth about women and still win the accolades of the publishing world. Women like Zona Gale and Willa Cather made their accommodations. "Willa Cather was absolutely seduced into that world. She absolutely gave away all of Nebraska she had in the awful book, **Death Comes to the Archbishop**."

From 1924 on, Meridel often wrote for the Communist Party and published in Party journals. Breaking out of one literary tradition to forge a new one that harmonized with her ideology was not an easy matter, however. "It was not so simple as saying you are joining the working class. You have to destroy the images. The problem is how to make this new image. To find the image of the oppressed instead of the oppressor is a violent, difficult thing "

The present selection of her work includes an unpublished novel, **I Hear Men Talking**, and two novellas, "The Bird" and "The Horse"—all products of Meridel Le Sueur's effort to achieve a class-conscious literature that was faithful to both her artistry and her ideology.

While these works do not always have the integration of ideology and artistry which the mature Le Sueur desires, they do have a power and intensity of their own. They are accomplished tales of the terrible entry of the young into the violence of reality. All the characters both seek and fear the violent transformation that will lift them out of the isolation and death of their worlds. Mercedes in "The Horse" fails completely; Floyd in "The Bird" learns to touch the living again and has hope of regaining his place in the human world. Only Penelope in **I Hear Men Talking** learns of the wholeness of life in its comm nal and political manifestations.

Mercedes in "The Horse" (*Story Magazine,* 1939) fails to translate her rhapsodic response to the animal into a basis for living in the human community because she rejects reality. Born into an upper-class family to a cold, vacuous mother, the headstrong Mercedes resists parental and social pressures to marry a proper young man, adopt the ways of that world, and be like "other girls." Before the Horse is born, her only glimpse of life based on other values is of the futile but persistent rebellions of her grandmother who "had a sharp way of contracting things outside herself, of suddenly becoming aware." In contrast, her mother was fragmented, "never opening to any word or gesture," hating to be touched by even her daughter. The Horse's birth one almond-scented Spring morning reveals to her "another world," where spirits are free and life is wonder. She directs all her energies and imagination to perfecting a "closed paradisiacal world" with the animal.

This delicate dreamlife begins to come apart when she unexpectedly finds herself attracted to Michael, the young man her mother insists she marry. But Michael is inevitably an intrusion into the closed world of the self and its external embodiment, the Horse. Mercedes is shocked to find "she knew so little about the real world" when she first hears Michael talk. Their relationship blossoms only when it is entirely private and cut off from human contact. Mallard provides the ruinous touch of the human world.

A cruel, leering man, he wants to break the Horse and tame the young woman. Mercedes' only way to react to him is to desire his destruction.

When he tries to ride the Horse, it tramples him to death. When she rides the offending Horse into town, she imposes her private world with the Horse, preserved at the expense of human safety, on the townspeople. They, like Mallard, want to stone her into submission. The fundamental destructiveness of Mercedes' solipsistic divorce from the human community is acted out when the Horse follows its own instincts and tramples Mercedes to death. The story's poetic lyricism captures both the momentary beauty of a private fantasy and the violent destructiveness of such an illusion. Mercedes' contempt for the human community and her rejection of reality doom all her bright instincts toward wonder, beauty, and love.

The progress in the story "The Bird" (*New Caravans*, 1936) is the reverse of that in "The Horse." Floyd Young is desperate for some "leverage that he might use to break out of himself" and fearful that he might have to "stay forever in this awful state of half death. . . ." He wants to reach out his hand to the world and give it his name, but he cannot:

> He thought he would have to be released from the outside. He could not do it for himself. His own world was fantastic. Some violence would have to pierce him. He wanted to run against it, to have it done.

"The horrors of World War I are part of what Floyd wants to escape," Meridel Le Sueur explains. "He s really a virgin being attacked by the world. He's really a young virgin girl."

The world of the ship seems fantastic. All its passengers show by caricature the gross and excessive in human nature, yet with odd touches of kindness, need, and gentleness. In their excess they include Floyd, who cannot stand aloof from their insistent appetites. When the storm literally tosses them into each other's arms, some offer comfort to the others and some exploit their fears. They find no transcendent moment, but they do grasp onto each other to survive the night. In his exhausted sleep Floyd weeps for them, suffering their sickness and fear, embracing "the foul crew, the sick girls." In his dream they are "the unformed stuff of the world, its invisible body" to which all belong:

> And the boat went on and their dreams reflected and surrounded them as the water reflected and carried the Salvor, and their own forms were reflected in convexity and concavity and echoed and reechoed until there was an intricacy of meaning, and a profundity in

the image that was amazing. What had been flat and stale only seemed so then, for the dream repeated it endlessly, reechoing and deepening what had been flat, repeating and enriching what had been stale.

The storm provides the violent experience which brings the passengers together. A storm will also be the climax of **I Hear Men Talking**. Le Sueur used the storm in the early stories because in her youth storms were the only force in the Midwestern towns that united the people. "Later I had the strike," she observes.

The use of the storm and strike as agents for violent transformation come together in **I Hear Men Talking**. Penelope's awakening to her womanhood comes with the Spring; her sexual desire parallels the burgeoning strike effort of the farmers, and climaxes in an afternoon in which strike, tornado, and birth sweep the community out of its usual pettiness and temporarily unify the people.

I Hear Men Talking is an early novel. Sections of it were published as early as 1933 and parts of it were probably drafted as early as the late Twenties.(3) The setting is Iowa. Milk strikes and penny auctions such as those in the text occured in Iowa in 1932-33, but Meridel Le Sueur remembers radical farm unrest in her girlhood in Oklahoma around 1912. The partly autobiographical Penelope is about the same age Le Sueur was during the Socialist fervor before World War I. She has apparently fused the real farm strikes in Iowa in 1932-33 with her memories from about 1912-17. While the story is not a specific historical representation of either time, the events of the novel are similar to those in many Midwestern states throughout the 1930's.(4)

While the focus of the novel is Penelope, the townspeople are crucial to the structure and meaning of the story. Their lives provide commentary on both Penelope's life and the corruption and destruction of the human community under the system of capitalism and in the name of individualism. These characters include Bac, the handsome but cruel young man who both fascinates and repels Penelope with his sexual force; Mr. Littlefield, the town's outcast, stripped of all self-respect but dreaming still of his rise to importance as a power among others; and Miss Shelley, tricked out of happiness forever by her romantic illusions. Meridel Le Sueur is at her best in the novel with these portraits. Less fully realized are the characters who guide Penelope in the direction of communal action and identity. Penelope's mother, Mona, remains a remote figure, except in the tender moment which she and Penelope share while hemming a dress. Lowell, the organizer whose shadowy sexual relationship with

Mona never clearly shows Penelope an alternative to self-centered men like Bac, lacks depth as a character. Still, his passionate insistence that people must stand together voices the alternative vision toward which Penelope is reaching at the end of the novel.

I Hear Men Talking attempts to replace the ideal of individualism with the ideal of the group. In 1935 Meridel published in *New Masses* (February 29) an essay entitled "The Fetish of Being Outside" which is interesting for the light it throws on her work and on her definition of herself:

> I do not care for the bourgeois "individual" that I am. I never have cared for it. I want to be integrated in a new and different way as an individual and this I feel can come only from a communal participation which reverses the feeling of a bourgeois writer. What will happen to him will not be special and precious, but will be the communal happening, what happens at [to?] all. I can no longer live without communal sensibility. I can no longer breathe in this maggotty individualism of a merchant society. I have never been able to breathe in it. That is why I hope to "belong" to a communal society, to be a cellular part of that and able to grow and function with others in a living whole.

This comment may also describe autobiographical characters such as Penelope. Even Miss Shelley and Mr. Littlefield, the most isolated people in the town, long to experience some unity with others. The pathos of their situation is that they are seduced by the illusions of happiness which permeate their culture: in Miss Shelley's case, through sexual domination of a man; in Mr. Littlefield's case, through individual power.

The sexual fascination Penelope feels for Bac, and its parallel in Miss Shelley's fascination with Hawk, give us an important study of the way female sexuality is victimized when male sexuality makes a commodity of the woman. Miss Shelley translates her desire to merge her virginal selfhood with some force outside herself as being "wed" to the cold and exploitive Hawk. Penelope also imagines sexual experience as the "initiation" into the "secrets" of life. Like Miss Shelley, she wants to lose herself in the force and being of Bac. At every turn, however, Meridel Le Sueur repudiates the notion that sexuality with men who make women into commodities holds any avenue for fulfillment. Such myths are part of bourgeois culture, she suggests: the Hollywood answer to the yearnings of the spirit and body.

At the Gem picture show, one sees "mythical girls and men, huge beyond any knowing and silken, distorting what was known but sweet to the taste as honey. . . ." Bac appears to Penelope as a "dazzler," a "confusion of light," but he tells her, "It's me and not

232

a motion picture." The description of Bac in Penelope's eyes illustrates the powerful but menacing nature of his sexuality:

> She saw the hot glance of Bac like a hound after her . . . and the strong curve of the haunch, the thigh, showing his strength, his slumbering back showing beneath the jersey, saw the way the muscles wedged down cruelly and swelled up to his neck and the hands large that went to his mouth and his face wide and cruel and handsome because of that a looking after her so she could not walk, like a noose crippling her, his glance like a dog going at her, confusing her walking.

Though Penelope hopes that Bac's embrace will be a transforming fire to which she can surrender herself, his caress feels like a "trap, a snare." Penelope is dismayed to find that when Bac "moves in," she resists. The metaphors all suggest that his sexuality tears, strangles, traps, and debases. Bac even lays bets with the other young men on when he will "make it" with Penelope, advising them of when and where to hide to get a good view. At one point when Penelope runs away from him, he calls to the boys to help him chase her down, promising that they will get their "share." Instead of initiating her into womanhood, this version of male sexuality only pins Penelope down to something "small, compact, and hard as stone." The exclamation "Men!" which most of the women characters utter at one time or another is spoken with all the amassed ambiguity of their wonder, desire, repulsion, and rejection.

Bac's sexual decadence is part of his moral corruption in embracing bourgeois values and betraying his working class ties. Bac betrays the farm protesters by tipping off the sheriff, thereby endangering both their lives and the success of their farm auction strategy. His act is a crime against his friends and his class. His self-serving individualism is expressed when he tells Penelope that Lowell, the protest organizer, has it "all wrong . . . you can't buck the game. . . ." Bac thinks that one should be "crafty" "inside the law" and brags, "I'm going to be worth a million dollars some day, amid the big guys. . . ."

Like Penelope, Miss Shelley is "warmhearted, want[ing] to touch," "waiting for the fulfillment of a strange ecstacy." When Watson Hawk, a man with "no bounty to give," rejects her love, she pleads, " 'Kill me . . . kill me,' " "tasting what could be between one person and another" but finding only that the "touch of men" was a "bright blade that bore disaster for women." Penelope consciously fears that she will wind up like the sterile Miss Shelley unless she learns to give herself up to something beyond her own fears and self-protectiveness. Unlike Penelope, however, Miss Shelley was not surrounded by people like Lowell and Mona or the farmers, who all suggest an alternative way to "step out" of the destructiveness of selfhood.

Penelope's first ecstatic escape from self comes when she helps Dr. Starry deliver Mrs. Fearing's baby. The doctor calls Penelope a "good soldier," and she feels like "an instrument" working to help him. Penelope is so absorbed in the struggle to deliver the child alive that she momentarily does not recognize as her own the tears she sheds for Mrs. Fearing's suffering and at the wonder of birth. At last she knows something important—"how it was to get into the world"—and the bond between her and Dr. Starry feels like it will last forever. The consuming emotion of the moment pushes Bac out of Penelope's thoughts and provides the real experience which guarantees that his falsity of emotion can never seduce her.

If Miss Shelley is the woman who sours and shrinks in an isolate selfhood, Mr. Littlefield represents the sterility of ego without the glamour of sex. Littlefield is a pathetic, ineffectual man whose egotism hides behind what he calls his "big outlook for humanity." He dreams he might have been "a Webster, a great man," but even the youthful Penelope sees that he is a "ghost," "slowly chewing himself off at the breast, knowing that he lived off himself. . . ." He is the inverse example of Bac, the weak, death-dwelling egotist cut off from the town while still dreaming of holding power over it.

The message of Lowell and the strike organization are alternatives to the individualism of Miss Shelley and Mr. Littlefield. Lowell is "teaching something beyond his words" in his organizing. In an elliptical conversation he assures Penelope that there are others like him "all over the world." Lowell's specific radical identity is unnamed, as the novel carefully avoids overt ideological details, but his message is clear: "It hasn't hurt us yet, has it, to be together?" "A man can't stand out alone when a tide comes up, now can he?" "A man like [Fearing] when he loses his job thinks he's all alone. He ought to come with us. We all ought to be together. The grass doesn't grow separate, stand alone, does it? Or the trees?" Still, since the action of the farm protests occurs offstage and is simply reported at home, Lowell's message lacks dramatic enactment and his words simply echo a theme characteristic of the 1930's novels of social realism.

The cyclone which hits the town at the end of the novel illustrates in nature the process of violent transformation which mixes death and birth. Though several are killed, the town is momentarily unified by the winds. Some had seen "a fire standing in the storm" and "voices fused together, talking, bearing witness to what they had seen and would see, of a tide they knew now carried them and did not separate them doing battle against each other. . . ." The feeling of "belonging" which Lowell finds in the political group and Penelope experiences in the birth of the Fearing baby parallels the experience of the town when the winds blow away the people's petty hostilities, along with their houses.

At the close of **I Hear Men Talking** Penelope has not yet found her political identity, but she has given herself to the instincts which underlie a radical identity. The town has not become a socialist hotbed, but it, too, has experienced a sense of community which underscores the dissatisfaction with the law of the self. In **I Hear Men Talking** the natural cycles of life, expressed in both the earth's fecundity and in women's bodies, are tied to both the desirable social harmony and to political action.

Meridel Le Sueur's vision in these works is communistic but not utopian. Her fiction analyzes the sickness of a bourgeois world which claims that human fulfillment lies in the economic and personal assertion of the self. She argues that the nature of capitalism isolates and destroys us, cutting us away from the communal identity that can save the soul as well as society. Penelope, Mercedes, and Floyd all try to reach beyond self for some fulfillment in the company of other living things, but no utopian world materializes in which such fulfillments exist for more than a moment. Mercedes briefly escapes the sickness of her class in her private fantasy with the Horse, but her dreamworld collapses because it is cut off from the vital but imperfect human world. Floyd Young does grasp hands with his fellow passengers, but they are men and women marred by the corruption of the world around them. Penelope, nearly bursting with an expansive young soul that wants to embrace the whole of life, is surrounded by petty gossips, dominant young men, outcasts, small-minded merchants, and cranks. Even the tenderness and intimacy she feels with her mother are momentary.

The maturity of these stories lies precisely in their refusal to suggest that the moment of unity is anything but fleeting, or that the human community is ever perfect. Like Lowell, the good radical must embrace the people as they are and work to bring about the ideals and the organizations that can create moments of cohesiveness. Penelope, while a target of the malice of the narrow-minded town, opens her heart to its Littlefields and Miss Shelleys. Without illusions about the town, she identifies with its people.

Meridel Le Sueur believes that fulfillment lies in belonging to the group, that political action is an expression of one's belief in humanity, and that the body's desires, the earth's cycles, and the life of the community are all part of a living whole. Since sexual repression and class conflict pit the individual against the group and reduce the life force to a commodity, she portrays the oppression of sexual relations as part of the pattern of corruption of human relations under capitalism. She rejects the notion that one's ideology is just a set of opinions affecting one's political views: it is, indeed, a set of values that determine a way of life. She offers us portraits of people whose lives are blighted when sexuality and spirit are defined by the same values that define success as money and personal power. Her desire for communal identity is set against bourgeois culture, which subverts, misguides, and distorts our fundamental human needs. In her world, the pull of the heart and the processes of nature move in a unity whose communal expression is the socialist vision.

—Linda Ray Pratt
University of Nebraska
Lincoln, Nebraska
May, 1984

(1) Meridel Le Sueur, interviews with Linda Pratt, September 23-24, 1983, St. Paul, Minnesota. All further quotations from Meridel Le Sueur are from this set of interviews unless otherwise noted.

(2) Elaine Hedges, ed., Le Sueur, *Ripening* (Old Westbury, New York: Feminist Press, 1982), "Introduction," p. 6.

(3) The exact date of composition of **I Hear Men Talking** is obscure. One section was published as "Fudge" in *Fantasy* (Winter 1933) and another section appeared as "Our Fathers" in *Intermountain Review of English and Speech* (Feb. 1, 1937). Hedges writes in her "Introduction" to *Ripening* that "Le Sueur worked on 'Our Fathers' through the twenties and thirties, and eventually the story grew into a novel, *I Hear Men Talking*, which she has recently returned to, revised, and completed" (p. 5). Le Sueur recalls that she probably completed the novel about 1945.

(4) The milk strikes and farm sales in Iowa in 1932-33 would have been in the news at the time Le Sueur was writing the novel; however, her girlhood years when she was Penelope's age were primarily spent in Oklahoma and Kansas. While the Socialist Party was active among farmers in these states, I have found no indication of farm strikes in these states this early. I note with appreciation the assistance of William C. Pratt in establishing the historical background of this era.

Publisher's note: The publisher has adopted the convention of putting "I Hear Men Talking"—the narrative printed in this book—in quotation marks, indicating that it is a story, in order to distinguish the narrative itself from the entire book which goes under the same title. We agree with Professor Pratt that it is generically a novel.

Afterword

I didn't want these short novels, written in the Thirties and Forties, to be published unless they would serve the purpose of illuminating the struggle between the dying class of the oppressor and the rising class of the oppressed. This is the crucial axis of our time, not merely an aesthetic. The artist's duty now is to recreate the new image of the world, to return to the people their need and vision of a world of a new birth of abundance and equality.

Cynicism, despair, alienation, hopelessness, paralysis of action and elitism are now seen in the deathly images of the bomb and of the destruction of the people and the earth.

These stories mark my painful search for a living image that could change my life. We are still searching for such an image, and it is appearing in the world struggle to survive. These stories are valuable if you see in them the struggle against this decay and despair. Their weakness is that I did not know what temperature broke the chains of the old images, cracked the egg of the 19th century image of the rise of the bourgoisie as a class.

Melville struggles to shatter the 19th century, old, rotting, dangerous images of the white whale and the oil industry. It is dangerous and painful to challenge old images, and live on the edge of the heated destruction of the high winds of change, to catch and record the heraldic cry of the new humanity. And it is so visible now, the old image delivering mass destruction.

The people in these stories see the old image coming to kill them. They are full of terror, ambiguity, and paralysis.

I don't want to add one grain of confusion, of despair, of death to the global struggle we now have to live. But it is valuable to diagnose the disease, and when necessary to do drastic surgery, cut out the source of contamination.

Since these stories were written, the disease has invaded the whole body of our society and is visible and horrible, the poison entering us from the earth, the air, as reality, as threat, as death.

I was trying to save our lives and the life of the earth and the society in which I lived.

I was trying to name the enemy. I was trying to find my allies and above all the action to extend the word into reality. I rebelled against the culture of the dissected, alienated, passive, and seductive, the philosophy and language of the oppressor, the splitting of the subjective and the objective, which leads to unreality and sentimentality, and takes us blind to the slaughter.

In these stories I gave narration and description of the corpse, but you cannot denounce without commitment eventually to transformation.

I did not know how to conjure this. I knew there would be no transformation without action. I knew you would be destroyed if the conscious and unconscious, subjective and objective did not find ways to unite. We cannot exist and be human under domination—these stories make that clear. The naming of the world is not possible unless infused with love. No one can say a true word alone. When the word, in bourgeois education and philosophy, is deprived of the dimension of action, the word becomes empty, suffers alienation, sentimentality, verbalism. We are not built in alienation and silence. We must somehow find how to be committed to others, how to express that love which is an act of courage, not of fear, but of bravery and of seeing the liberation in each other, that makes us proud and human. I was trying to find that action—that love.

I think these stories do show the entrapped person silenced, and the necessity to oppose the loveless violence to the heart, to discover the oppressor as an enemy outside oneself . . . they show submersion in the terrible muffling of the oppressor, being drowned in silence, and the necessity to be reborn of the resolution of this contradiction, as oppression gives way to liberation.

I show this death, this terror and this longing for freedom. I saw paternalism, exploitation, aggression and death. I saw young women unable to make contact even in love. I saw men and women, all creatures, and the earth itself dying in the Midwest from exploitation, from being consumed without love, and dying without hope, the people evicted from the land and separated from each other. . . .

These stories show that . . . maybe a little too lyrically, obscured, not sharp enough, due to my not knowing how to see and unite in the human hope and trust and love. I did not know how to make, enlarge, and limn the image of solidarity, I did not know what the action of transformation was. This was what I did not know and it is now·appearing over all horizons.

There were other insights I was struggling with . . . the manipulation by the author of the reader who is a consumer, the brazen and often brutal design of our literature to intensify the image of brutality . . . wars, and elitist individuals. The "whodunnit" narrative style which I follow in these stories, and am now trying to break open into more storytelling, was an effort at alliance between writer and reader, and a lifting of consciousness into the new transformation, not the greedy, decaying, agressive and brutal.

In a new reality we cannot use the forms or even the language of the old oppressor. We must be bold, open to new structures, new forms, relationships, images of being together. I even have to see and feel what kind of lyricism and style serves the new reality.

These stories are of the time when dominating and exploitative relations were concealed in the bourgeois economy. The people in these novels cannot see, they are blinded. They are literally killed by this cruel dichotomy.

Reality is not property relationships, is not property relations. These stories in a crippled way try to show this. Dreiser, Norris, Twain, Whitman also tried to show this cry-out against the predators. Now we can express the true relationship of the exploiter and the exploited, in our own language and with our own storytelling genius.

The image is of the new child within the body of us all. This must include the girl and the horse, the boy and the prostitutes, Penelope and the corrupt town and the strike and the cyclone. The image the writer must now develop is the synthesis.

This action was unknown to me and to the people in these stories.

I was also struggling against how thought can become non-dialectical and purely logical, how there can be a breach between thought, need and action. This breach conceals the relationship which is determined by productive forces outside the characters' knowledge. So they end in disaster.

There follows a series of comments on the meaning of each story printed in this volume, as Meridel Le Sueur views them today.

"The Horse"

I was influenced by D.H. Lawrence, a very revealing writer of the Twenties. He wrote of the trashing of the body in our civilization, of Puritan attitudes toward the body as commodity, and of male aggression towards the woman-as-property. He was very important to me because he described the body as alienated by economic necessities and the dominance of property rights over human rights, especially oppressive to women.

This is in "The Horse," but not sharply enough focused. Mercedes rebels against her role as a commodity, being sold off for profit by her family. I could see how important her rebellion might have been. But her relation to the Horse is hardly a solution. It is the flight from the dangerous reality of her family and class into this phantasmagorical unreality that kills her. She is driven to fear, terror, and death, killed by the contradictions. . . . The shadow of the oppressor is over and in us.

The women's movement cannot use the Horse as an image. It is a symbol of nature and the exploitation of nature and woman. But it is obscured by lyrical descriptions. There is an evasion of her sexual response to being a commodity. And I have tried to depict natural relations by means of a force not actually using her. It's a good story to study critically—to see how mysticism and vagueness can blanket and obscure a good social image.

I always used some natural force to awaken the character. In one story the wind coming in a window awakens the lost girl. How many girls I have in my stories, too . . . did I evade growing up? Or have we many women grown from girls?

"The Bird"

Before and during the Second World War, I wrote two short novels with the main actor a young man. I think this came from two sources, first the envy I had that I could not have the experiences men do, go to Alaska on a boat or play pool in a public tavern or have any number of experiences in street life . . . and second I wanted to show that young men suffer brutality and terror and loss of belief the same as young women. (Every young man I knew before the First World War never came back from Europe . . . also they suffered sexual brutality.)

Here again I feel the main theme is mitigated by lack of depth of understanding, and lyricism and sentimentality—the climax, the change is brought about by a storm! The characters have a moment of human solidarity, but you know it is only a moment and that the boy has no future, nowhere to go to continue this moment, and it is liable to get worse for him and for all of them. I also do not think the young prostitutes are fully realized, nor the racial relationships, and it is all certainly obscured by a kind of vague mysticism. There is an attempt to show the brutality of the society that has created them all. There is a certain truth to the fatalism, of course, but this is not what I feel is true image-making. We must search out the class and social elements that illumine even the misery of humans, that show how their memory, their proximity can make them brave with another possibility of human relationship.

When the first Russian delegation came to the farm country after the War, some of the farmers refused to meet them in the park. Hundreds followed them everywhere, but these old codgers, sitting in the tavern, asked what the Russians had done and said. A young farmer told how he had seen these people who never had a mortgage, and this shook them, and the young farmer said, "You old codgers are like the stupid fellow still in the cocoon who pointed to the butterfly flying in the sky and said 'Look at that damn fool you'll never catch me up there!' " I feel that when we see the cocoon we must be able, by science or history or memory, to know that the butterfly is inside and will someday fly free. If you don't know or believe in the process, you can only write that the butterfly is captive, lost, doomed.

I Hear Men Talking

This novel shows some growth, in depicting the relationship between the townspeople, who may be said to be in the cocoon still, the struggle of the girl to find a newer reality than the one killing the townspeople, and the struggle of the farmers to retain their land and their security. The role of women and their consciousness enters my work here in a more realistic and vividly told story.

I think the lyricism of the writing here begins to function as part of the action, as part of the subjective feelings of the people and above all in the interaction between their feelings and despair and the events of their lives and the life of the town.

External and real events are told in active prose, in contrast to the poetic and lyrical song of the girl trying to find her place in the world. There is also an attempt to show the conflict of Jennie and Penelope in relation to the corrupt Bac and the social dangers of male supremacy.

There is more relation between the lyrical and poetic and the harsh and oppressive. The lyrical is used as reaction to the deathly action of the economics and history of the town. There is more of a social action, and research into the social reality of their lives and their hurt from it. It is much more clear that the enemies are appearing . . . the oppressor and the oppressed at last are clear. And their interaction with each other causes the life and death of the participants. (Here again it is a natural event, a cyclone, which brings them to consciousness, but there is also the strike, and the class dialectics begin to come out quite clear.)

I have begun to rewrite this story. Having the original version printed, along with the history I have now lived with my country and people, makes me very enthusiastic about rewriting it. Now I have seen what changes people. The Depression probably was the climax of this understanding. It was clear who were the oppressors and the oppressed. Our writers began to reflect this more sharply than ever before. Now the global struggle adds an even more literal, enormous drama of life and death, in which to tell the truth is revolutionary.

These stories were all blemished by my not going far enough in spelling out their historical relationship. The Horse might have been saved, along with the natural power of the woman, and turned against the enemy, cutting through the romantic picture of herself, like Nora in "The Doll's House" leaving the rotting family based on property and greed. In "The Bird," what could have illuminated the boy beside the storm? or the storm can be a symbol of change, of transformation. . . . The real storm of "I Hear Men Talking" is in the struggle of the farmers and her grandmother and mother. I didn't look deeply enough historically to see what growth is in society and the individual, or in the honing of necessity in their lives, plunging them into hunger and vision.

Now we need to be sharp and clear. In these stories you have one foot in the non-world of seduction and power and the other foot in the world of loss, indignity and hunger. My later stories show I moved from one world to the other, or saw their interpenetrating struggle.

There is the question too of literary style. I now question the lyricism of my early stories, as if they were covering the horror and the loss, the terrible sewage of bourgeois life. We see in them no poisoning of the earth and blasting of the humus, dooming the individual to violence unheard of. A farmer in North Dakota said to me once, "You write too beautiful." Now I am always watching out for that. For years I read Ruskin, that beautiful prose, till I found out it was a lie. Now I look behind beautiful prose very sharply. Before, I defended myself by saying we should not leave the beautiful, lyrical use of language to the ruling class—the workers must have, and do have, beautiful language. But I often remember the farmer's words, and he is partly right. Someday we will have a new kind of lyricism in a just world. Yes, language will also be freed and global. . . . We have to think about it. It seems I was both revealing and covering up . . . this is the terrible dichotomy of our society, and it causes deep confusion, illusion and wounds.

The events and struggles of my people have taught me. I have stayed close and paid attention. They have to react, revolt, to save our lives. I have learned from them as their struggle has sharpened, and we must now, as image-makers, be alert, alive to the rot and seduction of the old and fresh to the appearance of the new. . . . Their solidarity is an act of love. We try to find the word out of the silence, what has been denied us.

The writer has to dive deep, come up with the bloated corpse, point out the death squads. We are deeply wounded, as Ezekiel and Isaiah, by the suffering of our people. The self is injured, isolated, confused. The writer is bewildered, reflecting the wrong and artificial and magical images. Withdrawal and disappearance, brutal disgrace and victimization, injure the oppressed person, while he or she is unable to see the enemy or appear as victor.

I learned to see this hope, this tiny sprig of green after the flood in the mouth of doves. I saw it flash from the flood in strikers, women in childbirth—from their bodies, their humanity, their love, their pure act of love, their pure hope and belief, their solidarity. The prophet-writer must be able to glean this from every harvest, event, struggle, encounter and destruction. Out of destruction comes the new. Out of silence the word is bound together.

Now this consciousness is emerging in global people. What stories there are to be written, not of the mystical or psychological or merely Freudian conflict but the visible, the real, the terrible and universal event now that is the culmination and ending of capitalism; to seek and find in all of us, especially in the most oppressed, not only the oppression but the green crowning of the protein of corn, the converting of horizons, the property turning into global food . . . purifying the creeping poison, converging and unifying. It is in us all. . . .

Meridel Le Sueur

243

Other works by Meridel Le Sueur:

The Girl (novel, 152 pp., $4.50). First written in 1939, published by us forty years later, this highly acclaimed novel of St. Paul in the Depression is an underground classic.

Harvest & Song for My Time (stories, 135 pp., $4.50). A combined edition of her early stories of the Thirties and the tales of the McCarthy period which were previously published in left-wing publications. Thirteen stories, eleven unique to this volume.

Women on the Breadlines (essay and three stories, 24 pp., $2.00). Proletarian writings of the Thirties, these four sketches focus on the effects of the depression on the women of St. Paul. Illustrated by Tecla, people's artist and Meridel's friend, who died tragically last year.

Worker Writer (pamphlet, 32 pp., $2.00). A manual of writing directed to workers, which also includes an analysis of the author's own story, "Biography of My Daughter." With additional remarks on writing added in 1981.

West End Press
Box 7232
Minneapolis, MN 55407